The Queen of Summer's Twilight

The Queen of Summer's Twilight

Charles Vess

NEWCON PRESS

NewCon Press
England

First published in September 2022 by NewCon Press,
41 Wheatsheaf Road, Alconbury Weston, Cambs, PE28 4LF

NCP281 (limited edition hardback)
NCP282 (softback)

10 9 8 7 6 5 4 3 2 1

'The Queen Summer's Twilight' copyright © 2022 by Charles Vess

Cover Art, logo, chapter headers and interior illustration copyright © 2022 by Charles Vess

All rights reserved, including the right to produce this book, or portions thereof, in any form.

ISBN:

978-1-914953-26-2 (hardback)
978-1-914953-27-9 (softback)

Cover art by Charles Vess
Interior illustration by Charles Vess

Text edited by Ian Whates
Cover layout and interior typesetting by Ian Whates

PROLOGUE

At the crest of the hill Janet braked the cycle, planted booted feet firmly to either side and studied the landscape of brittle, knee-high grass flowing away from her in every direction.

Struggling to balance the heavy machine, she cut its engine. In the sudden silence that followed, Janet became uncomfortably aware that this strange world was utterly devoid of any bird song or the low jangle of the telly in another room or even the drone of a distant car. A light breeze, though, stirred the bone-dry grass, striking each blade against the other, producing an insistent rattle that was the only sound that broke the profound silence of that awful plain.

For as far as she could see there was only that vast sea of dead grass, broken occasionally by a blackened tree, until in the far distance it swept up against a high, sharp ridge of dark rock.

Above her the sky was a deep twilight-blue expanse sprinkled with a multitude of stars and a crescent moon that gently illuminated everything beneath it, turning her chocolate skin a shade darker.

Coughing suddenly from the acrid smoke that began to billow around her, Janet turned to look back the way she'd come and saw a long black ribbon of charred grass that marked her cycle's passage. At her feet, it was still burning.

"Bloody hell, if this is Elfland, then that damned queen can keep it, because its shite!"

The smoke triggered another spasm of hacking that brought tears to her eyes and left an oily grit on her face. Wiping her eyes with the back of one hand, she squinted into the distance.

Damn, where did they go? Have to be here somewhere!

Grimacing with the effort, Janet forced herself to once again master the unfamiliar weight of the cycle. Kicking it back into life, she tore across the endless plain followed only by that ribbon of flame and the blackened track she left behind.

ONE
Twelve days earlier

When the man appeared, Geoffrey was the first to see him. It was a quiet Saturday afternoon, and the boy hovered at his favourite spot, the sweets aisle of the small newsagents, greedily eyeing a packet of milk chocolate toffees. The clattering of the bell over the front door announced a new customer and Geoff glanced up eagerly, hoping it was one of his mates with some spare coin. And there he was. A man in a floor-length leather coat with a high collar and flashing buttons plainly proclaiming, as if over the loudspeaker at a local football match, that he wasn't from around here.

When the stranger spoke to Mr. Graferty, the owner of the shop, his accent was so thick that Geoff doubted he could have cut it with his Gran's sharpest knife, the one she used to slice the Sunday roast. Boredom slipped away as the lad immediately slammed out the door looking for his mates.

Fortunately, they were close by, so all five boys followed the stranger as he exited the shop, and walked behind him all the way to the end of the pavement on the outskirts of the village. They paused there, uncertain if this new game would have any payoff. But the intricate tooling on the stranger's full-length leather coat and its flashing silver buttons looked so unearthly that it practically begged them to follow. So they did. All the way along the tarmac of the single-track road out to the abandoned estate, miles from the small village.

At first, they kept a few steps behind, just in case the mysterious stranger got angry at their crude jokes or the occasional small pebble they tossed at his high leather boots. But once they realised that the man was paying no attention to them at all, they grew bolder, playing games of tig using the man as base.

Their youthful persistence appeared to pay off when he stopped before the tall rusted iron gates of the old Lynn place. And then, when he pulled a key out of one of the leather packets laced through his wide belt they caught their breath. Somehow each lad instinctively knew that the heavy, ornately fashioned key he held in his hand was never made to unlock any door except this particular one.

Inserting it in the enormous metal lock, encrusted with rust and bird droppings, the man struggled for a moment before successfully twisting the key. Then, with a sharp metallic groan, the gate finally swung open, leaving the boys whooping in shared delight.

Of course, each one of them had listened to a hundred different stories about the Lynn Estate as their parents and their friends gossiped over a slow pint at the pub. They already knew that before the last of that family, the old Dowager, passed away, she had established a trust fund that still paid the estate's property taxes while far distant relatives in Australia and Canada continued to argue over exactly who would inherit the place. But none of them had the legal right to move so much as a single stone. So, here it sat, slowly returning to the ground from which all the stone had been quarried so many years before.

"Da will have my hide if he finds out I've been out here!"

"Won't tell if you don't."

"Besides, this is like a personal invite, innit?"

"Yeah, one that no one else in the village ever got!"

"It's not like we're gonna threw any rocks at the windows."

"If there was any left to break…"

"Just sayin'."

"Right, right…"

Following the stranger inside the gates, they watched as he paused to stare up at the derelict ruins of what must have once been a large, rambling manor house made of dour grey stone. The scatter of broken slate tiles from its collapsed roof and the charred timbers strewn across the yard all stood evidence to a long-ago fire. The dull fragrance of burnt timber still clung to the rain-soaked wood, but it was the abundance of mould that caused first Geoffrey and then Jamie to sneeze. In turn, they both wiped their hands on their trousers.

Deep in thought, the man carefully picked his way through the rubble to the far side of the building and walked into the family graveyard, filled with headstones once inscribed with proper names but now too weathered to read. Then, when he sank to his knees and began to weep, the boys almost lost patience with their afternoon adventure.

The stranger's emotional outburst made them feel uneasy, as if they were witnessing something too private for them to understand. Except for Geordie, whose own father had recently passed away and who, although he would never tell his mates, had run straight to his bedroom after the funeral service and bawled for hours.

His younger cousin Jamie, swinging from a limb of an ancient yew tree that bent protectively over the graveyard, let out a low howl of triumph when the stranger got back to his feet. Still curious, they followed the man as he walked back toward the house. This time, though, he paused before a low stone shed whose windows had been bricked up for as long as anyone in the village could remember.

And then, when the man fumbled for yet another key to unlock the heavy, metal door of the shed they all become electric with excitement.

Every village boy or girl that had ever trespassed on the estate had made up stories about what was in this shed, swearing that they knew the truth. Lately, village folklore claimed that the mummified body of the Dowager's brother was hidden inside, murdered with a cup of poisoned tea served from her own wrinkled hand. Moments later, when the door swung open and they followed the stranger in, egging each other on and still completely ignored by the man, all their bloodthirsty fantasies were dashed by the banal truth.

It was simply a garage, packed tightly with old motorcars, each missing various parts, some entirely without their engines, lined neatly along one wall. There was even an ancient wooden carriage, decaying in the damp; velvety moss cushioned the hard edge of its enormous wheels and filled the interior of its cabin with a gentle carpet of soft green.

However, sitting in the midst of that ruin, wrapped tightly in thick oilcloth, as if it were a present waiting for the proper person to come and claim it, was something else entirely. When, with some difficulty, the man unwrapped layer after layer of the cloth, what they saw was a curious looking motorcycle, clearly built for an age long past, though its chrome still shone even in the dim light of the windowless garage.

To the boys' delight, the stranger, his face set with determination, pulled a leather helmet from the satchel hung over his left shoulder and slipped it on his head. The boys scattered from the doorway as he wheeled the cycle out into the yard, and then followed him into the middle of an enclosed field not far from the house.

From his first awkward attempt it was clear that the man didn't know how to operate the machine's complex controls. Geordie, whose father owned the garage in town and who had taught his son how to tinker with engines, thought he could show the stranger how to kick the cycle into gear.

Anticipating a long afternoon spent watching the man falling repeatedly off the bike, he sent his cousin back to the storage shed for the can of petrol he'd noticed sitting just inside the door. Unlike everything else there, the metal container was shiny and new, obviously not a long-term occupant of the dank room, perhaps even renewed periodically by the estate's agent against this very possibility.

The trip was successful, and after unscrewing the cap Geordie filled the cycle's fuel tank. Then, shyly pointing to each control in sequence, he showed the man how to start the motorcycle.

But with the first ferocious roar of the engine and a long belch of black smoke from its exhaust pipes, the man took control of the enormous black machine. He and Geoffrey scampered back toward their chosen spot on top of the wall to sit and watch. Lithe and agile, Geordie easily scrambled up to the shared perch then looked down at his friend's pleading face.

"Hey. What about me?"

"Right. Grab my hand then."

Straining with effort he pulled the heavyset boy up to join them.

"Oof! Geoff, if you want to keep up with us, you've got to stop eating every biscuit yer Gran offers you."

Geoffrey settled himself on the top of the rough lichen-encrusted stone before replying, "Yeah. But them oatmeals of hern put me right in heaven." Then looking back at their incredulous faces, he protested, "Well, they do!"

"Lard butt, they don't let fatties in there."

"Hey, who told you that fibber?"

Geordie cut through their chatter, hissing, "Shut it and pay attention, there's plenty of laughs right in front of us."

All five heads snapped around to look out at the several acres of fallow grass sprinkled with remnants of stubble from some long since harvested crop that formed the backdrop for their entertainment. The field, enclosed by the same high stonewall they straddled, was accessed only by the narrow door that they'd all come through and a sagging wooden gate that had long since shed any paint that might once have graced its surface.

To their continual delight, the man succeeded only in falling off the powerful bike again and again, so that he was soon covered head to toe with mud and torn grass, and the ground around him a jumble of muddy tire tracks. Much later, as he wearily set his foot on the clutch once more, the man grimaced as the young boys' hoots of laughter filled the air.

Gasping for breath, Geoffrey exclaimed, "This is way better than any of those daft shows on the telly."

But just when the boys began to get nervous about what their mums would say to them for staying out so late, they clapped their hands with relief. The stranger finally succeeded in getting the great black machine in gear and managed to stay upright long enough to steer it across the field directly under them. Guiding it cautiously out through the gate that he'd propped open earlier, the man waved his thanks for their help.

Then, as the drone of the motorcycle faded into the distance, each boy looked at one another and grinned. That same grin was still on each lad's face long after he was back home.

Thomas Lynn wiped the mud from his eyes, and, firmly gripping the controls on the handlebars of the great metal steed, concentrated on carefully guiding it along the strange surface that covered the roads of this new world. One gloved hand reached up to briefly touch the small pendant hanging from his neck. As he did so, Thomas remembered what the old witch in the Land of Summer's Twilight had said after she gifted it to him. "This will serve ta guide you in your quest. It once belonged ta your Queen and will lead you ta Her lost self, if you listen ta what it tells you."

Indeed, all afternoon Thomas had felt the pull of someone or something coming from the city that loomed now out on the horizon, far across the moor. The lights of that city beckoned to him as if they were a jewelled diadem on the brow of The Lady Herself.

There was just enough light left in the sky for Thomas to see far down the road to where dense storm clouds raced to greet him. Still caked with the mud and grass of that woeful field, he welcomed the certain deluge, wanting to be clean and fair-smelling when he greeted whatever it was that called out to him so strongly.

Around him, the rolling landscape looked tantalisingly familiar, but the jumble of buildings crouched across its surface seemed, to him, out of place and ugly. As he encountered more and more of the strange metal machines that flew past on the road beside him he forced himself to accept them as an expected part of this strange new reality.

Thomas, though, in his time, had seen stranger lands than this, so he leaned into the wind and, feeling the first light touch of rain, smiled.

TWO

Snip!

Janet stared into the mirror and watched a crooked smile play across bright crimson lips that accented the warm brown of her skin. Still furious with her father, her brows were creased, her eyes dark with seething anger.

Snip!

"My guests will be here soon."

Snip!

"Put on some nice clothes and for god's sake fix your hair!"

Snip!

Maybe I should just tell him I'm having another one of my spells?

Oh no, Father, I've fainted again… I could just swan across the bed here in my own damned room.

SNIP!

I have to get out of this bloody house. Now!

From under ragged tufts of hair that jutted from her freshly cropped scalp, Janet's hazel eyes looked curiously back at the 'new' her as she whispered, "Okay, guess I should have found a proper clipper to use for this shearing. Still, Da will let out a howl when he sees me like this!"

Janet placed the pair of scissors on the polished marble table in front of the vanity, surprised at the sheer volume of what surrounded her.. Strewn on the plush carpet at her feet was a mound of what had been, until moments ago, the thick black hair that she'd worn for as long as she could remember.

"I wonder what mother would say."

That is if I even knew who she was? That is IF I'd ever even meet her…

Janet stood and shrugged into a leather jacket. It was new and black and just slightly too big for her, but she liked the way it looked. Most especially, Janet liked the way it made her feel.

Looking at the mirror again, she was excited by the young woman who stood there gazing defiantly back at her in the drab, lifeless room with its heavy dark wood furniture, the cream-coloured walls, and the canopy bed that had always taken up more space than it should. It was a room that

Janet had lived in all her life, without ever having any input into how it looked.

That bastard still thinks I'm his little girl!

Their latest argument had begun after Janet had returned that afternoon and found her new painting plucked from its place on her bedroom wall. Days earlier she'd been in the attic, rummaging through a massive pile of boxes on her never-ending quest to find some trace of her mother, and had discovered instead a small painting wrapped in layers of dusty fabric, tucked in alongside a jumble of meaningless curios. After carefully unwinding the cloth wrapping, Janet had been delighted by what she saw and immediately hung the canvas beside her bed, replacing the dreary abstract piece that had always been there.

The new, brightly coloured painting had been a comfort to fall asleep with, and it had brought a smile to her lips when she opened her eyes this morning. Now, just like that, it was gone. For some reason it had infuriated her father, and that, in and of itself, had pleased Janet. However, the anger that had contorted his face when she'd confronted him about his latest 'theft' had surprised even her. His voice had thundered back at her after she had demanded its return, "That painting was not yours in the first place."

"But I…"

"There's nothing you can say, I've had it destroyed."

"*Destroyed?*"

Soon both of them were screaming at each other.

Again.

Their argument had finally ended when Janet slammed the door of her father's study behind her just after he demanded she clean herself up in time for his dinner party that evening.

I've put up with this kind of shit since forever, but I don't have to take it anymore, do I?

She glanced out the wide bay window that filled almost the entire far wall of her bedroom. If it weren't pitch black outside, she would have seen the precisely manicured grounds of her father's estate that had in recent years felt more like a prison than a home.

If I stay here I'll never grow up. Never. Ever. NEVER!

Janet's angry, impatient gaze focused on the too familiar painting that once again hung to one side of her vast beige bed. "Boring! So bloody *boring!*"

Her new canvas had featured a small figure of an exotically armoured knight posed in a landscape filled with impossible colours that shimmered under a soft twilight sky strung with an uncountable number of cascading stars. She had ached to be a part of its beauty.

Fuck you, Father!

Before she could think better of it, Janet bent down and scooped the wiry tangle of cut hair at her feet into a small waste container which she tucked under one arm. Turning, she strode to the door and paused there. Her free hand hovered over the light switch for a second as she whispered, "Goodbye room," before plunging it into darkness.

Trying to look more confident than she actually felt, Janet followed the jangle of conversation that drifted up from below and hurried down the broad, curving staircase to the ground floor where her father was hosting his large, formal party. Then, just before Janet stepped into the great room, she paused and peered in as if it were some kind of treacherous alien environment, which, of course, it was.

The room's high, vaulted ceiling rose above elegant furnishings and richly panelled walls that were interrupted at intervals by brightly-coloured abstract paintings, framed in shining metal. Precise looking young men and women filled the room. Unlike Janet, they were dressed in proper evening clothes, the men in dinner suits and the women in what looked like very expensive gowns.

I'll bet every one of those dresses cost more than their entire month's salary.

Her father stood in the midst of the crowded room, easily keeping his guests entertained. John Ravenscroft was a tall man, still handsome, but going slowly to fat, though still exuding raw energy as well as a natural assumption of his superiority. When Janet finally walked through the crowd toward him, the first thing his attention focused on was her newly shorn hair.

Letting out an exasperated sigh, he asked, "Janet, what have you done now?"

To which she replied, "Nothing that I shouldn't have done, ages ago."

Then he took in her leather coat, the ripped jeans and the slogan slashed in bright red ink across her raven black t-shirt: ***Just Do It!*** An even darker scowl creased the usual symmetry of his face.

Most of the party guests had heard at least a few tales of Janet Ravenscroft's more outrageous escapades, so they nervously stepped aside as she sauntered toward her father, dark face cocked to one side. After she got close enough to smell his cologne, Janet spat out, "Here, this is for you! You always loved it so." Abruptly, she emptied the contents of the waste container onto his intricately tooled Italian leather shoes. Janet's newly shorn hair fell on them and spilled across the carpet at his feet.

Looking down, the elder Ravenscroft grunted with distaste and stepped back, shaking away the dark wiry strands of hair. When he looked up at his daughter, she smiled at him and then let the waste bin drop, too. It hit the carpeted floor with a dull metallic clang that punctuated her angry words.

"Consider it a going-away present, Daddy dearest!"

Janet turned then and strode from the room, heading across the imposing entrance hall and out through the front door, casually leaving it open behind her. Beside the drive there was a tight circle of men and women braving the cold autumn night for a smoke. Their heads turned with curiosity as Janet stalked past and hopped into her own car, a red convertible Ferrari that she had parked at the very end of the parking area earlier that day. The keys were already there, in the ignition, so she started the engine, shifted gears and headed down the long driveway, which ended in the massive gates that dominated the entrance to the Ravenscroft estate.

Those gates were open now, allowing a late arriving guest to enter. Janet flashed past the startled driver and out onto the long drive beyond that eventually emptied onto a public street.

Glancing in the rear view mirror she saw her father, one hand raised. She could imagine him yelling, "Janet, come back here this instant!"

She shook her head, enjoying the novel sensation of the cool night air whipping over her freshly shorn scalp and yelled back over her shoulder as loudly as she could, "Not on your bloody life!"

THREE

Hours later, Janet walked unsteadily down a deserted lane in downtown Inverness. On either side of her, parked cars lined a street packed with shabby apartments and ground floor businesses, shut tight this late at night. Occasionally, overhead streetlights soaked the urban landscape around her with their yellow sodium stain. An unpleasant odour from one too many overflowing garbage skips curdled the cool night air. Oblivious to her surroundings, Janet was deep in a very one-sided conversation with every car that she passed.

"I was just havin' some fun.

"Never been much for drinkin' though. Mostly it tastes bloody awful! Mostly…"

A grin lit up Janet's face then and without her almost habitual scowl her features were soft and lovely. "'Sides a drink in the face is nothing, 'specially when it's one of daddy's little army men. Thought he was gonna take me back to the castle for my own good, did he?"

Janet plucked regretfully at the torn sleeve on her new leather jacket. "Gave 'im the slip, though, right out the window in the loo."

She laughed, lurched over to a sleek sports car and sat down on its hood. There was a loud hollow thump as a shallow dent formed beneath her. Janet tilted toward the car parked beside her Ferrari and whispered, "Okay. Is mine, a gift from my darlin' daddy don't you know?

"Ha! Bribe more like…"

Janet glanced blearily at the dull glow of the sprawling city beyond and sighed. "Fucking ugly ain't the half o' it." Then she stared into a puddle of oil stained water just below her dangling feet, trying to focus on the rippling streetlight reflected in it. "I get it, though. This is where I live… so get used to it…"

Just then a loud, insistent buzzing caught her attention. A few lines from her current favourite song played loudly from an inside pocket of her leather jacket before fading away into the night air. She fumbled for her mobile, and then squinted at the screen, trying to read the text, "Oh. What a surprise! A message from his highness."

One hand to her forehead, she performed a mock swoon, "Come back. Come back. I will do anything for you, daughter, if only you return." Not even looking at the screen, Janet continued to talk back to her father's thumb-typed words, her voice getting higher and louder as each confused thought tumbled out. "So, why didya take my painting, old man! Why?

"Got no answer, have you… Then how about a few kind words instead? Maybe a hug goodnight? Or, just plain be there when I need you." Her voice lowered then, imitating her father's, "No, can't do that dearest, I'm WORKING!

"Then how about telling me where my mother is, you wanker!"

Angrily, she brushed away a tear from her cheek. "I just want to see her… Wanna talk to my own damned mother… got so much I could tell her, don't I? But that's just not ever gonna happen if he has anything to do with it!"

Least I'm pretty certain she's still alive. He'd have told me if anything serious had happened to Mum… wouldn't he?

Janet looked up into the night air and shouted "You would have told me about that, wouldn't you, father? WOULDN'T YOU?"

Abruptly a gravely voice interrupted her personal soliloquy, "Hey, looks like we might have us a wee Pakki here."

Janet slipped to the pavement and lurched around to see two men stalking toward her.

"Got yourself some trouble with yer old man, have ya' luv?"

The nearby streetlight clearly illuminated them both. The first sported an ugly buzz cut, revealing heavy tattoos that completely covered his scalp and disappeared under his frayed leather jacket. His companion was tall with shining blue-black skin and an Adam's apple that looked so sharp that it could slice a sheet of paper. His long dreads were partially gathered under a loose wool cap.

God, Janet why weren't you paying attention!

Suddenly, fear and adrenalin tore away at the thick alcohol-induced curtain that smothered her thoughts.

Now I could use one of father's little helpers… but you left him back at the bar, didn't you?

The taller man, with the filthy dreads, smiled at her, his mouth full of rotting teeth. When he leaned toward her to speak, she could smell his rancid breath.

"Hey, nice phone."

Helpfully his companion added "Real nice."
"Looks like you're gonna drop it, though."
"Give it here."
"We'll take care o' it."
"And you too come ta that…"

Janet watched, mesmerised, as the tall man casually began to wave a long blade under her face. It glinted sharply in the streetlight. His companion was now holding a tire iron tightly clenched in his fist.

Desperate, Janet threw her mobile up into the air and turned to sprint down the street as fast as she could, fumbling in her purse for the can of mace or better yet the knife that she always carried.

They're in here.
Somewhere…

Throwing the phone seemed to have delayed them momentarily, but soon enough Janet heard the pounding of their boots on the hard pavement close behind her. Certain that she was unable to outrun them much longer, her fingers frantically scrambled through everything that was jammed inside her purse. Finally, pushing aside her buried car keys she grasped the small aerosol of mace.

Got it!

Before she could pull the spray out, though, Janet lurched around a corner and abruptly slammed into a young man sitting on a large motorcycle. A Vincent Black Lightning. 1952. Its engine rumbling with eager life. The driver steadied the bike and smiled back at Janet, staring deep into her hazel eyes.

Unable to tear her gaze away, in that moment Janet forgot about the danger in the rough urban landscape around her as her world shifted abruptly on its axis. Drowning in the man's soft gaze she felt, for the first time in her life, completely and utterly safe.

And unaccountably, she remembered the knight in the stolen painting.

Looks like him, kind of…

Then, as the pounding of heavy, booted heels skidded to a halt a few feet behind her, Janet was jolted back into a world filled with would-be muggers and indifferent fathers. The man on the motorcycle, though, paid no attention to her pursuers. With his eyes locked on Janet's, his handsome face creased into a broad smile before he spoke for the first time, "Would you join me on my noble steed?"

Impulsively, Janet jumped on the bike, her arms clinching tight around the young man's waist. The cycle's motor revved, and suddenly they roared directly between her two pursuers and flew on up the street.

Craning her neck, Janet watched the hapless thieves quickly grow smaller in the distance and howled a delighted victory cry into the night.

Suddenly, in front of them, a short, heavyset man launched himself from between two parked cars directly at the cycle, making a desperate grab for Janet as she flew past. Her still nameless saviour leaned casually to one side, tilting his bike, easily distancing them both from the intruder's outstretched arms. As the man stumbled and rolled to his knees, she recognised the security guard she'd escaped from earlier in the bar and delightedly screamed, "Faster! *Faster!*"

Picking up speed, the powerful machine surged between several oncoming cars, carrying them both finally to safety. Still laughing, Janet's attention returned to her rescuer and she studied his profile for a moment, as he turned a little to look back at her. It was then that she realised his leather helmet wasn't like any she'd ever seen before. Intricately tooled, it fitted tightly around his head and was open over his eyes and mouth, more like a medieval knight's than the usual bulky helmet a biker wore.

He spoke loudly enough to be heard over the exhilarating sound of the wind and the road, "Where would you have me take you?"

With her cheek pressed comfortably against the back of his coat she relaxed. The coat smelled sweetly of herbs that she couldn't quite name, but they soothed her frayed nerves. Janet's face broke into a wistful smile before she said simply, "Drive. Just drive."

"It would be my pleasure."

FOUR

As the bike glided past the bright lights of oncoming cars and the cold, fresh wind rushed over her newly exposed scalp, Janet felt her old life fade away. At that moment she was certain that everything would be all right.

But that's crazy. I don't know who this man is or even where he's taking me!

Arms clutched tightly around her rescuer's waist, she considered the young man. From the quick glimpse she'd had he seemed handsome enough: bright dark eyes and high cheekbones. Laced cuffs fluttered from the sleeves of his long leather cloak that flapped around her in the wind like raven's wings. His long dark brown hair tied back with a red silk ribbon flew out from under the back of his leather helmet. Unexpectedly her heart fluttered, and she had to stop herself from wondering what his hair would look like loosened from that ribbon.

Bloody hell, I could have fallen into his gaze and stayed there...

Finally, leaving the city far behind, he brought them to a stop on the edge of the heather covered moor and cut the engine. To her right, Janet could just make out the dim curve of an ancient stone structure. All around them the landscape rolled and swelled into darkness, lit only by a star swept sky.

She smiled when she recognised where they were. "Hey, I know this place. That's the old bridge that's the start of Ye Old Jacobite Trail. Plenty of tartan clad ghosts or snoggin' teens if you go that way."

Trying, unsuccessfully to suppress a shiver from the cool night air, Janet leaned in close to her rescuer, "Listen, the least I can do is introduce myself to my gallant saviour." The man turned back to her, and on his shadowed face she saw him smile, "If it pleases you."

"Well, yes. Yes, it does please me. My name is Janet Ravenscroft. Thanks for saving my butt back there."

The young man stepped off his bike and, facing her, presented a courtly bow. "A Knight must always stay alert to the dangers on the road he travels."

"Really?" Janet smiled and continued, "Just like in a fairy tale then, you're going to be my knight in shining armour."

"Perhaps. Now, it pleases me to give you my name as well. I am Thomas Lynn, and I am at your service."

Janet shifted uncomfortably, "Thomas. That sounds so damned formal. Can I just call you Tom?"

"I have been known by that name as well."

"So, Tom, what's with you sounding like you've stepped out of a production of The Princess Bride?"

"My Lady, I…"

"See! Just like that. Nobody talks like that. Nobody."

Tom's face twisted into an impatient grimace, "Where I call home, all speak in like manner."

"Okay, I get it, you're playing a game… Want to maybe tell me what it is?"

"I can assure you, this is no game."

They stared at each other awkwardly for a moment until Janet grasped Tom's ungloved hand to climb off the bike. Her eyes widened then, as the world around her twisted and shimmered. Suddenly the blackness of the night gave way to a softer twilight and the stars above began to pulse in time with her rapidly beating heart. She was overcome by the intense, saturated colour that infused every spray of heather and every rock and small tree around them and most particularly, the person standing so close to her.

There, in that strange new world, Thomas' eyes seemed to actually glow.

That intense flood of sensation as well as the lingering effects of the drams of whiskey she'd so carelessly knocked back earlier that evening caused Janet to sag helplessly against Tom.

Gracefully, Thomas Lynn lowered the now unconscious mortal girl to the heather at his feet, unwilling and unable to pull his attention away from her beautiful, soft features.

Most of all it was Janet's rich brown skin that surprised and delighted him. His own, pale as alabaster from living so long in a land lit only by the moon, made a vivid contrast.

Behind them both, in a wild tangle of heather and an occasional stunted tree, strange twisty creatures with tiny folded wings began to chatter amongst themselves, leaping from branch to limb and back again. Finally two, bolder than the rest, dropped to the ground and crept slowly toward the Knight and the sleeping mortal. Tom, although he was aware of their presence, ignored them, whispering to himself, "In her own way she is as beautiful as the Queen herself…"

"All right matey, we heard that!"

Tom impatiently turned his head, acknowledging their presence before hissing, "Come! See for yourselves if you think I lie." Curious, the two fae creatures crept closer and peered down at Janet. A look of perplexed wonder filled both sets of slanted yellow eyes.

"Thomas, what you speak is true!"

"Yes…"

"But is she the one the witch woman sent you looking for so far from home?"

The man continued to gaze raptly down at the soft features of the unconscious girl. "I am almost certain that this mortal woman is why I am here this night. But I must test her to be sure."

Tom hunched his shoulders. "In truth, I like it not. But my duty to The Queen is my only purpose here until I restore Herself to Her land and Her court."

Scratching his head, one of the small fae creatures glanced curiously up at Tom, "Is that what's been keepin' ya busy out here then?"

Blustering, Tom continued, "Yes, that for a certainty…"

"Now, Tommy boy, nae more of your malarkey we'll be hearin'."

"We seen ya out here 'n the mortal lands fer th' last few days larkin' 'bout. As ye say, on the Queen's business or more likely on orders from the ol' witch woman, who's to tell which?"

Both small creatures glanced sideways up at Thomas. Then the first one slyly added, "It's a dreary place and that is fer sure."

Sudden enthusiasm lit Tom's eyes, "Indeed, it is not. My memories of it have done this land no justice at all. I was born close by, and my love for this moorland runs deep inside my bones."

Nodding to each other, as if his words only confirmed what they already knew, the tallest of the spindly creatures suddenly grinned, "Ah, well then, Thomas, we'll nae try to dissuade ye of any false notions ye might have an that's a fact."

His companion looked back down at the human girl and grimaced, "Don't think much o' tha' hair though?"

"Awful ain't the half o' that."

"We could fix that up quick, though…"

Thomas ignored the nattering creatures as he gracefully gathered the unconscious girl in his arms and carried her to the crest of the arched bridge. There the Knight gently lay Janet down. Quickly shrugging off his long leather coat, he folded it several times before using it to pillow the young woman's head from the hard granite that paved the ancient structure. Then, while the stars continued to wheel across the sky overhead, he stared raptly down at the mortal woman.

"There is such innocence in you. Later I will beg your forgiveness for what will happen now, but I must be certain that you are the one I was sent to find."

FIVE

A short time later, Janet stirred, then stiffly got to her feet before leaning quickly down to pick up the coat that had been left under her head. Shivering from the cold, she slipped gratefully into it, her arms clutching the leather close to her body as she looked around.

In the pre-dawn darkness, Janet could just make out an almost treeless landscape that rolled away into upland glens and tumbling burns without a single soul moving across its surface.

Well, there's absolutely no knight on any black bloody motorbike to be seen out there.

"Thomas. Tom!"

A few meters away was a small parking lot, now completely deserted, where this section of the old highway began its leap up and over the ancient stone bridge and the racing burn just below it in what was the first leg of an extensive walking path that stretched all the way to Cairngorns National Park.

"*Tom!*" she shouted.

Janet buried her hands deep into the coat's pockets and began to stride briskly back and forth along the short span of the bridge trying to loosen her cramped muscles and jumpstart her circulation. After a few minutes, though, she called out again into the darkness.

"It's way too cold to play games. Where the fuck are you?"

To her left, far out across the darkness, she could just make out Inverness, the towers of its high-rise bank buildings and ancient cathedrals now dimly lit by the nearing promise of dawn. To the south there was only a broad expanse of moor rolling into the distance, disappearing into thick clouds and mist and far away, heavy rain.

"No bloody mobile to call for help and it's too far to try to walk back to the city. And at this time of morning the traffic out here is almost nil. So, I can't even chance a bit of hitch hiking."

Janet stood in the centre of the bridge and let out a very un-lady like bellow.

"Tom! Thomas! Or whatever you want to call yourself, I'm right fucking here. Where the bloody hell are you?"

Charles Vess

Some shining knight you turned out to be. Just another bloody wanker, like all the rest of them.

Seething with frustration, she suddenly grabbed a bit of loose granite and hurled it as hard as possible at the rushing stream below. The loud, mostly satisfying splash that followed momentarily soothed her nerves. Letting out a harsh laugh at herself, at the world in general, but most importantly at her current location in it, Janet propped both arms on the rough stonework and peered down into the deep shadows that still gathered under the arched bridge.

Hey Mum, what do I do now?

Janet had found herself asking that same question many times during her life and always imagined the look of warmth and love that would be on her mother's face. Or at least, what Janet imagined her mother looked like.

Because good ol' Daddy won't even allow a picture of her anywhere in the house, will he?

She looked down at her slender arms, wiggling her fingers in the darkness of the night as if she could actually see their rich brown colour.

Sure about one thing, though, Pops is as white as white can be, so Mum must have been dark skinned like me.

Right?

Anyway, it's always felt good to talk to the ghost of what she could have been. Tell her how stupid my latest A level tutor was or how bloody hard my math homework is or even, what I should wear on whatever date I might have.

But if she'd really been there... in the same house, would I have been able to talk to her about this kind of stuff or would I have had as little to say to her as I do to father?

Sure do wish I'd had a chance to find out...

Her wistful musings abruptly came to an end when Janet sensed rather than saw an immense looming shadow climb out from under the stone bridge and vault onto the rough paving in front of her. In the darkness she couldn't make out any of its features, but whatever the thing was, it blocked out every star above her.

"Tom?"

Only a deep, guttural, rumbling voice answered her, "Say the password or pay the forfeit."

The words weren't spoken in English but instead some strange language that Janet had never heard before, yet she could understand every syllable that had been spoken. Janet was dumbstruck. Though only when she found herself able to reply in that same language did Janet begin to truly panic.

"What? What password..."

"Say the password or pay the forfeit."

"Please, I don't know what you want!"

"The password or the forfeit."

"Okay, okay then... swordfish?"

"The true password or the forfeit."

"How about, 'please' then?"

Ominous silence followed her frantic guess, leaving Janet with a desire to run away as quickly as possible from whatever shadow-thing confronted her. Her fingers clutched for the reassuring can of mace but her shoulder bag was gone and with it her knife as well as the can of noxious spray.

The creature, whatever it was, stood solidly between her and the vague promise of safety that the public motorway offered. Her only other option was to run out onto the dark moor. Indecision froze her in place. But after hearing another deep animal grunt, Janet dodged forward, around the shadowy creature, trying to run back across the bridge.

Immediately there was a whoosh of air above her and the solid stone of the bridge quivered with the weight that landed on it. Again, the great beast blocked her escape.

"The password or the forfeit."

Terrified, Janet spit out, "I don't know your bloody password."

"Then you must pay the forfeit."

For a moment the unseen creature's words seemed to hang visibly in the cold air of the bridge until a slight breeze caught them up and stroked them across Janet's skin, where they clung for a moment before fading away. She shivered. Then, deep within her, complex memories of a place and a life that Janet had never known existed before this night began to quicken and take on shape here in the mortal world.

Janet managed to gasp out a few words before her body shuddered uncontrollably as if from some kind of great physical impact.

"I will not pay your bloody forfeit!"

Her mind then, not her body, reeled from the onslaught of some powerfully aggressive otherworldly intelligence that subsumed every human sense she possessed. An insidious primal force against which no mortal was able to offer an adequate defence flowed unabated into Janet and took form.

The woman, who moments before had been a mere human, now looked through other eyes and saw the dark creature for what it had always been. Towering above Her was a giant pig-like beast, clad in rough layers of leather and fur, with a wide black belt cinched around its waist above two short legs ending in cloven hooves. Below a pair of tiny bloodshot eyes, long sharp tusks distorted curling lips that stretched from ear to ear.

"Beast, I need no password. Do you not know your Queen? And why do you still stand before me? Kneel and show your fealty."

Gazing below him at what still looked like a young mortal girl, the beast hesitated.

"Now!"

Squinting its beady eyes, the beast somehow saw through the illusion that now cloaked Her and knelt, its snouted head bowed low, touching the stone pavers.

A cruel smile lit The Queen's face when She looked past the grovelling creature to the end of the stone bridge, where, suited in leather armour burnished a deep red, with a helmet clutched under one arm and a great sword in the other, a familiar figure stood awaiting Her pleasure.

Words in that unknown language fell easily from what had been Janet's lips, "Thomas, my Knight of the Rose, what do We do here in this dreary place? Where is My hall? My palace? Where are My gardens filled with roses blooming red, as red as your blood?"

Although neither her velvety chocolate-coloured skin nor the crude cut of the young mortal woman's hair spoke to any aspect of his Queen, it was unmistakably Her voice, Her presence. Tom fell to his knees, arms spread wide in a gesture of abject humility. "My Lady, I am yours to command. What would you have of me?"

Before this strange queen could answer, the body that She inhabited shuddered and stumbled against the side of the bridge. She cried out, "Thomas, to my side!"

Janet had never stopped her wild struggle with the intelligence that had taken control of her will. And the Queen, surprised at the mortal woman's fierce resistance, simply backed away from it, biding Her time, to watch and to study Her mortal host.

Suddenly, the mind that had trampled so easily over Janet's true self was gone, leaving her bewildered and furious, but most of all frightened. She screamed her anguish into the night sky, "What was that? Who was that? Whoever she was, that bitch thought she owned me!"

Total exhaustion forced Janet to once again crumple into Tom's waiting arms. She buried her head against his chest for a moment until remembering what happened earlier that evening her head jerked up. There were sparks in her eyes and little chance for her anger to cool.

"You wanker! You left me on this bloody fucking bridge. Why?"

In her fury, Janet paid no attention to his white face or his sombre eyes looking at her full of concern, and wonder as well. Instead she slapped him as hard as she could.

After a moment of stunned silence, he murmured softly, "Truly I cannot tell you."

At that same time, Janet became aware once more of the shadow-beast that until now had silently watched the strange drama playing out below it. The creature shook its broad, hairy shoulders, as if to say, it had seen stranger things than this before and on this very bridge as well. Only now, when Janet looked up at it, she could clearly distinguish its shape and form where before it had been merely a creature spun from shadow and darkness. Abruptly she realised that the alien presence within her had effected some kind of fundamental change in her perception of the world around her.

Just before those strange visions began to fade away, she looked out on a world that was not cloaked in deep nighttime shadows but in soft twilight with a brilliant crescent moon riding high in the sky.

The creature continued to look down at Janet curiously for a moment, before turning and, without haste, climbing back over the edge of the stone bridge to disappear into the darkness below. For a moment Janet stood staring back across the now empty bridge, the sight of Thomas's huge black bike leaning against its railing somehow reassuringly normal.

She asked, "Tom, what was that thing... what kind of world would make such a horrid creature?"

The Knight of the Rose looked inscrutably at Janet for a moment before offering a completely unsatisfactory explanation, "That, my lady, was a troll."

"A troll? Really?"

Janet stared at him until he sighed and offered her a more detailed answer. "That was The Troll under The Bridge. He always bides here, under this particular bridge, and has done so for the last age and more. He counts it as honour to challenge all who pass this way."

Tom grinned at her, trying to charm away her anger. But nothing eased Janet's primal fear that that otherworldly mind would find her again and imprison her inside a body that she had absolutely no control over. "Tom, I have to know who or what was just inside me. I looked through someone else's eyes and what I saw was not this bloody Earth… you, for one thing…" Remembering Thomas kneeling before her, clad in armour, Janet frowned. "Hey, where's your armour? How'd you stash it away to so damn quick?"

With a casual shrug of his shoulders Thomas stood mute, offering no explanation for what had just happened. That profoundly awkward silence continued until it became an almost bottomless pit that needed to be filled somehow. Infuriated, Janet filled it with her anger. "You bloody well brought me here, so you must have wanted me to meet that god-awful beast. Why?"

"I had no wish to visit harm upon you and would have defended you against it if I had to, but on my honour, I can tell you no more than that."

"Why… why do you keep talking like that? There aren't any knights any more or ladies for that matter. After all that you're still playing some stupid game?"

When Tom still offered no explanation, Janet turned away and stalked toward the road.

Ignoring the tittering laughter of the small Fae creatures around him, Tom followed close behind the frustrated mortal girl.

Sensing him by her side once more, Janet turned. There were fresh tears streaking down her cheeks now. Her face twisted with rage, she shouted, "I'm absolutely not hanging around some asshole I can't trust. So, do I stay out here where there's a monster from my worst bloody nightmare or do I somehow find my way home and put up with the creature that lives there?"

Thomas stared back at her a moment before reluctantly nodding his head. When he finally did speak, there was a ring of bleak finality to his words. "Janet, you speak the truth, at least as far as you know it. There is but a thin curtain that cloaks your world from another where the beast you saw tonight is as common as the metal vehicles that fill your strange paved roads."

The handsome knight smiled then, as they were both buffeted by a blast of rain and wind, and began to speak, "And lady…" but seeing the quick scowl on his companion's face, he thought better of his choice of words. "Janet, I will spend this night here on the moor and you are fit for far more comfort than I can offer you. Where would you have me take you?"

"Right! I guess it's the monster I know because your troll buddy absolutely bloody terrifies me."

Janet's shoulders slumped wearily. "I'm so tired of fighting… with you, with my father, with everyone. And that's all that's waiting for me if I go back home, more fighting. I'd made a promise to myself tonight that I was done with that life, but now…now, I don't know what other choice I'm left with."

"Perhaps you could just explain to your father what it is that you so earnestly desire?"

With both arms wrapped tightly around her body, Janet replied, "He won't listen to reason, especially not from me. He never does." Understanding her frustration, Tom replied, "I, too, have dealt with one whose will is unforgiving of what others may want or even need. It is ofttimes difficult to reason with such a person."

Janet stared out at the impossibly huge landscape around them for a moment, then back at Tom's implacable face as a tight smile slid across her lips, "I really didn't plan my escape very well, did I? And, I sure shouldn't have stopped for that drink to calm my nerves." Resigned, she whispered "Okay, take me home. I'll tell you how to get there."

Moments later Janet climbed astride the Vincent and clasped her arms once more around Tom. As the bike picked up speed across the gravelled lot and out onto the motorway, she couldn't help but bury her face into the broad back before her and try desperately to push away the empty feeling that had been growing inside her for too many years. That afternoon, Janet had almost been overwhelmed by the certainty that she was drowning in a world where John Ravenscroft's every wish was absolute law.

How can I go back there and not go fucking crazy?

Janet opened her eyes and watched the dark moor slip past them as the cold night air-dried the tears that she hadn't even noticed were on her cheeks. Improbably, with all that had happened between them tonight, warm thoughts of the man she clutched so tightly fluttered along the edge of her mind.

Then I must be crazy! For whatever stupid reason, he helped make what happened here happen. I could have been hurt or even worse.

But without her habitual anger, Janet felt lighter, as if that anger had been simply weighing down her spirit.

Just who or what are you, mystery man?

Dawn's full light coloured a sky thick with rolling grey clouds as Tom brought the Vincent to a stop before the gate that opened onto the Ravenscroft estate, and Janet stepped away from the huge black motorcycle. Both she and Tom had been so deep in their own thoughts that neither had spoken on the long drive there. Janet stood beside the bike for a moment before slowly shrugging her way out of the long leather coat that she was still wearing. Tom's arm came to rest on hers. "Keep it, the morning is still cold."

Her simmering anger momentarily resurfaced. "No, it's bloody yours. I don't want it. Just take the damn thing!"

Reluctantly, Thomas handled the coat, folding it over into his lap before reaching his hand under his shirt to carefully unclasp the small pendant that hung by a delicate silver chain around his neck. Tom placed it, still warm with the heat of his body, in Janet's outstretched hand. "Then please accept this token as an apology for all that you have endured this night."

Without waiting for an answer, Tom revved the engine of his cycle and flew down the long tree-lined drive, never looking back.

"What a flat-out wanker."

It was only after she no longer heard the roar of his bike that Janet thought to look down at what was cupped in her palm. A delicate silver pendant with a beautifully sculpted rose, entwined with thorns, rested there. Janet gripped the pendant securely in her hand and grimaced.

Fuck him if he thinks a bit of bling is going to buy my forgiveness.

Turning back to the high iron gates that opened onto her father's estate, Janet was about to punch in the key code when she paused. Through its massive bars she looked up the long drive and even with the heavy morning mist that still clung to the overly manicured lawn the dark hulking spread of the house she was raised in was visible. In the cold morning air beads of sweat formed on her brow.

"No. No. *NO!*"

"I just bloody will not do it."

Okay, Ms. Janet, let's try this again. I have to escape this bloody prison, so... I need my car.

Janet turned her back on the gate, but not before producing a defiant hand gesture for the security camera that her father was sure to see long after she was gone.

"See ya later, Pops."

Maybe if I drive fast enough and hard enough I can leave all the bloody monsters behind me.

At that moment, she stopped dead in her tracks as wave after wave of intense pain shot through her body. Desperately gasping for breath, Janet staggered back against the massive iron bars of the gate. Just before she passed out, Janet clenched her eyes shut as the colour of every single object around her intensified far beyond the capacity of any normal person to focus on. Overwhelmed, she collapsed in an ungainly sprawl on the tarmac and lay there oblivious as the sun continued its slow crawl up over the horizon.

Six

Later that morning, within a small circle of standing stones, far out on the heather-covered moor, Thomas leaned back against the rough granite surface of the tallest of those dolmens. His face creased in thought as he stared at the heavy, black motorcycle leaning against the stone opposite him.

With practice I've grown accustomed to riding that strange construction of metal as I ever had any living steed. And, for certain, it gathers far less attention here in this world than any stom,ping warhorse would.

Though, if I were not truly human, the metal that fashions it would burn my flesh and diminish my strength till I counted death a rare blessing.

Above Thomas and the vast moor that surrounded him the wind howled in fury, sending ominous clouds scuttling before it. Those clouds were filled with the promise of heavy rain that wouldn't be long in coming. But inside the ring of stones the air is warm and still, as it has always been for those that knew the way of it.

When first I stepped through this door of stone back into the mortal realms of my birth the heat of its sun welcomed me like a long-forgotten friend.

The simple joy of walking this once familiar landscape, one that had nourished my people for hundreds of years, stirred such longing in me that I am eager to linger among its wonders.

Thomas had been so consumed then by that curiosity that he'd briefly considered stealing a horse to ease his exploration. But the thought of so base an act had twisted darkly at his mind. So, when Thomas had found the motorcycle left at his family's estate and the young lads who had been so eager to show him how to use it, he'd been pleasantly surprised. The discovery had felt like a gift, left there especially for him.

I could not have asked for a better one.

The thoughtfulness of that unknown and unnamed family member had eased the darkness that had all but drowned his thoughts after seeing the elaborate stone markers rising above the graves of his mother and father, indeed, his entire family. effect of time and weather on the outlines of the lettering on each of their head stones had given him some vague idea of the passage of time since last he had walked these hills.

Abruptly, the memory of Janet's vivid features brightened his sombre thoughts.

When not consumed by anger, the warmth of her eyes... the rich colour of her skin... offered such contrast to the golden beauty of my Queen...

His hands plucked guiltily at the heather that gathered at the base of the largest of the great standing stones.

"Perhaps I should not have put the mortal girl through such an ordeal and instead brought her to the Summer Lands this very night?" he pondered out loud. "After all, quickest done is soonest mended."

Looking up into the windblown sky that hurtled, twisting and turning above him, Thomas heard again the old witch's words when he had found her there in the midst of the rank devastation that now laid claim to the palace that had once been sacred to his Queen.

"Thomas Lynn, Knight o' the Rose, why have you cast aside your sworn duty and strayed from Her presence for sae long? Why were you not here ta prevent tha destruction that you now see all around us?"

Sudden shame filled his heart as he pleaded his long absence.

"Is it not also my duty to be a steward of Her realm, ta keep safe its far-flung borders, to cast down any malice or wrong-doing that I find there?"

Silently the witch stared back at him.

Gesturing round about them both, he had cried out, "Crone, know you how this pestilence came to be? What savage will has brought such utter ruin to my Queen's city?"

The crone had laughed softly at his outcry, "Sir Knight, still speaks o' Her as his Queen, even after he has abandoned Her and their love bower so very lang ago."

Brow knit in consternation, Thomas continued, "But I have been gone only a short time..." The ancient witch smiled slyly back at him, "Surely you kin that time flows differently along th' border twixt this Land o' Summer's Twilight and any other."

Fixing him with her cold gaze she continued, "Flowing, slipping, from one side ta the other. Aye, but a single hour there could be repeated here again and again o'er the slow passing o' this land's moon into its fullness. A moment there, can last an eternity here."

Thomas was silent then, remembering how often this creature had stood beside his Queen, offering Her advice and the wisdom that only great age can bring with it. In the end his choice had been a simple one: to put his trust in her words. Remembering the crone's name, he called her by it, "Mother Hainter, bottle witch, you who are said to be a keeper of the old wisdoms, where then will I find my Queen? If she were taken against Her will, then I will go to Her wherever She may be and deliver Her from that place of evil. For, has She not named me Her champion?"

The wizened crone continued to stare silently at him for so long that Thomas began to wonder what he might have said that had made her angry. When she did speak again, he was horrified by what she said.

"In a manner She is safe, for She now bides within th' bleak halls o' Th' Lord o' Death and o' Darkness."

Thomas had sprung to his feet, reflexively gripping his sword hilt.

"Calm yourself, Sir Knight. It is Her body only that is his prisoner. Rescuing Her now would nae offer any o' us any comfort, for She is moon-mad, her mind lost ta all rhyme and reason. Her mind borne away on terrible winds ta bide in some other's body."

Although Thomas had never suffered under that Lord's cruelty, he remembered clearly all that his Queen had told him of the evil heart that held sway over that empire. Clenching the hilt of his sword harder, the Knight pledged an oath, "Then with all speed I must find Her true self, wherever She may be gone, and speed the healing of Her mind and spirit!"

The crone had again smiled to herself, evidently pleased with her own secret thoughts, before she answered, "Well, Knight o' th' Rose, then you must return ta the land o' yer birth and find there th' human who now possesses th' mind o' your broken Queen. And once found, it needs be brought here into Her land and in th' presence o' Her physical form for th' healing ta begin."

Vivid memories flew then through Thomas' thoughts. "The mortal realms... it has been long and long since ever I ever thought of the simple life that I once lived there."

Ignoring his discomfort, the witch woman's brows furrowed in thought. "Sir Knight, I also have it in mind that I have watched this tale o' love and war played out twixt your Queen and this Lord far, far ta many times in my lifetime, and that is a very lang time indeed. Always it ends in despair and loneliness for them both as well as their lands. So, Thomas, I think that between us, we must write another, more natural ending ta their eternal tale o' woe. Would you also make that your quest, Knight o' th' Rose, as dangerous as it may well prove ta be?"

Thomas had struggled then and now to understand the witch's words but, finally, he asked only, "Who are you creature? How do you know of such matters?"

"Ah Thomas, it's old I am, older even than the Fae.

"I have walked through th' world's stories since before there were mountains. Since before there were oceans. Before even th' winds that blew between th' stars."

Then her strange slanted eye stared straight at the knight, "Indeed, it was my song that birthed this world out o' black chaos. My stories that made every creature that walks this circle round, whether they be from th' mortal lands or o' Faerie.

Thomas rose then to his feet, "Truly, I understand little of what you say, and yet you also spoke of a quest that will restore my Queen and heal all that is Hers and that, with all my heart, I do willingly accept." Unsheathing his sword, he grasped its hilt with both hands and kissed its blade before intoning, "Here I do swear as the Knight of the Rose to accept this quest and only my death will keep me from the fulfilling of it."

With those words a pleased smile spread across the bottle witch's lined face, "So be it then."

"And after I have brought that which you ask into the presence of my Queen, what must I do then with this mortal who has played host to Her spirit?"

"As ye will, Sir Knight. As ye will."

Thomas had nodded grimly and turned to leave but the witch woman had grasped his arm, and so he turned again to face her.

"Thomas, I fear th' Queen's mind is too powerful ta be contained in a single mortal shell. If that were ta happen then that person would become as mad as she and no use ta either o' us. So, be mindful that there may be more than one mortal that you must find."

I have no other choice but to accept the little mother's words to be true so there is at least one more piece to this puzzle that I must find in order to make the Queen whole. For I am cert that Janet is of sound mind even though her anger causes her to lash out at all that come near.

I must secure all who are needed to complete this queer tangle if I am to restore The Lady's wits.

His features twisted with guilt as he considered what he had done that night.

The witch's pendant will tell me where young Janet bides or if she is in danger. So, my quest for this other mind will not be hindered on her account...

Later that same morning, Janet jolted frantically awake, throwing her head from side-to-side trying to dislodge the nightmare memory of the pig beast's fetid breath as well as the presence of the woman that had so completely violated her mind. Then, when Janet felt the familiar weight of the padded restraining straps that crisscrossed her chest and legs, she tried to calm her wildly beating heart.

Those bloody creatures wouldn't have the nerve to come knocking on my father's door.

Another wave of panic arose, though, as she remembered collapsing out on the drive earlier that morning. For a moment, she again struggled with her restraints; humiliation, frustration and then anger replacing her panic. Craning her neck, Janet was relieved to see that she was in her bedroom, if not in her own bed. Then, looking directly up at the ever-present surveillance camera mounted over the door, she successfully kept her emotions sufficiently in check to call out in a reasonable tone, "Hey. Hey! I'm awake... Get me out of these straps. Please!"

Her bedroom door immediately swung open, and a familiar male nurse hurried into the room, a concerned look on his face. Still, Janet gritted her teeth, straining against the straps that held her down, "Curt, please, please, please get me out of these damned things."

"Hold on, miss...we only strapped you in because the doc and your father were worried that you might begin sleepwalking again..." Ruefully, Curtis pointed to the carefully bandaged abrasions on both her elbows. Then, seeing the look of resentment etched on Janet's face, the nurse continued. "You know you could really injure yourself during one of your spells."

As he moved to unhook the restraints, Janet wearily responded, "Yes, I know. But it's just so freaky waking up strapped to a bed." Then, managing a strained smile, she asked, "You ever tried it, Curt?"

"No, Ms. Ravenscroft, I haven't."

"It's not any bloody fun, you know."

Once her arms were free, Janet pulled her robe tight against her body and looked up at the nurse, "It's okay, you can leave now. I'll dress myself."

When he hesitated, Janet did her best to smile and spoke as calmly as possible. "Curt, I'm okay. Really. I just need a bit of privacy, that's all.

Please." She paused, then looking up again at the security camera, added "Well, as much privacy as I'll ever get in this bloody place."

Curtis' eyes followed her gaze and then looked back at her. "Now, miss, you know that it's there for your own good. Imagine if you were to have one of these episodes and you were in here where we might not find you for hours."

Janet's shoulders sank wearily in on themselves, "Okay. Okay…"

After the nurse shut the door softly behind him, Janet slipped into fresh clothes and walked over to the bay window. Cautiously, she looked out over the grounds below to the city just over the hedgerow that bordered her father's estate. Even though the sun was shining high overhead, warming the autumn day, she shivered.

Does it even matter how bloody sick I am if those fucking monsters are out there waiting for me?

Janet's thoughts were interrupted by the soft swish of her bedroom door opening once again. With a sigh, she turned to greet the man who had been hired four years ago to be her personal physician. Janet tried not to let her impatience or any residual terror get the best of her, because she knew from far too many past episodes that Doctor Nehran had to make an official, but seemingly useless, examination as soon after each incident as possible.

Accordingly, the good doctor patiently conducted a thorough checkup, which he performed as efficiently and with as much good humour as possible. And Janet, with every bit of good grace that she could summon, did her best to cooperate with him. The tests were soon finished and Doctor Nehran once again declared her well, or recovered, or at the very least as healthy as he and his colleagues had ever determined her to be. No medicine they ever prescribed or gruelling series of tests that they conducted had done anything to identify, much less fix, whatever might be wrong with her.

Janet gave him a quick, forced smile, "Doc, don't you ever get frustrated never knowing what the problem actually is? I know I bloody well do!"

The soft-spoken Indian man looked down at her, frowning, "I wish that there was something new to report, but unhappily there is not. Your blackouts continue to be as erratic as they've always been. I certainly hope that this new tendency toward greater length and severity won't continue because if it does, your condition will begin to severely disrupt your life.

"If you were to ever have one of these attacks when you were driving or even if you were by yourself somewhere, you would simply collapse. What would happen then? Who would help you?"

At the door, he turned back, a worried smile on his kind face, "I'm afraid that there will always be unexplained mysteries in our lives, and it looks like you, Miss Ravenscroft, will continue to be one of them. You really should thank your father for providing you with the care that you need. He's doing the best that he can."

And paying you handsomely not to report my condition. Janet's eyes hardened. "Right, Doc. And thanks for doing whatever you can to help me."

Living for so long, though, with an illness that had done its best to reshape her life, had left her deeply frustrated as well as angry. But when she noticed some of that same frustration etched on the doctor's dark brown face, she dampened her impatience and tried to pay attention to what he said. Immediately she was sorry she had.

Still lingering in the doorway, Nehran added, "Your father did ask me to tell you that he'd like to speak with you this afternoon… as soon as you felt strong enough."

"That would be now, wouldn't it? The King mustn't be kept waiting too long."

"Miss Ravenscroft, please don't judge your father so harshly, he really is very concerned about your well-being."

Biting back a reply, Janet waited for the doctor to close the door before sinking back into her real bed and trying her best to not let the black depression that wanted to smother her win.

She let a long hour crawl by trying to keep her disordered thoughts from spiralling back into the remembered depths of Thomas' dark eyes. When Janet left her bedroom, it was more to escape those thoughts than to comply with her father's order.

Bloody damned if I do and bloody damned if I don't.

Then, she quickly made her way down the long hallway to his office and without knocking on the door, slipped inside.

Her father looked up at her from an expansive desk covered in neat piles of paper, "Good afternoon. Slept well, I hope?"

"Certainly. Weren't you watching me?"

Ignoring the sarcasm, John Ravenscroft's reply was as soft as silk. "No distraught dreams brought on by your most recent prank?"

"I slept very well, thank you."

Looking defiantly back at her father, she watched him attempt to contain his own anger. "And I suppose you're not going to tell me where you went after leaving my security guard sprawled behind you on the street last night? Or who, exactly, the young man on the motorcycle was?"

There were grown men and women in boardrooms all over the world who trembled when they heard the same edge of anger in John Ravenscroft's voice. Janet, though, continued to stare silently back at her father, stubbornly refusing to explain any of last night's supposed indiscretions.

If I tell him about the monster out on that bridge he'll say I'm mental and fucking lock me up and throw away the key.

"Well, I thought you'd like to know that we've already located your, shall we say, 'abandoned motor'. I had it brought back and parked in the garage.

"But Janet, I have to tell you that you will not be allowed to drive again. Your medical condition has grown far too serious, you could do some very real harm to yourself and to others as well."

"Fuck! Just fuck, *no!*"

Ignoring his daughter's distressed outburst Ravenscroft continued, "I will however be happy to provide a driver whenever you need to leave the estate."

Then I'm trapped here, probably bloody forever!
But... damn it, he's right I shouldn't be driving.
Still, it feels like I'm being forced into doing whatever it is he wants me to do.

Without taking his eyes off Janet, her father reached into a drawer on the side of his desk and held out a shiny object that appeared tiny in his enormous hand. It was Janet's stolen mobile phone. "You left this behind in your hurry to get away last night. Hamish asked me to tell you that the man who found it said that he was grateful for the loan before returning it to you."

"Really?" Janet delicately plucked the mobile from her father's hand and slid it into her back pocket, "Please thank your Mr. Hamish for me, okay?"

I'll bet that creep with the dreads got his face smashed in.

They stared stonily at each other for a moment, until Janet swept her hand over her freshly shorn hair and broke the silence. "In case you haven't noticed, I'm not a child any more. I had a birthday last month. Remember? I'm eighteen. I can drive... well, I used to be able too. I can drink if I want. I don't even have to get your permission to go on a date any more. And I swear, if you keep trying to manipulate every bloody second of my life, I will find some way to escape this damned prison of yours no matter how hard you make it, and you'll never see me again. Ever!"

Janet was surprised to see the sudden fear reflected deep in her father's eyes and was almost shocked by his reply. "I... I simply want to do what's best for you... to protect you, as I always have. I know that sometimes it might not look like that to you, but I do love you, Janet." His wide shoulders sank for a moment before he continued, "It would be a great help to us all if you could just follow a few basic rules."

Ignoring her father's concern, she spat, "Don't you mean it'd *help you*? It certainly wouldn't bloody well do to have John Ravenscroft's daughter sprawled out on some floor, looking unseemly in public. That would make all the news feeds, wouldn't it? And that would make you look like a right idiot!"

The venom in his daughter's words seemed to leave Ravenscroft momentarily speechless. Guiltily, he looked down at his desk just as Janet asked testily, "Okay, do I have your permission to leave now?"

With a curt nod of permission, Ravenscroft replied. "Yes, of course. Please remember that in this house I can easily keep you safe. But outside its gates there is more danger than I hope you will ever know. I simply can't let you just wander off without all the protection that I can provide.

"Janet, you should be pleased to have a driver," her father said by way of a parting shot. This way you'll always have someone to carry your shopping bags for you."

SEVEN

Two days later, Janet was seated at one of a long row of benches that lined a small triangular park at the junction of two streets in downtown Inverness. The park was filled with bright, multi-coloured playground equipment, being enthusiastically and thoroughly abused by a half dozen gleeful screaming children. Along the other benches, adult guardians sat patiently watching their charges to exhaust themselves.

Beside her was a small mountain of shopping bags, which, with one slim arm, Janet casually kept from tipping over and spilling onto the pavement. She smiled and waved pleasantly at two men standing about six meters away, tasked by her father with following her whenever she left the estate. Even at this distance Janet saw the look of absolute boredom on their faces after accompanying her through store after store over a long, uneventful afternoon. Their arms were laden with even more shopping boxes and bags. Both men looked so uncomfortable with such a domestic chore that Janet almost laughed but thought the better of it.

At first, it had seemed like a good idea to get out of the house and in the process give her room a thorough makeover, but what began as an angry response to her father's suggestion, didn't feel at all satisfying now.

Binge buying all this frivolous crap seems pretty childish now. He was right about one thing, though: I do need help getting all these packages back home.

I wonder what today would have been like if I had any friends to share it with instead of those two stiffs.

Behind her, on the other side of the small park the furious yapping of a small dog cut above the happy laughter of children at play. Without turning she contemplated what it would be like to actually own a pet.

Dog or cat, I wonder?

To her annoyance, the high-pitched yapping continued to steadily increase in volume.

Why is it always the littlest wag-tails that make the most noise?

I suppose the little yapper thinks it's protecting its mistress.

With a sigh, Janet glanced at the two men whose duty it was to protect her.

More like they're here to keep me from running away!

They do their best, but don't they ever smile or have any fun?

When the dog's frenzied barking only increased in volume, Janet looked casually over her shoulder to see what was causing it. A short haired, pedigreed poodle stood stiff-legged just to the side of the fully occupied swing set, barking its carefully cropped head off. The sharp insults on the edge of her tongue were left unsaid as her eyes snapped wide in terror. Just to its side there was a great hulking beast, certainly not of this Earth, slinking, belly to ground.

Its tail twitching spasmodically, the black, cat-like beast inched forward, intent solely on its prey. There could be no doubt who that was. Without pausing, the great hunting creature batted the small dog aside and continued to head straight toward Janet.

"Bloody Hell!"

Yet no one else at the park seemed to be aware of the huge creature. No one that is, but the wee dog. *No one.* Her gaze jerked back toward her bodyguards who continued to stare at her with studied indifference.

They. Can't. See. It!

With the beast only a few meters from her, Janet frantically made a split-second decision.

I can't get those men killed just because I wanted to go bloody shopping…

Out of the corner of her eye, Janet saw the snarling creature gather itself, ready to launch its muscled bulk over the wrought iron railing that separated the park from her.

But where do I run?

At that moment, Janet heard her name called. Turning, she spotted Thomas astride his bike, balancing it at the nearby curb. Surprise and relief poured over her.

Yes!

Dropping her bags, Janet lunged away from the bench, and in two quick steps leapt onto the back of his Vincent, shouting urgently, "Go! Go! Go!"

As they roared out into the heavily trafficked street, Janet glanced back but now saw absolutely no sign of the stalking beast. Her two frustrated guards, were frantically trying to force their way through the shoppers that thronged the crowded pavement. Tom gracefully manoeuvred the motorcycle down the street, quickly picking up speed before there was any chance of their being caught by man or invisible beast. Her arms grasped firmly around Tom's waist, Janet let out a gasp of relief.

Fuck me!

Then, shouting over the sound of the wind whistling by, she asked, "How did you do that? Be right where I needed you at the moment I needed you?"

Tom turned his head to briefly look at her and grinned, "Janet, you are too young to have such enemies." Janet's sarcastic response was cut short as the bike jumped up onto the pavement and bounced down a steep flight of stairs.

Janet shouted back at him, "Enemies? They're just some guys trying to make a living. My real enemy is my bloody father. He's wants to suffocate me in that damn house of his!"

"No. They are of no concern, but the hunting beasts had almost found their prey."

"Beasts? I only saw the one. You mean there were more of those bloody horrible things?"

"They always hunt in packs…"

Janet clutched Tom's waist harder and continued, "But why did I see it when no one else could?"

The eloquent shrug of his shoulders only served to ignite Janet's anger.

"Right, Mr. Tall and bloody silent, when are you going to explain what's going on here? Just thinking about those awful creatures gives me the creeps. I need some answers, Tom!"

After her outburst, they rode in silence through the streets as sunset began to touch the sky with colour. Occasionally, she reached up to rub her hand over her newly shorn scalp, ruefully thinking,

Janet you're an idiot. Here you are, your arms around this handsome stranger again, going… where? But for some reason I feel safe when I'm with him… despite all my unanswered questions!

After they crossed the River Ness by the Young Street Bridge, Tom manueuvred his bike into a parking space along Ness Walk. Running alongside the embankment of the river with easy views of Inverness Castle and the various cathedrals that top the low downtown skyline as well as a multitude of cafés and restaurants, it was very popular. Tonight was no exception.

They climbed off the Vincent and slowly threaded their way along the crowded thoroughfare. After Thomas noticed that Janet was compulsively looking over her shoulder, he stopped and smiled at her, "Have no concern for your safety now. I will protect you."

"Really? Just like that, I'm supposed to believe that the wanker who left me stranded out on that damned bridge is my what…my champion?"

And yet somehow, I do want to.

At that moment they were both distracted by the loud jangle of music that erupted from deep in her purse. Janet dug deep into it and pulled out the offending mobile device. Its screen was lit by a text message from her father that she barely took the time to read.

"Janet, where are you! I want you to text me right NOW!"

Without hesitation she hurled the device out over the River Ness, where it dropped beneath the surface with a soft splash. She turned back to the handsome young man close by her side and smiled at the look of confusion on his face, "Just a gift from my father that I don't really want or need."

And his bloody army can't trace me so easily if I don't have that damned thing on me.

They fell silent then and continued their stroll between the city and the river, simply enjoying the night and each other's presence.

By the time they came to a stop under a huge spreading elm that leaned out over the water's edge, the sun was disappearing in a burst of orange and yellows. Thomas looked solemnly into Janet's eyes and broke their shared silence.

"I fear that I have brought an undeserved evil upon you. Because of me, you have seen the door slip open onto a vast world that is sometimes needlessly cruel and quick to visit very real danger upon the unsuspecting.

"It is a world that few mortals ever chance to see."

"Few mortals! What do you mean? You're as mortal as I am…" Even as Janet spoke those words, doubt began to creep into her heart. Especially after what she had seen in the last few days.

"You are human, aren't you, Tom?"

"Yes, but one that is inured to the habits of this other world, a world that I have promised to protect you from. With my life, if need be."

Flustered by the obvious sincerity of his words and the soft look in his eyes, Janet's heart unexpectedly began to beat faster. Gathering her thoughts, she turned away and looked down for a time into the darkening water below. Suddenly, she realised that what started as a casual adventure was struggling to become something more.

Do I really want that to happen?

She smiled to herself.

Maybe.

Then Tom asked a question that startled Janet. A question asked of her many times before, one that she had always before chosen to simply ignore. This time, though, Janet realised that she wanted to tell this man everything she could about herself.

"What of your mother, then? What does she have to say about you being imprisoned in this castle of yours?"

Janet stared for a moment at the fading reflection of the sunset in the slow flowing river and the silhouette of the cathedral looming just across it before answering. "I never knew my mother. She's always been a ghost with no face, one that constantly hovers in my thoughts. There's only been my father for as long as I remember. And he's always remained distant, aloof... as if it somehow pains him to even see me. We've never got along, and lately its only grown worse.

"When I turned twelve, I started to have these weird seizures or blackouts or sudden panic attacks or whatever my father's very expensive doctor was calling them that particular week. In the last year, they've gotten worse, both in length and severity.

"After forcing me to put up with every test that my father's considerable wealth could afford, my doc determined that the blackouts were the cause of my memory loss, the constant walking in my sleep, my personality shifts. They even recorded me talking in my sleep in a language that no one understood."

She smiled ruefully. "At least until last night out on the bridge, and there I was speaking that same language. Only this time I knew the meaning of every word I spoke....

"Which is so bloody weird...

"Anyway, my father has always tried to keep a pretty tight leash on me. As I've got older he's become even more obsessive about keeping me under lock and key. But Tom ... I'm eighteen years old. Eighteen. I shouldn't still be living with my father. I need to be out in the world finding out who I am and what it is that I really want from life. Shouldn't I? Right now, I feel like a huge, empty hole waiting for something to fill me... And that's not right. I should be the one choosing what I want to learn. Shouldn't I?"

Unexpectedly, Tom lightly held both her hands in his warm ones. "Surely your father is concerned with your wellbeing. After all, doesn't he want what's best for you?"

Janet's eyes filled with troubled memories before she leaned comfortably against his shoulder. "A number of years ago, he enrolled me in this posh private school. Of his own choosing, of course. It was very exclusive, all dark brick and high walls and sturdy gates. Only the best families sent their daughters there. I think he was hoping I'd make some friends in the right sort of crowd. But most of them were horrid and their families even worse.

"Except for a few halfway decent ones, my schoolmates made the same stupid comments about my skin that I've heard my entire life.

"Bloody gollywog or whatever you are!"

"What are you even doing here, black girl!"

"There was more of the same, sometimes even worse, but I tried to ignore them all.

"Until one afternoon, out on the football pitch, a group of the meanest girls surrounded me, spitting slurs right at my face. I couldn't stop myself, I screamed right back.

"That made them even more pissed, so they began to kick a bloody soccer ball right at me… as hard as they could, over and over again. For probably the only time in my life I blessed my 'health problem' because I suddenly collapsed and they all just ran away.

"In a flash my father brought me back home. I still don't know whether it was to protect me or to hide me from the world because he was ashamed of the colour of my skin."

"I think not. You… you are quite beautiful, Janet Ravenscroft."

Eyes wide with surprise, she paused for a moment, trying to digest what this compliment might mean and sensed another subtle shift in their relationship.

Flustered, she continued, "Anyway, since then it's been private tutors and home schooling all the way through my A levels. He may call it home, but it feels like prison to me."

She looked up at Thomas, uncertainty clouding her hazel eyes. "It is safe… it's comfortable. I don't need a job or have to pay rent or even worry about money… or have to put up with any bloody name-calling. But if I stay there, I won't be allowed to live my own life or make my own mistakes, will I?

"And that is maybe even more terrifying than those bloody creatures of yours."

Listening to Janet, Thomas felt troubled because he had asked himself the very same questions for more years now than he could remember. Indeed, those questions were what had led him to stray from the Queen's court for longer and longer spans of time.

His thoughts were brought back to the woman beside him when a sharp laugh burst from Janet lips. "And in case you were even wondering, all that extra security really puts a right spanner in my social life. Any bloke I'm with just runs off straight away after looking over his shoulder and seeing some massive goon intently following his every move.

"Lately, I've felt like I'm going to go mental with frustration, so I started playing a game with Father and his men. I work out some kind of elaborate plan and escape to somewhere interesting and then, for a few hours I pretend to be a normal, healthy young woman with normal, healthy problems. But all those stupid games I've been playing at are beginning to make me wonder if I really am the spoiled little girl that my father thinks I am."

Janet stopped talking for a moment and looked intently around at the now darkened city crouched close along the river at their side before she whispered, "Sometimes I catch my father looking at me like he's absolutely certain that I'm just going to go right off my nut, totally barmy... maybe it's because he can't do anything to fix me that he's so bloody paranoid about what I'm going to do next?"

Her mind raced furiously, trying to imagine how she could possibly frighten a man like her father with all the resources his wealth and power gave him.

When she looked up, she caught Tom in mid-sentence. "... indeed, there is meaning for me in your words that is most familiar. In my life as well, there is one who has tried to keep me in a cage. It is, as you say, a beautiful cage, but one that nonetheless has stout bars that prevent me any real freedom." Hearing his words Janet smiled to herself, grateful to have someone to talk to who understood at least some of her frustrations.

Suddenly, from the café just beside them, there was a sharp explosion of noise. Clutching at Tom's arm, Janet began to breathe again, only when she realised that it was caused by a waiter at a nearby café who had spilled an over-stacked tray of dishes onto the pavement at his feet – not some loathsome creature. Looking at Thomas she asked, "Can we go somewhere a little less public?"

"As you wish."

EIGHT

A light rain began to fall as Thomas pulled his bike into the loading zone in front of a busy downtown music club. As she hopped off, Janet whispered into his ear, "Meet me inside, okay?"

Tom nodded and then, as he threaded his bike through the busy traffic looking for a place to park, he began to wonder why he'd allowed himself to spend so much time with this mortal woman.

May The Queen forgive me for shirking my true duty.

Janet had chosen the Club 320 because she was reasonably certain the only kind of monster that might lurk inside was the human kind, and she'd had more than enough experience handling those. Also, its owner was a good friend, maybe her only one.

Inside, the beamed ceiling was low and there were no windows save for the two on either side of the club's entrance. An old-fashioned oak bar extended along the wall of the long room back into semi-darkness where it ended, leaving just enough room for a well-lit stage that had, over the years, seen its fair share of performers. Two dreadlocked young men with high, penetrating voices that carried easily over the raucous audience led the small band now playing enthusiastically from it.

Relaxed, Janet leaned comfortably against the bar listening to the song, idly studying the crowd. Directly in front of the band, its more enthusiastic admirers were on their feet, gyrating to the intense rhythm of the music. The rest of the floor was closely packed with tables, most every chair filled with young people of every shape, size and colour. Right away Janet felt herself relax.

Never get any bollocks about the colour of my skin from folks here.

Wonder if Tom even noticed how many bloody people were staring at us back by the Ness?

Then she heard a familiar voice and eagerly turned toward it. Standing behind the bar, cleaning a pint glass, the owner greeted her with a warm smile, "Couldn't keep away, cud ya?"

Janet grinned. "No. Easy company, good tunes. What's not to like?"

The owner of the bar was in her early 30s with tats trailing up the black shining skin of both arms, disappearing under tightly rolled sleeves. Her head was an explosion of hair, dyed in various shades of pinks and blues.

"Like the band?"

"Good lyrics. What do they call themselves?"

"The Waydown Wanderers. They're over from the States making a quick tour around the Isles. Lots of chatter about them on the net, so I thought I'd snag 'em before they get too famous for the likes of this place."

On stage there was a lengthy pause between songs as an instrument was being tuned. The blondest of the dreadlocked singers filled it with idyll chatter. Throwing back his long dreads, he spun out a cheeky story about a banjo and a mandolin going on a date. When he reached the punch line, both women grinned.

"Cute boys, those two…"

Janet's smile grew even wider at her friend's comment but quickly disappeared as she continued, "Just so ya know, had to nail the window in the loo shut after your escape act th' other night. You bunged up the lock something awful…"

"Sorry. You need me to pay for that?"

"Wouldn't hurt. Not much cash to be made these days from bands that don't get at least a bit of radio play. Me Da ran this place for years on a hope an' a prayer and now I'm followin' the same tradition. They can't kick us out, 'cause we own the damn building."

"We?"

"Da and me. That's him down at the other end. "Hey old man, say hi to my friend Janet." Fifteen feet away, a thin grey-haired older man was too busy serving up pints to stop to say hello, so he waved enthusiastically in their direction without pausing.

"If we weren't so slammed tonight, I'd give you a proper intro, but without the drinks we'd be out of business in double time. Speaking of which, need something…"

"A tonic then."

"Hittin' it heavy tonight, are we?"

"Want to be careful, I've a bloody date. Well… sort of."

"Right you are then."

Drink in hand Janet leaned back into the bar and considered where she was and the day that got her here.

Good. Don't see anyone from my father's private army here tonight. Wonder if any of them could actually take down that troll or the creepy cat thing?

Probably. But not without a lot of damage happening first.

At the far end of the bar, talking casually to the young woman sitting beside him, was an affable looking young man, Tad Lockerby. He was new to John Ravenscroft's security force, so his face was unfamiliar to Janet, which was why he had been assigned this job tonight.

All over downtown Inverness there were recruits just like Tad waiting for Janet Ravenscroft to appear, but she'd walked into his particular stakeout, and that pleased him.

Earlier, a quick Google search for the club had clued him on how to blend in with the crowd that hung out here. Dressed now like most everyone else in ragged jeans, a black 't' and Nikes, he was just another warm body at the bar nursing a pint and keeping up a flow of casual conversation.

He barely noticed as the loud thumping bass line of the band's current tune travelled up his legs from the polished wooden floor at his feet. Lockerby looked at the faces clustered around him at the packed bar, all a part of the vibrant multi-cultural ethnicity that in recent years called Inverness home. He smiled to himself, enjoying his job tonight. Turning his body away from Janet's sight line, he carefully tapped out a message on his mobile letting his boss know that he'd located their quarry. Then he settled back to wait for his backup to arrive.

Fifteen feet away, Janet was deep in thought, oblivious to her secret escort, doing her best not to freak out.

Tom just shrugs off these bloody nightmare creatures as casually as I go shopping, and he appears to be on speaking terms with the bloody bitch that wants to trample through my head whenever she pleases.

Who or what exactly are you?

Unable to stop herself, she pictured his handsome face, easily recalling the small laugh lines around his mouth and eyes.

Just then she saw Thomas step lightly down the three short steps that descended from street level. He paused for a moment inside the front door, his eyes adjusting to the dim light in the club. Watching him, Janet realised just how out of place he looked standing there. It wasn't just his ornate leather coat, but also, apart from the members of the band, he was practically the only white male in the club.

The bartender gently rapped on Janet's arm, "Whoa! That him? He looks like a real find."

"Hey, don't get any ideas. He's mine, okay?"

"Yeah. Sure."

After he slipped through the crowd to the bar, Janet shyly introduced Thomas to her friend. "Lottie, this is Thomas. Tom, this is Charlotte. Say hello, the both of you."

Barely listening to their conversation, Janet was completely distracted by the fragrance of sweet herbs that always seemed to cling to Thomas. Even worse was the effort needed to stop herself from stroking her fingers through his long, glossy hair.

After a moment, Tom ordered a whiskey, a single malt, and turned his attention back to his companion.

Under his scrutiny Janet grimaced, then murmured, "I thought you might have driven off..."

Thomas' face turned serious. "No, now that I have met your enemies, I was curious where you would feel comfortable and who you might consider friends."

Flustered again, Janet quickly asked, "And music? What do you think of the band?"

"They are loud for cert."

Gesturing at the pulsating crowd pushing in close to the stage, she glibly suggested, "We could always dance?"

"Is that what you call dancing in this world of yours, Janet Ravenscroft?"

Janet shouted back over a crescendo of applause for a just finished tune, "What would you call it then?"

"A dance is a formal courtship between two people. Their hands touch. Their bodies touch. So that they can feel each other's blood moving as one. Nothing I see out there suggests anything close to that intimacy."

Janet looked intently at Tom for a moment before asking, "Are you for real?"

"I am as human as you. I laugh. I cry. I will grow old and die. What more do you need to know?"

"Oh, lots and lots of things. In the last few days I've seen creatures that should only exist in a bloody fantasy film, and I've had some bitch tap dancing through my skull without any invite from me. So, what the fuck is happening?

"Am I going stark raving bonkers?"

"Janet, you are not moon-mad, only seeing for the first time a world that has always been here, all around you, but hidden from sight until now. You must forgive me my part in revealing that world to you, but does it not make you even a little curious of what more it has to offer?"

"Curious? No, not when all I've seen of it are grotesque monsters."

"But there is more... so much more that I could show you..."

The eager, guileless look on his face at that moment made Janet slowly shake her head. Her rational mind was already working overtime, trying to turn everything that she'd experienced in the last few days into some kind of crazy fever dream.

Suddenly, she grinned at her companion and, slipping her hand under his arm, nodded toward the dance floor, "I don't want to think about any of that right now, so why don't you show me what you mean by real dancing?"

"If that is your wish."

She smiled as Tom put his hand gently behind her waist and began to walk her across what little space there was on the crowded dance floor. There, he led her to an entirely different beat than anything coming from the band. Looking back, she saw Lottie watching them and mouthing, "Go for it!" Laying her head on Tom's shoulder, she determined to do just that.

It's as if we're totally alone out here.

How can that be?

Just as she surrendered to their shared pleasure, Tom's eyes snapped open and his body grew rigid with tension.

Looking past him, Janet saw five huge, cat-like beasts sliding through the mass of pulsing bodies as if the dancers weren't even there. Keeping pace with the stalking creatures was a dark, olive-skinned figure, dressed in elegant black leather. The stranger's eyes flickered deep red in the stage lights, and he held a drawn sword in one gloved hand.

"Bloody hell that fucking madman's got a sword!" Janet yelled, closely followed by: "Why isn't everyone running away?" Then she realised the answer. Only she and Tom actually saw the swordsman and his pack of wretched beasts.

Tom pulled away from Janet, his face a grim mask. Suddenly there was a long thin blade in his hand. Seeing the flash of that blade, the other man hesitated. The feral beasts at his feet, though, continued to circle their prey, simply ignoring the crush of people that crowded the floor in front of the stage. Then Janet heard the leather-clad figure call out over the pounding music. He spoke in the same other-language as the troll on the bridge, and understanding every word the stranger uttered caused Janet to break into a cold sweat.

"Well then, at last the hunter has found his quarry."

A grim smile slid across Tom's lips before he replied. "Huntsman, you have no business being in this mortal realm. Why come you here?"

"For you, Sir Knight of the Rose. My master commands, and so I must obey."

Before he even finished speaking, The Huntsman launched himself directly at Thomas. At once, The Rose Knight leaped forward to meet his opponent. Their swords glittered, arcing through the air, flashing in the glare of the multi-coloured spotlights from the ceiling above. Their blades glanced off each other with a harsh rasp. Again and again Janet heard the shriek of metal against metal. Then the two figures sprang apart. The Huntsman paused, clasping both hands firmly on the hilt of his sword.

He cocked his eye at Tom, "I was mistaken then, I thought perhaps you would listen to reason and simply let me take you from this unnatural place?"

"Unnatural? Have care, Huntsman, you speak of the land whence I was born."

Janet grasped Thomas' arm and spoke in that same unnatural tongue, "Tom, who is this man?"

Hearing her speak in the language of the Land of Summer's Twilight, understanding flickered in the coal black eyes of the Huntsman. Still, he looked slowly past the pulsing crowd of gyrating bodies and sneers, "Spoken as only a mortal would, Thomas. But my gracious Lord has tasked me with finding a piece of a puzzle that is dear to his heart, so you and now this mortal girl will most certainly have words with him this very night.

"In truth, after my master is done with this human child, my blood quickens at the thought of flaying the tawny skin from her body to look for the Queen beneath."

"Never! Not while I live."

"As you wish, Sir Knight."

Janet was unable to tear her gaze from the great stalking beasts that casually wound through the legs of the oblivious crowd around the two duellists. All four creatures were larger than full-grown panthers, but instead of fur their entire bodies were covered with stiff bristling quills. Protruding from each huge footpad were long talons that with each step left furrows in the linoleum surface of the small dance floor.

Tom, seemingly unconcerned with the beasts that circled him, raised his sword and shouted, "Sir, you shall have neither!"

In answer, The Huntsmans' blade arced through the air once again. Janet was astonished watching Tom leap lightly aside and then twist before he hit the ground so that his blade deflected his opponent's next thrust. Each move spoke to years of practice. Moments later, Tom stumbled back into Janet, a thin gash of blood cut down the length of his chest. He grabbed at her arm to steady himself.

As if his touch were some spark to fan an unknown flame within her, the room around Janet began to ripple and shift as another reality subsumed it. Now a great multi-tiered courtyard with a lush garden of fragrant rose and dense with apple trees resplendent with their white blossoms rising around her on every side. Beyond the garden, an ancient marble hall lifted to touch the clouds, its rose-coloured walls dappled with iridescent turquoise shadows cast from the trees of a surrounding forest that stood even taller still.

She had a single coherent thought before she lost consciousness.

Like a fucking migraine...

Suddenly the mind of the mortal girl, Janet Ravenscroft, was once again consumed by the inhuman will, known in Her own world as The Queen of Summer's Twilight. Regardless of Her actual appearance, She stood, oblivious to the crowd, the lights, and the pulsating music to indignantly consider the Huntsman and his stalking beasts. Unconcerned with the injuries Her knight sustained, She stepped regally toward the deadly intruders.

The Huntsman saw only a mortal girl of no consequence standing before him, yet when she spoke he became even more certain that he had found the very thing his master had sent him in search of.

With a thin, hard smile The Queen said, "Huntsman, why are you here in my hall? I gave you no such invitation, for your presence repels me."

A look of consternation flowed through the warrior's narrowed eyes. "This place? You name this slovenly sty your great Hall? It is a place fit only for mortals and their useless entertainments…"

The great beasts, fawning at her feet, The Queen stared at The Huntsman and replied, "Creature, hold your tongue. Are you jealous of the court you once called home…?"

Deep in the recesses of her mind, Janet had never stopped struggling against the usurper who clutched so eagerly at her soul. At last she succeeded. Abruptly, there was only a young human girl standing amidst the swirl of oblivious dancing bodies. Then, seeing the Huntsman's great snarling creatures gathered so closely around her, she screamed.

Only moments before Tad Lockerby had been enjoying himself. Once the mysterious boyfriend had appeared and attached himself to his quarry Lockerby had smiled to himself thinking that apprehending them both would put him solidly in his new employees' favour.

But once he saw the man leap about by himself on the dance floor, shouting at some fucking ghost, he suspected that he was in for a long night. Then, when his client's daughter started to gesture frantically, pantomiming something incomprehensible, Lockerby shifted into full work mode, even though his backup still hadn't arrived.

Bolting to his feet, he pushed his way into the densely packed crowd. Tad has no idea what was actually going down here tonight, but he was absolutely certain that his immediate job was to get Ms. Ravenscroft safely out of this place as quickly as possible.

Then, over the roar of the music he heard Janet scream and he bellowed at the people in front of him, "Out of my way. Now!"

Roughly pushing aside a still oblivious couple, he grabbed his client's daughter and attempted to shield her with his body from whatever she was screaming at. Immediately there was a sharp, tearing pain in Tad's right leg, causing it to collapse under him. He hit the floor, hard.

Momentarily dazed, Tad rolled away and desperately struggled to pull his gun from its shoulder harness.

"Fuck! I should have done this before I even got out here…"

Sweat burned Tad's eyes as he tried to locate the assailant through the tangle of legs and shoes and Doc Marten's that surrounded him.

But there was no assailant to be seen.

"What the hell… has to be the dude she's with … who else?"

Gripping his gun firmly with both hands, Tad drew down on his client's boyfriend, who was now just a short distance away. But before he could squeeze off a shot, invisible jaws, filled with impossibly sharp teeth ripped away his arm. Whatever his tormentor was, it coughed once, spitting his gun out onto the floor.

As the guard's body went into shock Tad collapsed in a pool of his own blood, his body splayed out on the floor.

Looking up, the last thing Lockerby saw before he died was a shadowy, leather-clad form towering above him with a satisfied smile on its lips.

Behind the bar, Charlotte noticed when the burly stranger lurched away from his seat, shoved into the crowd and then abruptly fell to the floor. She was pretty sure she'd seen him pull a gun before the excited crowd had blocked her view. Lottie didn't know what was going on, but damned if she was going to let anything awful happen in her bar tonight or any other. Pushing past her father and out from behind the bar, she headed straight for her friend.

Ten

Unconcerned with the dead man at his feet, The Huntsman kept his eyes locked on Tom. "Have you chosen then to remain in this dreary realm?"

Ignoring the taunt, Thomas shouted over the music to Janet, "Find the rear exit. My Vincent is parked in the alley. Get on it. Leave, Leave now!"

Shocked, Janet stared at the dead body of the complete stranger who had just tried to save her life. "What about him? Can't we do anything…?"

At that moment Lottie grabbed her arm, pulling Janet toward the back of the club. "You heard the man. There's an exit back there. Use it!"

Janet was still frozen with indecision. Directly in front of the two women Thomas engaged The Huntsman again, their swords glittering through the air. As calmly as possible the Knight of the Rose kept on speaking to Janet, "This is what I do. Please go!"

At that same moment, a still oblivious dancer slipped in the spreading pool of blood on the floor and grabbed his partner to keep from falling. He looked down and saw the body of the dead man sprawled at his feet. Beside him his friend let out a high-pitched scream.

Alerted by her reaction, other revellers began to notice the body and soon there were more screams as people started to panic, desperately trying to shove away from the dead man on the floor, running and scrambling over each other toward the front door.

Janet watched in horror as her knight with no visible armour leapt over all five beasts as they lunged after him, teeth bared. His blade slashed down, glittering brightly in the dim room. Two of the enormous beasts collapsed, spitting blood, their throats cut cleanly through.

She was still looking desperately at Tom when Charlotte's father grabbed her other arm and shouted, "Lottie, see to the band! I'll get your friend out of here." And abruptly her paralyzing shock dropped away.

Janet turned to follow the older man, but first she scooped the dead man's gun off the blood-smeared tile. Frantically shoving their way through the crowd, as all around them, people were running blindly, they scrambled away from the stage. When she heard the hunting scream of one of the huge beasts close behind, Janet was consumed by panic and hit the exit door running as fast as she could, only to bounce off its hard, unyielding metal surface. Close by her side, the older man grunted. "Hold on. There's a latch here somewhere."

She glanced behind to see the beast clawing its way straight for them. Janet turned back to the door and threw all her weight against it again. It still didn't move. Something above her caught her eye, and she glanced up. Along the top frame of the door there was a dimly lit sign that read: Emergency Use Only!

She screamed hoarsely to her companion, "Look! Up there…"

"Damn! Must be a new security bolt!"

Hefting the gun, Janet whispered to herself, "Well, Father dear, you taught me how to use a gun so thank you, just this once."

Backing against the door Janet steadied the borrowed firearm with both sweaty, blood streaked hands, took aim at the charging beast and then emptied every chamber into it.

With a wet grunt the beast collapsed, its dead weight carrying its great carcass to stop a few inches short of her feet.

Janet turned back to the door just as Lottie's father reached up to yank the bar away. With a squeal of metal against metal it grudgingly moved, triggering a shrill alarm that barely cut through the rising volume of screams behind them. The older man grimaced, "My daughter's way more security conscious than I ever was…"

This time when they both threw their bodies against the heavy door, it gave way. But as she stumbled out into the alleyway, Janet felt needle sharp talons rip the boot from her left foot. Then with a harsh cry, the second beast backed away. Beside her the wiry older man hefted the security bar in both hands ready to strike once again.

"Can't see the bloody thing, but it left tracks on the floor."

Janet cried, "No, don't!"

Suddenly the man screamed as the hunting beast's talons raked the arm holding the steel bar, almost tearing it from his shoulder. Slapping the frail human to the side, the creature pawed at its damaged eye, licking at the generous flow of blood falling from the long cut across its skull.

"Fuck!"

Turning, Janet sprinted across the rough cobblestones to Tom's bike. Clutching the handlebars, she tried to kick start it. But when the engine refused to sputter to life, she looked behind her again. The beast was crouched by the exit door, spitting her boot from its cavernous mouth, preparing to launch itself after her. Without thinking, she brought the gun up once more. Again and again Janet worked the trigger. But its chambers were spent and useless.

"Fucking hell!"

Suddenly Tom's skillfully thrown sword jutted from between the beast's shoulder blades, and it collapsed onto the cobbles, blood pumping from the wound. In the brief moment of life left to it, the beast rolled ponderously over on the sword and grew still.

Through the exit door Janet watched as Tom turned and leaped into the air. His arms caught at the tower of the heavy stage amps, bringing them smashing down on The Huntsman, leaving the leather-clad figure sprawled senseless across the tiles. Tom, though, hit the floor, rolling with the impact and came to his feet in a single graceful movement.

Moving toward the open back door, he helped Lottie shepherd the band safely out into the narrow alley but stopped at the battered exit.

As around them the night around began to fill with the sound of approaching sirens, the band looked at each other, exhaustion and relief etched on their faces.

Eyes wide, the first singer gasped, "Man, that was weird!"

"What the fuck happened in there?"

"Hey man, our instruments…what's up with them?"

Charlotte did her best to calm them down, but all their nervous chatter was cut short by a single sharp outburst.

"Oh Lottie, I'm so, so sorry…"

For the first time, the club's owner noticed Janet astride the bike and cried, "Hell girl, you okay?" But she faltered at the abject look of despair on the young woman's face.

"What?"

Janet points to the open exit door where Thomas stood looking defensively back into the darkened club. At his feet was the crumpled body of Lottie's father, his arm lacerated with teeth and claws marks. With a desperate wail Lottie collapsed beside her father's still form, taut with grief.

The dark-haired singer cried, "Look! I think he's still breathing…"

"Needs a doctor, we have to get him to hospital right away!"

"The sirens are getting close. Must be ambulances coming."

Janet gestured frantically at the singer that stood closest, "Your belt. Give me your belt, we need to help him right fucking now!"

Wiping tears away with the back of her hand Lottie grabbed for the makeshift tourniquet. A moment later she and Janet fumbled awkwardly to cinch the leather belt securely around the unconscious man's upper arm. When the blood flow began to slow, Lottie's body shook with relief.

Janet spared a quick glance up at Thomas. He still stood defensively at the open doorway ready to grapple whatever danger might come through it.

That bloody madman is after us, not them. If we leave, they'll be safe.
And Tom better not get tangled up with the police.

She caught at her friend's arm, "Lottie, listen. We've got to go… right now."

"Now?" The older woman turned, her face a mask of grief, "What about whatever is in there? And us? Are we safe?"

From the doorway Thomas answered without turning, "It is after us. If we leave, you will be safe."

Standing to one side in a tight protective circle, the drummer muttered nervously, "Yeah, what the hell was in there, man?"

Thomas shrugged his shoulder, "Nothing I think you will ever need to know about."

Then, hearing the emergency vehicles slam to a stop in front of the club, Charlotte stared at Thomas with a million questions. With an obvious effort, the older woman's face cleared, "Of course. Get out of here.

"But, Janet, you owe me. I want some explanation for all this, and I expect to get it. You hear me, girl?"

"Yes, I bloody promise." Looking down she heard the injured man's labored breathing, "He saved my life back there. If there's anything I can do, just ask me."

"Right." Then hearing the harsh shouting of police and emergency personnel inside the club Lottie cried, "Out here! We need help. Now!"

Looking up at Janet, her friend muttered, "Lord knows what I'm bloody going to tell them happened here tonight…"

"Lottie I wish I could stay!"

"No, I got this. Go on. Get!"

Moments later Tom kicked the engine into life, and they roared up the alley and out into the city beyond.

Much later, after the alley was thoroughly photographed and then cordoned off with a generous amount of crime scene tape, The Huntsman walked out. Casually brushing aside the bright yellow tape, oblivious to the chaos that still gripped the interior of the club, he sheathed his sword and looked back into the club. Thinking of the dead hunting beasts, he felt discomforted for the first time. Conveniently, they had all disappeared from even his sight in a swirl of writhing shadows long before any mortal could stumble over their bodies.

Stroking the head of the remaining beast, he whispered, "What an eventful night, my pet. This Knight of the Rose gives us an interesting chase, don't you think?" After pausing for a moment of thought, he continued, "Though my master will not be well pleased by the death of so many of his favourite pets..."

Dim lights from the virtually deserted music club washed over The Huntsman as he stooped to pick the knight's blade from off the cobbled surface of the alley where it had fallen under the body of the now vanished beast. He paused a moment to inspect the sword more closely. "Well, a mere mortal sporting an elfin blade. A present from his loving Queen, no doubt? She does enjoy giving Her little gifts... but I doubt that he is worthy of such a blade as this."

Directly across the street from the entrance of the alley there was an ugly two-story building whose windowless side was painted with a 'Welcome to the Highlands' mural, filled with kitschy renderings of characters out of folklore: Nessie, various giants, and several so-ugly-that-they're-cute witches. They were all smiling, all urgently welcoming the visitor to enjoy their stay and to please spend lots of money.

The Huntsman and his remaining beast walked straight toward it, and without hesitation stepped through its crudely-painted surface.

Moments later, two silver foxes scampered from under a car that was parked in front of the same building.

"Curious."

"Indeed."

"We've never seen this part of the tale before."

"Let us follow and see how the web spins its story this time."

Then, gracefully, they too jumped through the unyielding surface of the mural and into the Land of Summer's Twilight.

ELEVEN

With both her arms clinched around Tom's waist, the crowded streets flashed by, offering Janet a barrage of sight and sound that blessed her with much needed distraction. But vivid images of the dead man lying in a pool of his own blood and then Lottie's father kept dominating her thoughts.

She clutched fiercely at Tom's arm and cried out, "The father of the only friend I've got might die because of me. And that other man, just who the fuck was he?"

Tom didn't reply, his concentration evidently elsewhere as they suddenly careered through a pedestrian-only thoroughfare. Skilfully avoiding the startled people in front of the bike, he replied, "Who?"

Janet screamed into his ear, "That man back in the club! The one who died trying to protect me.

"Maybe he was one of your father's men? A new one whose face you didn't recognise?"

Janet cried out, frustration and fear making her voice crack, "Whoever he is, he's dead… and I don't even know his name.

"That world you wanted me to see is absolutely fucking terrifying! Then there's you…with the sword. Where did that come from? And that weird language we were both speaking… Who talks like that, and why do I understand it, now?"

Then she leaned in close to Tom's ear and hissed, "Tom, are you listening to me? What is going on?"

His determined silence only made Janet's frustration grow, so by the time Tom pulled the motorcycle up to the gate of her father's estate she was tight with anger. Tom turned to look back at her. "My lady, it is with my deepest regret that I must leave you now."

Janet's hands clinched even tighter on his arms, "Leave? No way! Not before I've got some fucking answers!"

Meeting her angry, disbelieving stare, Tom replied, "Where I go this night you cannot follow."

"And where the hell is that?"

Tom's lips set hard. "You must trust me when I say that I cannot give you the answers that you deserve. You must understand, I am the Knight of the Rose and my life is pledged once and always to the Queen that I serve."

Janet exploded, "Bollocks! Knight of the bloody fucking Rose... what's that supposed to mean? And this Queen of yours, she's the fucking bitch that's kicking her way through my head, isn't she?"

Tom answered through clenched teeth, "There is still much that I must learn about the mystery that now holds your life in its grip."

"So, you're going to dump me off at my father's home and ride away again, just like that!"

He softened his voice, "You will be safer here than with me."

Exasperated, Janet clenched her fists and cried, "Bloody hell!" Then her hazel eyes narrowed as she pointed at the elegant gates to her father's estate, "If you drive off now, I promise you, I will never walk through those gates again. Ever!"

After a brief struggle, Tom managed a grim smile, "Then I will escort you to your front door."

"Yes, you will indeed."

Under the eyes of her father's all-seeing security cameras, Janet turned and punched in her key code. Immediately the gate swung wide, and they drove through. A moment later, Tom brought his motorcycle to a halt in front of the enormous garage that housed John Ravenscroft's cars as well as any vehicles his private security force might need.

Turning back to Janet, he waited silently for her to dismount. Janet, though, leaned in closer to Tom as if to whisper in his ear and then, like many before, completely surprised him.

In one smooth motion, Janet jerked the key out of the ignition switch, cutting the bike's powerful engine, and jumped off the Vincent. Backing quickly away, she glared at him, her face a mask of steely determination. "Look, you're not leaving here until I get some answers." Without another word Janet slipped the keys into her purse and walked away.

Tom followed her through the door and then along a stone pathway that circled around the exterior of the house and emptied onto a terraced patio at the back, looking out over the sprawling grounds of the entire estate. Once they were standing on the patio, Janet began to pace back and forth across its carefully laid stonework.

Not wanting to force the keys from her, Thomas waited for Janet to speak and looked around curiously at the home that she had named a prison more than once. Close beside them was an ornamental pond. From its centre rose a plinth of marble with an elegant bronze statue of a stag bounding from its top. Surrounding the pool and the patio was an extensive formal garden that rolled away into the darkness of the night. In the near distance, the lights of Inverness silhouetted the extensive fence line that separated the Ravenscroft's home from the outside world.

It was only then that Tom realised the massive iron-wrought gates guarding the entrance to the estate were only a small part of an imposing fence line that completely enclosed all the land the estate called its own. That fence looked like some kind of massive medieval defence system with its sharp spikes rising out of the dense hedge of trees that closely entwined it. Lining the patio was another row of those same trees, laden with large clusters of reddish berries hanging low from their boughs.

Tom casually reached up and broke off a single berry, rolling it in his hand before inhaling its fragrance and then whispered to himself, "Interesting...a good defence, surely. But who planted it here and why?"

At that moment a burly security guard walked briskly down the same path that they had just taken. Reaching the patio, he looked suspiciously at Thomas, his fingers nervously tapping against the side of his holster and the pistol inside it, before speaking, "Evening, Ms. Ravenscroft. Everything okay here?"

"Yes! Yes, it is. Now just go away!"

Hesitating, the guard continued to eye them both. Until Janet somehow forced a smile to her lips, "It's Reilly, correct?"

When the uniformed man nodded, she continued, "Look, Reilly, this is my boyfriend, and right now we're working out... some issues. We need our privacy, okay?"

A high-pitched, mechanical beeping from the mobile phone on the security guard's utility belt interrupted them. Rolling his eyes, the guard offered an apology before answering it.

His face grew strained as he listened. Replacing the phone on his belt, the guard looked grimly at his employer's daughter. "There's been a bit of trouble in town with one of our men. I'll have to go." He paused, studying Tom for a long moment, as if considering what he should do with this man. Finally, shrugging his shoulders, he reached a decision, evidently choosing to accept Miss Ravenscroft at her word. "You sure you're going to be okay, miss?"

"Yes! Yes! YES!"

As the guard left, Janet heard yet more distant sirens. Crossing her arms over her chest, Janet looked hard at Tom. "I expect they're dealing with the dead man back there at the bloody club, aren't they? And Lottie's father as well."

He nodded, "I fear so."

"Tom, you know exactly why all that horror happened back there, don't you?"

After a prolonged silence, Thomas finally replied, but it was not what she had hoped to hear. "I am not permitted to answer your question. To do so would break my oath and render my word as worthless as disappearing smoke."

"So, you're saying that you won't give me any reason, any reason at all for what happened tonight?"

Thomas, The Knight of the Rose, stood straight and tall and grim, offering no sign of the confusion in his heart. "I cannot."

Janet clenched her fists again and whispered, "How can I trust you when you offer me nothing to base my trust on? Tom, I need to know why all this horrifying stuff is happening to me. I need to know who that guy in leather was and what his creepy creatures were, Why didn't he care if any of the people in that club were hurt or maimed or... killed... It could have easily been me. I could be laying in my own pool of blood right now!"

Her face twisted with doubt, she cried, "And yet you're telling me to simply trust you."

"My lady, I..."

"I. Am. Not. Your. Lady. Thomas Lynn or whoever you say you are, we're done. Leave! I... I never want to see you again."

Janet reached into her purse and threw the keys to the Vincent into the shallow fountain beside them. Then she turned away, stalking toward the house. Thomas watched her leave, pondering what he should do. His heart told him not to let Janet go, to offer her at least some explanation for what was happening to her. He knew she deserved nothing short of a complete explanation as to why he, the Knight of the Rose, was here in the mortal world, but his absolute certainty that she would never forgive him for it staid his impulse.

After a moment he whispered into the damp night air, "Janet, I too have questions. How came this fence of Rowan here? It will surely protect all those inside it, but only if they remain inside." Ruefully he shook his head, "And I fear that you will never be held a captive here for long.

"I must find in whom the rest of my Queen's mind resides... How will I do that if I stay by your side, I wonder?"

He leaned over the lip of the fountain, one hand holding back the lace of his cuff as he fished for the set of keys. They were easy to find. With them clutched in his dripping hand, he paused, looking up at the dark pile of brick and stone and slate that was the Ravenscroft home, squatting on the grounds of its estate like some great primordial beast that would protect hearth and home and all those that lived in it at any cost. Musing, he whispered into the silence of the night, "Janet, though you cannot hear me, I lay myself at your mercy, and when I return I will tell you everything that I know. Even though that knowledge will surely divide us once more, all that you ask I will give an answer to."

Tom turned away, determined to return as quickly as possible, and walked back to the parked Vincent. Once there, however, he saw a strange device attached to its rear wheel. Tom crouched beside the cycle trying to puzzle out the mechanism, musing to himself. "It would seem that there is a wish by many that I not ride away from here this night?"

When he heard the scrape of a boot heel on the pavement near him, Tom looked up to see a tight circle of Ravenscroft's security personnel surrounding him. Every one of them wore a hard, grim look. And each carried a weapon in his hand.

TWELVE

Janet pushed against the massive French doors, but when they wouldn't give way she noticed the red blinking light in the darkness of the room inside. Briefly glancing up at yet another of her father's security cameras, she casually offered it a two finger salute.

"Bloody stupid codes…"

Furiously she punched in a set of numbers and threw the doors open, letting them bounce against whatever they met, then impatiently slammed them shut behind her. Unconcerned, she tracked mud and leaves across the elegant Persian carpet that covered the floor of the room and ran quickly toward the stair. Aware that she was crying and desperate to be in her room, she took them two and three at a time.

Her father, though, was waiting at the top of the stairs, his expression flitting between worry and anger. Very quietly he asked, "Janet, can you join me in my office for a moment?"

Hastily wiping away her tears, she turned to face her father, "No! I bloody will not. I'm going to bed."

Her father's face set with determination as he firmly took hold of her arm, "Come along, this won't take but a moment."

When both Janet and her father were inside his expensively appointed office, John Ravenscroft gracefully eased his bulk down into the leather chair behind his massive oak desk. He gestured for Janet to sit as well. Ignoring his suggestion, she continued to stand, hoping that she'd be able to leave that much sooner.

But just as her father was about to speak, his mobile buzzed. Janet was surprised by the growing look of apprehension on her father's face as his terse conversation with the caller continued.

Trying to ignore what was being said, Janet paced across the carpeted floor in front of the desk, wondering if she really did just send Tom away. Forever. That inner turmoil was compounded when her gaze fell on the door at the end of the room leading off of her father's inner sanctum. Not once in all her life had she been allowed through that door.

Just another fucking secret!

So, when her father slapped his mobile onto the desktop and almost growled at her, she was ready to meet his anger with her own. "Exactly where did you go after you eluded my men this afternoon?"

Through clenched teeth Janet answered, "Downtown."

"Why?"

"I needed some space!"

"And tell me, where exactly did you find this space of yours?"

"A bar... downtown."

"That would be the Club 320?"

Before she answered Janet shivered, remembering the blood pooling under the dying man, the swordsman and his hunting beasts, and then, Lottie's father labouring for breath.

"Y...yes. Why?"

"Because one of my men was there tonight. I had my people all across Inverness looking for you and this boyfriend of yours or whatever he is. But one of them had the misfortune of being at that particular club and now I'm told that man is dead."

"Father, what... what was his name?"

"Why?"

"Because I want to know the name of the man who died trying to save me tonight."

"Tad Lockerby."

Janet's hands gripped the edge of her father's desk. "Yes, I saw him... die at my feet... but, but I promise you... it wasn't my... our fault."

"I find that hard to believe because my people are telling me that this man of yours was in a brawl in that place that turned violent, very violent indeed."

"Yes. And my friend's father was badly injured as well."

"Your friend?"

"Charlotte Parsons. The owner of the club..."

"Dan Parsons was hurt?"

Momentarily Janet was confused, "How... how do you know his name when even I don't?"

"Never mind that. Is he okay?"

"He was still breathing when we left. Lottie was getting him to hospital. His arm was nearly ripped off by those..."

Janet bit her tongue, fighting both remorse and deep guilt.

He wouldn't believe me if I told him the truth.

John Ravenscroft continued to speak to his daughter, only now his voice assumed the tone he might use if he wanted an unruly child to do what he thought best for it.

"Stop trying to explain your mistakes away. I'll look into it soon enough and get the truth."

"Well fucking great! 'Cause I want to know how he's doing. I want to visit that hospital, okay?"

Janet dropped into the wooden chair in front of her father's desk. She was prepared for more unpleasantness but not for his fury.

"Why do you do these senseless things?" he roared. "You tell me that you want me think of you as an adult and then you do something as stupid as this! I have my men around you for your own protection. If you keep running away from them, how can they do their job? How can I be certain that you'll be safe?" Ravenscroft turned then, balled his hands into fists and brought both down, hard, onto the top of the oak desk. Everything on it leapt into the air as if a small earthquake had struck the room.

Janet was terrified by the look on her father's face.

"Why do you simply ignore my wishes? I only want what's best for you! All your life I've had to be both father and mother to you. And that's not been easy."

She stared at her father a moment before replying, acid dripping from every word. "And whose fault is that?"

"Fault?"

"That I have no mother."

"Janet, how many times must we go through this?"

"As many times as it takes for me to understand why it is my loving father will not let me meet my own mother!"

He glanced back at Janet bleakly, "I've told you before, your mother isn't well. There is simply no point in your seeing her."

Her face twisted with suppressed emotion. "You've been saying that ever since I was old enough to ask. So, father, where is she?"

"Janet, I…"

"If she's still alive, why won't you let me at least visit her?"

"Soon enough…"

"Great. Fucking great! Except your idea of soon is more like bloody forever."

"Enough! I have nothing else to say to you about your mother."

Janet was surprised to see deep tenderness etched on his features. His voice was thick with suppressed emotion when he finally spoke again. "Janet, I would never, ever let anything harm you. I couldn't stand to see anything like that happen to you as well…"

John Ravenscroft's shoulders sagged, as if the confrontation had exhausted him. His eyes closed as if in prayer, perhaps willing himself to not hear Janet's expected but softly whispered question. "Happen to me… as well?"

"Never mind, just… never mind…"

"Okay, Father dearest, why don't we ever talk about this other thing? Look at me!" Janet held out both long, thin brown arms offering them as her evidence, "We don't look the same, do we?" Her father wearily turned his face away from Janet. "It must be a gift from my mother because it sure isn't from you, is it?

"Nothing to bloody say? Sometimes I even wonder if you're really my father at all. Did you adopt me? Are you so ashamed that you can't even tell me what happened to my mother?"

Her father, in a blatant attempt to change the subject, said, "So, tell me about this young man of yours."

But Janet's jaw set stubbornly.

When John Ravenscroft realised that she was simply not going to answer him, he continued, "Well then, there must be something special about the boy since you've seen him twice now."

"Why Daddy, whatever do you mean?"

"You know precisely what I mean. You've never been out more than once with any of your young men before."

Janet stared into his deep brown eyes, determined to keep her face clear of any emotion. Her father didn't seem to notice that fierce struggle as he continued. "Whether it was a date that I'd arranged or some unlikely person that you'd met at a random social event, there has only ever been the one date, and then you've abandoned the hapless fool."

"Maybe they were just bloody stiffs?"

"All of them? Is there never any pleasing my daughter?"

Janet surprised herself with her answer. "Yes. Tom does."

Determined, her father leapt on that small scrap of information and asked, "Tom? Just Tom? Nothing more?"

"Thomas… Lynn. And you and your army of goons are not going to chase him away! Do you hear me, Father? Do you?"

"And just when have I ever done such a thing?"

For a moment her cool facade dropped away, "This is my life. Mine! Why can't you just let me live it?"

He scowled, "Because you've always made such a hash of it when you do."

"Of course I have. I've made mistakes. Lots of them... But how can I ever learn anything if you're always following me around, sweeping them into neat little piles so that I don't ever have to deal with them again?"

"I'm only protecting you... our family... our name."

"Yes, of course, a Ravenscroft must never let anyone see that we've made a mistake. I so don't care about that..."

"You should. This estate will be yours one day..."

"I. Don't. Bloody. *Want*. It!"

John seemed taken aback by his daughter's emphatic reply, but she hadn't finished. "How many times do I have to tell you? I won't hide in this fucking prison one more minute than I have to!"

Bluntly turning aside her anger, John Ravenscroft asked instead, "So when will I meet this new boy of yours then?"

Janet bristled, "Boy? Really, father..."

"All right then, this young man..."

She was suffused then by a sudden flood of memories of her brief time spent with Tom, warm as well as horrifying, and had to quickly blink away tears. So much so that when she looked at her father again, Janet found it difficult to assume her customary mask of barely controlled anger. "Didn't I tell you? He's gone. I won't ever see him again. So, no need to get territorial about him, okay? Now, I'm exhausted and I'm going to bed. If that's bloody well all right with you."

"By all means, I've got to talk to some friends and try to keep your name out of this nasty business. And then I'm going to have to deal with something a bit more serious than the usual messes that you leave behind, because this time one of my men is on a slab in a morgue downtown.

"In the meanwhile, do you think you could promise not to leave this house unescorted again?"

The monstrous hunting beasts and the implacable swordsman clawed their way through her mind and she nodded, "Agreed. But I insist that you keep me informed about Lottie's father. I have a right to know."

John Ravenscroft's eyes narrowed with calculation even as he nodded his assent. "I won't forget."

Without another word Janet left the room.

After what happened out there tonight, I'm not sure I even want to leave here again.

Not far away Thomas got slowly to his feet, preparing to confront the tight circle of determined men. One large, heavyset man, the guard that had interrupted them earlier out on the patio, gestured at the mechanism on the bike's rear wheel, "That's a lock down."

The man beside him flexed his arms, corded with hard muscle, and continued, "Yeah, you're not going anywhere without having a conversation with us first."

Tom sighed and slowly turned, looking at each man in turn. "Must I try to answer everyone's questions this night?"

The first man spoke again, "Me, I've got no questions. It isn't just about keeping you away from the brat any more."

One of his companions, slowly swinging a short section of pipe in his hand continued, "Tad Lockerby was one of us."

His companion added, "Yeah, he was new…"

"But now he's ended up dead on a downtown dance floor."

"And you were there."

"In fact, we expect you did it!"

"Okay…"

"Let's get started."

"Nothing too serious, though."

The first man confirmed what they were all thinking. "Yeah, the boss is going to want to ask this guy some questions before the night is over." Then quickly and efficiently they closed ranks around Thomas.

These men were all veterans of Iraq, Afghanistan. And some had even fought in the Falklands. They had been trained thoroughly in the art of war, so what happened next should not have happened. Tom launched himself directly at the tight circle of men and seemed to easily glide past every punch and evade each fist as if this were just a friendly game between good friends, which it most certainly was not. Moments later he was free of the circle without a single blow landing on him. And then, just as quickly, he was off, running toward the back yard.

Suddenly, the dark lawn and gardens around him were illuminated as bright as day by dozens of high intensity security floodlights. Every tree and shrub and statue stood in stark contrast to the immaculately cut lawn, now shining silver gray in the artificial light. With absolutely no hesitation, though, Tom ran toward the fence that lined the perimeter of the Ravenscroft estate. It was twelve feet high and topped with razor sharp spikes. Yet in one fluid motion, Tom leapt over the barrier and continued to run flat out, disappearing moments later into the night and the city beyond.

The yard Tom left behind, however, remained a beehive of frustrated activity.

After Janet had finally stumbled into the sanctuary of her bedroom, she fell, exhausted, onto the bed, too tired to even struggle out of her ruined clothes. But any hope of sleep was shattered when her windows blazed suddenly with light followed by the frenzied shouts of voices echoing from the yard below.

Janet lunged to the windows just in time to see a figure running swiftly across the rolling grass below her. Then, in one graceful movement, like a great stag, it vaulted over the entwined hedge and fence perimeter, disappearing into the night and the city.

She watched, fascinated, as her father's men scurried below her like a nest of disturbed ants, directed by the elder Ravenscroft's bellowing voice.

With a sigh Janet turned back to her bed, but, as tired as she was, she tossed and turned for hours. Eventually, through bleary eyes, she watched the dawn begin to push back the dark edge of night.

Thomas… where did you go?

Then, pulling a pillow over her head, she tried to block out the brightening world before, finally, sleep came to her rescue.

Until the early hours of the morning, John Ravenscroft devoted himself to wiping any suspicion that his daughter may have been a part of the bloody violence at the downtown music venue off the official record.

When left on hold at the hospital that Daniel Parsons has been taken to, he made a note to call again and then hung up, ready for the next task.

One by one, the men who confronted this Thomas Lynn told him the same story: that the man they had been tasked with finding had been here on his property but had slipped through their collective fingers. Which made him even more certain that his daughter's new friend, whether she said she wanted to see him again or not, was a person of interest. Afterward he sat there for hours, mulling over all that he knew.

It was almost dawn by the time John Ravenscroft placed a call to the chief of his security force. He rubbed his tired eyes as the phone rang several times before a muffled voice answered.

"Sir, do you know what time it is?"

"I don't care, Mac. I really don't. You are in my employ, and I expect you to be available whenever I need you. Am I correct in that assessment, Mr. Mackintosh?"

"Yes, sir. Absolutely!"

"Now then. Thomas or Tom Lynn. That's the boy my daughter has been with for the past two nights, the one who so easily slipped through your men's fingers tonight. You'll find pictures of him on our security cameras. I expect there to be a complete file on my desk early this afternoon. Am I clear on that?"

"Yes sir. Of course, sir."

"And Mac, have a pleasant morning."

THIRTEEN

The sense of satisfaction John Ravenscroft felt as he picked up the new dossier that waited on his desk faded quickly. The extremely thin folder contained exactly two digitally enhanced pictures of a pleasant-looking young man. That was it.

Both were taken with his own security cameras. In the first he sat on a motorcycle with Janet's arms wrapped tightly around his waist. They were at the front gate. In the other, the same man was leaping impossibly over the estate's fence, all twelve feet of it. Underneath the photos were several text pages with a scant typed profile of a particular family, once prominent in the Highlands, named Lynn.

Quickly reading through the brief outline, he found that at one time the Lynns had been wealthy, but now their estate was bankrupt and fallen into ruin. The family had indeed produced a son named Thomas who, it seemed, had disappeared over 100 years ago in mysterious circumstances.

Grimly he muttered to himself, "What utter, useless nonsense!"

Immediately Ravenscroft hit the speed dial on his mobile. When the call was answered he hissed at its recipient, "Mr. Mackintosh, am I to understand that you and your team could find nothing on this man?"

"Yes, sir. But we're still looking. We're hopeful that something will turn up by the end of the afternoon."

"Hopeful? *This afternoon?* Am I to be kept waiting an eternity then?"

"Sir, we are going through every database in our network. And hacking into others as well."

"I should think so, Mr. Mackintosh. It is the future after all. Everyone's life is an open book if you know how and where to look."

"Yes, I am aware of that, sir. We will find him."

But by that late afternoon deadline when there was still absolutely no record, public or otherwise located anywhere, in any database, on this particular Thomas Lynn, John Ravenscroft began to grow increasingly agitated.

Absently leafing through the short file that contained every known fact about the Lynn family and their runaway son only infuriated him further.

At the other end of the hallway, Janet balanced a cup of steaming tea in one hand as she stared out her bedroom window. What had become obvious last night was even more so now that she'd had time to contemplate all the possibilities.

I'm stuck here for a long, long time.
Too many of those damned monsters prowling around out there past that fence.

Then, for the first time, Janet noticed the purchases that she'd made during yesterday's abruptly abandoned shopping trip stacked against the back wall. Reluctantly she walked over to what now seemed like a useless vestige of anger directed at her father. But when she opened the first of the boxes and held a lengthy roll of brightly coloured batik fabric out against the sad beige lace canopy of her bed, her spirits lifted, causing her to smile.

Okay, if I'm stuck in this damned prison, the least I can do is make it look better. What else did I get?

From one heavily padded package Janet removed the painting she'd so carefully selected yesterday at one of the galleries on Bank Street. Eagerly, she replaced the dull abstract painting that, except for one brief day, had always hung by her bedside with her new purchase. The canvas was by English artist Brian Froud. It pictured a woman clothed in an elaborate medieval dress holding up a mask that obscured her features. Her deep-set eyes stared out through the leaf mask directly at the viewer, as if questioning the meaning of the world that she looked at. Directly behind the mysterious woman was a lacework of leaves and vines, filled with a multitude of tiny faerie creatures.

I like it almost as much as the painting Father stole from me.

Satisfied, Janet walked out into the hall with the old canvas and left it, face against the wall beside her door as if to proclaim her newfound sovereignty.

She let out a subdued whoop when she stepped back into her room, pleased at the transformation that had begun. But a moment later, a sudden flicker of movement outside her window ripped through her giddy mood, sending Janet's heart pumping into overdrive.

Bloody hell, not here!

Expecting the worst, Janet braced her hand on a pane of glass and looked down onto the terrace. What she saw there brought relief, of a sort.

Okay, no monsters this time... just father's private army marching to his orders...

Below her window a half dozen security personnel headed purposefully toward the estate's garage, and almost immediately after, she heard the roar of vehicles rumbling down the driveway.

My father's sent them after Tom.

If they find him someone may end up seriously injured... again... because of me... I don't ever want that to happen again... to anyone.

Unconsciously fingering the delicate pendant hanging from her neck, Janet considered what she could do about it.

After several hours, the scurry of security personnel along the hallway ceased, and Janet cautiously made her way to just outside her father's office. She used to play this same game when she was much younger so Janet knew that John Ravenscroft's raised voice carried even through the thick oak door. But this was no longer a childish game.

She listened, puzzled, as her father run through a very long and very specific list of his chief security officer's faults. From experience, she knew just how efficient his men were at ferreting out information. But now, after working diligently all night and day to uncover anything about Tom, they had found nothing.

How is that even possible?

On hearing yet another outburst from her father, Janet shook her head and then quietly slipped back down the hall to the relative safety of her own room. His voice still rang in her ears. "If this Thomas Lynn has the kind of resources needed to wipe his identity this clean, then I want him found and brought to me in any condition that leaves him able to answer my questions.

"And Mac, I want that to happen as soon as possible! Do you understand me?"

When Janet finally closed the door to her bedroom she pressed her head against it for a moment, lost in thought.

Fuck! Wouldn't I love to hear Tom answer those exact same bloody questions...

Memories of Tom leaping gracefully through the air, deftly trading sword thrusts with the leather-clad man and his creatures played through his thoughts. But most of all, it was the confident smile that seemed so at home on his handsome face that burned itself into her thoughts.

Will I ever see him again?

Because, I don't think my mysterious Mr. Lynn will be found unless he wants to be.

FOURTEEN

Rain thundered down from a dense, sullen sky so endless that it seemed to swallow the plain of heather and granite boulders spread out below it. A great black mare surged across that moorland, regardless of the sharp broken stones or treacherous mire under its hooves. The hot breath of both rider and mount plumed out behind, leaving a momentary trail of white mist in the frigid morning air. The rider was soaked to the bone and without saddle or bridle, but his knees, clamped firmly into his mount's heaving sides, kept him astride the horse. And regardless of the danger, he urged the mare to go even faster.

Just before each narrow strip of tarmac the mare gathered itself and leapt, never touching the man-made asphalt. Then, far off in the rain swept darkness, a flash of lightning revealed the small ring of standing stones that was their destination.

Inside the tight ring of stones, the storm was no longer of any concern to either rider or mount. Still, the mare nervously reared and pawed the air in front of the largest of the seven stones, ears laid flat against her head. Thomas slid off the mare's back. The horse turned her dripping head and looked directly at him before speaking, "Where have you brought us this foul night, friend?"

"Only where I must go."

"Go?"

Steam rose from the dripping coat of the horse as Tom stroked her heaving flanks. "I must step through the stone and find the witch woman, Mother Hainter. There are questions I would ask of her, for I fear that the quest she tasked me with has brought grievous harm to those I sought and is cert to bring more if I continue."

He looked back into the rain swept moor for a long moment. "In truth, my heart no longer yearns to return to the Lands of Summer's Twilight."

The great horse shook its mane, scattering a torrent of water over the dry earth around them. After considering the tall man standing beside her for a moment, she asked, "Thomas, that damned Queen of yours always falls too quickly into pettiness and anger. She would much rather shout commands than reason with her subjects."

Tom smiled. "Yes. It was foolish of me to pledge my fealty to one such as Her. But I was young then and did not know what I do now. But what is done is done. I cannot simply forswear my given word."

If a mare could be said to laugh ruefully, this one did just that before speaking again. "Rumour has it that She no longer sits her throne or even possesses her rightful mind?"

Tom reached up to wipe away a last rivulet of water that flowed down between the mare's eyes. "Even so, I thank you for a morning well spent in your fine company. But now I must be about my business."

The horse, as black as the storm-thick sky, stamped her hooves. Only a flicker of her ears betrayed any unease at Thomas' answer.

She looked on as he walked closer to the largest of the standing stones and slowly reached out to touch it. Tom spared one quick glance toward the city he'd just expended so much effort escaping from. Through the lowering clouds, the dim glow of Inverness coloured the far horizon. Turning back to the stone, he stepped through it, leaving behind heartfelt words trembling in the air. "Janet, please forgive me."

The moment Thomas disappeared into the stone, the Pooka plunged away, back outside into a world that was still lashed by storm in search of mischief and yet more foolish mortals.

Only the great standing stone remained, resting there as it had for ages without number, blindly watching bird and beast, mortal and fairy, cross the swelling heather-covered land around it. And there it would stay, waiting patiently for the end of one story or the beginning of another, its rough granite surface, as ever, listening in utter silence.

Within that stone or on the other side of it, Thomas stepped into a world entirely different from the rain swept moor that he just passed through.

The untroubled sky above him was the same eternal twilight that had always gently illuminated the Land of Summer's Twilight, but instead of falling on a lush verdant landscape, it cast its soft glow over a great, endless plain of dead grass. Deep in thought, Thomas paused for a moment.

How foolish. I had hoped that what greeted me before was simply a passing illusion and that returning, I might see Her lands replenished... thriving.

His shoulders were rigid under the weight of the complex task that lay before him, one that he had gladly accepted, little realising the consequences of that choice. As quickly as he could, The Knight of the Rose picked his way across the blighted landscape that surrounded him, knowing that he must find the witch woman as soon as possible.

All the way across that almost endless field, sombre memories twisted through his thoughts.

Once I rode across this plain at the head of the Queen's army, my armour shining brighter than the moon above.

On the kingdom's farthest edge, we met a vast horde of goblins come to lay waste to all that was rightfully Hers.

There was blood then and slaughter and at the last, we claimed a great victory.

Returning, Her city was bedecked in banners and filled with song for all of us who had served Her so well.

The smile She welcomed me with set my heart a flame.

Much later, when Thomas finally stepped onto the broad stone thoroughfare that led into his Queen's city, his thoughts were no less tangled, no less troubled. Before him the great marble arches from which elegant carved doors once swung wide to admit any who wished to share in that glory, now lay broken in the dust. All about him the soaring towers of the Queen's city had fallen into ruin. Nowhere could he see life of any kind.

Hurrying down the long-deserted avenues, his footfalls echo back at him from a silence that held complete dominion over the once-blessed city.

Above the Knight, still clinging to the marble walls that lined every avenue, were the withered husks of a thousand times a thousand ancient flowering vines. Pausing, Thomas reached out to touch the trunk of one and watched in dismay as it crumbled into fine dust.

Her roses once made this city a vast bower cascading with colour and filled the air with a fragrance like no other place.

Confidently threading the complex weave of avenues, the knight finally entered The Queen's throne room. But, as before, only brittle leaves and scattered windfall greeted him. Forcing himself to look he saw, high above, the Queen's throne sitting cracked and empty and he was tormented by a cascade of memories.

It seems but yesterday that She brought me here to live in Her shining city.

Warm were Her arms and warmer still the bed that we shared in our passion.

I believed then that I was forever blest.
And for a time, I put away all thought of my true home and family.
Why, then, did I begin to long so for escape from Her dominion?
Why?

Thomas quickly left the hall and walked out into what was once a verdant garden forbidden to all save the Queen and Her consort, The Knight of the Rose. But there, too, only death and decay rose to meet him. Overcome, Thomas fell to his knees and cried out, "Mother Hainter, where are you? I would talk with you. Now!"

But the echo of his anguished cry was the only sound that broke the silence that cloaked the ruin of everything he once thought he loved. Until, after a moment, he heard the soft tread of booted heels on the marble walkway. Looking up, he saw a short, wizened figure with wrinkled skin the colour of burnished mahogany standing before him – not a resplendent, and somehow, still hoped-for Queen.

"Witch woman, what must I do?"

The crone's deep-set eyes peered long and hard at the knight. "Did you expect th' quest I tasked you with ta be an easy one?"

Slowly then, Thomas began to unburden himself of what he had seen and done in the mortal lands and of his newly awakened desire.

"It was never my desire when you sent me into the mortal realms once more, but now my heart longs to stay in the land of my birth... with the mortal woman named Janet... the same who holds at least a part of The Queen within her.

"Last night, after my stubborn silence had provoked such richly deserved anger from her... after she had sent me away, telling me to never return, I realised that it was she, not the Queen, who was now at the centre of all my thoughts and my heart.

"It was my certainty that I would cause great harm to Janet if I brought her here that caused me to flee. There will assuredly be no honour for me if that were to happen, yet neither will there be any honour if I do not do all that is in my power to restore the Queen to Her rightful mind and so make whole once more The Land of Summer's Twilight.

"Janet, though, is made of soft mortal flesh, and I fear the creatures that call this place home will feast upon her, mind and body."

For some time, Thomas continued to unburden his heart to the withered crone before falling silent. The witch considered Thomas for a moment, a thin smile twisting her lips.

"Surely a Knight o' the Rose can protect a single mortal from any that might do her harm?"

"And greater danger still awaits both her and yourself than all the formidable creatures of this land. Th' Queen's anger will be great indeed when She learns o' your wish ta leave Her court and o' your presumption ta regard any other than Herself with affection.

"Perhaps, though, your Janet is made o' stronger mettle than you presume? Women so often are. So, tell her what you will, but fetch her here you must. For it is only in this garden, that th' Queen can be fully restored.

"Now go. Return quickly ta the mortal lands and give your charge what service is yours ta offer, for th' Huntsman will not hesitate long ta secure Janet for his master. And even though her father's home offers great protection, how long will she bide within it?"

Thomas nodded grimly and turned to leave.

Still the witch stood a moment longer in the midst of that immense, wasted garden that was once filled with life and beauty and, wrapping her thin arms around herself, she smiled. Within her deep-set eyes hope bloomed where there had been none at all. And with that rekindling, a single rose bloomed in that garden where there had been no life for so long.

Turning, she called out to the absent knight, "My blessings upon you, Thomas, for I fear you will need all I can bestow ta bring us to a proper ending."

Neither close nor so very far away, the Huntsman walked silently toward a vast castle, made entirely of stone and brick, that was the domain of his master, The Lord of Darkness and of Death. The enormous structure sprawled limply across the barren landscape as if it were patiently waiting for something or someone to bring it back to full, vibrant life. It had been waiting an age and more for such.

Twisting piles of rubble, cast-offs from the hovels of every manner of creature that had ever pledged their service to the Dark Lord, littered the ground at his feet.

Wide pools of reeking sewage gathered at the base of each broken building, which were themselves skewed at odd, disturbing angles, one from the other, and set with windows that were all either too big or too small and placed at uncomfortable positions in the walls that they served. Towering above all this desolation were huge chimneys spewing thick streams of black smoke into the darkening air, making his Lord's court seem more like a machine-age factory of the mortal realm than any castle out of Faerie.

Deep under the blackened earth there was a chamber of dense, shifting shadows that wailed in hollow anguish. There, the Dark Lord sat astride a throne fashioned from the bones of a vast multitude of creatures, both two-legged and four as well as others, stranger still, from the far distant land where mortals dwell. All had only one element in common: they had once been his enemy and now their remains constructed a blasphemous throne that perched high above the floor of that awful chamber.

Barely seen in the deep shadows that clung to his throne, two enormous horns rose from his wrinkled brow, spiralling into the darkness above. Astride that throne, The Lord of Darkness and of Death presided over his realm but wished for more power, always more.

To come to that inner chamber, a supplicant must descend one thousand and one brick-laid steps, set so steeply one to another that many had fallen and died there. As a reminder to others, their bones remained scattered at its base, slowly being ground to dust under the feet of all those who were more blest in making that difficult passage.

The Huntsman, followed closely by his remaining hunting beast, passed into the inner chamber and crossed its vast floor carved from a single piece of rock. The room was alive with shadows and faintly echoed with their whispers. Standing directly below the figure that sat upon the great high throne, he bowed and did not rise until, after a long silence, he was spoken to.

Above him his lord and master whispered, "I see only one of my pets. Have the others remained behind to hunt yet more human prey?"

"No, my Lord. They perished in your service."

The Huntsman's hard face masked all emotion as he continued to speak, "As was charged me, I found the mortal that you sought, and it was he that killed your beasts."

"Ah, then, why is he not here that I may punish him for so unwise an act?"

"He escaped me, my Lord."

The Dark Lord's voice thickened with barely suppressed rage, "So you tell me that this human killed four of my beasts and evaded you with apparent ease?"

"Indeed Lord, your Queen named this same man Her Knight of the Rose and has had him trained at Her court. He must possess many abilities to recommend him to that title."

At the Huntsman's casual mention of the Queen, the Dark Lord rose to his feet, and the writhing shadows in that vast chamber began to swirl excitedly in every corner of the hall, filling it with their urgent wails. When he finally spoke, it was in a whisper barely heard above their hollow cries. "Huntsman, I consider all your past service to me and am mindful of it, but if you speak of The Queen again, before you have completed your task, I will tear your tongue from your throat and feed it to my shadows here."

Wisely, the figure in armour held his silence, continuing to supplicate himself before his lord and master.

"Even so, Huntsman, whether he be called Knight of the Rose or naught, he will be bound and at your side when next I see you. Will he not?"

The Huntsman whispered, "Indeed. And…there was another…"

"Another?"

"She looked to be a mortal girl, yet I heard her speak with the voice… of She whose name you would not have me say."

The Lord of Darkness and of Death's taloned hands clutched hard at the gilded arms of his high chair before he spoke again, "And Huntsman, you would know the sound of Her voice, would you not?" The Dark Lord contemplated his minion, "This human must be another piece of this strange puzzle, however small. Bring her to me as well. I would speak with her. Go now. Be about your work!"

"With pleasure, my Lord."

FIFTEEN

After eight seemingly endless days of pacing down one long hallway after another, a reluctant prisoner in her own home, Janet was finally free of her cage. She ignored the wind that pulled at her black dress as she stood at the top of a short flight of marble stairs that opened onto the vaulted doors of one of the city's oldest cathedrals.

We wouldn't be in this place today if it weren't for me...

Her gloved hand brushed nervously through her cropped hair, gelled back now and looking far more elegant than it had a right to after what she'd done to it. Janet's gaze nervously swept across the façade of the building behind her and then out into the night beyond.

Thomas told me to stay inside my father's estate, that those horrid beasts wouldn't be able to reach me there. So, I bloody did just that.

But now here I am, in public because I have to be.

Hey, any fucking monsters lurking out there tonight?

Behind her, the cathedral was packed with people she didn't even know. Except for two. One lay in an elegant coffin and the other sat in the pew before it, racked with grief, her face streaming with tears.

The mourners inside were gathered for the funeral service of Daniel Parsons, father of her friend Lottie. They filled the cathedral almost to overflowing. When Mr. Parsons had somehow miraculously survived his injuries that night, his family had breathed a collective sigh of relief. Only to have their lives shattered when he had succumbed to a virus, caught in the same hospital that had made such heroic efforts to save his life. Afterward, Lottie had insisted over and over again that it wasn't Janet's fault, but her friend's sincere forgiveness had brought her no relief, only more guilt.

Still, what perplexed Janet was that her father had insisted he attend the funeral as well, and even pay for it, if needed. When the members of the Parsons family had quietly accepted his unlikely offer, she hadn't known what to think.

He doesn't even know these people... does he?

Just another bloody mystery to add to the list.

In what had quickly become an unconscious habit, her fingers reached up to stroke the pendant that hung around her delicate neck.

Where did you go to, Thomas? A rueful grin flickered across her lips. *Well, Janet, you did scream at him to leave, didn't you?*

She spared a quick, furtive glance down to the street where several black SUVs full of her father's men were parked.

All armed and very bloody dangerous, I'm certain.

If Thomas came here tonight, someone would get hurt... because of me. And I already have too much to fucking forgive myself for.

Janet's last moments with Tom came vividly to mind. *Just let it go. If you ever see him again, you can apologise for all the bitchy things you screamed at him.*

Trying to shake off her nervous energy, Janet began to pace back and forth along the top step of the stairway; which doubtless put the four bodyguards looming close beside her even more on edge. They probably had a bet going on exactly when that evening she would make a run for it.

Janet, however, had no intention of trying to escape. She knew that her father's men offered her the protection she needed. Not from Thomas, of course, but from the monsters. More importantly, she wanted to speak with her friend Lottie again.

Better go in.

Walking through the great doors, she heard the soulful voices of the choir that had filled the atrium only moments ago, fade into silence. The minister's solemn voice began to echo throughout the immense hall.

Janet threaded through the dense crowd, making her way to the empty seat beside her friend, marked reserved.

Bloody hell, look at this mob.

Mr. Parsons must have touched a lot of people's lives for this kind of a turn out.

Wish I could have got to know him.

Reaching her seat, she listened half-heartedly to the remainder of the minister's eulogy, unconsciously scanning the throng of people standing in the church, making sure that there were no leather-clad swordsmen or unlikely beasts sliding through them. When she realised what she was doing, Janet shivered.

Later, after the sombre service was over, the voices of the choir again filled the lofty space. Their hymn should have soothed Janet's jangled nerves, but only irritated her instead. One hand clutching Lottie's, she watched suspiciously as her father spoke to the widow, Mrs. Parsons. She kept staring, wondering what someone like John Ravenscroft could possibly have to say to the very frail, elderly black woman.

He looks like Moby Dick beside Lottie's family.

It was then she realised, despite the awful circumstances, how comforting it was to be surrounded by faces like her own. The sea of faces, shaded from light brown all the way to a rich blue-black, were compelling and vivid.

No one here will be yelling slurs at me...

Caught in her thoughts, Janet almost missed what Lottie said when she leaned in and whispered, "They're old friends..."

"Friends? He's never once mentioned your family to me..."

"Well, from what you've told me you don't exactly talk much, do you?"

"No, I guess we don't."

Janet struggled to escape the tangle of her thoughts before she enveloped Lottie in a fierce hug.

"Hey, enough about me. Are you going to be okay?"

"Yeah, yeah. It'll be rough, but I'll survive. The Parsons are a hardy lot."

"Really?"

"Really."

"Lots of repair work to do down at the club, which should keep me busy for a bloody long time. The 320 is father's legacy, after all"

"Okay, anything I can do to help?"

Lottie pulled away to look Janet in the eye.

"Listen. I know you don't want to hear this, but your father is putting some much needed cash into the club, and I for one, am grateful.

"He really doesn't seem like the monster you make him out to be. Maybe you should go easy on him?"

"Yeah. Okay. I'll think about it."

Lottie's brow wrinkled with concern. "And Janet, what about this Thomas of yours?"

"Gone. I told him to leave, so he bloody did."

"I don't blame you. He's at least partially to blame for the mess down at my club... and... two men are dead because of it... one was my Da."

Hastily wiping away the fresh tears that ran down her cheeks, Lottie kept talking. "Could you even trust Thomas if you saw him again?"

Before Janet could answer, Charlotte was engulfed by a wave of close family and many more tears were shed. So Lottie didn't hear her friend, standing to the side, feeling lost, whisper, "I don't know... I just don't."

After what seemed like an eternity full of unexpected bursts of noise that kept Janet constantly on edge, she saw her father begin to make his goodbyes. Grateful to be leaving, she linked her arm under his and said, "Okay, can you take me home now? Please."

Bloody hell, every single laugh or cry or even a hard pat on the back is making me jumpy as fuck. Never thought I'd want to get back to my personal prison so soon.

Surprised, the elder Ravenscroft looked down at his daughter. When he replied, his usually stern face was softened by a paternal smile. "With pleasure, my dear… with pleasure."

Across the street from the funeral, high in an ancient oak, Thomas had been carefully observing events unfold below him that evening. He had seen the abundance of guards and considered simply swooping Janet up as she stood on the steps of the building, but had decided against giving in to the pleasure of rescuing her.

He was certain that John Ravenscroft's security force would have been only a momentary nuisance; his real concern that evening had been The Huntsman. Thomas had expected him to appear at any moment, especially now that Janet was far from the safety of the unusual wall around her father's estate.

Choosing to bide his time, Tom considered the enormous effort involved in planting and maintaining the hedge of rowan trees that completely circled the extensive grounds of Ravenscroft's estate. Most of them were mature trees, planted long ago, perhaps by whoever had built the estate in the first place.

Who would have had the knowledge to do such work?

Janet and her father flanked by four security personnel emerged from the cathedral and started down the broad front steps toward their waiting SUV, Tom's gaze followed them. A vehicle just like it stood in front and another behind.

Packed with the father's soldiers, I'm certain.

But as many as there may have been, they would offer no protection at all from the servant of The Lord of Darkness and of Death.

As he carefully considered his next move, the rough bark under his hand suddenly began to twist and turn, forming itself into a wrinkled face that blinked up at Tom for a moment before speaking.

"Hurrrrrmmmm.

"Weeeeeeeeeeeeeeeeeeeeeez.

"No, don't tell me. No! Wait! I've seen you before. Nonononono, don't tell me, I know it well. Your name is Duncan. No? No... "Lacklan then? Or was it Dylan? Ah, there it is, right on the tip o' my tongue. I've got it now. You'd be called Thomas.

"Am I right? No need to answer, of course I am, I'm always right.

"And how sir, are you this fine evening. Well, it might indeed be fine if I were somewhere else other than this miserable city, breathin' its foul air. Stunts my limbs ya ken? I should be leanin' up against a wee house out on the moors or nestled in a bonnie glen beside a bright blue burn, chocked full with the salmon, it would be. Yes, that would suit me just fine, indeed it would.

"I'd no be breathin' this black air then. Weel, I expect it's a bit late for a' that jist now.

"So then, if you please, Mr. Thomas Lynn, what's going on doon there that has so caught your interest that you can no speak to me at all?"

Without a word, Tom winked at the ancient green man and then sprang across to the next tree that lined the long, stately street.

"Well then, it's goodbye, is it? Here is my best good luck to you with whatever you may be up to this fine night. I expect you'll be needin' it before tha dawn's light comes again."

Moving quickly, Thomas dropped from the tree to a nearby rooftop and continued down the street, not hearing the old green man's blessing.

In that same manner, Tom continued to shadow Janet and her father all the way back to their estate.

SIXTEEN

Less than an hour later, the caravan of black SUV's turned off Culloden Road and onto the long private drive that bore the Ravenscroft estate's name. Huddled in the back of the middle vehicle, Janet had pushed herself as far away from her father as possible. Her thoughts a tangle of half-truths and revelations, she hadn't spoken for the entire length of the drive across downtown Inverness.

Finally, attempting to find the answer to at least one of the multitude of questions that all but consumed her, Janet asked, "So, how do you know them? The Parsons, I mean. You talked with his widow for a long time, and out of the fucking blue you offered my friend Lottie the money to rebuild her music club. But you've never said word one about any of them to me."

John Ravenscroft surfaced from his own thoughts to briefly acknowledge his daughter with an ill-considered comment. "I can't think of any reason that you need to know why." Then he turned back to the long in-coming text that he was studying on his mobile. It concerned his wife and the secret that had for too long helped build a wall between father and daughter. Lately Janet's ceaseless effort to tear down that wall had produced an abundance of absurd antics that only served to drive the elder Ravenscroft into frustrated anger.

Finished, John looked up, his gaze lingering on his young daughter, who was quickly transforming into a woman as strong-willed as her mother. He'd spoken too harshly, he realised.

"Forgive me. I..."

But Janet was staring intently out the window After a moment she quietly whispered, "My mother, what was she like? At least you can tell me that, can't you?"

John was taken aback the question, so close to his own thoughts. But years of high-stress situations in boardrooms all over the world had prepared him for moments just like this. "You are very alike. And you only become more so with each passing year."

"And that's all you're going to tell me, isn't it?"

"Janet, now is simply not the moment for a lengthy discussion about your mother."

"Then when is?"

Ignoring the strained silence that followed, Janet lost herself in childhood memories of hours spent playing in the Privet hedge that ran the length of both sides of the drive. Then it had been an enormous barrier surrounding the castle just inside, and she the heroic prince come to rescue a sleeping princess within.

A sharp metallic clang brought her back to a bleaker present, where she fought against waves of rising panic, watching the gate into the estate begin to slide open.

Now I'm going to be that sad sleeping princess, a prisoner in her own father's castle.

Trying to push that panic aside, Janet asked her father another question as casually as she could. "If Tom had come tonight, what were you planning to do?"

Ravenscroft smiled, "As I've told you, I only want to ask the young man a few questions."

"Really? That's all…"

He looked up at Janet, asking quietly, "And why shouldn't a father be concerned about any man that courts his daughter?"

Janet tried but didn't succeed in suppressing her laughter. "Bloody hell! Now my mystery man is some kind of old-fashioned gentleman caller?" Then she grew serious. "I don't really know how I feel about Mr. Thomas bloody Lynn. I've only seen him twice, but I seem unable to get him out of my head for the last eight days. Believe me, I've tried." Janet put her hand to the pendant at her breast. "So, he's got completely under my skin. Maybe someday it could be love. I don't know, I've never been in love before…"

Janet was even more surprised by her impulsive words than her father appeared to be, but then she smiled to herself, suddenly knowing that they were true.

Any hint of compassion vanished from John Ravenscroft's face. Instead, he reacted as he always had to anything that threatened his interests. "Really? So, I'm to believe you this time when you say that your Thomas is more than just another random annoyance you want to throw under my feet?"

"Oh, yes. Much, much more."

A strained smile struggled across her father's face. "Well then, in that case, I really do need to know more about this Thomas Lynn of yours. Do you happen to know where he comes from or even who his family is? That would be a good place to begin, I should think. After all, I have to make sure that your Tom isn't just playing a canny game because he's after our estate."

Shocked by her father's words, Janet spat out her reply. "We'll only know if I actually ever see him again, won't we?"

Ravenscroft frowned. "Janet, I only want to protect you from any unpleasantness. Just as I always have your entire life."

Her anger swept aside any fear of whatever monsters might lurk in the night.

"Protect me? You've made me a prisoner in my own bloody home, that's what you've done!"

Ravenscroft stared intently at her, before saying, "Whatever I've done has always been for your own good." But in the face of Janet's incredulous stare John Ravenscroft looked away, for the first time showing some discomfort. When he finally spoke again, it was in the soft, comforting voice that she dimly remembered from her childhood, a tone he almost never used any more. "Daughter, how many times must I tell you that, no matter what you may think, I do love you?"

Janet opened her mouth to hiss another sharp retort when the vehicle in front suddenly lurched forward and twisted over on its side, as if it had been hit by something large and very heavy.

"No! Not again."

"Again?"

The driver slammed on the brakes, grinding to a halt inches from the overturned SUV before yelling, "Both of you, get down!" Pulling his gun from its shoulder holster, he prepared for whatever was going to happen next. Immediately, John Ravenscroft began to issue a series of commands into his mobile to the security personnel in the vehicle behind them. "No, I did not see what's caused this. Get out of your vehicle and find out. Do not, I repeat, *do not* call the police until we know exactly what is happening here. Do I make myself clear?"

Both father and daughter peered intently out at the scene of destruction in front of the car. Neither saw anything that could have caused the massive impact that jammed the lead vehicle between the front gate and the stone pillar it was no longer attached to.

At that moment, Janet felt a sharp wave of nausea and pressed her face against the cool window looking for relief.

No! No! Not now. We were almost safe…

Suddenly, she was looking at the chaotic violence outside through the Queen's eyes. The darkness that had shrouded the road around the car moments earlier was no longer black but suffused with the soft glow of twilight. The hedge along the drive and the stately trees beyond, the overturned lead vehicle, and the men trying to escape from it, all seemed over-saturated with unnatural shimmering colours.

Janet shuddered before being completely overwhelmed, as once again that alien presence claimed dominion over her body. Disdainfully, She buried the useless remnants of the human girl deep within the recesses of her mind. Then, only The Queen remained, watching with anticipation as a dozen giant cat-like hunting beasts circled the three SUVs.

She smiled as one of The Huntsman's great beasts slashed a long gash through the side of the overturned vehicle in front. Not able to see their attackers, the men inside began to fire wildly into the air. But one by one, each man was pulled through the gaping hole on the side, their bodies torn to bloody strips by the serrated edges of the ripped metal. For a split second, they hung suspended in the air flailing their arms, their legs, as if they were children's hand puppets. Then they were literally ripped apart by the beasts. As the blood sprayed across the tarmac and the grass beyond, She began to laugh, entertained by the slaughter.

Horrified by that laughter, John Ravenscroft stared across the seat in disbelief. What he saw there convinced him that someone or something *other* sat inside his daughter's body, because whatever it was that wore Janet's features, it most certainly was not his daughter. The creature that stared back at him barely even acknowledged his existence. Its face, possessing none of Janet's softness, was filled with more implacable cruelty than even John Ravenscroft could muster.

Desperately, he hissed at this impossible impersonator, "Who are you? What have you done with my daughter?"

His questions remained unanswered, as the vehicle behind was abruptly lifted from the ground and slammed back down again with enough force to shatter every window, scattering a shower of glass across the drive. Jerking around at this explosion of violence, John stared in horror as those men, too, were yanked from the SUV by whatever invisible force attacked them.

On the roof above him, Ravenscroft heard a hollow thump and looked up, preparing for the worst. Seconds later, through blood-splattered windows, he saw a figure that he recognised from the surveillance footage as Thomas Lynn leaping toward the remnants of the third SUV. Confused, John cried out, "What is he doing here?"

Beside him, The Queen of Summer's Twilight watched with delighted anticipation as Her Knight of the Rose stood calmly in the midst of the circling beasts, preparing for battle. A satisfied smile lit Her face when She announced to the stunned human across from Her, "That is my Knight, my champion and my consort, come to perform his sworn duty and protect his Queen."

To John Ravenscroft, who still saw nothing of the great beasts or the Huntsman that led their attack, Her words seemed utter nonsense. His angry retort thundered above the mad screams of his dying men. "What? That madman must somehow be causing all this slaughter, and I'm going to stop him. Now!"

The woman who had once been his daughter reached out to clutch Ravenscroft's hand and whispered, "Do you see them now, mortal? My champion and the other? From this moment we will both be suitably entertained."

At Her touch, Ravenscroft instantly saw the creatures that were tearing apart his well-trained force of men with so little effort.

"My god, it is real then? "Mairi spoke true when she swore to me that there was a world other than our own, but I never for a moment believed her.

"Only now… And… Thomas, he's trying to save us…"

Clinching the handle of the jammed door, he tried to wrench it open with all his considerable strength, to no effect.

Outside, a dozen beasts, blood dripping from their enormous jaws, prowled through the grotesque tangle of bodies that littered the pavement around each vehicle. Then Ravenscroft saw a figure standing atop the overturned vehicle in the rear: a tall, thin man, dressed in black-tooled leather, holding a bright sword in each hand.

The Huntsman casually tossed one of those blades into the air, calling out as he did, "Here. I did not think it proper of me to fight you again without returning what you claim to be yours." Thomas caught the twirling blade without pausing and leapt toward his opponent.

Still held in the Queen's iron grip, John Ravenscroft lunged toward the front seat, desperately bellowing at his man, "The gun! Give me your gun!"

Oblivious to Ravenscroft's command, the bewildered guard gripped his weapon firmly in both hands but couldn't take his eyes off his dying friends.

When their SUV shuddered and the roof and front door punched inward, shattering every windshield with the impact and covering them in a shower of glass, it was too late. The guard's head was gripped by the jaws of a great ravening beast that only Ravenscroft could see and the whole body was flung from side to side, arms flailing uselessly.

Frantically, John Ravenscroft tore his wrist away from the Queen's grip and lunged over the seat, both arms grabbing for the man's gun as it fell into the pool of blood collecting in the seat below. After a mad scramble, Ravenscroft gripped the pistol in his hands and prepared to fire off as many rounds as it took to stop the impossible creature. But now he could no longer see the great beast that ravaged his driver. Only the mangled body dropped back onto the front seat, covered in fresh blood and the sharp, overwhelming scent given off by the beast, assured him that it was still there.

With a snarl, John turned back to the rear window, but the figure in dark leather was nowhere to be seen either. There were only the remnants of the SUV with dead, twisted bodies slumped on the pavement around it, and Tom swinging his sword gracefully through the empty air.

Ravenscroft bellowed, "Of course!" before lunging for the hand of what had once been his daughter. Grasping it, he saw everything again. Sweeping his gaze across the chaotic scene out on the driveway, John brought up the gun with his free hand. Several of the beasts lay sprawled across the drive, dying, their throats sliced completely through. The remaining creatures formed a circle around both the leather-clad stranger and Tom, who continued to exchange skilful thrusts with their blades.

The Queen of Summer's Twilight looked coldly back at John Ravenscroft. "Mortal, unhand me!"

With an easy twist of Her wrist, She freed Her hand from the human's unwanted grasp. Again John could see nothing more significant than Thomas jumping wildly from one elegant stance to another across the top of the crumpled vehicle behind him. Only now, there were long slashes torn through his clothing that showed fresh blood.

Beside him, the Queen's calm voice did nothing to ease Ravenscroft's anxiety. "Foolish mortal. Do you think there is anything that you can do to determine the outcome of a conflict you cannot possibly understand?"

Ravenscroft scowled back at the alien creature sitting across from him and said, "There's far more that I understand about all this than you know. Now, please allow me to help your champion, if I can. Give me your hand!"

The Queen smiled coolly back at John before replying simply, "No." In one smooth flowing motion, She turned away and seemed to slip easily through the car's shattered window and walk toward her champion.

A few feet beyond, Tom rolled to his feet to see what he thought was the young mortal girl, who had won his heart standing close beside him. His eyes narrowed, though, when he saw the great hunting beasts fawning at Her feet. Her dress whipped around Her slim legs, driven by a powerful wind that touched no one else. When She spoke, Her voice was pitched soft and low, Her words not in any language heard in the mortal realm.

"It is I, Thomas. Do you not recognise me?"

Instantly, Thomas dutifully prostrated himself, "My Queen…"

Still in the car and without the Queen's aid, John Ravenscroft only saw Thomas and the woman who had been his daughter standing in the midst of the wreckage of the two SUVs and the twisted bodies out on the drive. Certain that the carnage wasn't finished yet, he whispered to himself, "There are still more of those damned beasts and that bloody bastard who's done his best to kill Thomas out there… somewhere close by."

Forcing himself to be calm, John hoped for the best, as he fired off his entire clip of bullets in a tight pattern in the air, close beside where Thomas and The Queen stood.

At the sound of the gunshots, Tom turned away from The Queen to see the leather-clad figure close at his side, with his slim blade poised for a killing thrust. The Huntsman clutched his chest and stumbled back over several bodies on the tarmac. Sinking to his knees, his face twisting with agony he shrieked, fresh blood welling from under his hand.

Although Ravenscroft couldn't see what effect his gunshots had, he could tell by the expressions on the two that were visible, that he'd accomplished something.

Crouching low over their master and sniffing at the shoulder where the bullet was lodged, the remaining hunting creatures looked up and hissed angrily. Then, snarling, two of them lunged toward the remaining vehicle where Janet's father was sitting. Thomas leapt to his feet, shouting, "Ravenscroft, defend yourself!" and sprinted toward the car.

Instinctively, John Ravenscroft raised the pistol again, but each rapid pull of the trigger only struck an empty chamber as the invisible creatures leapt toward him. He felt their huge bodies strike the door of the armoured SUV and then could only imagine their great jaws open and ready to snatch the gun away, and with it, his arm. But a sharp, commanding voice rang in the air, "Enough. This game is over!"

At her command, the beasts stopped their attack and slunk away, spitting out their impotent fury.

Stepping gracefully over the sprawled bodies of Ravenscroft's men, The Queen stood, staring down at The Huntsman as he writhed in agony at her feet. For a moment, She gazed at him, knowing that for any creature of the Fae the touch of iron would quickly prove fatal. Her hand gently stroked the prickly spines of the hunting beast that brushed close by her side, calming it. "Take your master home. His death will not be long now, and it would not be seemly to leave him here in this dreary land where these wretched mortals dwell."

The Huntsman, though, looked up at Tom and snarled viciously through clenched teeth, "Know this, Sir Knight, no matter Her words, I will survive. I must. This hunt is merely delayed by my wounds, not ended before its proper outcome."

Opening his great jaws, the largest of the beasts carefully cradled The Huntsman's limp body between his bloody teeth and backed away. The remaining beasts followed its lead, their heads still bowed, and disappeared into the night.

Tom turned, determined to give chase, but at that moment, Janet finally succeeded in beating away the mind of The Queen. Collapsing onto the tarmac she cried out, "Tom! Help me!"

And there, in the midst of ravaged human bodies soaking the hard pavement with their life's blood, Thomas knelt and wrapped his arms around the trembling girl, doing his best to comfort her.

When he felt a heavy hand fall on his shoulder, he looked up, startled. John Ravenscroft stared straight at them both. Through weary eyes, Janet tried to focus, "Hello, Father. You're okay then?"

He held her gaze for a moment, as if to confirm that it really was his daughter looking back at him now, then he breathed a long sigh of relief.

Clutching at Tom's strong arms, Janet began to cry, "You're safe! All of you are safe."

Thomas gently stroked her shoulders before speaking. "You spoke again with my Queen's voice, and in the language of Faerie…"

He was taken aback, though, by Janet's violent reaction to his words. "Your Queen? Fuck your bloody Queen. Why the hell is she doing this to me?"

Her father looked down at her, concern and fear shifting across his face. "Janet, calm yourself. Without this Queen, whoever she may be, none of us would be alive now…"

Thomas held her tighter, and thinking only of the advantage that The Queen had given them, spoke hastily, "Was it so terrible?"

Janet's face twisted with loathing when she answered, "Yes! Yes it was. No matter how hard I fought it, she controlled my body, my mind… my whole self. I feel like she…like she was *violating* me, Tom. It was horrible!"

Looking at the destruction around them, Ravenscroft added quietly, "We may be alive, but my men were not so lucky."

There was a low moan then from the front of the car, still mostly intact, as a blood-spattered figure struggled to his feet, swaying unsteadily. Janet's father moved quickly to keep his chief of staff from falling back to the tarmac. Holding the dazed man's arm, Ravenscroft murmured, "Ah, Mr. MacIntosh, good to have you with us still."

Ravenscroft's head of security struggled to wipe the blood away from a long gash on his forehead with the cuff of his shirt before answering. "Yes sir, I'm still here."

In the distance they all heard the steady scream of multiple sirens moving rapidly closer to the estate. Ravenscroft asserted his usual command of any situation and quietly but firmly explained to each of them what they were to do next, in a voice that was very used to being obeyed.

"Mac, would you be so good as to go to the office and secure this evening's surveillance tapes? It would not be wise to let prying eyes actually see the unfortunate events that I'm about to lie so well about." The still dazed man nodded assent and quickly picked his way through the scattered debris, stepping carefully over the bodies of his men, and walked briskly up to his office alongside the garage.

Turning back to Thomas and his daughter, he noticed that Janet's body has begun to shake uncontrollably, and calmly explained to Thomas,

"My daughter is going into shock. We need to get her into the house as soon as possible. I have a more than adequate medical facility there to deal with her injuries. I just wish that I hadn't given my physician and his staff the evening off. Still, he is on call."

Looking curiously at the man who held his only daughter in his arms, he asked, "Will you take my daughter inside for me?"

Ravenscroft turned his attention to the approaching sirens and added, "I'll join you as soon as possible." Pausing for a brief moment, he considered his next words carefully. "We have so much to tell each other, don't we?"

When Tom still didn't move but simply continued to stare back at him, Ravenscroft offered a more compelling explanation. "I am staying here to wait for the police. I will offer them something logical, however far from the truth, to help explain this tragedy.

"But you," and he looked Tom straight in the eye, emphasising his words, "you should not be here when they arrive. First, they will ask you questions that you can't or won't answer, and then they'll run a background check on you. When they find, just as I did, that there's nothing in any database to tell them who you are, they'll throw you into a cell quick as you like.

"Go. Now! I can take care of this. I've had plenty of practice."

"If that is your wish." With Janet gathered in his arms, Tom turned to walk through the ruined gates and on up to the great house.

SEVENTEEN

A full hour later John Ravenscroft walked into the great room of the house. Janet lay unconscious on the plush couch, her arms still tightly wrapped around the mysterious man who had helped save both their lives. Thomas looked up at Ravenscroft, cautiously following his every move as if he were ready to bolt like a wild animal caught in a trap.

The older man cleared his throat before speaking. "Well, I suppose you have no idea where the medical unit is located here, but I think it might be better for my daughter if we took her there now."

Thomas' face implacably hardened, "No. My Lady... Janet, before she succumbed, made me promise that she would remain here, in this room, until she awakens. It seems that your daughter has little trust in her own father."

"I see. Janet, you will find, can be quite stubborn." Ravenscroft suddenly felt bone weary. He rubbed his eyes before continuing. "Well then, I placed a call to Janet's physician, Dr. Nehran, and without giving away too many incriminating details, asked his advice. There's really not much we can't do right here in this room. Just keep her quiet and warm and let her body heal itself. Assuming, of course, that there are no serious physical injuries?"

"I have checked. There are none."

"Under these particular circumstances, I told the good doctor to remain at home. I have no wish to cause yet another death this evening."

Quietly then, John slid an over-stuffed chair across the room closer to the couch and fell tiredly into it. Calmly looking at the young man who meant so much to his daughter, he began to evaluate their uncertain future. He carefully noted Tom's shredded leather jacket, the peculiar old-fashioned shirt, and what he would call leggings that were all soaked with blood and stained by a long road travelled quickly. Bloody welts mixed with deep bruises were now beginning to show on what otherwise he might say was a handsome face. Ravenscroft cleared his throat. "I think you would feel much better, though, if you cleaned yourself up."

When Tom nodded agreement, Ravenscroft pointed to the arched entrance into the room they sat in and continued, "The washroom is down that hall on the left."

Gently disentangling himself from Janet's arms, Tom left her huddled on the coach and walked to the wide doorway that opened into the hallway beyond. Her father held out a neatly folded set of clothes that he'd brought with him. "Take these. I believe they will fit."

After a moment's hesitation, Ravenscroft chose to elaborate. "They're mine, or were." Then with a rueful grimace, he continued, "I was much fitter in my youth. And you will feel better in clean clothes."

Grateful, Tom took them but still hesitated before leaving the room, to offer a courtly bow, wincing from his still fresh injuries. "My name, sir, is Thomas Lynn, and it is my pleasure to meet you, Mr. Ravenscroft."

"It's John... please just call me John." Janet's father continued to look up at the odd young man, and attempted to smile. "And the pleasure is most certainly mine. My daughter and I both owe you our lives, and for that I am in your debt."

Thomas paused at the doorway a moment longer before replying, "A debt answered swiftly by your own service to me."

Ravenscroft looked at the young man quizzically, "Service? I only did what needed to be done."

"Nevertheless, the Huntsman would have killed me if you had not stopped him. Also, you prevented the guardians of your law from holding me captive, even now, deep within their iron dungeons."

Ravenscroft's left eyebrow arched in wry amusement, "Our guardians of the law, as you say, have a certain amount of respect for me and what is mine. It was not easy, but I think they are going to accept my rather fantastic story. For the moment anyway..."

The older man settled gratefully back into the soft chair, "I offered them no mythic beasts or duelling swords, just a simple Earth-bound terrorist attack, perhaps brought on by an extremely disgruntled international partner of one of my many business transactions. Of course, there have been more than a few of those, and it will take some time for the authorities to trace them all."

Then Ravenscroft's expression grew more serious, "In a few hours, perhaps less, there will be a visit from any number of proper detectives, and they, I fear, will be much harder to misdirect.

"But, let's say they do accept my somewhat implausible explanation and just go away, what are we going to do about that man and his creatures? And what of this person who is apparently hell bent on consuming my daughter's mind?" He held up his broad hand when Tom began to protest. "You cannot tell me otherwise. I looked into her eyes and there was not a shred of Janet within. And I heard her speak as well, with words that were certainly not of this Earth."

Nodding at Janet's sleeping form, he continued, "There is a shadowy world whose existence I've spent my entire life denying. Long ago, creatures from that world took my wife or at least her mind from me, and now they've come back for my daughter."

John Ravenscroft pressed his hands once more against his tired eyes and didn't see Thomas' entire body grow rigid at the older man's bitter revelation. "They drove my wife mad, and now they're trying to do the same to Janet. I will do anything… anything at all to prevent that. Do you understand me?"

Thomas, looking every inch the knight that he was, even clothed in torn, blood-splattered clothes, solemnly gave his pledge. "Sir, my life would be forfeit before I would allow any to harm your daughter."

Taken aback by Thomas' unequivocal answer, John quietly asked, "You would do that? You'd give your life for Janet?"

Thomas drew himself up to his full height, "Sir, do you doubt my word or my honour?"

For all of his life John Ravenscroft had ruthlessly judged men and women, dismissing as useless any that he found lacking for his purpose. He looked at Thomas now with growing respect, and replied, "No. No, sir, I do not. But Thomas, what can we do to prevent a repeat of what happened out there tonight?"

When Thomas offered no answer, Ravenscroft sighed and gestured toward the washroom down the long hallway. "Hurry back. We still have a lot to discuss."

After the improbable young man left, John Ravenscroft brought all of his considerable focus back to his daughter. There were large, dark red stains splashed across her once-elegant dress, and Janet's face and hands were scratched with deep welts that still seeped blood. But he saw no serious injuries. "Right. I'll need to take care of those cuts myself then." Fighting against his own exhaustion, John got to his feet to fetch the disinfectants and bandages. Pausing, he looked tenderly down at Janet for a brief moment before turning to walk down the hall.

When Ravenscroft returned, he gently lowered himself onto the couch beside his daughter and began to apply the first aide that he'd brought with him. But at his touch, Janet groaned and sat up, instinctively sliding away from her father as far as she was able, huddling at the far end of the couch, seemingly lost in thought.

With the palm of her hand, she wiped away tears that ran down to the cuts on her face and asked a question that, after everything that had happened that night, startled him. "Father, why do you try so hard to keep any remnant of my mother out of sight?"

John Ravenscroft remained stubbornly silent as she continued. "There's not a single photograph of her in this entire house, and that's just bloody weird because you've told me again and again how much you loved her!"

He was surprised when she moved closer again and gathered both of his massive hands in hers. Staring into his eyes she said, "We live in the same damn house, but we never, ever talk to each other. Practically the only conversations we've had since I turned thirteen were screaming matches." He dropped his gaze as she continued, "And a nod when we pass in the hall doesn't count!"

The medication and bandages forgotten in his lap, Ravenscroft's massive hands clung tightly to Janet's, and yet he still felt unable to offer her an explanation for his actions.

Janet continued, in the face of his silence,. "It must be so damned hard keeping all those secrets bottled up inside. Doesn't your tongue ever trip over them all? I know mine does, and I haven't had half as long to collect my own.

"You'll never know the half of who I've imagined my mother is. When I was younger, I expected her to just walk through the front door at any moment and rescue her kidnapped daughter from the dark castle that imprisoned her. She was my Fairy Queen. I was her long-lost daughter, the princess.

"That will never happen, will it father?" Janet's voice grew suddenly hoarse as she cried, "Why won't you tell me anything at all about her…?"

Lost in thought, John Ravenscroft wrestled with memories of his wife that for so many years he'd kept as far away as possible. Visions of love and happiness and pain… so much pain, cascaded through John's tired mind. He looked at his daughter, "There's no purpose in being angry with me. There's nothing you could say now that I haven't told myself over and over your entire life.

"Anything… anything at all that reminded me of your mother would only reignite my anger. I refused to believe there was any truth to her ravings about another world that existed alongside our own, because fairy tales never had a place in my life.

"Until tonight, that is.

"Janet, every day you look more like her." An involuntary shiver ran through his solid frame before he continued. "And in the last several years, you'd even begun to act like Mairi as well. At times, when you spoke in the same strange language that she had screamed at me so long ago, it seemed that her madness was consuming you as well. And that absolutely terrified me."

He slowly shook his head, "But now, after what happened out there tonight, I know that your mother was frightened by a world that is as real as this one, only I couldn't see it."

A soft voice startled them both, "Indeed."

Standing at the entrance to the room, Thomas' sombre gaze rested on each of them for a moment before he continued, "I have lived in that invisible world for most of my life and seen the beauty… and the terror that it has to offer. Any mortal who chooses to walk in The Queen's court must be careful, indeed. For there will come a day when you must decide whether to stay there in that land of eternal summer or return here and then eventually grow old and finally, pass away."

EIGHTEEN

Resplendent, even wearing cast off clothing, Thomas, The Knight of the Rose looked intently down at Janet. Meeting his gaze, she felt a pleasant shiver prickle the flesh of her arms and neck.

John Ravenscroft noted that deeply intimate look and uncomfortably shifted his considerable bulk on the couch. "Well, yes… of course, but we have other matters to discuss, don't we? All my life I've discounted anything that smacked of the imagination or fantasy. It was all nothing to me, fit only for weak minds or young children. Now, I find that I must throw away the rules that have always determined my life and accept that a vast unseen world exists as a matter of hard fact."

He grasped his daughter's hand more firmly and looked seriously up at the young man who had just pledged himself to her. "It will be difficult, so please have patience with me."

After a moment, Ravenscroft moved back into his own chair, leaving the sofa for Tom to sit beside his daughter. Janet whispered a question, then, so softly that both men had to strain to hear it. "Tom, the world that you come from, the one that I saw through this Queen's eyes, is it always as ugly as that huntsman and his creatures make it seem?"

"No, my Lady, not always. There is danger there, of course, always great danger, but also more beauty than will ever be found on this Earth. The inhabitants of that land are called the Fae. You call them fairies and have diminished your terror of them by making them small creatures that inhabit your nursery tales, living at the bottom of your gardens. But, as you've seen tonight, they are so much more than that."

Janet clasped her hands together. She glanced at her father and tried to relate the events that had led them here. "Tom and I met on the stone bridge near Aviemore last week," she said. "A troll creature attacked me there. I reacted then just as I did tonight. Spoke that same bloody language. Saw that same totally freaky world."

Startled, John Ravenscroft remembered his wife insisting that she had seen the same things in the days before she was lost to him. It recalled the greatest tragedy of his life as he whispered, "Tonight…when I…I looked into your eyes, daughter, you were not there."

He looked up, wanting desperately to believe what his daughter and Thomas were telling him was the truth, "I called it madness when I saw that same look in your mother's eyes."

Janet nodded. "Why wouldn't you? When that horrible creature is in my head I feel like I'm going to explode. Crazy isn't even the half of it… You saw me out there with those horrible creatures cowering at my feet. Why didn't they just eat me and be done with it?"

Listening to Janet, her father pressed his hands to his eyes trying to block the painful cascade of memories that still haunted him.

After a moment, Ravenscroft quietly commented, "I think we need to know who exactly this spirit woman is, if we're going to keep her from hurting you."

"Bloody hell, yes!" Janet turned to Thomas. "So, who is this Queen of yours? What kind of creature can just casually make me do whatever she wants? And why did that bitch pick me to be the one to torment like this?"

"It will serve us ill to name Her with such vile epithets as seemingly trip so lightly off your tongue."

"I don't fucking care. Just tell me who she is!"

After a startled pause, Thomas began to carefully answer that question.

"She? She is The Queen of the Land of Summer's Twilight. Her smile brings joy and delight to those who live in Her court and strikes fear into those that do not.

"Mortals have seen Her in their most vivid dreams and named her Titania or Mab, Meave, Gloriana or the Morrigan, Diana and Ishstar. By whatever name they give Her, She is more glorious than ever they can imagine.

"She is the ruler of all the lands of Faerie, from the broad fields of Morningstar, even unto the impassable mountain called Sorrows Ebb. And to Her, I have sworn my life and my honour to do all that She commands of me."

Ravenscroft was shocked by that, but what must Janet be thinking? He watched as she tore herself out of Tom's arms and stood defiant, "You… you've sworn yourself to this creature! Why? Do you expect me to just sit here and wait for her to tell you what to do next?"

Staring steadfastly at the young woman he loved, Thomas proclaimed, "I have sworn a solemn oath to obey Her in all things that She asks of me, for She is my Queen. Or was, till madness overthrew Her."

"That's just stupid!" Janet began to pace across the room, trying to calm her thoughts, making a desperate effort to remember exactly what The Queen was thinking for the brief moments that she occupied her body. Abruptly, she halted in front of Thomas, "Well, my Queen is certainly not crazy. Cruel and inhuman, but not crazy. So, are you sure it's the same person?"

Quietly, with great dignity, Thomas related The Lady's recent history as he had come to understand it. "While I was absent, a great evil came upon Her kingdom, trying to force its will upon Her very being. To escape, She cast Her conscious mind far, far away, leaving behind only a hollow husk that even now shrieks madly at the moon.

"Because of this madness, my Queen can no longer maintain the balance of life and death. Now Her kingdom, the eternal Land of Summer, is slowly fading to nothing and all of its inhabitants as well.

"To preserve that Land, it is essential that I make Her whole once more. Once She is restored, I will have fulfilled my quest and fulfilled my avowed duty to The Queen. Only then will I have the right to beg that She release me from my vow of obedience to Her will."

Facing sceptical looks from Janet's father and outright derision from his daughter, Thomas continued, "Through some strange sorcery, Her mind has been lodged within yours, untouched by the madness that has consumed the husk of flesh that remains of Her."

"That is utter bullshit!"

Her father, perhaps fearing another emotional episode, got to his feet and reached out to comfort his daughter, saying, "Janet, please calm yourself." Then, looking uncomfortable, he continued, "Shouting at each other won't make this problem go away. We both know that by now. There's so much more that we need to understand before those creatures return." Turning to Thomas, he asked, "I am right in assuming that this huntsman and his beasts will return, aren't I?"

"If The Huntsman survived your bullet. Or if not, some other chosen one will continue these attacks until they have accomplished their master's will, or we are all dead.

"Does this master have a name?"

"Yes. He is known as the Lord of Darkness and of Death. His kingdom is vast, and the creatures that he calls his own bow to no other will but his."

Ravenscroft simply said, "Well, whatever he calls himself, we must prepare ourselves…"

Thomas, calmly leaned back into the sofa and looked up at both father and daughter before replying, "Indeed, that is so, but I believe that we have an advantage there." What Tom asked next clearly startled the older man. "Master Ravenscroft, who built your estate?"

"What... what has that got to do with any of this?"

Thomas smiled at the older man, "It is a mystery to me who could have woven into the building of it as many subtle safeguards, enabling it to withstand all the creatures of the Fae that have come against it."

Before answering, John Ravenscroft lowered his head in thought. "Well... this estate was built by the first to lay claim to the Ravenscroft name. As it happens, his name too was John. Our family has lived here ever since his time."

He looked up at Thomas then. "There has always been a family rumour that he possessed the second sight."

This was news to Janet. She was about to ask a question, when Tom's grip on her hand tightened, and one quick look into his eyes convinced her to remain silent and listen quietly as the older Ravenscroft continued to speak, "By that I mean he could sometimes see into the future. The sight was once claimed as a common heritage amongst those of Highland decent. Tradition says that he used that ability to guide all of his business dealings and because of it, they always prospered.

"After he had amassed a great fortune, even for those times, the first Ravenscroft began to construct this estate. Overseeing every detail himself.

"My family has always said that he saw some future doom that would come to either himself or one of his descendants and prepared for it in his own inexplicable way."

Janet was aware of Tom hesitating and studying her father before he replied, "Your ancestor did do just that. If I was not truly human, I could not stand here beside you now. The wards that he wove into the making of this place are strong and deadly to the creatures of Faerie."

"This house is built on one of the great Meridians, on a conjunction of two Ley lines that gives the estate a powerful protection all by itself."

This time Janet couldn't stop herself from asking, "Ley lines. Really? Aren't they just some kind of new age joke? You know, totally spiritually radical. Now, you're telling us that they're real?"

"Yes, my lady. All my years spent in Faerie have attuned me to the presence of true magic. And at this very moment, I feel the vibrations of those lines of power weave their way through my body as clearly as I now hear your words." Thomas smiled reassuringly at Janet and her father before he continued, "But it is the hedge of rowan that is your ancestor's true masterpiece. I have never seen it's like before. No creature from the lands of faerie could ever cross such a barrier."

Thomas stood for a moment, clearly lost in thought, before he spoke again, "And behind its protection both of you must remain, until I've dealt with these creatures of the Fae."

Ravenscroft looked incredulously at Tom before he thundered, "Do you really expect me to hide behind these walls and do nothing?"

Thomas, the Knight of the Rose, had commanded vast armies and was as used to issuing commands as the man that stood before him. He suggested coolly, "John, would you send someone into one of your meetings knowing nothing about either the business at hand or those who sit across the table from them?"

"Hardly."

"Then please allow someone who understands the Fae to be about their business. Your presence would only hinder my quest."

A palpable tension filled the room as both men looked warily at one another. Before either could say anything to escalate that tension, Janet reached out to rest her hand on Thomas' shoulder. "Why me?" she asked. "What have I done to attract this horrible Queen's attention anyway?"

As Thomas began to explain what Mother Hainter had told him, they were interrupted by the shrill beep of Ravenscroft's mobile. Janet felt visibly annoyed when her father took the call, but Thomas watched the older man curiously as he spoke into the small metal object held in his hand. When a dark frown spread across his brow, Thomas grew concerned.

After Ravenscroft ended the call, he looked at them and smiled grimly, "It seems that there are two detectives at my front gates, or at least what's left of those gates. These gentlemen expect me to come down to my security office in ten minutes and answer all their questions about what happened tonight. Afterwards, I expect they will ask to search the estate."

His eyes hardened as he said, "And I am going to give them that permission." Janet's eyes widened, and she reached out for Tom's arm again as her father continued, "Really, it's the only way to avert the outright disaster of a horde of police camping out here for the foreseeable future." Thomas' body stiffened at the thought. Ravenscroft looked carefully at them both, "It would be so much easier for all of us if both of you could just vanish into that invisible world of yours."

His daughter's hold on Tom's arm tightened, "Not on your life." Janet looked at her father, "I'll think of some place to hide us, okay? I haven't lived in this house all my life without finding a few secret lairs."

Ravenscroft held up his hand, "It would be better if you didn't tell me exactly where." Then he smiled again, "Good luck, I'll see you both in the morning, yes?"

After they left. John Ravenscroft's face settled into a sombre mask, almost as if he were preparing to go into battle. And he was. Ravenscroft was certain that the detectives would grill him for answers to the bloody mess that still lay under the front gates of the estate. Those detectives would consume many hours tonight, and he knew that he'd be lucky if he saw his bed before first light.

NINETEEN

Janet took Thomas' hand and led him along the long, carpeted hallway that ran down the length of the west wing. Part way, she pushed open a door, revealing what looked like a simple closet filled with cleaning supplies and boxes stacked against every wall. For a moment, Janet fumbled with a catch set almost invisibly in the elaborate wooden dado rail that adorned all four walls. From the floor beneath their feet came the rumble of a mechanism turning, and a section of wall slid back to reveal a narrow entranceway opening on to a metal stairway, which descended into total darkness.

With one foot on the stair, Janet turned back, and, clearly noticing the quizzical expression on Tom's face, grinned, "Never underestimate the stubborn curiosity of a young girl." Moments later, they stood in the midst of complete darkness, their feet on a solid stone floor. Before she flicked a switch to illuminate the windowless room, Janet whispered, "I was twelve years old when I discovered this room and immediately claimed it for my own."

At one end of the long narrow space was a plush chair that sat beside a small table with a reading lamp. A large, comfortable bed piled high with quilts and pillows was pushed against the wall. Most of the rough stone walls were covered in intricate tapestries. The stone flagging at their feet was made comfortable by layers of thick Turkish rugs. All along one wall was a single, floor-to-ceiling bookcase crammed with books, puzzles, and board games.

Tom looked down into her smiling face and spoke for the first time. "There was a bolt hole like this in my family's home as well. We used it for the smuggling of whisky and sometimes even to escape religious persecution. Though ours was certainly not as comfortable as this."

Janet shrugged, "I spent so many days here – and nights too – reading and thinking and imagining what my future would be like…" She blushed shyly. "Those daydreams were never even close, though. I never saw anyone like you waiting for me in any of my possible futures."

She cleared her throat before continuing, "Trust me, no one will find us here."

Thomas smiled warmly. "Janet, I do trust you." She sat down on the soft bed and carefully judging what she saw in his face, asked, "If you do – trust me that is – then tell me who you really are."

Settling beside her, Thomas spoke, "Janet, accept now that my heart is yours and with it my soul. Know, too, that I will use every talent I possess to protect and serve you as long as you may live."

Once more Janet blushed, but stubbornly chose to continue her interrogation. "But who do I thank, who are you?"

Tom was silent for a time, gathering his thoughts, before he spoke again. "It was a day of days, long, long ago. I was hunting… a hunt that was not of my own choosing but insisted on by Father. The day ran long and come the setting of the sun. We still had not flushed a single stag. Nor had we seen a fox or even a stray hare. Although by then, those poor wee creatures would not have settled my father's blood lust.

"Our horses were on their last wind when we finally sighted an enormous stag and gave chase. My father's face shone with a mad light, certain that he could see its great horned head mounting the wall of our family's keep. I took the lead trying to slow my too-eager father from injury. Then I pushed my steed over one hard jump too many and, exhausted, he stumbled. I fell from my saddle. My only thought was of the sharp stones that would greet me on the ground below."

Janet murmured, "It must've hurt."

The Knight paused for a moment before continuing, remembering his father and their last hunt together. "No, it did not, for I did not hit the ground. Two strong arms caught me, and when I looked to thank my unexpected saviour, I beheld the most beautiful woman that I had ever seen – until short days ago – The Queen of the Lands of Summer's Twilight."

As if preparing to hear the worst, Janet gripped the quilt with both hands, staring hard at Thomas as he continued. "She took me to Her palace fashioned from marble and stone. There, I was overcome by the beauty that surrounded me, but most of all by Herself." He paused, carefully choosing his words. "Janet, you must forgive me this but I became her lover then. One in a long line of many, I think."

Thomas' voice hesitated at a question that Janet suspected he'd asked himself many times before. "I do not know why She chose me. I suspect that if you've lived the almost eternal life of the Fae, the quick, hot beating of a human heart is an irresistible attraction." Janet leaned closer and whispered, "Perhaps it was because of who you are, a knight of old, whether you wear a suit of armour or not."

He shrugged. "But as the years stretched before me ever longer, my heart grew restless. I began to take every excuse to stray from Her court. Hunting and adventuring. Tracking goblins in the mountains. Felling giants in the great forest that covered most of Her twilit lands.

"There came a day when I returned, and She no longer sat upon Her great throne. And for all my searching, neither She nor any of Her court were to be found. I was sent here then, into the mortal realms of my birth, to look for Her. And, acting on sweet memories of my previous life, I sought out my father and my family, thinking that their arms would be open and their greetings warm."

Janet shuddered then when she saw Tom's face crumble with dismay. She reached out and took his two hands in hers as he continued. "When, at last I found our family home, Carter Hall was its name, it was in ruins and all my family long since dead and buried. Their gravestones were ancient, the names on them worn away by the wind and the rain."

Janet asked, quietly, "Thomas, just how old *are* you?"

Thomas lowered himself to sit close beside her. "I do not know. There are no passing days in Faerie. No months or years. Only a single, eternal twilight, with only the slow waxing and waning of Her moon to gauge any passage of time. I was barely seventeen when I went hunting with my father that last time, but I am certain that I have now lived longer than any human is meant to."

Seeing a hint of a smile on her lips, Tom asked, "You take this well, my lady?"

Janet smiled more fully. "It's funny, I've never much liked younger men, and here you are, just gone seventeen… a year younger than me, yet… that's only in human years, isn't it?"

He gripped her hands and continued, "It was on the very day that I first beheld the graves of my family that I later came upon a young woman who needed my aid. I gave it to her. Gladly. I know now that at first it was seeing the fleeting glimpse of my Queen in her eyes that sparked my interest. But it was the woman within that afterwards captured my heart and my every waking thought as well."

Remembering that night, Janet asked carefully, "But are you still in love with this Queen of yours, Thomas?"

He smiled gently in return. "Once I was, long ago. But no mortal can ever truly love a Fae creature that will live for a thousand times a thousand years. I pondered then why my heart grew restless. I wondered why it was that I spent longer and longer away from the delights of Her court. I've found my answer now. I was seeking someone to fill my heart with joy and gladness." Tom's gaze never left Janet's. "Now I know why it was that I wished to leave Her court."

With a catch in her voice Janet murmured, "Tom, no matter how bloody awful I think this Queen of yours is, I have looked through her eyes and seen her reflected in yours. She... she is very beautiful... her features so golden that they almost shine. How can you even look at me after knowing her as you do?

"Yes, She is beautiful but so very cold. I see in the depth of your eyes, and past your quick anger, such warmth is in your heart...

"So, it is you, Janet Ravenscroft. Only you that I love."

Janet leaned against his neck, nuzzling his long, loosened hair. "Thomas, I've so much to tell you... so many more questions to ask, but right now I'm so damned exhausted that I can't even think straight."

"My lady, I am yours to command."

"Then hold me Thomas. That's all, just hold me, and don't ever let me go."

Janet turned her face up to his, her lips trembling, and with tender hands, she pulled him down to her. Their kiss seemed to last forever and was followed by many, many more.

Leaning hard, up against the inner wall of the rotting brick and stone keep of The Lord of Darkness and of Death, there was a curious hovel where a certain root witch named Mother Hainter sometimes lived and practiced her trade.

Inside, she crouched close beside a small fire that burned continuously, night and day, in the centre of the single room that the witch called home. The smoke from that fire twisted slowly upward past heavy wooden beams and eventually found escape through a hole in the blackened roof.

Lining the shelves that filled every inch of space on her walls was a bewildering multitude of small glass bottles. Some were green and some blue, but mostly, they were the dull brown of dead leaves in winter. Each bottle contained at least a few drops of a liquid that would, in the best of times, earn the witch a meagre living and even, on occasion, help those who came asking for it.

Set in one wall was a small recessed chamber. And in that, her bed of covered straw, where the witch spent most of each long day that she endured in that bleak kingdom of darkness. Waiting patiently, for what?

Mother Hainter was wiser and more cunning than all but a few who came to visit her, so when the door to her neatly kept room slammed open and The Huntsman sagged against its sill, she did not seem unduly surprised.

With her one good eye, she took in the leather-clad figure, his wound, his urgency, and the four great hunting beasts that prowled restlessly behind him.

Greeting him with a high reedy voice that cut through the still air, she asked, "Huntsman, whatever you want, I will do. Within reason, of course, always within reason. But do not, I beg you, bring yon beasts in my home. They'll piss my rugs, and that is the very devil to wash out."

The Huntsman slammed the door shut behind him and fell helplessly onto one of the rugs flung across her dirt floor. Only one word escaped through his tightly clenched teeth. "Iron."

Smiling at her patient, the witch allowed herself a shallow display of sympathy, "Tisk, tisk, that is a bother, isn't it?" When there was no answer from the man sprawled before her, she continued, "Well, then, let's have a look, shall we?"

As wide as she was short, Mother Hainter looked down at the shaking figure at her feet. His agonised face was clenched in pain as she bent over him, carefully examining his still weeping wound. The root witch had seen the same injury before and knew just how quickly death could follow on its heels. And yet, there was no hurry in her movements. "First, sir Huntsman, there is my payment ta consider. A poor wee widow woman such as myself should nae be asked ta do such a thing as this for free. That would nay be right, now would it?"

His jaw set hard as he struggled to reach a small pouch that hung tucked under his belt. Impatiently, he threw six dull gold coins from it down at her bare feet. She snatched them up, first testing the coins in her teeth, and then she cackled with glee.

Under her long matted white hair, her good eye shone bright, and a pleased smile played across her broad, wrinkled face. She muttered to herself as she turned to consider the thousands of small bottles that perched on shelf after shelf after shelf of the room, waiting to be used.

"Boyo, just lie there, and I'll do what needs ta be doing. Now, where did I put the wee silly drop o' the creature…?"

The Huntsman continued to writhe in silent agony, his skin slowly turning grey as long black veins of poison crept from the raw and bloody wound.

After what needed to be done was done, with the root witch's tinctures applied and proving most effective – on this occasion at least – the Huntsman struggled to his feet. He looked down at her through blood red eyes that calmly calculated whether she should live or die for her service to him.

"Witch, I will remember what you have done this day, both good and ill."

He leaned heavily against the rotting wood of her door and spoke through teeth still hard set against the pain. "Speak of this to anyone, anyone at all, and my beasts will come looking for you to teach you such games as you've never played before!"

"Huntsman, do you threaten me? Mother Hainter has been about her business since lang before you began your service with that Dark Lord, and for certain I'll be here after you are nae more."

"Beware..."

Capering with glee, the root witch ignored his threat, "What? You fear what your master will do if he finds that you have failed. Again."

"Woman, what have you heard?"

"Nay a thing." Then, slyly cackling to herself, she added, "And everything o' course. So many beasties both large and small come ta speak with Mother Hainter. They tell me all the things that they have seen. And they see so very much."

The Huntsman hissed, "Not a word. To anyone!"

Choosing her response carefully, the root witch bowed before the tall, thin figure of The Lord's Huntsman. "If that is your wish, my lord, for we all have our parts ta play in this lang sad story."

TWENTY

After a dreamless night, Janet slowly opened her eyes, squinting at the dim room around her. Languidly stretching under the heavy, hand-made quilts as a cascade of memories from last night swirled through her thoughts: Thomas stroking her hair, her body. Her fingers brushed across slightly swollen lips, remembering the endlessly slow, intense kisses that only made her want more. Soon, though, she was aware that the blissful cocoon of warmth generated by their two bodies was melting away, and suddenly she was wide awake.

Clutching the quilt around her, she remembered how their bodies had fitted together as if they had been made for each other, each arm and leg shaping comfortably over the other's. They had slept, still clothed, tightly wrapped in each other's arms for the rest of the night. And now he was gone.

Pushing the tangle of quilts aside, Janet shivered in the cool air of the cellar room.

Must be upstairs… with my father.
Better go make sure there's no serious bickering going on...

Minutes later, Janet stepped into the hallway above, and, hearing the murmur of voices, followed them into the great room. Here she found Tom and her father deep in surprisingly civil conversation.

"Thomas, those detectives were absolutely insufferable. They kept asking me the same questions over and over again, trying to catch me out in a lie, I suppose. But I knew what I had to tell them, and I stuck with it even if I didn't get to my bed until well after dawn."

"Were they really so awful, father?" Janet interjected by way of hello. "Sounds like hell."

John Ravenscroft glanced up and smiled on seeing her. "Ah, Janet, there you are."

She crossed the room to sit on the arm of the sofa beside Thomas. Protectively, she laid one arm across his broad shoulders, then kissed the top of his head and, breathing in his scent, asked, "Has my father been treating you well?"

Across the room, John considered the casual intimacy on display between his daughter and this man that he hardly knew and successfully adjusted his reply, "We've just been discussing my round of cut and parry with the two gentlemen of the law that came to see me last night."

Remembering the difficult conversation, Ravenscroft said, "I've bearded bigger and better adversaries than those two, before either of you were born..." He cleared his throat. "Well... perhaps not you, Thomas."

He quickly recovered his accustomed poise and continued, "Yes, Thomas has been telling me the most fascinating tales about himself. If I didn't already know better, I would find them hard to believe, very hard indeed."

Janet didn't even try to hide her smile. "So, does my gentleman caller suit you, Father?"

John Ravenscroft returned that smile, warmly. "More than satisfied."

"Good. I was just on my way to make myself a cup of tea. Would either of you like one?"

But before she could leave the room her father called to her, "Janet, hang on a moment, I have something for you." Reaching out, he pressed an old-fashioned skeleton key into Janet's hand. "I'm very sorry that I've prevented you from knowing anything about your mother for so long."

Janet turned the key over, hoping against hope that it was what she thought it might be. "What...which door does it open?"

Ravenscroft cleared his throat again. "As you know, there is a locked door in my office." At the mention of that particular door, Janet went still. Then her father continued. "That key will open it." He looked steadily at his daughter for a moment. "Everything I still have of your mother is in that room."

Clutching the polished brass key to her breast, Janet was stunned and just as suddenly dismayed by what she might find there. "Thank you! Thank you, Father..."

John Ravenscroft nodded. "Well, I'm sure we can forgo that drink for now. Off you go. We'll join you there later."

Unable at first to face whatever she would find behind that door, Janet wandered aimlessly through the house, restlessly sitting for a moment in a particular chair or at a desk. In the library, she ran her hand along shelves of leather-bound books, all with their titles stamped in shining gold leaf.

She randomly pulled a volume down and flipped through it, only to slide it back into place a moment later.

I've spent endless hours imagining what would happen if my mother were to suddenly step out of my dreams and become real...

What if I don't like who she is?

Finally, she paused by a long row of windows and stared out at the mysterious hedge, hoping to see a small elfin face peering back at her.

But Tom says that would be impossible here...

Turning, she walked determinedly upstairs to her father's office at the end of the long hallway on the east wing of the house. For as long as Janet could remember, her father had forbidden her to ever enter it.

Maybe this bloody house is finally ready to give up some of its deepest secrets?

She had stood before this door so many times when she'd been growing up, her imagination fired by the mystery of what could be hidden behind it. Janet couldn't begin to count the number of times she'd tried to unlock the door. But she'd always been caught, and the punishment meted out by her father had become severe enough that Janet had finally quit trying. Now she was standing in front of the only door in the entire house without a keypad access code.

Janet inserted the key. Turning it, she heard a decisive click before the heavy oak door swung open on well-oiled hinges. Inside there was a clean, well-kept bedroom.

Father must come here often.

She was immediately drawn to the far wall, which was covered in framed photographs. Most of them featured a small woman, dark-skinned like Janet, displaying a wide, pleasant smile. Overwhelmed, her daughter burst into tears.

Mother. Why did he take you away from me?

She reached out to touch one of the photographs, then another and another. They were all so real: Her mother graduating from university, diploma in hand.

... singing in a café.

... smiling at her father, looking very much in love.

... holding a newborn infant.

That's me.

When Janet looked closely at that particular picture she saw a troubled, confused look on her mother's gaunt face that made her feel uncomfortable. The slightly faded photograph showed her mother, shoulders tense, sitting out on the garden patio, directly beneath where

Janet's bedroom window was now. Through the shade trees the sun cast a soft dappled light over everything in the picture. On either side, amongst the leaves of the two trees she sat between, Janet thought she could see a multitude of grotesque faces with tiny bodies sporting wings and short curling tails.

But how could that be if Tom is right about the Rowan hedge?

Janet shivered and placed the photograph face-down on top of a nearby dresser. Beside it was an instrument case that held a well-worn guitar, carefully preserved. Curiously, she studied the dresser and then slid out one of its drawers. It was full of neatly folded clothes, still suffused with a faint fragrance.

Janet collapsed onto the bed clutching an armful of blouses, her face pressed into them, crying.

After her tears had finally dried, Janet began to explore the rest of the small room, and she found a bin of old vinyl albums. Every one of the cardboard jackets showed the same wear as a well-loved book that had been read again and again, but was still well preserved.

Curiously, she thumbed through them. There were recording of singers that Janet had never heard of before: Jeannie Robertson, Ray Fisher, Lizzie Higgins and so many others. In a cabinet above the set of albums, she found an old record player. After several fumbling attempts, she succeeded in getting one of the records to play.

At first, she was disappointed to hear only odd scratchy pops, but when a gorgeous singing voice suddenly filled the room, and she was mesmerised. Fascinated by the songs, Janet eventually listened carefully to each record. Until at last she played one that had a huge scratch running across its surface, making the needle jump at every revolution. Still, the lyrics of the song entranced her.

Bloody hell! *It's the same story that Tom told me last night.*

She turned the jacket of the album over and looked for the title of the tune. She read: Tam-Lin.

Tam-Lin.

Of course, Tom Lynn.

As the damaged record continued to play, Janet leaned back and carefully looked around at her mother's room, thinking about Tom and the song and her mother.

Somehow, they all add up to one answer, don't they?

Lost in thought, Janet felt another presence in the room, and startled, looked up. "Mum?" But instead, she saw her father standing awkwardly in the doorway with Thomas hovering close behind him.

His face stricken, John Ravenscroft slumped heavily into an old-fashioned lace-covered chair before burying his face in his hands. Tom remained standing quietly, directly behind the older man. As the record continued to play, her father placed a small, carefully wrapped package into his daughter's hands. She stared at it for a moment before removing the covering and mutely gazed down at the mysterious painting that her father had said he'd destroyed.

> "There's none that goes by Carterhall
> But they leave him a gift,
> Either their rings, or green mantles,
> Or else their maidenhead."

The surface of the canvas was worked with wide, crudely handled brushstrokes, as if the painter had been well-meaning, but an amateur.

The dense woodland scene was of leaves and twisted vines framing the small figure of a knight. Here and there a smear of bright red or orange paint indicated ripe fruit hanging from a tree that remained unseen, as if it might grow just past the picture's edge. The colours of the fruit hanging from the dense canopy of trees and the twilight sky beyond, alive with a multitude of stars, were saturated, intense, lending what would have been a conventional landscape a unique quality that was other-worldly and strange.

> "Oh tell to me Tam Lin" she said
> "Why came you here to dwell?"
> "The Queen of Fairies caught me
> when from my horse I fell"

Janet looked up at Thomas, her face twisting with a sudden, intense realisation. "This is the world that I see when I look through your Queen's eyes. It is all liquid edges ... nothing is in focus... everything... everything there, shimmers with an intensity of colour that we don't have here in our world."

> "But tonight is Halloween

> and the fairy folk do ride,
> Those that would their true love win
> at mile's cross they must bide."

Janet felt a tentative smile struggle across her face as she remembered visits to museums in London and Paris, "Maybe Van Gogh and Gaughan were simply fairy painters?"

John Ravenscroft reached out and gently held his daughter's hands. After a lengthy silence that threatened to grow into something more ominous, her father cleared his throat and answered the unspoken question his daughter seemed to be afraid to ask. "Your… your mother painted it."

Janet's eyes shone with that acknowledgement. "Of course she did."

"It is the only painting of hers that I kept. I've burned all the rest…"

"You… *You burned her paintings*?"

Ravenscroft looked straight into his daughter's eyes before continuing. "Janet, you will never know how much I regret that now, and… and there were so many other unpardonable actions as well. But what is done is done and can never be undone."

"Only forgiven, if that is even possible, daughter?"

However, her father's fumbling attempt to explain his actions only filled Janet with anger. Other emotions rose then, to eagerly greet that anger like the familiar escape that it had been for most of her life. With sudden insight, Janet realised that if she let herself give into it, and the sharp words that would follow, then the fragile understanding that had just begun to build between her father and herself would shatter. Shaking her head, she asked instead, "But why would you keep one of my mother's paintings and not even tell me it was hers?"

> "In the middle of the night
> she heard the bridle ring
> She heeded what he did say
> and young Tam Lin did win."

Her father remained silent, perhaps replaying the past in his thoughts. After a moment he began to speak again. "That song was her favourite. Mairi kept singing it the day I sent her away… That was so long ago now that it almost seems like a dream." He shook his head trying to dispel those thoughts. "More like a nightmare really!"

Janet whispered, "Mairi?"
"Yes, that is your mother's name."

> "Then up spoke the Fairy Queen,
> an angry Queen was she
> "Woe betide her ill-faired face,
> an ill death may she die."

When the song finished, her father spoke once more. "She loved the old ballads. Sang them any chance she got. I could never understand why. Most of them seemed filled with fairy tale make believe. I've never had any time for such foolish nonsense. And none of them had anything to do with the people or the island where she was born and raised.

"She was singing those old ballads the first time I ever saw her in a little café on Bloer Street." He paused for a moment before continuing, "It was Club 320, owned then by Daniel Parsons. We all became great friends. And soon I fell so helplessly in love with your mother that I didn't care about the colour of her skin or what songs she sang.

"My parents had passed by then and all my other relatives lived far away. So, there weren't any outright objections to my marrying a woman whose parents had emigrated here from Jamaica with skin the colour of deep, rich chocolate. Anyway, that didn't concern me at all. I would love to have met her mother and father, but sadly they had died as well.

"After your birth, though, when your mother came home from hospital, everything changed, most of all Mairi. Physically your mother was still here, but she moved through this house as if she could hardly see it around her. I was forced to hire a nurse after Mairi couldn't take care of herself or even her own daughter.

John began to weep, prompting Janet to kneel at his side, trying to comfort him.

"When I tried to talk about what was happening to her, Mairi just looked right through me as if she couldn't even see me. Only when your mother sang her ballads did she show any semblance of her old self. I was jealous then and began to actually hate those songs. It was as if they had stolen her away from me. Even just a few short verses would fill me with such desperate anger and despair.

John's eyes opened wide then, no longer focused on his daughter, as if he were seeing again the last few weeks that his wife had spent in the house.

"Soon after she came home from hospital there was a great storm. A hundred feet or more of the fence and the hedge were swept away. I planted them again, of course, using the instructions passed down from my ancestor. But Rowan takes many years to mature. Afterwards your mother began to express an almost hysterical fear of anything green and growing.

"She threw the plants and flowers that she had loved so much out the windows to shatter on the patio. Mairi refused to even look out on the lawn or the gardens and hung thick drapes over every window.

"I thought then that her madness had begun to infect me, because I too began to see odd things flicker through the leaves in the trees outside our home. Me; who had never believed in a spook or goblin, even as a child. Now suddenly I thought I could see strange creatures peering through the gap in our temporary hedge, or, God help me, flying above it, and I was certain that I was going mad as well."

Janet held up the photograph from the dresser in her hand. Her father looked at it for a moment and then shut his eyes when she murmured, "Of course, that's why they were able to enter. The protection you had was gone."

The elder Ravenscroft's eyes grew shadowed. "I kept telling myself that it was all just a trick of the light…

"One day I came home to find the kitchen in flames. Your crib was in the very next room. You were screaming, frightened by the smoke. And your mother was hiding behind a wall of chairs that she had stacked in front of her in the bedroom, claiming that the fairies had come looking for her. That's when I decided that she would be better off in a place that could take care of her properly.

"And, after she was gone… I saw no more faces in the leaves."

His eyes haunted, he continued, "Now I know that they've always been out there, just past the edge of that wall of Rowan, haven't they?"

Janet gripped her father's knee again and spoke quietly. "And it's up to us to make them go away again."

John Ravenscroft looked seriously at his daughter. "Yes. Yes, of course. If I'd accepted that truth before this evening, then my men wouldn't have been slaughtered and left to die in their own blood out on my drive.

"And… and perhaps, my daughter would not hate me so much?"

Janet got to her feet and gently placed the small painting of her mother's on top of the dresser, alongside the photographs. Then she turned to put her arms around her father, kissing him on his rough, unshaven cheek.

"Then all this..." Janet gestures around them. "The house, the guards, the bloody security cameras everywhere, they were to keep those creatures out, not me in. Weren't they?"

His eyes closed tightly, "Yes, and none of it did me any good, did it?"

After a moment of silence, Tom's hand reached for Janet's, "I must tell you both that I have been told by one who knows of these things that there is yet another caught with us in the web of my Queen's madness."

With sudden clarity, Janet's hold on his hand tightened, "And... and you think that this other could be my mother?"

"Yes. Your father's story all but confirms it."

Janet stood deep in thought, considering everything she'd just heard. Then, looking straight at Thomas, she said, "So all my blackouts, my sleep walking, my speaking in bloody tongues and my mother's madness are down to this Queen of yours?"

Her father looked stricken. "Of course. Of course, they are..."

She turned back to him. "So it shouldn't be news to you, then, that I *have* to see her now... my mother, that is. We absolutely have to find out what she knows about all this, don't we?" Gazing at her father then, she realised that the man she saw slumped in the chair, looking fragile and almost lost, was a far cry from the John Ravenscroft she'd known all her adult life.

Silently, he handed Janet a crisp business card before speaking again. "I want you to know that I love your mother... I always will. Mairi was my life. If there had ever been any way to bring her back here, I would have done so. Whatever it would have taken." Holding the card tightly in her hand, his daughter stared at him as he continued. "That is her address... where she resides now..."

Janet frowned, "You mean, the institution that takes care of her?"

Her father sighed. "If you must call it that, yes. But, Janet, I own the facility, so there's no question that her every need is taken care of."

Crouching close beside him, Janet lightly kissed his cheek again. "Thank you, Father. And please... I don't want to see any of what remains of your army following me when I visit my mother."

John looked up at his daughter. "There are none left. Early this morning, I asked everyone who was still alive to leave. Catastrophic assaults by invisible fairy creatures aren't something I'm willing to wager anyone's life on but my own."

He looked at both Janet and Tom. "So, you will be careful? Both of you, I mean."

"Well, I do have The Knight of the Rose with me. If he can't protect me, then I don't know who can?"

Janet regarded her father ruefully. "And Father, one more thing: can you tell me the code for the lock on Tom's bike?" When he spoke a string of seemingly random digits, the smile that lit Janet's face seemed to lift the grim expression that had settled on his own.

Minutes later, they were in the garage. Janet knelt and punched in the code to unlock the Vincent. Curious, Tom asked, "Is there something special about these numbers?"

Janet looked up at him and smiled. "It's my birthdate."

Tom laid a hand on her shoulder. "Yes, of course."

Afterwards, Janet climbed on behind Tom and he kicked the machine into gear. Soon the wind was whipping past them as they flew down the road toward the nearby coast. She buried her face in the long brown hair that escaped his leather helmet and tried hard for a moment to will away all the responsibilities that threatened to overwhelm her life.

Couldn't we just run away to some desert island and hold each other forever? If I was still that same selfish girl who refused to grow up, I guess I might even want to…

A worried frown creased her brow as she stared out at the landscape that flashed by them.

My mother… after all these years, I'm finally going to meet her… talk with her… what will I say?

Twenty-One

An hour's drive from Inverness, on the southern shore of the Beauly Firth, stood a sprawling single-storey building with extensive grounds enclosed by high hedge of yew. A discreet sign just off the motorway, at the entrance to a small parking lot, informed Janet that she and Tom had arrived at their destination:

Greenhaven, a rest for those weary of the world.

Thomas cut the engine, and they sat quietly for a moment. Janet breathed in and out, trying to calm her nerves, preparing for whatever she would find inside the institution. The air around them was fragrant with the nearby sea, and the sky above was thick with heavy clouds that threatened an early afternoon rain.

Just before she climbed off the bike, Tom put a gentle hand on her arm, saying "Janet, I do not know what will happen within this place…"

"You mean in what condition I'll find my mother?"

"I hope she will be responsive to you. But even if she is not, we must get both of you back within the protection of your father's estate as soon as possible. You are in great danger outside its protective walls. If the Huntsman has survived, he will find us wherever we are."

Janet's hold on his shoulder tightened. "And you think he survived, don't you?"

"Almost certainly."

"Then I promise I'll be as careful as possible." She felt a surge of hope, of confidence, despite everything. "And I do have you with me, don't I?"

"Yes."

"Then let's go."

An earlier phone call from her father had cleared the way for the visit, so at top of a short flight of stairs a pleasant-looking woman wearing a trim fitted suit greeted them. Their guide led them through the wide glass doors into the facility, with a never ceasing stream of inconsequential conversation. They followed her through another set of secure doors, with its own key code, into a small, well-lit waiting area.

Janet looked curiously around the facility that had incarcerated her mother for so many years, her grip tightening on Thomas' hand. It was clean, orderly and surprisingly peaceful. Several attending nurses walked purposefully up or down the long hallway, some wheeling small carts filled with various medications as well as their patients' charts.

At least it doesn't look like a fucking loony bin...

Their charming guide led them into a large office and introduced them to a trim, efficient-looking older woman sitting at a broad desk littered with paperwork. Dr. Lindeman, the chief resident of the institution, brushed a strand of sandy blond hair away from her eyes and looked up to greet them. The pause that followed was momentary but still made Janet uneasy.

Yeah, I know I'm my mother's daughter. I bloody don't look anything like my father.

Then, shrugging off whatever surprise she felt, the doctor quickly got to her feet and held out her hand. "It so good to finally meet you, Ms. Ravenscroft. Thank you so much for coming."

Janet nervously shook her offered hand. "I've thought of nothing else for years and years."

"Then I'm surprised you've not visited before this."

Uncomfortable, Janet shifted from foot to foot, "You'd have to ask Father about that."

There was a slight pause before Dr. Lindeman continued. "I think I understand.." Still smiling, she released Janet's hand and turned to Thomas. "And who is this handsome young man, your fiancé perhaps?"

Janet was startled to realise that she was blushing, "This is my friend... my good friend, Thomas Lynn."

Thomas, unable to supress his ingrained courtly manner, greeted the doctor with a flourish, bending low over her hand and lightly kissing it. The two women looked awkwardly at each other, and Janet smiled to see that Dr. Lindeman's cheeks were now flushed as well.

The doctor cleared her throat. "Well, enough of that. I expect, Ms. Ravenscroft, that you are rather anxious to see your mother?"

"Yes. Yes, I am."

The doctor walked them into the hall and indicated a room, three doors down, labelled Mairi Ravenscroft. "Before you go in, Ms. Ravenscroft, let me explain. We have very few restrictions here as most of our patients are low-risk and extremely non-violent. The doors to their rooms remain unlocked except at night, so that they come and go as they please. In the rear of the facility, we have an extensive garden that allows our clients to enjoy the sun and feel a breeze on their faces.

"We find it especially beneficial to their well-being. Unhappily, throughout your mother's stay with us, she's absolutely refused to leave her room."

That sounded worrying. "Always?"

Doctor Lindeman's look of concern was far from reassuring. "Yes, ever since she arrived here eighteen years ago. And be warned, Mrs. Ravenscroft keeps her shades drawn, so it is a bit dreary in her room. The few times we've attempted to open them she has become so agitated that we've acquiesced to her desire."

"Thanks for the warning."

Hand in hand, Janet and her knight walked down the corridor. They paused in front of her mother's door as Janet glanced at Thomas, holding his hand a little tighter. "Could you wait here? I want to see my mother by myself, okay? At least to begin with…"

Tom smiled. "Of course. Call for me if there is need."

At first, there was no answer when she knocked hesitantly on the door. Waiting a few moments, Janet slowly pushed it open. After her eyes adjusted to the dimness inside, she saw an older woman, barely five feet tall, her dark skin a startling contrast to her long pure-white hair, sitting in front of a sturdy easel. The woman had several brushes held in one hand and a paint-loaded pallet in the other. Spots of bright colour were flecked across the otherwise tidy green smock she wore.

When her mother looked up, a gentle smile lighting her face, Janet had to restrain herself from impulsively throwing her arms around the small woman. After a thousand imaginary meetings and as many imaginary conversations, tears began to course down Janet's cheeks as she realised that this time, it was real, very real.

Wiping her cheeks with the sleeve of her jacket, Janet began to speak. "Mother…it's me, your daughter Janet." Not saying a word in response, Mairi continued to stare up at her as Janet continued, "I…I've waited so long… so long, to meet you. And now that you're here in front of me, I don't know what to say first…"

She tried her best to fill the silence. "Well, okay. Dad says hello, of course… and, I'm eighteen now… and grown up, I guess." The woman continued to stare blankly at her daughter, giving no sign that she recognised the young woman standing in front of her. "So I've… I've got a boyfriend. His name is Tom, but I think he likes to be called Thomas better… he's really nice, even Dad seems to like him. And, trust me, that's never ever happened before."

Nervously she continued, "Tom... Thomas is out in the hall right now. Do you maybe want to meet him?" But Janet's confused attempts at conversation seemed of no interest to her mother. Mairi quietly turned back to her easel and softly began to hum to herself.

Janet wiped ineffectively at the tears that continue to run down her cheeks. "Mother, won't you say something... anything?" But Mairi was totally absorbed in brushing paint onto canvas, oblivious to her daughter's emotional turmoil. Whatever Janet had expected to happen when she came here, being met by a wall of silence was not it.

In that uncomfortable silence, Janet began to study her mother's room. Pinned to the wall were hundreds of crudely painted pictures, layers and layers deep. Each obsessively depicted minutely rendered scenes, crowded with vast groupings of strange creatures both large and small. Some had wings. Some tails. Some had both, but all of them had long slanted eyes, solid black with no pupils, reflecting a world that was not of this Earth.

The crude paintings began to stir memories that Janet had been trying very hard to forget.

Fuck me! I see these same creatures every time I look through that damned Queen's eyes.

Janet's bleak thoughts fell away, though, when she recognised the tune that Mairi hummed. Under her breath, she begins to sing softly along with the older woman, astonished that she remembered every word of the song.

> "I'm as brown as brown can be
> My eyes are as black as sloe
> I'm as bright as a night-time nightingale
> As wild as the forest doe.
>
> My love was high and proud
> A fortune by his side
> But a fairer maiden than ever I'll be
> He took to be his bride."

This is so weird. I can remember every bloody lyric I heard in mother's room like I've been singing those songs my whole life...

Hearing Janet sing the ancient ballad, her mother turned back to her, eyes suddenly lit by joy. She rose from her chair to clasp her daughter's hands and joined her voice with Janet's. But when they finished the verses of the song, her mother grew silent once more, the joy draining from her eyes, the smile from her face. Once again, Mairi looked straight through her daughter as if she weren't even there.

Desperate to regain their connection, Janet began to sing another ballad, and when that song was finished, another and another, her mother joyfully harmonising with each. When Janet stumbled over the lyrics of a long border ballad, her mother's voice grew stronger, leading her on. However, when Janet had finally sung every song she could remember and the last notes of their harmonious voices faded away, her mother grew silent once more. A look of worry filled Mairi's dark green eyes as she feebly tried to pull her hands from Janet's grip.

Reluctantly, Janet let go and gently helped the older woman back into the chair in front of her easel. There, Mairi sat, staring inward at a world of quiet madness where Janet couldn't follow.

Frustrated, Janet walked slowly along the wall of the room, marvelling at the strange world that moved across the surface of her mother's paintings.

When she carefully lifted one edge of the heavy curtain that blocked the world outside, Janet caught a brief glimpse of the gardens and the sea beyond. At the far end of the distant rocky beach, she was surprised to see a tall thin standing stone. But hearing her mother's startled, high-pitched cry, she immediately dropped the curtain back into place and turned. Mairi's eyes were wide and full of fear, her hands holding the brush in front of her face as if it were a sword that could protect her. The older woman dropped to the floor and jammed herself between the bed and the corner of the room, scattering around her on the carpet tubes of paint and brushes. The sharp smell of spilled turpentine filled the room.

Clearly terrified, Mairi cried, "No! Don't let them in. They'll steal everything from me. Again! Again! Again!"

Immediately, Janet crouched beside her mother and tried to comfort the frantic woman. "Mother please, it's okay. There's no one out there that will hurt you. Let's put you in your bed, okay?" The older woman's body still shuddered with emotion as her daughter helped her up into the bed. Janet, looking into her mother's wide, unfocused eyes, tried to smile, "There, that's more comfortable isn't it? But once in her bed, Mairi frantically pulled a quilt over her and curled into a tight ball, leaving her confused daughter staring down at her muffled form.

Outside in the hall, Tom and an attendant, who waited by the door to the room in case they were needed, both heard Mairi's startled cry. They looked at each other. Worried by the low wailing cry from within, the nurse pushed open the door, to see Janet seated beside the huddled figure of her mother in the bed.

Thomas quickly crossed the room and gathered Janet into his arms as the attendant calmly took charge of the situation. "Right. This has happened before. I'll just go and get her medication. Won't be a minute."

After the nurse left, Mairi peered cautiously out from under the thick covers. Her face lit with joy when she saw Thomas. Throwing the quilt off, she sat up and eagerly reached toward him, clutching her daughter's hand in her left and Tom's in her right. Instinctively, Janet reached for the support of Tom's other hand and gripped it firmly. The instant the circle was complete, Tom sensed the presence of The Queen deep within both the older woman and her daughter, aware and struggling for release. At once, all the accumulated guilt he'd kept locked inside flashed through his mind and Thomas whispered, "Forgive me, I did not intend to abandon you…"

Looking past Janet's mother, he saw the hundreds of paintings fixed haphazardly to every available space on the walls. Raptly, he scanned the obsessively scrawled eyes, the gnarled hands, the small pearlescent wings, the long, tapered ears, the multitude of odd, misshapen faces that he instantly knew as creatures of the Fae, all staring back at him. The images were so compelling that he began to look closer and see that behind the minutely rendered mass of rolling, tumbling, dancing figures were bits of soaring architecture that he recognised as the great hall, the court of The Queen of Summer's Twilight.

Then, hearing the song Mairi began to sing, Thomas was astonished.

> "Oh I forbid you maidens all,
> that wear gold in your hair,
> to come or go to Carter Hall…"

With a smile brighter than any summer's morning spreading across her face, Mairi continued to lend her voice to the lyrics of the ancient ballad.

> "First she plucked the red, red rose…"

Beside them, Janet began to choke and her body to convulse. Oblivious to her daughter's emotional trauma, Mairi sang on.

> "Then came young Tam-Lin,
> saying 'Lady pull no more'."

As her convulsions grew more violent, Janet felt her face flush with heat. Sweat trickled down her cheeks. Against her volition, her mouth snapped open... to disgorge a single red rose.

The crimson bloom with its long stem fell end over end to the floor, landing at her feet. Utterly entranced by the fallen rose, Janet pulled her hands away from her companions and slipped off the edge of the bed, to fall to her knees. There she cupped the remains of the already wilting flower with both her hands, crushing the petals to her breast as if they were something unimaginably beautiful that she had now lost forever. The withered petals fell through her trembling fingers, floating softly to the floor.

Janet looked up at Tom, her eyes wide with fright. Her lips were streaked with blood where the thorny stem had torn at them. She wiped the blood away before speaking. "Again, I saw through that damned Queen's eyes." Her own eyes wide with astonishment she gestured at her mother, who stared back uncomprehendingly at them both. "And bloody hell, you were right. She is there within my mother as well."

Before Tom could offer any explanation, the window beside them burst open, showering them all with shards of glass. And The Huntsman and his beasts stepped into the room.

TWENTY-TWO

With a satisfied smile, The Huntsman clutched Mairi's arm as she screamed and screamed again, her worst nightmare come true. With his other hand, he cast a hunting-net over the heads of both Janet and Thomas. Lunging forward, Tom pulled it away before it had settled on the mortal girl but was himself immediately caught in the fine mesh of its weaving. Struggling, he cried out, "Janet. Run!"

She hesitated, though. "Mother! Tom! I can't leave you both!"

The Huntsman laughed, "No, stay with us, I will have all those that I seek this time." At his command, the foul beasts stalked towards Janet. Desperately, Thomas tipped his tightly-bound body in front of the creatures, tangling himself and the net in their legs, slowing their charge. He shouted once more, "If he binds us all, we are truly lost!"

"I'm not going to bloody well run away again!"

But four red-eyed beasts, mouths full of enormous razor-sharp teeth, continued to move toward her, offering no alternative. Jumping back into the hall and nearly colliding with someone immediately outside, she slammed the door shut and wedged a nearby chair under its handle. Adding her weight against it, she screamed, "Security! Help!"

"What's going on?" Janet had been so focused on barring the way she hadn't realised it was the nurse returning with Mairi's medication that she had so nearly bumped into. The nurse grabbed at the chair, trying to pull it away, insisting, "I have to get to my patient." Then the door shuddered from the impact of more than one heavy body, followed by the awful sound of something sharp and very determined tearing at its hard surface.

"What in God's name is in there?"

Janet hissed back, "You wouldn't believe me if I told you! But we need help! Now!"

Abruptly, the door buckled out toward them as the hinges gave way. They redoubled their efforts to prevent it from bursting fully open, when they heard a terrified shriek behind them, and, looking over her shoulder, Janet saw another resident standing by his open doorway, screaming. Scattered down the hall were more patients, their eyes wide with terror.

Janet pleaded with the attendant, "Get them back in their rooms and lock down this damned hall!" With a quick nod, the nurse turned to grab the elderly man and guide him as gently as she could back into his room. Slamming that door, she ran back toward the others, frantically waving them inside and shouting, " Security lock down now!" Then, with one quick backward glance, she took off running for the front office. Moments later Janet heard the alarm sound, followed by the decisive click of all the doors in the facility being securely locked.

The frenzied shrieks from the beasts on the other side of the door snapped Janet's attention back to the matter in hand. The widening gap between door and wall reminded her that one flimsy chair and her own tiring body were all that stood in the way of disaster. Through that gap, blood and wood and metal splinters showered her face.

One final violent impact knocked the door completely free, and Janet turned to run down the now-deserted hall.

Behind her, the lunging beasts slid helplessly across the slick linoleum floor before regaining their footing. They bounded down the hall pursuing their prey, throwing deserted carts to the floor and tearing through anything else that got in their way. Over the pounding of her shoes Janet heard the shrieks of the pursuing beasts and pushed herself to run even faster.

Through a glass door just ahead, she saw Dr. Lindeman with her hands gripping the terrified attendant who was trying to explain what had panicked her. The doctor stared out at the corridor wide-eyed.

As Janet sprinted past Lindeman's office, she screamed, "Get down and stay there!"

Running as fast as her legs would carry her, Janet slammed into the now securely locked front doors. Desperately, she turned to look back. Snarling, the beasts bounded up the hall toward her, slowing now that they had her trapped. The energy drained form Janet's body, and exhaustion took hold as despair threatened to overwhelm her when, from behind her, there came a sudden audible click as the doors unlocked. DR. Lindeman, it had to be her!

Janet didn't hesitate. She pushed the doors open and jumped through, closing them immediately and hearing the click of the locks sliding into place once more.

She saw the beasts crash into the heavy plate-glass doors and bounce away. Spinning to a stop, they roared out their frustration and blood lust.

Revitalised, Janet turned and leaped down the short flight of steps, sprinting toward Tom's Vincent as fast as she could.

That glass won't hold them for long...

Swinging her leg up over the Vincent, she clutched the gas throttle, but it took two fumbling tries before the engine roared into life. Lurching away from the curb, the bike flew through the parking lot and out onto the deserted highway. A moment later, Janet sensed that the creatures were no longer pursuing her, and she eased off the gas. Slowing down, she looked back toward the clinic, concern for Tom and her mother sharp in her mind.

The alarm still shattered the still air.

Then over the hedgerow that lined the road she heard her mother scream. Through a gap, Janet saw down to the long beach. The Huntsman had his two captives bound securely and hanging over each shoulder. Followed closely by the four beasts, he moved quickly, straight toward the distant dolman that towered over the wind-beaten grass just above the beach.

"You're not getting away that easily!"

She turned the bike off the road and jolted wildly down a long flight of cement steps before finally reaching the pebbled beach. "Wanker! You'll have me to deal with if you hurt either one of them." Keeping the Huntsman in view, she guided the Vincent, a little awkwardly, across the loose pebbles on the beach. But she was dumbfounded when she observed her quarry, without a pause, run headlong into the tall standing stone and simply vanish.

Fuck!

Without any hesitation, Janet topped the shallow rise and gunned the cycle's motor, heading straight for the hard, seemingly unyielding surface of the same stone.

Where you can go, I can bloody follow.

TWENTY-THREE

Janet clenched her teeth as the Vincent jolted across a vast plain of withered grass and dead, twisted trees, leaving a burning trail of smoke and ash in the bike's wake.

There was nothing living to be seen. No creatures. No birds or beasts. Nothing. Above her, only an endless twilight strewn with glistening stars.

Damn, where are they?

Janet floored the bike, hoping to catch up to The Huntsman and his captives. But, hours later, when dead black mountains rose up all around, she was still alone in that vast landscape.

Time in The Land of Summer's Twilight was always strangely mutable. So it could be just hours that passed but it might also be that long days lapsed before the last of those dark crags disappeared behind her. The air around her grew increasingly dense, until billowing clouds of thick black smoke blotted out the stars that tumbled through the sky above. And before her, sprawled across an endless, pitted plain, was a forbidding castle of brick and stone.

Fuck, I'm guessing that's where The Huntsman was taking them…

Bringing the Vincent to a stop, Janet looked up at the decaying brick walls, misshapen and ill built, reared high above her. The castle was huge beyond anything she had ever imagined, and yet, just as the vast landscape she passed through, it seemed deserted of any life. The windows in every turret and parapet and madly-shaped tower stared back at her like empty black eyes.

After navigating alongside the wall for what again seemed like hours, Janet grew certain that there was no entrance, only an endless brick parapet that disappeared into the dim twilight that cloaked the far horizon. And her gas gauge was running ominously low.

No bloody petrol stations out here.

Still bound in The Huntsman's netting, Thomas was thrown roughly to the stone floor beneath the throne of The Lord of Darkness and of Death. On her knees beside him Janet's mother, oblivious to the strange world that now surrounded them, continued to sing softly under her breath a tune that seemed to comfort her.

> "There was a knight in Scotland born
> Follow, my love, come o'er the strand-
> Was taken a prisoner and left forlorn
> By the great lord Earl of Northumberland."

The Huntsman stood over his captives, expectantly gazing up at his lord and master, as if waiting patiently for some manner of thanks. He received none.

Instead, a shade of annoyance filled the Dark Lord's voice when he chose to speak, looking directly at Thomas. "You mortal… you were The Queen's lover?" When the Rose Knight gave no reply, he continued, barely suppressed anger tinging every word. "That She would choose such as you to share Her bed beggars belief. For that, I may forgive Her, but not yourself, Sir Knight.

"For a mortal to willingly consort with the Fae is at the very least unwise but always dangerous.

"Your Queen and I have a contract, sealed in our blood. Once every hundred years She must gift me with a tiend, a tithe of fealty to myself, in order that She and Her pretty kingdom remain, or She must pay the forfeit and diminish.

"Perhaps, Sir Knight, she was grooming you for that very purpose."

Goaded beyond measure, Thomas shouted angrily, "Never!"

Barely controlling his fury, the Dark Lord replied, "Why this reluctance, Knight of the Rose? I have much to offer those who enter my service and would delight so in bestowing those favours on one who richly deserves them."

Thomas' face paled. He was certain that the only favours he would ever receive from this creature would strip away his honour, layer by layer.

Hearing his master's taunt, The Huntsman's body grew rigid. His eyes narrowed as he calculated their meaning for his own future. In the heavy silence that followed, only Mairi's sweet voice was heard, echoing softly down the length of that great and awful hall.

> "There he was cast into prison strong,
> Follow, my love, come o'er the strand-

> Where he could not walk nor lie doon,
> Even by the great lord Earl of Northumberland.
>
> And in his sorrow thus he lay,
> Follow, my love, come o'er the strand-
> The Earl's sweet daughter walked that way,
> And she the fair flower of Northumberland."

Her words leavened the despair in Tom's heart as he looked about at the gloomy hall that could become his new home. All around, black rivulets of moisture seeped down dull brick walls to gather in standing pools of shallow oily water. The water reflected dimly the light of a thousand torches that ran haphazardly along the length of the Court of Shadows. The smell of death and decay filled his senses.

High above Thomas, the Dark Lord gestured out at his hall. "Do you not admire my court? Do you not appreciate what those that I call my own have made manifest besides mere beauty?"

The horror that filled Thomas' eyes was evidence of his thoughts.

"No? A pity then, but your opinion is of little concern to me, Sir Knight. My only desire is to have my Queen sit beside me here, on this throne."

Through gritted teeth Thomas asked, "And was it not that same desire, my Lord, that brought The Queen's madness upon Her?"

"Silence!" The Lord of Darkness and of Death bellowed, and, rearing to his cloven feet, his great twisting horns struck the ceiling above, sending a shower of sparks out into the gloom of that chamber.

The massive figure that stood far above him was an impossible mixture of both animal and Fae. Its body was a hideous distortion of each, made somehow worse by the evident effort with which the creature had clothed its lumpen form, perhaps trying to affect the elegance of some noble lord of the Faerie. An attempt that was wholly unsuccessful.

His mouth, a ragged slash cut across a singularly despoiled face, opened to reveal blunt yellowed teeth before closing again as the creature tried to affect a smile. "So that you might know the humility of your once and future Lord, I will tell you, Sir Knight of the Rose, how I paid court to your Queen." He continued his tale with evident relish. "With every manner of courtly gesture and elegant gift, I made my devotion known to her.

"For our trysting feast I gave to Her a thousand times a thousand head of swine, their mouths stuffed with apples more red than blood itself.

"As my wedding gift I presented Her with a gown made from the silky pelts of a perfection of rats, more lustrous black than even the darkest of nights. And too, I sent Her other goodly gifts without number, equally fair and most pleasing, I hoped, to Her eyes and to Her heart."

Thomas was baffled by the note of bewilderment that began to shade the creature's voice as it continued, "Yet, when I came near, She ran from me. Fleeing into the very heart of Her sacred garden where The Queen's enchantments were strong indeed.

"It was only with the most profound patience that I was able to peel away each thin layer of that glamour, till there was left naught except that which I sought, Herself. Though when at last I held Her in my arms, She was shrieking mad and lost to me. I brought Her here, hoping that the blandishments of my home would offer Her at least some comfort."

Shocked, Tom raised his voice, "Here! The Queen is here, in this place of filth and pestilence?"

The Dark Lord's mouth twisted in a cruel semblance of a smile before he spoke again. "Mortal, you are merely a piece of inept meat, some cast off gristle, so take care with your impertinent words or I will rend your body. And truly, I would delight to do so at this very moment, but I believe that you are a most valuable pawn in the game I play. One to be treasured and used when it benefits me most."

His long, grizzled fingers gripped the arms of his throne as if they were instead wrapped eagerly around Thomas' neck. "I think it most fitting that though She now lives within these walls, you human, will never look upon Her again."

With great satisfaction, the Dark Lord watched the colour drain from Thomas' face. The great horned creature looked down at the figure clothed in red armour far below and noted with malicious pleasure the effect his words also had on his Huntsman. "Take this mortal away, but keep him well. As for the woman, I will give her in service to The Queen. For they are of a kind, moon mad and raving."

Once more, the Huntsman slung Tom's tightly bound body over his broad shoulder, and with a satisfied smile the creature turned to leave. Despair tore at Thomas when he saw the ungainly shadow creatures that called this court their home clutch at the wrists of Janet's mother and lead her away.

The Dark Lord's final words echoed down the length of the court of shadows. "Huntsman, know this. The mortal girl, too, must be mine. I know not how or why, but they are all pieces of a single game, a single puzzle: the girl, this simpleton woman, and my Queen. And I would soon see this mystery end to my advantage.

"Bring me this young mortal girl or you will surely find yourself in a cell beside the knight. There you will stay until your flesh falls from your bones and your bones become dust, and you will become but a forgotten actor on this stage upon which we play."

Close beside him, Tom saw The Huntsman's dark face blanch, his step hesitating a second before continuing across the floor of the great hall.

More than a thousand were the steps, cracked and uneven, that The Huntsman carried Thomas down and long and twisting were the narrow hallways beyond. He needed no torch, for the Dark Lord's creature could see in the utter darkness of that terrible place. An eternity later, there was a sudden clatter of keys turning in a rusty lock, and then the rush of torpid air as an unseen door swung open.

Tom felt the net peel away from his body as he was swung easily through the air. A moment later, he sprawled across the stone floor of an unseen chamber that was to be his cell. After the door shut, through the small grating cut through it, Thomas heard the sibilant hiss of The Huntsman's voice in the utter darkness that surrounded them both. "Knight, know this. Before you came to the Land of Summer's Twilight, I was The Queen's chosen consort. But with your arrival She cast me aside as if I were a simple broken toy to be rid of at Her whim.

"None, then, in Her realm would even speak my name. Stricken, I wandered far from Her hall until I found this place of death and decay. A place certainly more suited to my own thoughts and whose Lord welcomed me with pleasure.

"He gave me a new name and a new purpose.

"I have not rested since that day of days. Now, all that once lived within Her realm bide here in the dark of this dungeon until such time as my Lord decides what he shall do with them.

"With those thoughts, sleep well, Sir Knight of the Rose. Sleep well."

Twenty-Four

Exhausted, Janet brought the Vincent to a stop and cut the motor. Instantly, she was aware of the dreadful silence of the land that surrounded her, disturbed only by the whistling of the wind past the red brick towers above her.

She reached up to wipe the sweat from her brow and looked again at the immense wall that stretched endlessly before her. *Bloody hell. How can I even try to rescue them if I can't get inside this damned castle?*

Without warning, a hand in a shining black leather glove clasped her shoulder and a sibilant voice spoke in her ear, "Perhaps, my lady, I may escort you within?" Terrified, she jerked away, to see The Huntsman, his face split with a horrifying smile.

Janet desperately twisted the gas throttle to start the motorcycle. But before the engine could turn over she and the machine were thrown to the ground, her right leg trapped under the weight of the bike. Crouched above her, putting its full weight on the machine and spitting down into Janet's face was one of The Huntsman's beasts. Its mouth was so close that she could smell the rotting meat that clung to its long, razor-sharp teeth.

Casually, the elegant leather-clad figure looked down at Janet. "It is a good day for hunting, for now all my birds are caught at last."

Leaning close, The Huntsman whispered, "There is no need to struggle, for I will certainly gift you with your heart's desire. Your lover… and your mother as well, await the pleasure of your company within my master's house."

Janet was horrified by the immense court of rippling shadows, and even more so by the creature that sat on the great throne of teeth and bone above it. The Dark Lord was evidently more than pleased, his body taut with expectation as he looked down upon the captive far below.

"You gratify me, Huntsman, with your swift return. Is this then the other mortal you spoke of?"

Still struggling to process what she was seeing, it took Janet a moment to realise that she understood every word he spoke.

I suppose I have that bloody queen to thank for that?
"Lord, from this woman's lips I have heard The Queen speak, even as your hunting beasts fawned at her feet. Surely she is no mere mortal."

His master's long face was a mask of satisfaction as he purred, "Indeed, I think not."

Defiantly she cried out, "Where is he? Where is Thomas? And my mother! Take me to them. Now!"

"You would give me commands? That amuses me, child."

"Where is my Tom?"

"*Your* Tom? Now you claim ownership of a Knight of The Lady's court, who has promised himself to Her, body and soul? For is not your Thomas the consort of The Queen of these Twilight Lands? What will She say, I wonder, to this new arrangement?"

The Dark Lord smiled then at Janet, and it was a hard, cruel smile. "Shall we ask Her?"

"Ask?"

Janet struggled frantically, but The Huntsman's grip was firm and never loosened. Holding her close, he hissed in her ear, "Cease! My master commands, and we both must obey."

Stubbornly, Janet continued to struggle as he dragged her through a bewildering maze of hallways and small courtyards. Hung on every wall they passed were ornate carvings and tapestries brought from worlds beyond her imagining.

Each room was of a different height, the walls set at uncomfortable angles, one to the other. Some rooms were mere passageways between others, their interiors consumed by stone buttresses or enormous marble pillars. There was so much here that was strange or grotesque that Janet's mind grew numb. Yet in that great building, she rarely saw any living creature and those she did were performing some menial task, with bent back and dull eyes. Every one of those twisted creatures cowered close to the wet brick and stone at their feet as their Lord and his retinue passed them by.

At last, Janet was brought to the very centre of that awful palace. An open space that sat at the bottom of a great well where dim light from far, far above filtered down onto blackened grasses, studded here and there with stones like jagged teeth. Its massive circular wall, inlaid with intricate mosaic designs, was all but obscured by a thick carpet of mould, alive with spore. In the centre of that perverse space stood a Willow, huge and ancient beyond years, it's massive tangle of roots coiled in the shallow pool of black, oily water that lapped round about it.

At the base of the tree, woven into the embrace of a hundred coiling roots, lay The Queen of all the Lands of Summer's Twilight. Close by Her side sat Janet's mother, plaintively singing an ancient ballad.

"It's remarkable," The Dark Lord said. "Her voice somehow eases the moon-mad mind of the Queen, holding at bay the violent screams that otherwise would consume this chamber."

Janet barely heard him. The jarring contrast of her mother's small dark-skinned figure and the golden queen made the moment surreal beyond belief.

> "For forty days and forty nights
> He rode through red blood to the knee,
> And he saw neither sun nor moon,
> But heard the roaring of the sea."

"What have you done?" Janet hissed. "Why have you brought my mother to this damned place?"

Hearing Janet's voice, The Queen's eyes snapped open, to stare fixedly at her with a gaze that for a split second had no hint of madness in it. Then, just as suddenly, that impression of keen intelligence shuttered, leaving only madness in its place.

> "Oh no, oh no, True Thomas, says she,
> That fruit must not be touched by thee.
> For all the plagues that are in hell
> Bide in the fruit of this country."

As if to demonstrate his point, The Lord of Darkness and of Death then deliberately reached out his long-fingered hand and placed it over Mairi's mouth, ending her song in mid-verse. Instantly, the Queen's mad shrieks began anew, startling Janet.. He then removed his hand and, with his great horned head sunk to his chest as if deep in thought, turned away. Mairi took up her song once more.

> "Don't you see yon narrow, narrow road
> So thick beset with thorns and briars?
> That is the road to righteousness

Though after it but few enquire.

Don't you see yon broad, broad road
That lies across the lily leaven?
That is the road to wickedness
Though some call it the road to heaven.

Don't you see yon bonnie, bonnie road
That lies across the ferny brae?
That is the road to fair Elf land
Where you and I this night must go."

Looking up at The Huntsman, Janet pleaded, "Let me go! My mother needs me... I must help her!" But there was not the least flicker of compassion on the face of the Dark Lord's minion.

What does this bloody madman want with us anyway?
And Thomas... where is he?

After a time, the horned Lord stirred and looked up again, his eyes cold. "I know not how, but I will find some manner in which to put the impossible pieces of this puzzle together once more. Only then will my Queen sit by my side."

The Huntsman impatiently shifted his weight from one booted foot to another. "My Lord?"

Janet shivered as she watched the monstrous creature rise to his full height, his great twisting horns scraping against the overhanging branches of the Willow above, sending a shower of thin leaves cascading over them all. "Huntsman, take this mortal girl and place her in a cell deep in my dungeon where she cannot escape, for there is within her some essential part of this damnable puzzle. As for the older mortal, let her stay here and continue to offer what comfort she may. Guard them both, keep them well, or your life will be forfeit."

Held in his iron grip, Janet flinched when the Huntsman bowed low before his lord and master and prepared to take his leave. Then, as they passed through the arched entranceway into the darkness beyond, she heard the Lord of Darkness and of Death mutter to himself, his obvious despair almost making Janet feel pity. "There must come a day when my Queen will willingly sit beside me. For each Lord has need of his Lady..."

Soon, though, the monumental walls of brick and stone that construct The Dark Lord's unholy labyrinth swallowed whatever else he had to say.

Much later, when she stood in a cell so utterly black that she couldn't see the arm that still throbbed from The Huntsman's grip, Janet fought the rising panic that threatened to overwhelm her. Flexing that arm, she let the pain feed her anger as well as her determination.

Stumbling blindly to the rough wooden door, Janet listened intently for any sound that could tell her that there was another living soul somewhere near. But the only noise that broke the oppressive silence was the faint rhythmic drip of seeping moisture hitting stone and brick. When the dank air of the cell began to make her body shiver, Janet paced the short length of the cell, hugging her arms tightly around herself, trying to regain some measure of warmth.

Bloody hell! How am I going to get out of this fucking cell?

Exhausted, she collapsed in a damp corner muttering to herself, trying to fill the silence that gathered around her. "Okay, Janet, back in the asylum, how exactly did you remember the words to those songs? You only heard them once... so really, how?"

Maybe there's a bit of good magic working inside me?

"Anyway, putting a face on the bitch Queen makes it so much easier to hate her, because beautiful doesn't even come close to describing that... woman... no wonder Thomas fell for her.

"Thomas... Where the fuck are you? I need you... Mr. bloody Dark and Deadly and his pet huntsman are sure to do something awful to us pretty soon, so we need to get out of here before that happens. But, how exactly is that going to happen?"

Stop it, Janet!

"Don't let this damned place get to you..."

Determined to listen to her own advice, Janet crawled slowly across the floor, feeling with her outstretched hands, until she found the stout oak door. Her hands moved up its rough surface to find a small opening securely sealed with a lattice of iron bars.

You know, just in case anyone could squeeze through a space the size of a bloody mouse hole.

Pressing her mouth against its unseen bars, she began to shout as loudly as she could, over and over again, a single name into the darkness.

"Tom. Tom. Tom. Tom. Tomm. Tommm..."

When only fading echoes answered her, Janet began to sing, hoping that it would at least lessen the oppressive silence of the dungeon.

Hope whatever bloody magic is remembering these songs won't mind me using it again...

> "The elf Knight sits on yonder hill.
> Fine flowers in the valley,
> He blows his horn both loud and shrill,
> As the rose does bloom."

Far down twisting corridors and steeply laid flights of steps too many to number, there was a small cell made of brick, each a different shape and colour from the last, whose walls twisted upwards into a grotesquely shaped vaulted ceiling above. The chamber, built against the outer wall of the Dark Palace, offered a high window too small for even a small child to crawl through. That window, though, did allow a hint of light to fall dully onto the man below, who paced the short length of his cell, consumed by frustration and fear of what may happen to the woman he loved as well as the Queen he still served.

His heart leaped then when Janet's voice echoed faintly out of the darkness. Joyfully, he joined it with his own.

> "He blows it East, he blows it west,
> Fine flowers in the valley,
> He blows it where he liketh best,
> As the rose doth bloom."

For more hours than either would ever know, they exchanged verse for verse, until, exhausted, Janet's voice began to falter and then fade. Devastated, Thomas slumped to the floor and then he, too, fell into a troubled sleep.

When at last the Rose Knight awakened, he exhaled a desperate groan. His dreams were a torment of anxiety. Time and again he had found himself bound with no escape. Before the vivid images began to slip away, he remembered a giant tree... a pool of water so black there was no bottom to be seen... and standing in that pool was his Queen, screaming out in her madness. Then all three women, The Queen, Janet, and her mother, stood waist-deep in the pool, holding each other's hands. As one, they turned to stare hard at Thomas, looking at him through three sets of identical eyes.

Blinking away the remnants of that dream, Tom gazed up into the dim light that filtered into his cell from the window above and ran his fingers through his hair. "Even in sleep, my mind is thick with mysteries."

TWENTY-FIVE

Far away, down long silent corridors, Janet tossed in her sleep. Abruptly, her eyes blinked open as two soft tongues began to lick her face. In the total darkness of the cell, she was unable to see whatever impossible thing it was, but from either side of her head, she heard soft panting. Small paws pushed at her arms, and soft fur brushed her face. Janet whispered into the utter darkness, "Who…What…what are you?"

"Well, then…." The first voice intoned.
"You are awake…" Another voice added.
"At last."
"Perhaps you were having…
"such lovely dreams…
"that you wished…
"to stay amongst them forever?
"But your story…"
"will never…"
"find…"
"its proper ending…"
"if you do."
"Trust…
"us…"
"now."
"And…
"close…
"your eyes so that you may see."

Hesitantly, Janet did as the voices instructed, and suddenly she saw a vision of two sleek silver foxes staring up at her, their eyes lit with curiosity. Janet rubbed her eyes and muttered, "Are you just more damned nightmares come to haunt me in this horrible place?"

Ignoring the girl's doubts, one fox creature spoke. "Janet…"
Followed quickly by the second, "Why do you bide here…
And then both joined together in chorus, "Still?"

Janet wrapped both her arms protectively over her chest, "Bloody hell, you think I want to stay here?"

The two turned to look at one another. The air around them seemed to shimmer, as if a second reality slipped softly over the first. Now there were two small, elegant women standing before her, one inches taller than the other, their slanted eyes a matching green. Their hair was long and silvery, held back from their brows by simple circlets made of brightest gold. Both solemnly considered the walls of the cell with only the mildest of interest.

Janet stared incredulously at the two women as they linked arms and chorused together. "Mortal, you interest us."

Startled, Janet whispered into the darkness, "Who the hell are you? Why are you here?"

Turning to face Janet once more, the first woman answered, "You may call me Delian."

By her side, the second spoke softly, "And I, Aellin."

"Okay... Can either of you get me out of this damned pit of crazy monsters?"

The first fox-woman purred, "Yes."

As did the second. "Certainly."

"Of course..."

"But first..."

"you must..."

"listen."

"The Dark Lord is mad."

"Quite mad, indeed."

"as moon-mad..."

"as The Queen."

Janet can't help herself, "Fucking crazy isn't the half of that monster!"

"You would be too..."

"if you were living the same story over..."

"and over..."

"again."

"Always reaching..."

"the same ending..."

"and it..."

"so sad..."

"Much, much too..."

"sad."

"Someone must..."

"tell it true,"

"or this Lord..."
"and this Queen..."
"and the very land itself..."
"will most certainly..."
"be doomed."

Just what I need, bloody hallucination spouting complete nonsense...

I have to get out of here! Then find Tom and my mother and somehow get all of us out of this damned place! But... how?

Janet struggled to her feet, pacing the small cell, still puzzled by whether her odd visitors could possibly be real. The two women, though, simply continued to stand calmly, patiently watching her as if they expected Janet to suddenly open the door and let them out.

Then she heard Tom's strong voice echo again down the dark corridors of their prison, intoning another ballad. Listening, Janet began to relax for the first time.

> "Was a knight in Scotland borne,
> Follow, my love, come over the strand,
> Was taken prisoner and left forlorn,
> Even by the good Earle of Northumberland."

Smiling at the words, she joined her vibrant voice to his.

> "Then he was caste in prison strong,
> Follow, my love, come over the strand,
> Where he could not walk nor lie down,
> Even by the good Earle of Northumberland."

Eventually, when the last words of the long, gorgeous ballad faded away, Janet leaned back against the damp wall of her cell. Down at her feet the two women, now foxes once more, sat on their haunches, patiently waiting as if they had all the time in the world, which they did.

If those two got into this damned cell then they can bloody well get out again too.

Desperation drove her to ask, "Can you help me? Please!"

A soft whisper answered her. "No."

Followed by a second voice that was equally frustrating. "That is impossible."

"We only..."
"tell stories."

"We never…"
"never…"
"ever…"
"become part of one."
"But we do see where your story will go."
"Oh, yes."
"And you already know how to escape…"
"this dark place."

And, once more they chorused together, "We are content. We will wait and watch. You and the Knight will know what to do when the time for doing it comes."

Then, wrapping their long arms around each other, they began to laugh, a guileless sound of delight, that would lift the hearts of all that heard it.

Janet waited, then, for whatever these two strange creatures would say next. But as silence stretched into long frustrating minutes she realised that she no longer heard their soft panting, Janet was certain that they'd gone in the same mysterious way that they appeared.

That was stupid crazy.
Well… am I?
Crazy?
You know, daughter like mother…
No!

And just like that, Janet was certain that she knew how to escape.
That damned queen will get me out of here!

Grimly. Janet pushed aside the almost paralysing terror that washed over her when she realised what she was about to do.
Okay, Queeny, come out, come out wherever you are!

And with that invitation, The Queen of Summer's Twilight slipped smoothly into the mind and body that was Janet Ravenscroft. The young girl's bones and muscles shifted uncomfortably as if there was suddenly too much packed into too small a space. For a moment, Janet clung to her true self as frantic, last-minute thoughts echoed through her brain.
I feel like I'm going to explode…

Then the mortal girl was no more. The Queen opened her mouth and words fell past Her lips, elfish words of great power. Immediately, the rusted lock on her cell snapped open. What was now The Queen of Summer's Twilight felt a brief flow of air as Her prison door swung wide. Stepping out into the corridor, She delighted in the soft light that pulsed from the diadem on Her brow, illuminating the darkness that had ever held dominion over the dungeons of the dark Lord.

Smiling at Her own cleverness, The Queen began to walk gracefully down the dimly lit hallway. But after only a few steps Her body collapsed against the rough brick wall. She slid to the flagging at Her feet and gasped in shock at the cold stone that greeted Her as Janet reclaimed her body once more. The young girl was startled, though, to hear an echo of The Queen's voice still lingering within her head, bargaining with her.

Mortal, it seems your body cannot sustain my radiant spirit for any length of time. Therefore, I will help you if you ask it of Me, but only if you promise to free Me from this kingdom of death. And for that I will certainly be in your debt.

Agreed?

Janet grunted, "Charming..." Desperation, though, made her accept the offer. "Okay, you've got yourself a deal, Queenie." Even though the implications sent a shiver down her spine.

I will probably die if she overstays her welcome ... or go crazy, just like my mom...

Without the Queen's light, the dungeon returned to complete darkness. Janet moved slowly forward, feeling her way one foot at a time down long twisting corridors and seemingly endless flights of broken stairs. Above her and on all sides, she sensed the crushing weight of layer upon layer of stone and brick that fashioned the enormous dungeon through which she now blindly groped her way.

After what felt like an eternity spent in that darkness, where time and distance lost all meaning and only despair prevailed, Janet raised her voice to sing once more.

> "It was in a pleasant time,
> Upon a summer's day,
> The noble Earl Mar's daughter
> Went forth to sport and play."

At first there was no response, but she continued, knowing that Thomas and her mother were somewhere in the vast maze of tunnels stretching before her. .

> "And as she played and sported,
> Among the lily flower,
> There she spied a sprightly dove,
> Set high upon a tower."

When finally she heard an answering voice, far, far away, trading her verse-for-verse, her heart leapt.

> "I'll put gold hinges round your cage,
> And silver round your wall,
> I'll make you shine as fair as a bird,
> As any of them all."

Using Tom's voice as a guide, Janet's pace quickened. But soon, in the brief pauses between each verse, she began to hear furtive rustling movements and muffled voices come from each unseen cell she passed. She conjured up all manner of strange and horrible beasts that might be imprisoned within. Panic threatened to overwhelm Janet and still her voice. She stumbled, dreading to take even one more step. Leaning heavily against the cold, damp brick of the wall, she was able to distinguish the multitude of insistent voices that filled the air around her, all urging her to go on. Their encouragement gave her the will to keep walking through that awful place.

Every cell in this stupid bloody prison must hold some other poor sod brought here by that damned Huntsman.

She started to sing again. Those strange voices around her joined in chorus with her, until the walls seemed to vibrate with their song.

> "Instead of dancers to dance a dance,
> Or minstrels for to play,
> Four-and-Twenty lusty men,
> Turned to birds of feathers grey.
>
> This flock of birds took flight and flew
> Beyond the raging sea;
> And landed near earl Mar's castle,
> Took shelter in every tree."

Minutes, hours, days later, weariness rose over her and plummeted down like a great crashing wave. Janet's voice faltered, as did her steps. She stumbled against a wooden door, sliding to the stones at her feet, unable to speak or sing another word. All around her, the other voices fell silent as well. Such a deep and lasting silence few would have ever encountered, if not for Thomas' muffled voice that Janet finally heard through the thick oak door against which her head rested. With it came the stirring of hope.

> "They flew out from every tree,
> And lighted on the hall,
> And from the roof with force did fly
> Amongst the nobles all."

As the last verse of the song drifted away, Janet whispered softly into the darkness that enveloped them both, "I love you, Thomas. I love you."

Then she gave her body over once again to The Queen. Immediately, words of power spilled from Her lips, and the door to Thomas' cell wrenched open, crashing against the brick wall. There followed a cacophony of yet more wood hitting brick and stone as every bolt and every latch on every door in that great and terrible dungeon burst asunder.

Again, light as soft as the moon's illuminated the hallway. Into that sweet radiance The Knight of the Rose strode out of his cell, a smile upon his lips, only to be greeted by The Queen's cruel laughter. "What strange clothes are these you wear? My Rose Knight should not ever be seen in the drab garb of mere mortals."

Thomas, reacting quickly, bowed low before the woman who should have been his Janet. "My Queen, forgive me, I…" But just as quickly as the light came, utter darkness once again swallowed them. She was gone, and with a cry, Janet fell forward into Tom's arms. He pulled her close, grateful that it was truly the mortal woman he loved that he now held. He whispered, "Come, we must find our way out of this place of death."

All around them a rising murmur of voices filled the stifling air of every long twisting passage of that place. Those whispers grew louder and louder still, until their tumult began to shake the walls of what was once their prison. But who or what had been released, neither Janet nor Thomas was able to see in the intense and utter darkness.

Holding each other's hand, Janet and her Knight of the Rose stepped carefully forward. All about them, anguished cries rose from the unseen mouths of all manner of wild creatures of the Fae. Janet understood every one of them, and all asked for just a single thing: freedom.

Deep within, the Queen's voice began to whisper insistently, once again telling the mortal girl where to safely take each new step in order to escape the unholy prison.

Determined to rid herself of her unwanted intruder as soon as possible, Janet confidently put one foot before the other, leading Thomas and the unseen host toward the freedom they all so eagerly desired. "Quickly Tom, this way…"

All around them, unseen hands reached out and gratefully brushed her hair or her arm or her shoulder as Janet led the knight through the long, crowded passageways. And as they passed, all turned and followed the one whose voice they recognised as their Lady's.

"It is the Queen."

"All thanks to Her."

"My service will be yours, forever."

"I lay my honour at your feet, do with it what you will."

Janet shivered and gripped Thomas' hand tighter, wondering what would happen when they saw it was not their Queen, but only a young and very mortal woman leading them away from this place of darkness.

A soft echo of the Queen's voice followed her thought. *Fear not child, I am with you.*

Now that's a comfort, isn't it?

Do you mock me, child?

Whatever…

Leaning closer into Thomas, Janet whispered, "Tom, every moment that I'm here in Her world, The Queen grows stronger. But my mind… my body… I don't know how much longer I can sustain Her being inside me. She's eating me alive, and I'm bloody terrified of what will be left when She finally gets her way.

"But… She did promise to help me… us, if I freed Her from this madhouse…

"Tom, can I trust Her?"

He held her hand, and paused before abswering. "I was Her Knight of the Rose… with my own eyes I have witnessed both Her great wisdom as well as Her great cruelty, and never have I known which to expect from Her or when. In truth, by giving my heart to you, I have dishonoured my service to Her… but my heart will lead, and I must follow. So, I can only say trust your instincts but remain most vigilant indeed."

His carefully chosen words, though, were followed immediately by The Queen's haunting, cynical laughter that threaded through Janet's every thought, making her even more uneasy regarding what might come.

Gradually, so gradually that at first it wasn't even noticeable, the darkness that pressed so closely around them gave way to a dim light. And at that moment, thousands of winged creatures, all once of The Queen's own court, took flight and burst past them both, flying with furious speed toward that growing light and freedom.

Finally reaching the entrance to the seemingly endless black dungeon, Janet paused under a stone arch that opened onto a large formal courtyard filled with brilliant light. Exhausted, she leaned hard into Thomas, and, knowing that she must, Janet turned to face the enormous crowd of Fae creatures that had followed close at their heels for so long. The narrow corridor was jammed, for as far as she can see, with thousands of creatures of every shape and size as they slowly faded into the darkness far, far behind.

Oh!

Janet's eyes grew wide with wonder and terror, too. For assembled before her was every lord and lady, every scullery maid and cook, every creature with one eye or two or however many they may have needed, everyone that had ever trod within The Queen's court, both those she might have imagined and those that were forever unimaginable.

And, in all the vast panoply of faces, both grotesque and sublime, and every station in-between, that stared back at Janet she was struck that only Thomas' skin was white. Red and green, yellow, black, and brown and rose so pale that it was almost no colour at all, the creatures of the Fae gazed silently, uncertainly back. Fearing rejection or far worse, Janet began to panic for, of course, they did not see their Queen but instead, only a young human standing hand in hand with their Lady's consort, The Knight of the Rose.

Janet leaned close in to Thomas and whispered, "There are so many… so fucking many! And I am not their bloody Queen. What do I do?"

"My lady, perhaps you should ask them to return home. Their escape will surely distract the Dark Lord and draw his Huntsman's attention, making our task that much easier."

"But bloody hell, will they even listen to me?"

Deep in her mind, though, Janet heard the sibilant whisper of The Queen's voice, *and yet, they will answer to me.*

Unable to argue, Janet relaxed her control and allowed The Queen's mind to flood back over her, smothering any vestige of independent thought. Turning to Thomas, She asked, "Sir Knight, is your word then as false as your foolish human heart? You have sworn yourself to my service, yet now, you willingly follow another. At the very least, may I depend on you to perform your sworn duty?"

"Yes, my Lady, I swear that I will do so."

Thomas turned away, thinking hard about his future, knowing that soon he must make a choice between keeping his sworn oath or protecting Janet.

Indeed. To make The Lady whole again is my sworn duty.

But, by what means will that be possible?

I cannot help but wonder at the harm such a thing may render unto my Janet as well as her mother. Can I allow even the possibility of that harm to threaten my beloved?

When The Queen reached out to softly stroke Thomas' cheek before She spoke, he flinched away. "Alas, now that I am no longer your chosen one, what am I to do with you?" Although the young woman that stood so close to him now, cupping his face in both her slender hands, looked like Janet, he saw only The Queen's cold gaze staring out of her eyes. Enduring a touch that now felt like betrayal to him, Thomas replied, "Perhaps my Queen, this is not the proper time to discuss such matters…"

"As you say." Then, turning away from the Knight of the Rose, She looked imperiously at the creatures of the Fae and at that moment, somehow there was truly an aspect of The Queen that enveloped the girl's slender mortal frame. Tall and stately, She stood and addressed them.

"Knowing full well that it was not your choice to leave my Court but The Huntsman's art that brought all of you to this dark place, you have my forgiveness."

As one, the assembled multitude bowed before their Queen.

"Therefore, now, I command you to return to that court and prepare its great hall for my arrival.

"Go, and be quick about your business."

Eagerly, the vast horde of strange creatures heeded their Lady's command, and soon the courtyard is empty of all, save Tom and the mortal who was once Janet.

With that, The Queen released Her mental hold over Janet, knowing that a moment longer might render the girl useless to Her. Shuddering violently, she fell to her knees on the dusty marble tiles. Gasping for breath, her vision a riot of swirling shapes and colour, she still heard the voice of The Queen whispering deep inside her.

You will fulfil your part of our bargain now or have no doubt that I will consume you and everyone you love.

I'll bet you just bloody would...

Climbing to her feet, Janet looked at Thomas. "That was the first time I'd ever seen so many of the inhabitants of this land at once. Their skin... there are so many tints here in this land, a myriad of colours with no chosen and presumptive hue."

"Indeed."

"I wish my world could say the same..."

TWENTY-SIX

In the interminable journey afterward, Janet became certain that when its long-forgotten architect had finally looked upon his construction of darkness and endlessly twisting passages, he must have been pleased by the success of his cruel art.

Because it was their only hope to find safe passage through the labyrinth, Janet gave herself over and over again to The Queen. Each time, no matter how brief, left her weaker than the last. Only Tom's arm, circled tightly around her waist, enabled her to stay on her feet.

Without The Queen's advice, though, she was certain that they would have wandered endlessly through the silent rooms and long passageways until, their strength depleted, they would have lain down where they stood and slept a long, final sleep.

Warily placing her trust in The Queen's all-consuming desire to be whole once more, Janet eventually found herself standing outside a tall arched doorway that opened into the chamber where the monstrous Willow tree reared from its pool of black water. In a tangle of hoary roots, Janet saw her mother asleep, nestled in the dark, honey-coloured arms of the moon-mad Queen.

Instinctively, Janet rushed forward. Her only desire was to gather her mother in her arms but, sensing another presence in that chamber, she stopped and looked cautiously around.

The wizened bottle witch, Mother Hainter, balanced on a long low-lying limb of the great Willow just above the sleeping figures, staring inquisitively back at her. Scattered across the root-floor at her feet were a multitude of small bottles, some blue, some green and some a dusky amber colour. She squinted her good eye, looking past Janet, and spoke, "Ah, it's you, is it, Thomas. You and the mortal girl have been lang in getting here."

Before he could reply, Janet's head began to swim with the now familiar sensation brought on by The Queen's insistent presence. When she replied, it was with Her voice, "And what is that to you, little mother?"

Recognising The Queen's voice, the witch's good eye narrowed with calculation. But mindful of courtly protocol, the witch lifted her considerable bulk and leaped to an enormous shaggy root whose surface just broke the black pool and bowed low in front of the slender figure of the mortal girl who spoke with The Queen's voice.

"My Queen, what is your wish?"

"What do I wish?"

Followed closely by Thomas, She stepped lightly across the surface of a long, twisting root toward the witch. And, standing over Her true self, She gestured at it and cried, "I wish to sleep no more in this place of darkness. I wish to sit once more on the throne in my great golden hall. But most of all, I wish to see no more of that fool, The Lord of Darkness and of Death. That is my most fervent wish!"

Glancing askance at the recumbent body of The Queen, the root witch answered carefully, "Then I will do what I can to fulfil your wish."

"Take Us from here, as soon as you may. Return Me to my court, and all that you desire will be yours."

Inured as the root witch was to the ways of the highborn Fae, Mother Hainter mumbled to herself, "Even with certain treachery, tis a fine offer." Then her face twisted into a sly, calculating smile as she watched The Queen once more exhaust Her host's body and collapse across the same roots that entangled Her true form.

As Thomas knelt to comfort Janet, angry words crackled across the dim chamber behind them.

"What I have hunted and caught should never have been set free without my permission! And this night you have let loose the work of a lifetime."

The Huntsman, his face a livid mask of hate, splashed through the shallow pool that lay between Janet's prone body and the Knight of the Rose. Standing over Janet, the leather-clad figure drew his sword, "I care not how you found your way to this chamber, but none of you will leave it again, unless it be by my will. Even you, root witch!"

At The Huntsman's words, the mad Queen again filled the dim courtyard with Her anguished screams. Hearing those tortured cries, the Dark Lord's minion froze just as Thomas launched himself through the air directly at him. Wrapping his arms tight around The Huntsman, he carried them both back into the black pool. Moments later, they staggered to their feet, still grappling each other, trying to keep their feet from slipping on the roots that twisted and turned under the surface of the water. Soon their clothes were soaked and dripping.

The Huntsman, wrenching himself free of Thomas' grip, brought his sword up in a glittering arc, straight towards the knight's neck. Twisting to the side, Thomas skilfully avoided the other's desperate slash. Kicking out his foot, he tangled their legs so they both fell back into the pool, splashing black, oily water into the dim air of the chamber.

Horrified, Janet scrambled away. Still the cascade of viscous liquid soaked her. Momentarily blinded, she stumbled over a jagged root of the Willow and with a sharp cry she fell across the bodies of both The Queen and her mother. The Queen's eyes snapped open, inches from Janet's own. Staring intently at the girl she wailed, "Mortal, remember your promise!" But before Janet could reply, those eyes shut once more.

Above them, dancing along the length of a thick overhanging tree limb, the root witch screamed suggestions and abuse at the two men fighting desperately below. "That's it, bite doon hard!"

Ignoring the witch's exhortations, Thomas brought his hand down on The Huntsman's wrist and wrenched the sword away. Their chests heaving, they began to circle each other, thigh-deep in water, only now Thomas held a blade in his hand.

Cackling with delight, Mother Hainter continued to offer advice, "Gut him, Thomas. Now!"

This time, heeding the bottle witch's suggestion, Tom thrust the blade straight for The Huntsman's chest. Before it could sink home, the other parried with a fallen tree limb, causing the Knight's blade to glance off its hard surface. With a sudden back swing, The Huntsman slammed the limb down across Tom's wrist. He gasped in pain, dropping the blade into the pool, where it was lost under the black opaque surface.

Without pausing, The Huntsman swung the substantial length of wood again, this time striking a hard blow to Tom's right shoulder. Awkwardly, the Knight of the Rose stumbled back, scattering Mother Hainter's precious glass bottles and shattering more than a few. In despair, the witch jumped down from her perch crying out, "Now you're for it. What was in them bottles cost me dearly, they did."

Paying no heed to the little witch's wail, Janet struggled to her feet, helping Tom get to his. Behind them the Huntsman struggled out of the pool and balanced on the closely-packed network of roots, casually swinging his improvised wooden weapon. With little warning he brought it whistling around in an arc straight for Thomas' knees. Desperately, the Knight leaped away, but not with his usual agility.

The two men circled each other again, each testing the other's readiness, only Tom had to lead now with his uninjured shoulder.

Ignoring the frenzied cries of the bottle witch, The Huntsman feinted, then feinted again, before charging at Tom. Janet, her face a mask of concentration, kicked out as the leather-clad figure lunged past. Her foot connected with his knee and The Huntsman's left leg collapsed under him, sending him sprawling across the tangle of roots.

Thomas turned and leaped into the lower branches of the great willow, then struggled further up into the tree's branches where he was safely out of reach of The Huntsman's crude weapon. He stopped, calling out, "Huntsman! What will you now?" His adversary snarled and lunged forward, clutching Janet's arm. Holding the struggling girl, he looked up at his tenacious adversary and hissed a challenge. "Come, Sir Knight of the Rose. Come you here, and let us finish what we have begun."

In answer, Thomas leaped to the ground, rolled, and scrambled to his feet, smiling grimly.

The Huntsman shoved Janet aside, his attention focused on the Knight before him. Off balance, Janet stumbled away, trying to catch at the twisting limbs all around. But her hands, still wet and slippery, were unable to grasp anything substantial before she fell, knee-deep in the oily pool. Panting for breath and clutching at the roots beneath her for balance, she felt the hilt of the fallen sword. Desperately, Janet flung the blade toward Thomas. The Huntsman made a frantic leap to intercept it. But his injured leg would not support him, and he fell roughly onto the thick mat of roots at his feet, lying still at last.

Janet watched as Thomas closed on the fallen figure, sword grasped firmly in hand. Her breath caught in fear of what he was about to do. And yet, standing over the leather-clad hunter whom he had just overcome in combat, Thomas hesitated. Instead of striking a fatal blow, he simply held the sharp blade against The Huntsman's throat, causing a fresh flow of blood to slowly drip into the pool below.

At that moment, Janet's body jerked away from her knight's side, and her pupils rolled back. When she spoke again, it was with The Queen's voice. Only this time, She sang. It was an ancient song, whose words served to uncoil the thick web of roots that held Her true body captive.

And without pause, moving blindly like some ancient worm, those hoary Willow roots inched across the uneven ground and slowly, enclosed the body of the Huntsman, binding him securely in place. Finally, only his red eyes could be seen, filled with hatred, staring out from between two tightly woven roots. When the song and what the song had made was finished, Janet collapsed to the ground, her face grey, her eyes dull and listless.

Kneeling beside her, the Knight comforted her as best he could. Looking up at him, her eyes weary with the task still before them, she muttered, "Bloody hell! When She has eaten Her fill of me, Tom, She'll spit me out to die. Will this never end?"

Thomas helped Janet struggle to her feet. Immediately she stumbled toward Mairi, wrapping her arms around her mother., Relief and joy helped sooth her weary body, and she felt tears run down her cheeks. The older woman, though, merely suffered her daughter's embrace uncomprehendingly, never releasing her tight grip on the hand of the mad Queen.

Beside them, the ancient bottle witch squatted atop a twisting root, her wizened face split wide with delight. "Did not I tell yon Huntsman? I promised to be there at his fall and here tis." Mother Hainter chortled happily to herself before she looked at the others and spoke again, "Now, we must leave this place in haste, before the great dark Lord comes ta destroy us all." Looking shrewdly then at Janet and her knight, she continued, "His desire for vengeance will be very grand indeed!"

Her arms trembling with fatigue, Janet rested her head against Thomas' chest, "She's right, but I just don't have the strength to let The Queen trample through my mind again to get us out of this damned maze…"

The bottle witch held up her small, wrinkled hand. "There is nae need. I have come and gone in this crumbling palace fer more years than can be counted. I kin every passageway and bolt hole that's in it, and I will lead us all ta whatever safety there is for us."

Thomas looked curiously at Mother Hainter, "All? Do you come with us little mother?"

She cackled, "His wrath will fall on me as well as you, Sir Knight, as this Huntsman will only remain captive until his master frees his best hound. Then they will surely come after us all."

Squinting up at Thomas with her one good eye, she continued, "And it's certain, I am, that I will be needed when th' Queen is finally made whole once more."

For a moment she gazed wistfully back at the multitude of small, shattered bottles that lay scattered across the surface roots of that chamber and loosed a sigh. "Many years o' my trade now lie there drained and useless. Perhaps my time grows shorter than I kin…"

Many were the doorways out of that inner courtyard, but Mother Hainter did not hesitate. Following her as quickly as they could, Janet clung to her mother's hand, leaving Thomas to deal with the still raving Queen.

Soon Tom's strong arms had to lend support to Mairi, for The Queen, deep in Her madness, proved biddable only if She was hand-in-hand with Janet.

And so, once more, Janet and Thomas stumbled through the utter darkness of the labyrinth, but this time they heard the witch's voice beckoning them on, not close, but not far ahead, either. "Follow me, donae stray from my path or I kin you'll be lost, an' there will be none else ta help you from this palace of shadows."

Several times Mother Hainter paused at a branching of the way, and they both heard the witch mumbling to herself, as if she were arguing over the path that they should take. Until, at the last, they stepped out and away, leaving the crumbling walls of that great and awful city behind them.

As fast as they were able, the five companions picked their way across the blasted earth of the Dark Lord's kingdom, until exhaustion began to claim them. Janet stumbled and fell, taking her charge with her to the stony ground. Squatting by her side, the bottle witch offered Janet a draught of a curious liquid that she carried in her girdle. Whatever tincture was in the bottle, it restored Janet's strength and she was able to get back to her feet. Then, after pulling her mother up again, she started forward once more.

When Mother Hainter offered that same bottle to Thomas, he shook his head and replied, "No, only when there is no other choice. As yet there is strength still in me."

"Suit yerself."

At intervals during their long scramble across that desolate landscape, the ravings of The Queen ceased abruptly. Curiously, Her brief moment of lucidity in no way affected the mortal girl. It was as if the land itself were trying to heal its Queen. During those moments, She looked around at Her companions with wonder and shuddered at the desolate landscape that surrounded them.

In those moments, too, Janet studied the Lady of the Fae, her eyes filled with dull resentment at having to protect the very creature that had tormented her body and her spirit for so long.

No potion, no matter how strong, lasts forever. So, when exhaustion overwhelmed Janet again, Mother Hainter muttered that a second drought of the potion would only cause her harm.

Reluctantly, Thomas halted their desperate flight, hoping that some rest – no matter how brief – would restore at least some of Janet's failing strength. The companions collapsed against a great stone that lay hard up against a crumbling tower standing by itself in the midst of the desolation.

Mother Hainter pulled Thomas aside and whispered to him, "You kin that the Dark Lord will be following close ta our heels. We canna afford ta rest for long…"

Looking at the witch's face, strained as it was with exhaustion, he knew the truth of her words. As Thomas wiped the sweat and grit away from his own eyes he replied, "And yet there will be no hope of escape if each of us falls to the ground and cannot go on. Rest while you may. I will see what follows behind."

Climbing the ruined tower that thrust itself like a lone finger out of the rotting mud of that plain, Thomas looked to the east, toward the great palace that they had gone to such effort to leave behind. Its walls still looked impossibly close for all their effort.

Suddenly, that palace with its looming walls was wiped away by an immense cloud of dust rising from the surface of the plain, raised by the feet of those who pursued them. In front of that cloud strode The Lord of Darkness and of Death. At his feet were his remaining thirteen great hunting beasts, and behind him, rank upon rank, was a great army whose tread shook the ground. Where in that vast crumbling city this multitude of creatures lived, Thomas did not even try to fathom.

But of the Huntsman, there was no sign at all.

Thomas leaped down the crumbling steps of the tower, and reaching his exhausted companions a single word escaped his dry, cracked lips. "Run!"

Twenty-Seven

On the far western edge of the ruined plain that was the realm of The Lord of Darkness and of Death, there was once a great river.

A deep river and wide, one that had once flowed swiftly.

This river was and ever had been all that separated the Land of Summer's Twilight from that of The Dark Lord's kingdom. Between its two high banks flowed all the blood that was ever shed on Earth or beyond, in the Faerie Realms. Without The Queen to renew the life of her land, the once mighty river was no more. Now resting between its banks was only a deep layer of fine, pale red powder.

Turning her gaze wearily away from the lands on the far distant bank that were The Queen's true domain, the root witch squinted up into the Janet's face. "I kin what you would ask, girl. This river has served ta separate the two kingdoms since time itself was born."

Her eyes wide with wonder, Janet asked, "*Two* kingdoms of Faerie? I… I don't understand."

Mother Hainter laughed, "And why would you, human? There would be nae need."

Thomas, carefully choosing his words, tried to explain something that was certain knowledge to those who called the Summer Lands their home. "The blood… it ran here to serve as a reminder that all things must die, even an immortal. Between the two lands it has always flowed. And it always will, or… should…"

Janet nodded, responding to his logic. "Until our bloody queen's mind was gone." Then, looking behind them at the steadily advancing wave of pursuers, she added, "After the fucking Lord of Darkness and Death tried to claim both kingdoms for his own."

Nodding agreement, Thomas continued, "Never was there a bridge built to span it. So, we are left with little choice but to walk through this hellish divide or to once again become captives of the creature who pursues us." He held Janet's hands, trying to provide a glimmer of hope. "In Her own lands, I believe The Queen may regain Her true self and perhaps be able to defend those that She has pledged to protect."

Mother Hainter shrugged her shoulders. "Aye, a comforting thought, that. Now, step lively, children. We must be the first ta the other side if your hope be true."

Glancing back across the plain at the army that approached, Thomas heard a whisper escape the bottle witch's lips in a hiss, "It is an army o' shadows I kin, born from his Court o' Shadows."

Turning back to Janet, his gaze locked with hers as she whispered, "I love you."

"And I you, my lady."

After that, not one of their company spared so much as a glance behind them at the vast army that drew nearer with every passing moment. Their only concern was where to put their next footstep as they scrambled down the bank, studded with jagged rocks as sharp as knife blades. At its bottom they plunged into what had once been a raging river but was now only the silted blood of untold deaths.

Even in her lingering madness, Mairi acknowledged where they were when she began to sing.

> "For forty days and forty nights,
> He waded through red blood to his knee,
> And he saw neither sun nor moon,
> But heard the roaring of the sea."

"I bloody well hope not!" Janet grumbled. "We haven't got forty days or nights."

Once their feet sank into the heavy red powder and they began to push their way through the accumulated silt, they found their progress more difficult than any of them had imagined. Janet gripped her mother's hand tightly. And Mairi, in her turn, led the still raving, moon-mad Queen.

Sometimes waist deep and sometimes up to their necks, they pushed their way through the thick sediment of red dust that clung to their clothes, their hair, their skin, and gathered in every pore and crevice on their bodies, making it almost impossible to see and even more difficult to breathe.

> "Oh, they rode on, and further on,
> Until they came to a garden green:
> Light down. Light down you lad so fair,
> Some fruit let me pick for thee.

> Oh no, Oh no, True Thomas, she says,
> That fruit may not be touched by thee,
> For all the plagues that are in hell,
> Blight the fruit of this country."

Any hope that they may have had for a quick passage to the far side disappeared as each step became an uncertain effort to blindly feel their way across an unseen riverbed below the deep carpet of red dust. The loose rock, worn boulders, and sudden drops into what once were deep pools made their path treacherous, their progress frustratingly slow.

Soon enough, with her short, squat body, the bottle witch wasn't able to keep her head above the surface. At Thomas' invitation she climbed atop his broad shoulders, and sat there, balancing precariously, offering a steady stream of advice peppered with choice invectives.

"His army is nearly on us, and we pick our way through this as slow as can ever be!"

Janet spat out a mouth full of red powder and cried, "Is there no fucking way to make this crossing any quicker?"

From the perch on her champion's back, Mother Hainter cackled, "Girl, you already kin the answer ta that. Let the Queen inside you and She will take care o' us right enough."

Despite the truth of Mother Hainter's words, Janet still shook her head emphatically, *No. She'd probably fly us across all this with a snap of her fingers... But not now.*

I might just crawl back into myself and never come out...

Janet rubbed the fine red grit away from her eyes and saw, far over the dried river of blood, two silver foxes waiting expectantly for them on the still distant bank.

The bloody foxes... they are real.
But will they help us?

The two small animals sat silently amongst what was once a flourishing orchard of apple trees, now blighted and dead. Rising behind was a great withered forest stretching from horizon to horizon. The pestilence that had come hand in hand with The Queen's madness seemed to have consumed every oak and thorn and beech and hawthorn within that great wood. There was no stir of bird or beast or any living thing amongst the vast sea of withered limbs and underbrush.

Janet's concentration narrowed. Casting aside the danger behind and the unknown path before them, she made herself think only of where to safely place her next step.

That loony bitch is going to pay for this!

Suddenly, her thoughts were scattered as Mother Hainter's screeching voice cut through the air. "I see our enemies!" The witch's words brought a shiver of fear to them all. "They gather now on the bank behind us. Faster, my beauties, faster!"

But the very real fear of falling beneath the surface of the fine red dust into one of the deep pools or of stumbling on an unseen rock and breaking an ankle was never far from their thoughts. So they forced themselves to continue their slow, deliberate pace even as the bottle witch's strident cries rung in their ears. "Now they come! Oh yes, they come!"

When at last they reached the far bank and climbed, exhausted onto its shore, they are greeted by the two exuberant foxes. With short, joyful barks they leapt about the bedraggled figures, pausing for only moments at a time to lick their faces free of the fine red powder.

Triumphantly, Janet embraced her mother. But Mairi, still in the depths of her madness, just stared at the girl, uncomprehending. Beside them, Mother Hainter spat her words out as if they were pieces of sour fruit. "Foolish girl, there be nae safety for us yet, not with th' army that follows. Yet it is The Queen's own land, perhaps it will hae a gift ta give us?"

Jumping from Tom's back onto the shore, the bottle witch danced lightly on her feet, shaking the red silt from her leggings and boots. The foxes paused and sniffed at her suspiciously, making the elderly witch grin. Her one good eye squinted at the two animals, and a delighted smile spread across her lined face. "For all o' my considerable life I've heard tales whispered o' yourselves, but nae once have I ever believed them."

"Until now."

 Gesturing at the two sleek foxes, she turned to Janet. "Count yourself lucky dearie o, they are one o' the great mysteries, come ta life." Mother Hainter's voice dropped low as she pleaded, "Can you nae help us, my lovely ones? We are in such need."

The first fox shook her head slyly before springing away. "We are outside of any story."

And the second leaped gracefully over the first and continued, "Always outside, never a part…

"of any tale."
"No advice given."
"No action taken."
"Except one."
"And this story…"
"has…"
"never…"
"come to…"
"that…"
"place."
"Let us hope…"
"that it may…"
"one day."

The foxes then stopped their leaping dance and wound their silver bodies one round the other, tighter and tighter till they appeared as one animal.

"But we welcome you anyway, little mother."

The witch bowed as gracefully as her ancient body allowed. "Delian and Aellin, it is honoured, I am indeed." And kicking up her heels, the bottle witch laughed gleefully, "Oh, what fun we shall have!" Then with her hands on her hips, Mother Hainter cocked her head to one side. "If we survive this very day o' days."

The two foxes looked up at the witch curiously before they both nodded their sleek silver heads towards the river of blood. Janet turned her head to follow, and what she saw took her breath away.

A vast army of shadow, wavering and insubstantial but commanded by The Lord of Darkness and of Death, flowed down the far bank that had taken Janet and her companions so much effort to negotiate, and in a great black surge the enemy was already far out into the river of silted blood. On the bank behind, surrounded by his thirteen great hunting beasts, the Dark Lord stared fixedly across at his quarry. Even from this distance, Janet clearly saw the smile that played across his face.

"Thomas, tell me the truth, can She really stop them?"

The Knight of the Rose was still on his knees, aching with the effort of the crossing and keeping the little witch balanced on his shoulders. "Janet, I know not. But it is our only hope."

Janet saw in his eyes that he wanted to comfort her but didn't know how. Exhausted beyond words, she looked away and stared at the ground, finding it impossible to make what could prove to be a fatal decision.

But I must. And I will…

When she felt a hand grasp hers, she looked up, angry at being prodded, to see The Queen staring back into her eyes. There was an unexpected, pleading look on Her usually hard, emotionless face, and Her voice whispered inside Janet's head.

It is the only way.

Yet Janet shuddered with revulsion, remembering the mental chaos that came with every assault from The Queen. Then she felt another small, dry hand grip hers. It was her mother's. The older woman pressed close beside her, smiling. As one, they began to chorus an old song, a song of love and loss and redemption.

> "Then he took out his pipes to play,
> But sore was his heart with misfortune and woe,
> At first he played the notes of harm,
> And then he played the notes of joy.
> And then he played the good gay reel,
> That might make a sick heart heal."

The song ended, and their gazes locked for a brief moment before Janet came to a decision.

Okay, I will bloody do what I have to do.

Janet smiled grimly at her mother before she took both of Mairi's hands in her own, softly whispering, "I love you, Mother." Then she opened her mind, preparing for what was to come.

What that damned queen did to my mother… to us, is unforgivable. She's ruined both our lives with her desperate desire to escape her own responsibilities.

But… I know something about that don't I?

Determined, Janet lowered all the defences that she'd built over the last few weeks and instead welcomed, without condition, that part of The Queen lodged within her mother.

At once she was overwhelmed by other worldly images and speech and music that all but swept away any rational thoughts. Clutching her arms tightly across her chest, as if she could somehow contain the totality of a being who was simply too vast, too powerful for any one human to bear for long. Janet looked within herself and saw only The Queen of Summer's Twilight, whole and complete.

Face twisting with torment, Janet shouted over the rising tumult within her mind, "Okay, queenie, you made me a promise. Remember?"

There was an instant of silence that terrified her, then a hollow voice answered her question. "A promise?"

"If I got you out of that damned prison, then you swore you wouldn't harm me or any that I love!" Struggling to cling to her sanity for just a moment longer, Janet's eyes rolled back into her head, and through clenched teeth she hissed, "No promise, no deal. I'll let myself go as mad as my mother was, before I give you what you want without that promise!"

Smiling slyly, The Queen acknowledged Her pledge to the mortal girl. "All that you have said, I will do."

Janet cried out, "Then go for it, you bloody bitch!"

At once the Queen began to gather to Herself all the scattered pieces of the puzzle that had taken so long to be made whole once more. Janet slumped against Tom as her body convulsed. It was as if a part of her were being ripped away – excruciating and yet at the same time joyous, leaving behind a glorious sense of relief as the Queen's essence departed.

In the stillness that followed the root witch cried out, "The army o' shadows is well nigh upon us!"

With a single nod to acknowledge the witch's words, The Queen of all Summer's Twilight rose gracefully to Her feet and stood, triumphant and whole. She turned to face the distant Dark Lord and his oncoming army, calling out words of subtle elvish magic, words of such power that they reached deep into the ground at Her feet and pulled from it that which was, after all, Her right to command.

On the far bank, The Lord of Darkness and of Death heard those words and, knowing their import, clenched his fists in impotent fury.

Through her exhausion, Janet watched as inhuman shapes reared from the surface of the great river of dried blood. Huge, primordial figures, resembling no monster that she had ever imagined. They towered above the Dark Lord's army before crashing down upon it, smashing, breaking, crushing, rendering it back into the shadowy nothing that it had been made from. The dry surface of what was once a true river heaved itself into blood red waves that crashed and broke, slowly subsiding into the stillness that had reined before their making. Made of blood, and to blood

The Queen's champions returned, leaving only the Lord and his hunting beasts still standing on the far bank.

The Queen gestured out across the river where they had all just witnessed the complete destruction of the great army of the Shadow Court. "My lord, we meet again, she said casually. "And yet, I see anger written on your face. What is it that displeases you so?"

Doubtless sensing his rage, the beasts that prowled restlessly about his cloven feet fought against their leashes, eager to hunt and to kill.

Ignoring them, The Queen spoke again. "If you have naught to say to me, then leave us, or the doom that I brought down upon your army will be visited upon you as well."

In answer, the Dark Lord whipped his pack of dark beasts to heel and finally found words to speak. "My Lady, I would only ask that you give me your promise that I may speak with you in the privacy of your chambers."

"Never!"

A mask of frustration fell across his features as he growled but a single word, "Kill!" Then he released all his hunting dogs save one, the largest.

The other twelve leaped out far into the river of dry blood, diving beneath its surface in a plume of powder. Horrified, Janet watched each creature run unhindered under that surface, leaving long runnels snaking behind it, closing the space between them with terrifying speed.

She glanced up as a smile passed fleetingly across The Queen's face. A gasp from Mother Hainter, though, brought Janet's attention back to the surface of the river below. There, the silted blood had begun to swirl faster and faster in hideous mockery of a natural whirlpool, its violent currents trapping the unseen hunting beasts, never letting them go. Janet caught fleeting glimpses of a leg or a haunch as the creatures struggled futilely in the throes of the unnatural tidal pool. And she heard only a single sharp yelp before the sands calmed once more and left the surface as flat and placid, as if nothing had ever happened here.

From the opposite bank, the Dark Lord thundered, "For these indignities you all will die. Perhaps not at this moment, but there are so many tomorrows to be considered, are there not?"

The Queen answered his threat, Her voice as sly as it was melodious. "Speak then. I await the pleasure of your words."

"Here? In this place? With those standing beside you that I fain would hear my most private thoughts?"

Silently, She waited for him to continue, as if he had not made any objection at all.

Even from this distance they could all see the visible effort it took the Dark Lord to cast aside his consuming anger. When he finally replied, he had stripped his voice of every emotion save unconditional love. "My Queen, the madness of the moon has filled you for longer than either of us would have ever desired. For that length of time, I have cared for you as best I could. Unprovoked, you have fled from me and what is mine. Some would call that ungrateful, but not I, my Queen.

"We must give our blessings to those who have played their part in making your mind whole once more. I would call myself very wicked indeed if I did not reward them with suitable gifts and join in a chorus of rejoicing."

She appeared to consider his words carefully before replying, "Come to my palace then, if you wish, and I will receive you there on the evening of the next new moon. We will speak again, at that time and at that place."

"My Lady, I will come then and speak to you of more gentle things."

Standing tall and straight, The Queen looked across the stillness between them and commanded, "Yes, of course. Now, leave us!"

The Lord of Darkness and of Death's face contorted into a mask of frustration and desire, but still he turned away with his one remaining hunting beast and simply walked away, leaving the company where they stood safely on the Queen's bank of the Lands of Summer's Twilight.

His last words, though, hung in the still air. "My Lady, that night cannot come too soon for us both."

Twenty-Eight

Stretched beyond the limits of her strength, Janet collapsed unconscious into Tom's arms. Gently laying her on the ground, he anxiously gazed down at her worn face.

Beside them, Mairi opened her eyes, and for the first time in too long, looked out at a world that should have been free from the taint of her madness. But what Mairi saw was the very world she'd looked at for the last eighteen years. With a moan she curled into a foetal ball as soft whimpering sobs wracked her body.

Her cries caused Janet to stir and then reach out for the older woman's hand. Blinking away her exhaustion, the young girl smiled, "Mother. It's me... your daughter... it's Janet."

Heart spoke to heart, and Janet saw recognition in Mairi's eye, in spite of the many years that had passed. The older woman reached out for her daughter until both, still overcome with weariness, curled their bodies protectively around each other and fell into a profound sleep.

Not far from the sleeping women, Mother Hainter brushed aside a scattering of shrivelled apple husks before she sat beside the two foxes, gently stroking their soft fur. The ancient witch's stare was fixed on The Queen, who still stood on the river's bank, seemingly lost in thought. Perhaps She contemplated all that had been lost to Her in the long years of madness.

The root witch mused shrewdly, "Such generous promises you make, my Lady." Then, squinting at Janet, the bottle witch considered the mortal girl's measure. "That was well done twixt you and Th' Queen, but words, even those spoken under oath, can be twisted, especially with th' practice o' a thousand times a thousand years that this Queen has lived."

Thomas, too, stared at The Queen. His long experience with both Her cruelty and Her anger filled him with foreboding. However, the guilt that still consumed Tom's heart for abandoning his sworn duty to his Queen paled beside his growing love for the mortal girl. Concern filled his thoughts as he asked, "Witch woman, what must we do to restore my Janet?"

"Och, she'll be fine you ken. She simply needs ta rest and then ta heal, sir knight. And nurturing, that is my job. It is why I endure this dreadful place and th' ungrateful creatures that fill it."

Kneeling beside Janet, the witch ran her gnarled hands over the girl's limbs, carefully examining the stricken mortal. After a moment, she looked up at Thomas and smiled, "Her effort ta contain the Queen's wilful mind, even for so little a time, has taken its toll on her. But your lady has such strength as I have seldom seen in a mortal before. Still, she would be all th' better for a few drops of healing tincture."

Thomas looked hard at Mother Hainter, "Do you have such a potion, little mother?"

"Alas, my bottles are empty. Only th' knowledge o' what is proper to fill them with can be found on me this day."

Looking behind them at the dense forest beyond, she mused, "And for as far as my good eye can see, th' Queen's wood is bereft o' any life within it."

Pausing, she nodded toward the Queen and whispered, "But that may change soon enough…"

Around Her feet, a rush of life flowed steadily into the earth. Small tendrils twisted and turned and grew and crawled across the ground, unfolding in a multitude of minute – fresh new leaves amongst the scattered litter of brittle flowers and dead grass. And then, as if to seal whatever bargain The Queen had made with the land that She called Her own, the first bright notes of birdsong filled the air. To be followed, from somewhere deep in the withered forest, by the bellowing of a great stag.

Soon, small waves of life began to pulse from where She stood, transforming the withered grass at their feet, sending fresh green shoots up in a tangled profusion of abundant growth. Newly born flowers tipped toward The Queen, as if their unfolding petals honoured Her with their vivid colour. The bottle witch grinned at what she witnessed taking place all around them. "Och then, I will go now, Sir Knight an' see what there is ta find." Then, without so much as a backward glance, she disappeared into the great wood that had now begun to breathe with life.

Thomas cradled Janet's head in his lap. Beside them her mother stirred as if returning life was awakening the senses of all it touched. Mairi's eyes opened again. She turned, to smile gratefully at her daughter, and began to sing.

> "Then he took out his pipes to play,
> But sore was his heart with weal and woe,
> At first he played the notes of harm,
> And then he played the notes of joy.
> And then he played the good gay reel,
> That might make a sick heart heal."

In a blur of silver, the two foxes circled them, once, twice, three times, before dropping to the ground and cocking their long soft ears.

Delian spoke first. "Your song…"

"It delights us so."

"Yes, it does!"

Their sing-song voices offered no distraction for Thomas, who stared silently down at Janet's sleeping face in his lap. Wishing that he could do more to help her recover, he ran his hands over her dishevelled hair as she tossed uneasily. But when Janet's eyes flickered open and she saw who was above, she struggled, however weakly, to get out of Thomas' arms before collapsing once again into unconsciousness.

Her actions baffled Thomas. Mairi, though, continued to sing softly to Janet, her voice soothing her daughter's agitation as it once did The Queen's. Until, with the snapping of still brittle twigs and a shower of dead leaves, the bottle witch stumbled back into camp and interrupted the song. Mother Hainter grinned, her short arms full of the potent herbs she'd gone looking for.

In passing, the witch ruffled the fur on the head of the first fox. Without a word, it simply paced a step away from the fragrant bottle witch to sit on its haunches again, wrinkling its snout at her scent.

Squatting on the thick carpet of grass that now covered the ground around them, Mother Hainter paused and looked thoughtfully into Janet's face. It was twisted in torment. "Well then, I have most o' what I sought." Her wrinkled hand stroked the tangled mass of medicinal plants in her lap. "My beauties may look withered o' life, but there is new strength blooming deep within their roots." She smiled, "Spring comes once again ta th' forest o' th' Queen."

Janet suddenly shuddered awake and angrily pushed Tom's hands away. Turning her head, she cried, "Leave me alone. Just leave me alone!"

The Rose Knight reached out to the woman he had given up so much for, but Janet frantically crawled away from him as quickly and as far as her strength would take her.

"Janet, what have I done?" Wiping her tears roughly away from her cheeks and choking back bitter laughter, she replied, her voice hollow, "Nothing…nothing more than a consort of The Queen should."

"What?"

The haunted look in the girl's eyes sent chills through Thomas when she continued, "Even as The Queen saw through my eyes, I gazed through Hers."

Not understanding the meaning of her words, Tom reached out for Janet once more. She violently slapped his hands away with her clenched fists. "Bloody fucking bitch! Thomas, when I let the part of Her that was lodged within my mother's mind flow into mine, I saw so much more of Her than I ever had before… so much that I…I saw you and The Queen locked in each other's arms…I saw you and Her laughing and talking and…and… you… inside her, crying out with pleasure!"

Bitterly Janet spat, "Was it good for you then?"

The bewildered knight offered the only explanation he had. The truth. "I was a mortal in the land of an undying Queen who was beautiful beyond all women I had ever known. I could refuse her nothing, nothing…" Then he shook his head at those distant memories, "But Janet, that was so very long ago."

"I… I know that it happened before we ever met, but… I was actually in the same room and I… I felt how you touched Her, and saw how you looked into Her eyes and said that you loved Her… I don't know if I can ever forget that…. I'm sure that bitch wanted me to see you in her bed, damn her! I don't know if I can ever forgive you.

"Damn. *Damn*. DAMN!"

Then Janet was silent once more, her face a mask of torment, both arms clutching her knees, staring at nothing but the awful images that kept reeling through her brain over and over again.

Seemingly oblivious to this drama, the two foxes began to scamper around the girl in ever tightening circles until their soft fur brushed against the skin of her arms and her legs.

When they both paused, they looked at each other. And then the first fox placed her soft paws on Janet's knees and hunched forward, looking the mortal girl in the eye before speaking. "It is ever the way."

The second fox climbed onto Janet's shoulder, nuzzling her face, "Ever, ever, ever the way…
"Our stories become…"
"so confusing."
"We don't know…"
"if we come…"
"or if we go."
They joined each other in chorus then. "The best way, is to be together, that, always, always makes for a happy ending."

Angrily, Janet shrugged the two foxes off and got to her feet, striding unsteadily over to Mother Hainter before dropping to the ground again and muttering under her breath, "Pests!"

All this time the witch had been busy preparing her posset, which she now offered to Janet. "Drink this. It will help you regain your strength and… perhaps too, some peace of mind."

But Janet paused as her fingers closed around the brimming liquid nestled on the bone cup. She looked at Mother Hainter a moment, trying to deciding whether to trust the small witch or not. When she raised the cup to her lips, the bottle witch stopped her, and cackling with mirth at Janet's evident distrust, said, "And save some for th' Queen herself, She will be needing it, I ken."

Janet grimaced at the mention of Her and muttered between sips of the dark, foul-smelling brew, "She doesn't need any fucking help from me."

Hearing what Janet said, they all suddenly became aware that The Queen had not moved from the bank or spoken for some time. She still stood there silently contemplating whatever strange impulses flowed through Her heart. But then she raised her graceful honey-coloured arms toward the moon and the faint stars that hung in the sky above. A soft breeze that only touched The Queen herself, drew Her dress tight against Her long legs and Her breasts. It whipped Her shining black hair, twisting it about Her beautiful face.

From The Queen's feet, wave after wave of vibrant green life began to pulse into the earth as if in time to the beating of Her heart. A multitude of rainbow-coloured butterflies lifted from Her hair past the falling profusion of lilies, lilacs, buttercups and hyssop, anemones and foxglove and primrose and daffodil and hollyhock. A heady mixture of their soft, abundant fragrances suddenly scented the twilight air on the river's bank.

Mairi cried out, as if what was happening to The Queen tormented her still fragile mind, too close to the mad visions that had tormented her for so many years. Janet crouched close to her mother, covered Mairi's eyes, and swore to herself that she would protect the older woman no matter what happened next.

Thomas was bewildered when The Queen of All Summer's Twilight fell to Her knees and disgorged a single rose from Her mouth. It seems to drop in slow motion into Her cupped hands. She stared at it as each rich red petal shivered and then become yet another rose and another and another until they cascaded to the ground in front of Her, instantly rooting there.

Her mouth gaped open, grotesquely wide, snapping the ligaments of Her jaw with an audible crack to emit a ceaseless flow of birds and snakes, frogs and bees and stag and fox, bear and deer, badger and dragon and sloth, cat and dog, mermaid and unicorn and every other manner of beast both on two legs or on four pour from her lips. And all followed the two silver foxes in a spiralling dance through the thick grass that now carpeted the entire bank.

Her outstretched fingers thrust deep into the still dry earth. Thomas tried to turn away, remembering their sensual strokes across his body, but he was transfixed. Mounds of thick moss topped with small delicate white flowers that gathered at the base of bright red mushrooms and sombre toadstools flowed around the pale flesh of Her arms, transforming them. Her shoulders, Her face, Her eyes. When finally Her mouth choked with trailing vines, wreathed with ivy and sumac and honeysuckle leaves, Thomas fell to the ground, trying to cover his face, but he was powerless and could not tear his eyes away from the primal transformation that played out in front of him.

Her now brittle hair dropped from her head and rooted in the ground, becoming green and grey and rust-covered grasses alive with every manner of insect and spider, lady bug and dragonfly, wasp and ant, grasshopper and cricket, black and brown and yellow and no colour at all.

From the hollow husk of Her withered body, a dozen saplings sprang: oak, willow, hawthorn and maple, alder and beach and apple, birch, ash and holly, and last of all, rowan. Feeding upon whatever life still remained within Her, the saplings stood a dozen feet high in a matter of moments, their crowns thick with tender green leaves that swayed gently in the soft breeze.

And everything that had fallen or spewed or grown or transformed from The Queen's body turned then and ate their fill from those tender, succulent trees, stripping the bark, and the leaves and the blossoms and the berries, eager to live and beget more of their own kind, until there was nothing left of them. Except only a small, tender rose cane that delicately reared from the lush green bank that lay beside the eternal river of all the blood that had ever been shed on Earth, a river that was previously dead but now flowed freely once more.

Overcome by what he had witnessed, Thomas screamed in frustration and in shame. His Queen, a woman who had once claimed his heart, whom he had pledged to protect with his life, had just been utterly destroyed before his very eyes, and he could do absolutely nothing to prevent it.

Still clutching her mother, Janet stared at the wretch of a man who had once been her Knight of the Rose, clearly struggling to understand what she was witnessing.

Mother Hainter, though, whispered into the silence that was left behind those screams. "Th' wheel turns, birth, death and then... perhaps, resurrection." The bottle witch left the others crouched in the now tall grass and pushed aside the teeming mass of creatures that clustered in a churning mass over what had been The Queen. At the witch's gentle touch, they begin to bound or hop or fly or crawl away. All except the two silver foxes, which remained there, eagerly waiting for what was still to come.

Reverently, the witch knelt in front of the single trailing plant which was all that remained of The Queen of the Land of Summer's Twilight.

The first fox barked, "Carefully now."

And the second continued, "The roots..."

And the first took up the tale again, "of every story told...

"are delicate."

"To begin anew...

"they must not...

"be damaged...

"only nurtured...

"so that what grows...

"from the old...

"will be strong...

"and flourish."

Panting in their eagerness, their tongues hung from their open mouths. Together they chorused, "A new story sprouting from the old will gift those living that tale a more gracious manner in which to begin it anew."

Mother Hainter testily replied, "You need not tell me my business. I ken it well enough."

With her aged hands, she carefully dug into the soft loamy soil around the newly sprung shoot. Lifting the pale green thing, the witch placed it in a curious leather satchel, slung from her belt, which she'd used for the same purpose many times throughout her long life. Finally, she packed the earth loosely over the plant's fragile roots.

Before she closed the flap of the pouch, though, the bottle witch poured what remained of her broth of herbs over the young plant and whispered words that none but the two silver foxes could hear. And they, excited beyond imagining, filled the twilight air with their barking.

TWENTY-NINE

In the profound silence that followed, Janet looked to the bottle witch and, feigning indifference, asked, "Okay, are we done? Can my mother and I go home now?"

Mother Hainter cackled to herself, "Nae, no yet I fear."

Janet felt frustrated, if not surprised, "Why not, little witch? What more can we do that hasn't already been done? My mother and I are weary to our bones." She gestured at Mairi and continued, "And she has a husband that she's not seen for far too many years." Mairi head lifted at her daughter's words, hope glimmering in her sad eyes.

The ancient bottle witch studied them both for a moment before replying, "My children, we must still make whole again what has been broken."

Looking at the forest, burgeoning now with new life, echoing with bird and animal song, Janet replied, "But haven't I…haven't we already done just that?"

"It is a tangled tale that still holds us all within its web." Mother Hainter smiled encouragingly. "Janet, you and Thomas and your mother – and yes, The Queen as well – are all but bitty pieces o' a tortured puzzle that must be restored before its story runs true. Until that happens, it would be best for us ta remain together."

Then the bottle witch called to her, "Janet Ravenscroft… look ta me. There are questions I must ask o' you now."

Sighing, Janet turned her attention back to Mother Hainter, trying to calm her disordered thoughts.

"Now then, child, when were you born?"

Janet grimaced, "What's my age got to do with any of this?" But when Mother Hainter continued to stare at her without speaking, she realised that there was, of course, something more than idle curiosity in her question. The foxes silently padded to her side and climbed into her lap. Gratefully, Janet stroked their soft fur and immediately grew calm.

The bottle witch continued, "I seek not th' year, for they are nae counted here in this land. I would have you tell me th' season only."

"Okay, fair enough. It was in the fall, at the end of October."

Growing even more serious, the witch queried, "An' th' exact day o' your birthing?"

Before she spoke, Janet had a sudden insight: all of the unfathomed mysteries that clung to her and her mother and the once moon-mad Queen rested on the answer to this one simple question. "It was Halloween night, just before the clock struck midnight."

The old witch danced excitedly on her bare feet before stopping to grin at Janet. "All Hallows Eve then. You'll be sure o' that girl?"

"Bloody hell, yes! My father always used to make a stupid joke about me slipping out of the turnip he'd carved for the lantern..."

The witch's face grew stark and troubled, "Only on that certain night is th' border 'tween our two worlds paper thin. And it was on that very day that th' Dark Lord cast aside the last o' The Queen's glamour's an' stepped sae eagerly through Her sacred wood. She despaired then, knowing that at th' last, Her strength was nae his equal. Certainly, She would have sought for and found some final refuge."

Janet murmured, "Her madness?"

"Yes! She loosed her mind then and sent it spinning far, far away."

Tears formed in Janet's eyes, "And my mother..."

"Regardless of what it might do ta any possible host th' Queen sent a great part of Herself out into th' mortal realms thinking that th' fell Lord o' Darkness and o' Death would surely nae find Her there."

Hearing the witch's words Mairi stirred and whispered, "I loved the old songs of my adopted country. Their fancies and phantoms were always a delight to me. But most of all I loved the muckle ballads. The tales they told were almost like fairy stories..."

The first fox intoned, "And like...

"...will call to like," finished the second.

Mairi seemed to stare within herself, into a well of troubled memories, slowly reasoning the mystery through, "So, somehow the Queen entered my mind at the moment of my daughter's birth... when I was weak... vulnerable." Tears began to course down her face, "And lodged there, within me..." She cupped her hand on Janet's trembling face before continuing, "And it seems, a smaller part lay dormant elsewhere..."

Overcome, Janet's head sank into her arms, still listening to her mother's soft voice tell their story, "It was She that drove me mad... and kept me, for so long, from my home and my family." In the silence that followed Janet looked up, as with just the barest of whispers her mother continued, "I think that She deserved to die."

For a moment both women stared hard into each other's eyes before Janet added, "I'm glad that She did."

Mother Hainter wisely sought to turn both mother and daughter's thoughts away from that vast, empty road that led only to bitterness and useless satisfaction of revenge. "It would make anyone feel th' same. Nae mortal can hope ta withstand th' full glory o' th' eternal Queen o' th' Fae an' walk away from it unscathed.

"Through perhaps nae planning o' Her own, a small part o' Herself became bound within Mairi's bairn as well. And that is what saved you. If She had given all ta you, that is th' moment you would have surely died.

"That at least is true." Mairi smiled, "I am alive and I have my daughter with me. And I'm most thankful for both."

For the first time since Janet had rejected him, Thomas stirred. Without looking directly at the mortal woman, he asked, "So, we must remain bound together until...?" Janet looked across at Thomas and saw the misery that had settled on his face.

I almost feel sorry for him... almost!

With a grim smile, the bottle witch began to speak again, and what she said surprised all, save the two foxes. "Th' Queen is nae truly dead, She only waits for Her rebirth."

Thomas' haggard eyes suddenly filled with hope, but Janet clenched her mother's arm hard as the witch continued, "Properly tended, Her story will begin anew as it hae many, many times a fore." The two foxes jumped up from Janet's lap and leaped around the four figures, crying out together, "Many times. Many, many times. Many times beyond measure."

The witch smiled at their frenzied antics a moment before continuing, "But that will only happen if we nurture Her carefully." She gently patted the satchel at her side then, "We must take what I have preserved here ta Her city an' plant it there, in the midst o' Her garden. Born again, She will perhaps have a new story ta tell us."

THIRTY

Janet never knew how long it took for their company to travel through the Queen's great forest. Only the moon above them, slowly waxing greater and greater until it was full and strong, spoke to any passage of time. Their steps, though, quickened as they saw all around them the once dead land of The Queen become lush with new life. Each blackened tree or withered bush and briar sported small fresh buds, shy with the first green breath of life after so long a season of death.

As if provoked by the burgeoning life all around, Janet's dreams became astonishingly vivid. Once she awakened, sitting bolt upright, her eyes still haunted by the cruel visions that had helplessly unreeled in her sleep. It was Mother Hainter who clutched the still-shaking girl to her breast.

Uncomfortable as she was sharing such intimate knowledge with a mother she hardly knew, Janet whispered to the witch, "I saw them again… Thomas and The Queen. They were together… in Her bed. Naked… their bodies entwined. I was in that bed, with them… for what seemed like forever…" The ancient crone wisely said nothing, just wrapped her arms around the young mortal woman, trying to ease the misery from her as best she could.

But in such close company nothing was ever truly a secret. Listening quietly to Janet's whispered confession, Thomas felt guilt tear at his heart as if it were trying to stop it from beating.

Acutely aware of the icy wall that Janet had constructed between Thomas and herself, the two older women watched helplessly as the Knight tried wordlessly to seek her forgiveness with a hundred unasked for acts of kindness and generosity. After each, the older women looked at other, shaking their heads at the foolishness of youth, and subtly contrived to bring the two together whenever they could. Occasionally, when there was no other recourse, the two did share words. But their conversations always spiralled into anger on Janet's part as Thomas stumbled through yet another futile attempt to explain what his sworn duty to The Queen was.

"My heart, though, is yours" Thomas insisted. "It will be with you always, wherever you go. But I will not abandon that which I have sworn my honour to protect, I would only be a lesser man if I did so."

Unable to let go of her anger, Janet clenched her fists and hissed, "Your Queen! You mean the bitch that you still love well enough to throw your life away for?"

"Janet, that love ceased to be, long, long ago, as you know full well."

Janet remained unmoved by his declaration. "Thomas, why do you persist with this? She's dead! Your Queen is dead. I was there. I watched Her loyal subjects gorging themselves on Her body until there was nothing left."

Thomas' face drained of colour before he said, "They only did what it is in the nature of this Land to do... as do I."

Looking in his eyes, Janet saw only confusion and wrenching pain, but that didn't prevent her from spitting, "Are you telling me now that you'll owe your service to this new Queen, whoever She might be?

Thomas lowered his head, saying nothing.

"Well *are* you? Because then you might as well have joined the other creatures at their feast!"

His head jerked up, a look of horror in his eyes. But when he opened his mouth to reply Mother Hainter interrupted. "Janet, your Knight is right. A new Queen will be born. The death o' the old ever gives way ta the birth o' the new. Always! It is the way o' this Land. Any land, even yours, mortal. Ponder on that, if you will."

There were many questions that a mother and daughter should have been eager to ask one another after a lifetime of separation, yet they all remained unspoken. Consumed with anger at what seemed to her to be a senseless choice by Thomas, Janet remained silent, endlessly repeating their arguments in her head and heart.

Not long after, Mother Hainter called to Thomas and asked him to go and gather wood for their fire. When he hesitated she cackled, "Be quick about it, dearie one. For I must brew more o' my herbs ta help keep the strength in us all."

After he climbed to his feet and walked listlessly into the now dense woods around them, the bottle witch joined the two mortal women. "Forgive me, I canna' but help ta overhear your angry words, Janet." She smiled at the older human whose face was drawn and worried, then looked searchingly into Janet's eyes. "That story o' our lives is a tangled, messy web, difficult ta make sense o' even at the best o' times." She smiled again. "We would all do well ta remember that as best we ken."

The ancient bottle witch wearily pushed aside the satchel that contained the fragile rose shoot that must, at all costs, continue to grow and prosper under her care. Its tender stalks, already coloured with a deep reddish purple, curled over the confines of the leather satchel. They were now studded with minute but very sharp thorns that had left long, bloody gouges on the older woman's wrists and arms. Mother Hainter began to rub a healing salve into her lacerated, nut-brown skin, smiling in relief.

Mairi's eyes widened with concern before she offered, "Can I help?"

"Nae, dear one. This is my task an' I kin ask nae other ta share in it."

Her eyes troubled, Mairi asked, "Oh, you mean this new Queen you spoke of? Is the little plant much trouble then?"

"Yes, small as it is it weighs on these old bones." The witch grunted then, thinking of the task ahead, "But I am equal ta it for I must be."

When the witch finished ministering her salve, both she and Mairi looked carefully at Janet, who still sat deep in her own thoughts. The bottle witch spoke to her then; quiet, carefully chosen words that startled the young woman. "There be few among us who would keep their pledged word as honourably as Thomas. He has made a choice that is perhaps hard for you ta fathom, but nae for me."

Janet laughed bitterly, "His promise seems absurd to me."

Her mother added, "Dear, you really don't give him credit for everything that he's done for us." Then she smiled sweetly as she continued, "Your Thomas seems like a good man... So much like John, at least as I once knew your father."

Janet's sharp laugh interrupted her mother's nostalgic reflections, "Those two... alike?" Then she added, as if recalling something, , "We'll have to see, won't we." Looking at the bottle witch, she continued, "That is, if we ever get home."

In answer, Mother Hainter gave them a promise with no closure, "In good time, my sweetlings. All in good time."

Mairi looked downcast at the witch's answer and longing filled her eyes, "I'd like to see my John again... feel his arms around me."

An edge of anger showed in Janet's words as she stared straight at the bottle witch, "Will we never be done with this Queen of yours?"

The witch chortled, "My Queen? I call nae one Queen. Or King for that matter." Then, laughing at their confusion, she continued, "I only try ta heal what needs healing. That is my duty, mortal. And never have I shirked it, though th' years grow long and th' stars grow dim and old. This land needs its Queen, and so I will do my part in restoring Her ta that purpose."

Mother Hainter paused for a moment before adding, her face haggard, "But I am the last o' my kind. When I pass away into th' west, who will remain ta help heal those in need? Who will put back together what has been torn asunder?"

The older mortal tentatively suggested, "The foxes perhaps?"

"Nay, those twa are ootside any story that ever was…"

Abruptly she shook off her melancholic thoughts and chortled, "But I tire o' talking about my own wee self… We have a tale before us ta untangle and set ta a proper ending, do we not?"

Mairi gestured around them at the forest that shimmered with strange flowing colours that weren't suited for human eyes to comprehend, "Even so, I'd very much like to return to my world… my home, again."

The witch grinned, "You will, dearie one, I think I can promise you that at least.

Rising to her feet she continued, "Now, our knight has been lang in the forest and I fear he may be lost. Rest your weary bones here until I return." Then she looked straight at Janet, "We have need o' all our company if we are ta survive our journey together."

A short time later the ancient bottle witch came upon the Knight of the Rose kneeling despondently in the midst of a small clearing. Strewn about him, as if dropped there with no regard for picking them up again, was a scattered armload of dry branches gathered for their fire. His hands were buried deep in the drift of dead leaves as if seeking to grasp the vibrant new life that pulsed beneath. Mother Hainter's nostrils filled with the fragrant aroma of tender green and growing things that still remained under the protective layers of rust-coloured leaves.

Hearing the crack of a twig beneath her feet, Thomas looked up, his face twisted with misery. "Will Janet never understand that I cannot simply walk away from my pledge to The Queen?"

"Nae, Thomas, she will not!

"She was born into a much different world than your own. Raised ta understand different values entirely. Somehow you both must bridge the divide betwixt yourselves if you wish ta live together as one."

Thomas gestured past the gentle swaying of the trees that encircled the glade. "Out there, in the lands beyond this eternal twilight, I was raised to be the leader of my clan. For all of my short life there, I was taught and truly believed that my worth as a man would be judged on the certainty of my given word.

"That word when solemnly pledged was never given lightly or in vain boast serving only to flatter the one who spoke them.

"I saw the respect and loyalty that my own father's words set in the eyes and hearts of all those who called him Laird. And I wished the same for myself. Learning from his example, I knew that I must hold to any promise given, no matter the hardship that choice brought me.

"Life, though, in my highlands, was hard with few simple pleasures to offer, even for the heir to its Laird. And the Kirk held sway over all our lives with an iron hand, frowning especially on all things that spoke of earthly pleasures.

"But I was young, with a young man's desires and so there was a girl – Anne, the blacksmith's daughter. We were enamoured. And I, foolish and innocent, pledged my life to hers without first seeking consent from my family or priest.

"When Father heard of it, his wrath knew no bounds. Furious that his only son would throw his future away by pledging himself to a woman of such low social degree, he locked me in a tower room and hung the only key from his own neck.

"I spent long wearying days in that prison. So at first I was relieved when they came for me, but they roughly bound my arms and dragged me into the church, where I heard both Anne and my own name read at the top of a long list of others that our priest had found wanting of our Lord's good grace. Any so named would no longer feel the welcome arms of the clan until they confessed to their proscribed sin. Father's insistence that I break my vow then and there to the girl was crueller yet, and to my mind an even greater sin. When I would not, he turned her family out of their holdings, banishing them from his lands.

"I was consumed by righteous anger, refusing to speak to my father, my mother, any of my family, wretchedly whiling away my days in that tower.

"Until a day came when they fetched me once again, put me to horse and sounded the hunt to begin. My father and I rode out together then for the last time. Perhaps he thought that my time alone on that tower had softened my heart towards him. Or feeling the entire clan round about me, I might come to realise the scope of what I was losing, I know not.

"Over the course of that long day my fury did not wane. But even that anger did not blind me to my father's folly. In his eagerness for the kill, again and again he took his exhausted mount over hedge and fence that were far too high. We approached another, one that I knew to have a steep bank on its blind side. So, even bound, I turned my mount, cutting him off, and made that difficult jump myself. I landed hard, slipping from the saddle. I expected nothing but the hard ground to greet me, but instead the Queen of Summer's Twilight brought me safely to a different place.

"She and Her court utterly bespelled me by the freedom that it offered.

"Consumed by my lust for the beauty of its Queen and the promise her eternally youthful body held, I cast aside any thought of my lost love, my family, and my clan. Revelling in the sensual joys of the flesh, I sought forgetfulness in Her warm and open arms.

"Yet eventually, even there in Eternal Faerie, the un-numbered years grew long and my heart began to ache. I knew not for what. Until you set me to walking between the worlds and I breathed again the sweet mortal air of my highlands.

"When I saw once more the raw fire that lit my fellow highlander's eyes and the avid curiosity that filled their hearts, it called out to me.

"I knew then that I truly belonged in the land whence I was born.

"Even so, I had pledged my service to the recovery of the Queen. Having forsworn my word once, I was not eager to do so again, certain that I would be truly damned if I did.

"That is, until my quest led me to the mortal named Janet Ravenscroft, and then all my certainty was for naught.

"My first attraction to her deepened quickly into love, and it seemed that she felt the same for me as well. Yet now – only confusion and anger lie between us.

"How then, witch, am I to serve the Queen and the woman I love at the same time?"

"A hard question indeed ta answer, Sir Knight. Let us both think on it, shall we?"

Thirty-One

When at last the companions emerged from the great forest to stand on a hill overlooking the vast rolling plain that swept toward The Queen's city, Thomas' heart leaped. Below, the blackened grass and withered trees were verdant once more. The gentle rolling hills spread for as far as his eyes could see, laced with sparkling streams and stands of towering oak in full leaf. Crowding the sky above, birds filled the freshening air with their sweet song.

Considering the vast distance there was yet to travel, the bottle witch shifted her burden uncomfortably from one shoulder to the other. For the first time, Mairi saw the raw red welts left from its straps and she asked her companion, "Surely now, you'll allow me to help?"

Mother Hainter turned to the mortal woman, a fragile smile on her face, "Nae dear. This is my burden ta bear for as long as I may." Then, looking at the other companions, she grinned, "Th' sooner started, th' sooner there."

However, the Moon above waned from full to crescent as the small company crossed the seemingly endless plain. As they drew closer to the Queen's City, they were surprised to discover that the grass around it was still withered, the trees blackened, and the walls rising before them cracked and broken.

Trying to push aside the despair he felt at seeing the now familiar destruction, Thomas' quickened his pace and was the first to walk through the ruined gates of the city. Janet looked away from his tortured face, saddened in spite of herself by Thomas' obvious torment. She turned to the bottle witch, "All that happened back there by that awful river of blood, didn't it mean anything? Was our effort for nothing, escaping his blighted kingdom, crossing that damned river, The Queen's death, everything! Was it for bloody nothing?"

The ancient witch chose to offer no answer. Instead, straining under her burden, she squinted her one good eye up at Janet and said, "Well, what did you expect, dearie? This city is but a reflection o' its ruler. It canna thrive again until She lives once more." And gently stroking the satchel with its precious contents that weighed at her body so, she continued, "That is our purpose here. And when it is done, then we will all be free ta go where we please."

With a muttered groan, Mother Hainter struggled to lower the satchel carefully onto the marble paving at her feet. She stood above it, swaying with relief, and exhaled. All of them looked down at the weathered pouch that had hung from her shoulders for the length of their journey. And they saw for the first time that the suppleness of the leather had faded, leaving it dry and cracked, barely able to support its burden.

Strong purple canes burst through every seam to wreath the small leather satchel in curling stalks, lush with new leaves and sharp with hardened thorns. Above it, the witch's aching shoulders sagged from exhaustion. She slowly flexed her gnarled hands, trying to work through their numbness. Those hands were also caked with blood from the multitude of fresh wounds lacerating her flesh,

The silver foxes circled the growing plant warily. They sniffed at it and then filled the still air with their excited barks. Mother Hainter grinned ruefully. 'I'm glad that someone is happy." Then the witch made a request that nobody expected. "Thomas, this new Queen grows too heavy, even for me, and these old bones must have their rest. Will you no carry Her for me now?"

"Why ask Thomas?" Mairi asked. "When I've offered to help so many times?" The old witch smiled and cupped her hand under the woman's chin. "Because, my dear, he is The Knight o' the Rose, and it is his duty ta serve The Queen, so it is fitting that he take up the task now."

For his part, Thomas eagerly accepted, grateful for anything that would distract him from the awful spectacle of destruction that loomed around them. He knelt beside the small leather satchel and solemnly intoned, "I swear by all that I hold honourable to fulfil the task that you have set me." Carefully he slid the straps of the satchel over his broad shoulder and, lifting it for the first time, winced at the unexpected weight.

They continued, making their way through the labyrinth of alleys and avenues that led into the great city. On the way they saw many who must have been fellow captives in the dungeons of The Lord of Darkness and of Death. They had kept their promise and returned to The Queen's city, but without Her glory to replenish its spirit, their feeble attempts to repair what had been broken was inadequate at best.

When the company finally reached the throne room at the heart of the city, the news of their coming had spread, yet the crowd that filled it to overflowing was ominously silent. The great hall had been swept clean and the shattered tile underfoot polished and shining. The throne room itself, with towering vaulted ceilings, was choked with every manner of Lord and Lady of the Fae, all hoping to celebrate their Queen's triumphant arrival.

But as Janet looked closer, she saw that their garments were shabby, their faces still haggard from their long confinement, and everyone within the great hall stared silently, uncomprehendingly, at the little witch, the silver foxes, and the two human women that stood beside their Knight of the Rose. Soon, though, a rising murmur of discontent began to echo through the hall. Thomas looked into many faces that he recognised from his long years spent in Her court and saw there only impatience and anger.

As he eased the satchel from his aching shoulder, its frayed strap ripped, and the parcel fell to the floor. The brittle leather of the pouch split open, spilling its precious burden onto the marble floor. Thomas' body shuddered with relief, but he stared down, horrified, at the plant's tender shoots splayed out on the tile at his feet, their fragile roots exposed to the air. The Knight cried out, certain that he had failed to keep his oath once more. "No!"

Terrified by Tom's anguished expression, Janet moved toward him as he fell to his knees, his breath coming in short, violent bursts. Ignoring the chorus of desperate voices around them, whose only concern was the return of their Queen, Janet crouched defensively beside Thomas as his own arms circled protectively around the fragile new growth.

No one there noticed when the foxes began to chase each other, flickering past Thomas, Janet, Mairi, and the bottle witch until they become a long, continuous blur of soft silver light. When they halted, instead of foxes, two elegant ageless women, their long silver hair bound at each brow by simple gold bands, stood before the assembled multitude of the Fae Court.

"Come."

"It is time…"

"at last…"

"for our part…"

"in this story…"

"at long, long last."

The two women knelt by each other's side and reverently lifted the fragile plant from the remnants of the leather satchel that had protected it for so long. Standing again, their slim bodies began to grow taller and taller, till they towered above the court. Held in their gentle hands, the small rose shoots began to grow and flourish, sending out a cascade of curling purple stalks along with a multitude of glistening red blooms that trailed beneath them.

Aellin and Delian gazed into each other's eyes and then down at the crowd, waiting for them to grow silent once more. When they spoke, their voices were soft and warm, hovering in the air of the vast hall, yet all those assembled there heard the two women's words as if they were whispered to them alone.

"You have spent…
"long years…
"in a place…
"of darkness
"and death…
"but once more…
"you live…
"in the Queen's own bright city."
"Now…
"You must…
"prepare yourselves…
"and your city…
"for her coming.
"Go now…
"with gladness in your hearts…
"and songs of celebration on your lips."

Silently heeding the two women's declaration, the court slowly emptied of all save the companions who had, against all odds, brought The Queen back to Her rightful place. Squinting with her one good eye at Thomas and the others, Mother Hainter cackled, "Now that was interesting, you ken?"

Then, looking up at the towering figures of Aellin and Delian, the witch cried, "Come! It is time we were about our business, is it not?" She took Thomas's arm, noting he was still staring in wonder at the two women who sometimes were foxes. The witch remarked, "You, Sir Knight, should be o' gae cheer. For in the heart o' Her kingdom She is too great a burden for any save such as they."

The ancient witch shifted her own aching shoulders once more. "Ta Her garden then. There is much still ta do."

THIRTY-TWO

Awestruck, Janet and her mother quietly followed the towering figures through the vast, empty hallways of the palace of The Queen. They passed elegant rooms beyond counting, all now standing empty, waiting for Her return. Although the broad hallways were cleared of rubble and each marble column and tiled floor was polished and shining, the decay that had set in during Her long madness still leached away at the enduring splendour that should have been evident in everything they passed.

Janet paused on the very highest of a series of broad terraces that stepped layer after layer down the steep hill and looked out at the sacred wood that has been a sanctuary to The Queen for time out of mind. From that high place, she saw what had once been an enormous wood of fragrant flowering rose and ancient apple trees was now devoid of any sign of life. "What a bloody dreary view this is."

Then, noticing that her companions were already several terraces below, Janet followed, hurrying down the broad shallow steps that connected each level to the next.

She found them again in a wide courtyard at the heart of the sprawling, unnaturally quiet garden. Four wide avenues bisected it, running north and south, east and west. In its centre was what had been a fountain, now dry and choked with dead leaves and shrivelled apples.

Beside her, Thomas stared hard at the fountain's intricately carved surface. Following his gaze she saw tier upon tier of figures, both animal and Fae, dancing across it. She could only imagine how magnificent the fountain must have been in its prime, and wondered what memories it stirred in him... Memories of Her, no doubt.

Towering above the blackened, stunted trees that bordered the courtyard, Delian and Aellin knelt on either side of the fountain.

Reverently, the two women used their fingers to dig a shallow hole in the dry earth near its base. Devoid though it was of any life, they placed their precious charge there.

Both fox-women bowed their heads and, clasping their hands together, slowly leaned toward each other until their foreheads touched. Faces suspended just over the surface of the soil, their mouths opened, and as one they exhaled a single soft, sweet breath. At once, the dead earth transformed, becoming rich and fragrant compost.

Then, slowly, as if some impossible part of each were now gone, the two figures diminished, slipping back into their animal selves. Soon they were once more only two small silver foxes, their fur gleaming in the soft twilight, sitting on their haunches amongst the rest of the company.

Her eyes wide with wonder, Janet clasped her mother's hand.

A little apart from them all, Thomas carefully watched the bottle witch scurry about, preparing for her part in the ceremony.

A faint fragrance of new sprung roses caressed the air then, making Thomas smile with sudden, vivid memory. He remembered his first days at the Fae Court, his senses aflame with the warmth of The Queen's embrace and the intense, swirling colour that saturated everything he looked upon.

The Queen beguiled me then with all manner of sights and foods and gifts beyond imagining.

Though bestowing Her eternal body, wondrous beyond measure, was, I thought, the greatest gift of all.

How then did the wonder of that glorious body and Her court grow so stale?

Why did I long so to see the lands of my birth once more? Indeed, why did I so readily fall in love with this mortal girl when I had all this to compare her to?

And looking about him, Thomas remembered The Queen's palace and Her gardens as they were before Her madness, resplendent with roses and endless polished marble halls.

Everywhere I looked, there was beauty beyond measure. But when all that beauty is restored, I will still gladly leave it for a life in the mortal realms with my Janet.

He studied the young girl standing next to him, as she waited anxiously, hand in hand with her mother for whatever may come next. Although he was certain that she paled in comparison to the eternal beauty of The Queen of All Summer's Twilight, he knew he'd made the right choice.

Heart will speak to heart, and gladly I have given mine to hers.

Would, that she could forgive me...

Suddenly Thomas felt an almost tangible weight of some profound but unseen presence, and moments later the air seemed to tremble with it, as if it were anxiously awaiting the coming of something desired beyond all things.

Whatever promise lay hidden quickly began to rise to the surface, called there by the slow keening tune that now trembled from Mother Hainter's weathered lips. It was a soft, slow song in a language, which had rarely been heard since before there was ever a moon and stars in the sky above.

Knowing full well the potency of that song, the silver foxes began to dance intricate patterns that twisted in and out and around the companions, scattering the rotting husks of everything that once grew in the garden under their soft padded paws.

Withered stalks of brittle grass and fern began to pulse with subtle colour, lifting whole again from the renewed earth to sway gracefully in the air as if dancing before a new Queen as yet unseen. Astonished, Thomas watched as new flowers unfurled from each fresh stalk, then bloomed magnificently in a profusion of white and orange and red petals.

The withered trees, so densely packed around them, began to sway violently, in a wind that no one could feel. Their blackened trunks returned to life; their twisting limbs pushed forth green and growing leaves that suddenly transformed the dead garden into a space, vibrant with life.

Out of this new greenwood bird song joyfully lifted into the air and they heard the cry of an owl. The soft stirring of a family of mice was quickly followed by the low humming of bees, and from deep within the heart of that sacred wood, the quiet song of the green man came to life once more.

Turning, Thomas watched with delight as a multitude of purple canes rose from the ground where the small rose was planted, then bent, twisted and curled again. Fiercely clinging to the nearby stone of the fountain, they snaked across its surface and burst forth in wild clusters of red, red roses and a profusion of rich purple leaves that covered the delicate carvings beneath. Continuing, they twined over and about the high fountain, creating a lush, fragrant bower. And then, stepping from the soft, dappled shadows cast by those new-sprung leaves, there came an infant with long hair trailing into the fresh green grass. Roses, trembling with dew, wreathed her brow.

With each new step the child took, She transformed as rapidly as the vegetation around her, maturing from infant to young girl and finally to a radiant golden-skinned woman, cloaked in glory, unaware of Her own nakedness.

Barking their joy and delight, Aellin and Delian leaped through the thicket of twisting rose canes that now towered high above all that stood there in the garden.

The eyes of the newly born woman opened and slowly focused on the world around Her. Then, on seeing Thomas, a delighted smile lit Her face. When She called out to him, though, Her voice was shaded with only a pale echo of Her usual authority, for now it was filled with a generous, beguiling tone that had never before come easily to The Queen of Summer's Twilight.

"Sir Knight... my heart rejoices to see you here... but why... why is my body so weak? My mind so confused?"

Still the Knight of the Rose bowed low before the beautiful woman, acknowledging Her as his Queen out of respect — and fear as well — but no longer with unconditional love.

"Lady, my heart celebrates that you walk once more amongst us."

Clearly delighted with his response, She gazed down upon Her consort. Then for a moment She turned Her gaze on his companions and briefly considered each of them. But Her interest was more captivated by the garden round about them with its abundant rose blossoms. And just above them, the apple trees were crowned with thick, fresh green leaves, laced with wave after wave of white, sweet smelling blossoms that showered upon the ground to leave each supple limb heavy-laden with red, glistening fruit.

Looking again at Her knight, She spoke softly. "What strange visions I have, filled with so much pain and torment and darkness. All about me the earth was packed close, and above, no moon at all." She passed one delicate hand across Her pale, green eyes as if to clear them and then leaned close into Thomas, kissing him full on the lips.

Quickly breaking the kiss, he stepped back, carefully studying this Queen's features. Thomas tried but failed to recognise the woman he had once been so consumed by. Yet with each passing moment, She gathered to Herself more aspects of that once and future Queen. Her soft, innocent face hardened, and Her mouth curved in a cruel smile before She spoke again, "What visions indeed... Have you been unfaithful to me, Thomas?"

In supplication, Her knight bowed his head so that he didn't see the sudden leap of hope in Janet's face when he finally answered, "I have wrought only the duty owed a Queen by any knight in Her service. Much, though, has happened since last we spoke. I would speak to you of it."

Coolly She laid Her slender fingers over his lips and looked long and hard at Janet before cupping Thomas' chin with one slim hand. Then, drawing a single razor-sharp nail across his cheek, casually leaving behind a deep, bloody gash, She said, "Indeed my memories of recent days are as insubstantial as passing mist, so I would have you tell me all that has come to pass here, and in the mortal lands you've spent so much time in of late."

Another and another and another deep furrow joined the first cut across his check and neck as the Queen continued to stare sidelong at Janet's horrified face. Seeing the mortal girl turn away gave her great satisfaction.

Mairi stepped closer to her daughter just as Janet's anger boiled over, "This? This is the thanks your knight receives for helping to restore your life? He and this witch have all but destroyed themselves bringing you here, and now you offer only this pointless cruelty as a reward. Thomas has already suffered more than enough in your damned service!"

The Queen studied the young woman. "Mortal, my rewards are for those that have earned them, not for any who may have once done so, but no more."

Reaching out, Mother Hainter gripped, Janet's hand in her own and with a subtle nod, silenced the girl. Then, preparing for the worst, the bottle witch turned back to The Queen. "My Lady, she is nae but a mortal, unused ta speaking in th' manner o' your court. Forgive her rashness, I beg you."

Helpless in the grip of her anger, Janet wrenched her hand from the witch's grasp and through gritted teeth, hissed, "This bloody bitch owes me, and I'm going to collect!"

Before The Queen was able to respond, Mother Hainter spoke again, quietly, reasonably, understanding that this new-formed Queen was as yet unable to call upon all the considerable resources and wisdom that Her past lives would soon grant Her. "Lady, even now, as we tarry in this garden, the Dark Lord waits impatiently at your gates. It is the new moon, and with its coming, you promised him the freedom o' your court. And he is most eager ta speak with you."

Reluctant to distract Herself from the pleasure this casual cruelty had brought, The Queen hissed, "But this mortal girl troubles me so…"

The bottle witch shrewdly positioned herself between The Lady and Janet before speaking again. "Please, there is much for you ta do and learn and little time ta school you in it, if you are ta prepare for the Lord's coming."

The Queen of Summer's Twilight stared icily at Janet until, with a dismissive wave of Her long, elegant hand, She turned and walked back into the palace, followed closely by the witch and the two silver foxes.

At the top of a short flight of stairs, She turned back. "Thomas, attend me. I will have need of my Knight of the Rose and soon, I suspect."

As Thomas meekly followed, Janet found her simmering anger hard to restrain. Her fists clinched and her mouth hardened. So she was startled by the gentle stroke of soft fingers along her cheek. Turning, she saw her mother standing close by, looking up at her with clear, loving eyes.

And, with a sharp cry, Janet pulled her mother into her arms and wept.

THIRTY-THREE

This time when The Lord of Darkness and of Death entered The Queen's city, none there sought to impede his progress. He brought with him no army of shadows but only a single companion, the last great hunting beast that stalked close by his side, fitted with an elaborate harness made of shining black leather.

Although the crowd filling Her throne room was relieved to have their Queen with them once more, as Her presence granted them some measure of protection, they remembered well their time spent in the dungeon of the treacherous Lord and trembled.

As for the great dark creature with his twisting horns, it was as if the onlookers were not even there. Ignoring the murmuring horde of Fae, he and his hunting beast strode the length of the great hall intent on only one person: The Queen of Summer's Twilight.

Clothed in resplendent samite, on Her brow a graceful crown of silver inlaid with green emeralds, and in Her slender hand an elegant sceptre of gold, The Queen of All Summer's Twilight sat upon Her great, high throne. One step below, in his acknowledged place of privilege, Thomas Lynn, Knight of the Rose stood, elegantly fitted in a freshly oiled suit of red leather armour, his unbound hair cascading back over the heavy red cloak that fell almost to his feet. With a troubled heart, he watched the Lord of Shadows advance toward Her throne.

Beside the knight, looking as if she would rather be anywhere else but there, even in her hovel leaning against the wall of The Dark Lord's crumbling city, stood the bottle witch, Mother Hainter. She spared a concerned glance at Janet and her mother standing two steps beneath, before murmuring under her breath to the two silver foxes that sat patiently by her unshod feet. "Well dearie ones, I ken the outcome o' the story that will be told this day an' all will end as it was meant ta." Aellin and Delian curled their warm silver bodies closer, perhaps seeking to lend some measure of comfort to the witch.

Clothed now in long flowing robes more suited to the manner of the court of the Queen, the two mortal women's hands were clasped tightly, as if they each needed to lend strength to the other in order to endure what might come. Rigid with anxiety, they watched the horned creature and his beast pause at the base of the steps.

The Dark Lord bowed low, as he greeted the living jewel he so desired. "My Queen."

Into the profoundly awkward silence that followed, She said impatiently, "Why then, are you here, and what would you speak of with me?"

Lifting his head, and with it the two twisting horns that rose from his brow, he smiled. "Why, my Lady, I bring a gift that I hope will be received with great gladness."

In Her private chambers Mother Hainter had described in great detail to the newborn Queen the like and quality of the gifts that The Dark Lord had given Her in the past. Remembering those descriptions, She could not help but suppress a shudder. "Again? You bring me more of your repellent gifts?"

"Alas my Lady, this gift is not for your radiant self, but for your Knight of the Rose. For is not he but a reflection of you and of your court? And is he not without the blade that you yourself gave him to defend your honour from all the dangers that may come against you in this land you've ruled for an age and more?"

In one long, sharply taloned hand The Dark Lord held out a slim sword of obvious elvish design.

Smiling slyly, he intoned, "This blade was taken some time hence, perhaps maliciously, by my underling, and I would return it to your Knight of the Rose with all good will."

A faint flicker of impatience played across the Queen's face then, but still she nodded towards Thomas, indicating that the knight should descend the stairs to accept the blade.

As Thomas cautiously drew near the Dark Lord, he heard the low rumbling growl that came from the hunting beast pacing stiffly at the Lord's feet. Close enough to smell the beast's foul breath, Thomas saw what others could not. The rose pendant he had gifted Janet suspended from the beast's collar.

With a grimace, the Knight of the Rose bowed stiffly before holding out his gloved hand to accept the proffered sword. "It was indeed a cherished gift and losing it filled my heart with sadness."

Still tightly grasping the blade, the Dark Lord looked up. "My Lady, I would, though, beg but one small favour in return."

"Yes. Get on with it. I have little time to waste this day."

The great horned figure gestured to Janet, standing only a few steps above him, "This mortal girl has angered me."

"Angered you? Indeed, how so my lord?"

"She has taken what was mine and defiled those who were in my charge."

A smile played across The Queen's lips. "And you would that I...?"

"Give her to me so that I might bestow on her that which her actions so justly deserve."

Thomas turned sharply, looking up to the woman who sat on the great throne as Her icy words fell down through the still air. "Indeed, I have no further use for the girl. Take her, if it is your wish... and the older mortal beside her as well."

The Knight of the Rose cried, "No!" and wrenching the elven blade from the Lord's grasp, he leaped forward, trying to put himself between the horned creature and the two mortal women.

A single bound, though, brought the Lord's hunting beast clawing to a stop on a polished marble step, blocking his path. The huge beast opened it jaws, exposing teeth like jagged glass, spitting its defiance before leaping straight for the knight in red armour. The impact knocked Thomas from his feet, their bodies locked together as they tumbled to the throne room floor, scattering frightened onlookers; but not The Dark Lord. Tom caught a glimpse of him calmly observing their bloody match as if it were of no possible consequence. Otherwise, the knight was oblivious to those who looked on.

Tom knew he was in a fight for his life. When the beast's teeth ripped through his boiled leather armour, cutting deep into his sword arm, he screamed. The blade dropped from his limp hand and skittered across the tiled floor, stopping only when it met The Lord of Death and Darkness' cloven foot. Smiling to himself, the Dark Lord placed one heavy cloven foot over the blade's hilt, making certain that it would not be used again.

Janet, shaking off her frozen horror, pleaded with The Queen, "Your promise...what of your promise to me?"

The bottle witch's hand grasped the her arm as she hissed, "Janet, this is no' the time ta waste a promise such as that. This is a right an' proper challenge between these two champions!"

She hesitated, "But that beast..."

The witch swore, "Child, let this be! Your man is armoured and would nae be named the Knight o' the Rose if he did nae possess uncommon skill. Let your Thomas deal with this wretched beast. He will have help if needs be."

Below them, tumbling over and over again on the hard marble floor, the two champions gained no advantage over the other. Tom's leather armour shielded his body from much of the frenzied creatures' attack, but the beast's talons and natural ferocity gave it an advantage in turn.

Back and forth along the length of the great chamber they fought with a primal violence that only escalated with each new injury. With an agonised scream, Thomas tore his body away and struggled to his feet. The beast crouched low, circling the man, hissing its rage.

No one in that vast throne room could tear their gaze away from the brutal struggle, nor did most even desire to. All save one, who tossed a slim dagger, better suited for slitting throats than gutting an enormous hunting cat. Flung from Mother Hainter's hand the small blade glittered and tumbled as it arced through the air. Bouncing once on the hard marble, it spun to a stop close by the two figures locked in mortal combat.

It was no sword but Thomas knew that any blade might give him the advantage. He dodged past the great beast and leaped forward to snatch up the dagger. The Knight of the Rose hit the tiled floor hard and then rolled to his feet, where he deliberately paused, bracing himself to face the monster's next charge.

With a sharp shriek that reverberated through the hall, the enormous cat-like beast sprang at the Queen's Knight. Thomas danced lightly forward between the cat's outstretched claws and then away, leaving the blade buried up to its hilt in the creature's broad chest.

Spitting blood, the hunting beast spun across the floor, its jaws snapping ineffectually at the blade. For a brief moment it paused, flashing a look of hatred and frustration at Thomas, before leaping away, up the steps as if seeking new prey. With a final burst of strength, the beast raked its needle-sharp claws down the bottle witch's chest and stomach. They both fell, tumbling awkwardly down the high marble steps, leaving a path of fresh blood in their wake.

At the base of the stairs, its claws sunk deep in the still body of Mother Hainter, the beast rose slowly to its feet before shrieking defiantly, once, twice. Then it collapsed over her near lifeless form and into the spreading pool of blood.

Thomas fell to his knees and with enormous effort rolled the great beast away. As comforting hands caressed his shoulders, Tom realised that both Janet and her mother were close beside him, anguish written plain on their faces. He looked again at the crumpled body of the witch as she stared back at him, then her gaze found Janet. Small creases formed at the corners of the little mother's eyes, followed by a faint smile. Janet caught and held the witch's cold hand as she wheezed a few quiet words, "Janet... even in death I will hold you ta our purpose. Here begins a new tale. Try ta steer it true... ta a better... ending."

With her long, thin lips set in a defiant grimace, life drained swiftly from her. And Mother Hainter, the Bottle Witch of all the Lands of Summer's Twilight, stared sightless at no one and nothing.

Thirty-Four

In the midst of that throne room, thronged with creatures of the Fae, Mairi sank to her knees beside Thomas and her daughter and gently placed her hands on either side of the witch's weathered face. "My friend... my friend, have you truly left us... left me?"

The two silver foxes came close as well and softly licked the fallen woman's face clean of all the blood that marred her features.

"One story ends."

"Another begins."

Then, even in the midst of their grief, they began to notice exclamations of surprise ripple through the crowd around them. Close by their side the great cat's bloody body shifted and rippled, slowly, painfully, transforming itself into the body of the Dark Lord's own Huntsman.

Through rapidly dimming eyes he gazed at Thomas, and whispered past blood-spattered lips, "Know, Sir Knight, that once I, too, wore your armour. The Queen called me Her Knight of the Rose as well... and promised me that it... it would be forever. Be certain... that you choose well... be certain that it is...what...your...heart...desires..."

And then he, too, died.

Recoiling from the death of a creature, who like themselves was well-nigh immortal, the crowd that filled the great hall cried out in one voice and shrank away, leaving the tiled floor at the base of the steps empty of all save the three mortals and The Lord of Darkness and of Death.

Thomas pulled the dagger from the beast's chest and carefully cleaned the blade before unclasping the delicate silver pendant from the leather collar that still circled The Huntsman's neck. Grasping it tightly in his gloved hand, he rose to his feet.

Beside him, Janet placed a tentative hand on the knight's arm and whispered, "Bloody hell, I will miss her. We all will. But I'm glad you're still alive at least." Her warm words surprised Thomas, for they were the first such she'd spoken to him since their argument beside the River of Blood.

Smiling grimly, he held the pendant out to Janet, who clasped it in both her hands. Answering the quizzical look on his face she whispered,

"Thomas, I'd never throw your gift away, the Huntsman took it from me before he dumped me in that bloody dungeon."

"Thank you, my lady."

"I…"

Unconcerned with their conversation, the Dark Lord looked at Thomas for a brief moment before stalking past him. Carefully avoiding the spreading pool of blood, he looked up toward the woman who sat the great throne above and addressed Her. "Yet again, what is rightfully mine is taken from me without thought or consideration. This errant knight of yours, this mere human piece of meat, has now killed a valued servant who had served me well, and, indeed, in his time, served you as well."

Although The Queen was more than pleased with the bloody death of The Huntsman, She was taken aback by the sudden loss of Mother Hainter. Her expression carefully schooled, She gazed down at the tall, horned figure in his red and black velvet finery. "What, have you no kind words for the little witch who ministered for so long to those that call your city home?"

"No, my Queen. She played a part in thwarting my desires as well, so I find little concern for her wellbeing."

Yet, in the short time they had been together, She had found the advice that the bottle witch gave to be of great use and was troubled by her passing. Petulantly, She twisted the gold sceptre in Her hands before speaking. "I trust that the transformation you fashioned upon your servant was for your own amusement?"

He sneered. "What of it? He was mine, no matter the circumstance that proved his death, and I still claim my forfeit!"

"Here, in this court you have no right to claim any of my subjects for your own!"

Before he replied, The Dark Lord smiled in a manner that chilled the hearts of all who saw it. "Yes, my Lady, I do. Our ancient contract, signed with our blood, grants me that right, even in defiance of your will. Therefore, I now claim this mortal knight to be my rightful fiend."

The Knight of the Rose was shocked by the Dark Lord's words. "My Queen," he said with deliberate calmness, "I am pledged to you and no other. How may I continue to serve you if I live in his Court of Shadows?"

Looking at Thomas for a moment, The Queen replied, "Thomas, I weary of this game you play. I have clearly seen that your heart is no longer mine, and that of itself displeases me." Implacably, She turned Her attention to the Dark Lord. "Perhaps you wish to accept your gift now, rather than on the eve of all hallows, even though that auspicious event comes upon us so swiftly?"

Great and terrible was the smile that settled then on the Lord's face. Looking on it, any hope for mercy should Tom fall into this monster's hands evaporated..

Fearing she was set to abandon him, he cried out, "My Lady, I beg of you..."

But his words were overridden by the The Queen. "For as long as there has been a Land of Summer's Twilight the contract between this Lord and I has been paid in full at the agreed upon time. Indeed, my kingdom owes its very existence to this transaction. So, he *shall* receive his due, and who better to pay this debt than my own Knight?"

Words fell from the lips of the Dark Lord like silk scraping over rough homespun. "Yes. It has ever been so! And ever will be. It is not fitting for any to question a tradition that has seen a thousand times a thousand years name it their own!"

At that moment, such a look of uncertainty crossed Her face that Tom felt a surge of hope. The Lord of Darkness and of Death clearly saw the same, because he hurriedly added, "Then at this time and in this place, I will accept your gracious gift. That is, if we may speak together for but a little, someplace where unworthy ears cannot hear the words I would speak. Perhaps in your garden, amongst the roses that you so admire?"

The Lady's reply was sharp with bitterness. "Sir, do not presume to order my thoughts with your velvet words. I am the Queen eternal of this land, and I will do what I must do when I decide it should be done."

Unheeded by the two ranting monarchs, the foxes bounded up the cold marble steps. Reaching the throne, they did not rest at The Queen's feet but, without pause, leaped into Her lap, to curl there in tight circles of warm silver fur, soothing Her wrath.

Clearly pleased as she was that even blessed creatures such as these showed Her their allegiance, The Queen still had difficulty masking Her indecision.

"I wonder then, can this ancient tradition, this *tiend*, be broken?"

The foxes gazed up at The Queen's face and saw lurking deep within Her pale green eyes a host of abiding fears: fear of another plunge into madness, fear of Her own downfall at the hands of this persistent Dark Lord, and even greater than those, Her abiding fear that someday She would truly pass away, never to be reborn. Unblinking, the two creatures stared up at the Lady and whispered to her so softly that only She heard.

"Indeed…"

"there are other stories…"

"ones that tell…"

"of such an ending…"

"by one who "

"has the strength to do so."

Because She was newly re-born and still uncertain of Her authority, She whispered, "What stories? I have not heard them."

Below, at the base of marble steps, the Dark Lord, clearly sensing Her, hesitancy, determined to act. Leaping toward the throne he bellowed, "I tire of the games we play. You will be mine. Now!"

Thus was ever his way and ever his greatest weakness.

Horrified, the Knight of the Rose leaped toward the horned creature and flung the Dark Lord down the steps. Where, in a swirl of velvet cape and fine clothing, the Lord of Darkness and of Death hit the intricate marble tiles and slid across the polished floor, only stopping when he came up against the body of his former Huntsman.

For a brief measure, there was complete and utter silence in the great hall. Then he slowly climbed to his cloven feet and stood in the pool of blood that lapped at the body of his fallen minion. His hands clinched into fists at his sides as he looked up at The Queen, his face contorted with frustration as well as calculation.

With his hunting beasts dead, his vast army destroyed, and his impulsive bid to physically take The Queen thwarted, he was certain that it wasn't the moment to force his hand yet again. Even so, he was not yet ready to accept defeat.

The Queen, reaffirming Her anger, screamed so that the vast hall echoed with Her voice. "Leave! Leave my City. Now!"

With a barely perceptible bow, he answered, "My Lady, it would seem that on this day, yours is indeed the winning hand in our game. My poor Huntsman murdered, and now, your Knight shows no love at all for his new master. I think it best to come another time and continue our discussion then."

The Lord of Darkness and of Death looked at Thomas from under heavily lidded eyes and quietly issued his first command to him. "Go and fetch the two mortals. I would take them with me as The Queen desires." Then, expecting to be followed, he turned and walked slowly through the crowd.

Tom was duty bound to obey his Queen's wish, no matter what it be. With heavy heart, he quietly stepped toward the two women still crouching over the body of the fallen witch.

Janet, though, noted the look of cruel satisfaction sliding across the long, sharp face of the Dark Lord as he turned away and screamed, "NO! That's not going to happen!"

At her protest, The Queen turned and smiled down at the mortal girl. "And what might you do to prevent it?"

To which Janet replied, "You swore a promise to me! Or doesn't that mean anything to you, Queenie?"

The new-made Queen sighed and raised Her voice once more. "Halt!" At Her command, both the Dark Lord and Thomas paused.

She laughed unpleasantly. "Perhaps one day you will learn manners more fitting to this court, but you are right. We did indeed make such a promise. And that oath must have some meaning, even if I am not that same Queen, even though it were made to a mere mortal."

The subtle recasting of Her words chilled Janet's heart.

Then, setting her face into a hard smile, The Queen continued, "You, and your mother will go free, but only at such a time and place of my choosing."

"And Thomas?" Hoping against hope Janet waited for the answer that concerned her most.

"Thomas? Why, I myself have done nothing to harm your Thomas, so indeed my word is not broken. However, what The Lord of Darkness and of Death may choose to do is not and never will be a concern of mine." She paused before adding, "But it would amuse me to look on the despair in my Knight's eyes while he awaits the coming of All Hallows Eve... Be it so. He will stay close by my side until that time."

Looking at the Dark Lord, who now stood silently in the hall below, She assumed an air of certainty Janet wasn't convinced She actually felt. "Now, I weary of this turmoil. So be gone. And quickly!"

Without another word, the Dark Lord turned and stalked from the hall. But before he turned away, Janet witnessed something that she would have said impossible a moment before. Fleetingly, in the dark creature's eyes, she had seen regret and longing and even love for The Queen that he desired above all else.

You stupid, stupid man, you'll never capture Her heart this way. Never!

Janet opened her mouth to speak again, but The Queen emphatically ended their discussion, Her next words twisting deep into the mortal girl's heart. "Now, I wish to be alone with my Knight. Will someone not take these women to my tower? For they are no longer needed."

Thomas, who was still for a short time at least, the Knight of the Rose, looked up at his Queen and bowed. "My Lady, I give my thanks to your mercy and your wisdom." Then he continued, "With your leave, I will escort the mortals from your court?"

Unconcerned with what any other might want there in Her court, the Queen snapped, "Thomas, let me hear no more from you on this matter. What you wish does not concern me. It never has. It never will."

He started to protest but The Queen was having none of it. "Silence! Have you not sworn your oath as a knight of this realm to do as I command?" Her beautiful face calmly considered his troubled future. "You will come with me now. Others will attend the human chattel."

The Lady of the Summer Lands paused then and looked into his eyes. "And know you this, when All Hallows Eve is truly upon us, I will surely commend you then into the service of that great Lord for so long as you shall live."

THIRTY-FIVE

Although the Queen's Tower was a place of confinement for the two mortal women, it was not for the others in their company. The two foxes, who were sometimes also women but never mortal, were able to come and go as they pleased. Sometimes, for days on end, they were absent, never saying goodbye or even hello upon their return.

So, for the most part, mother and daughter were left to themselves, and in their long confinement many conversations came, both easy and hard, between them as they tried to fill a lifetime of absence.

Mairi's kind but shrewd advice made Janet realise just how different her life would have been if her mother had been there for her. Every conversation left Janet cursing the madness that made her absence necessary as well as the person that caused it. Though her eyes were often clouded with tears after speaking with Mairi, the young woman began to see more clearly who she was and what she could become. Until finally, she accepted that The Queen's wanton desire to escape her responsibilities as well as her ever-present anger were kindred to her own.

Giving into that anger feels so damn bloody good.
Well, most of the time...
But what does it really get me?

Janet's thoughts came back to the present when she heard her mother say, "I can only try to imagine how much has changed in our world after so many years... since... I was... was put in that... that *asylum*."

Without thinking, bitter words tripped from Janet's lips, "You do understand that it was your husband, my father, who put you there?"

Mairi cupped her daughter's face in her hands, "I... we shouldn't blame him for that, my dear. My mind had flown far, far away, and I was a danger to anyone near me, most of all to you." The older woman looked sadly at the younger. "It's just that losing all those years I could have spent watching you grow up torments me. Being there to help my daughter become the woman she is today is a privilege that I'll never have."

Dismayed by her mother's attitude, Janet continued, "You can't just ignore that Father put you in that place and then wouldn't tell me where you were until the day I came to visit you... Bloody hell, that... that seems so long ago now, but how can you tell time in this damned twilight world with no days or nights?

Then, after a moment's reflection, "But in our last few days together he seemed different, caring even. He despaired at what he'd done to you... and to me. I could maybe love the man he was then."

Her mother's voice was certain when she replied, "Janet, despite what you tell me, your father is a good man. I remember what he was like before my... madness. When I met him, I worked in the city library. It was on the shelves there that I first discovered a book with the old ballads printed in its pages. I fell in love with the stories they had told.

"My own mother had sung to me all the time, they were the songs of her youth, old songs from our island, from Jamaica. I guess that I'd heard them so often that I'd grown too used to the stories they had to tell. Then, when I found recordings of those songs... and the library had quite a collection of LPs... do they still make things like that... albums I mean?" Mairi waved her hand, dismissing the detail. "Anyway, when I heard those beautiful voices making the old tales new again, I was certain that I wanted to be a part of their tradition.

"After that I was always busking on the street or singing in whatever little club would let me get up on stage."

Then, looking at Janet with a gentle, trembling smile lighting her face, Mairi said, "It was in one of those cafés that I first met your father."

"The Club 320?"

"Yes. However did you guess? Oh, never mind. We had such good times together and soon became good friends with its owner and his family..."

"That was Daniel Parsons, wasn't it?"

"Oh yes, Dan was a delight to work for. Do you know him?"

"Did..."

"He's passed away, then."

"Yes." Janet sighed, then shrugged her shoulders. "There's still so much to tell you, Mother."

After a moment's reflection, Mairi continued, and what she told her daughter surprised Janet, "It was so very easy to fall in love with John. Tall. Handsome. He was so full of life and didn't care that we were from two completely different cultures.

"It was only later, after we had fallen in love, that I found out how very well off his family were. When he first showed me the Ravenscroft estate I was a bit overcome. Though I never met any of his family... they, just like my parents, had passed years before." Her mother's glistening eyes studied Janet for a moment before she asked, "Did you know that he was an only child?

"Anyway, barely a year later I fell pregnant with you, and by then your father's new business was flourishing. Both of us were excited about our daughter to be and what she would bring to our lives..."

"My very last memory is of looking up into his eyes as I lay in the hospital bed, waiting to deliver you, Janet. There was so much love in those eyes… We were so excited to have you…" Her voice trailed off, as Janet realised anew just how many years had been wasted due to The Queen's madness. Mairi reached out for Janet's hand and said, as if reading her mind, "I will never forgive that Queen for making me lose those years. Never."

Afterwards, Janet began to tell Mairi something about growing up, alone, in the vast Ravenscroft estate and what kind of father John Ravenscroft had been to her. Mairi assured her that every story described someone that she would never have wanted to know, much less loved.

Seeing the look of distress in her mother's eyes, Janet began to worry. "But I'm not being fair to the man that I was just starting to know. I hope he's still there when we get home."

Mairi wore a tired smile on her face. "Dear, after all these years I'll have to get used to a new John Ravenscroft anyway. That is if… *when*, we get back home. We will get home, won't we?"

Janet mutely nodded, hoping that it was true.

Smiling bravely, her mother asked, "And your life? What are you interested in? What have you been doing with it?"

Janet looked away, embarrassed by how very little she has actually done with her life.

Why did I waste all those years playing stupid games with my father? There's so much more I could have done…

And, if I hadn't met Thomas I'd be playing them still, wouldn't I?

When Janet answered, she felt particularly self-conscious. "Ever since I was thirteen all I ever wanted to do was to break every rule that Father threw in front of me. Making him as angry as possible was all that seemed to make me happy." She felt a little guilty as she added, "And I was really good at it! But I didn't know what else I was supposed to do. I just knew that I had to live my life as far away from him as possible." Their lofty prison gave them spectacular views over the great otherworldly forest. She gazed out at it now before adding. "I guess that would pretty much be here, wouldn't it?"

Her mother's eyes crinkled in a gentle smile, "Life always reaches out and grabs you whether you're ready for it or not."

Her mother's next question, though, caught her off guard. "So, have there been many young men in your life?"

"Thomas, there's only ever been Thomas."

"Surely there were others? You're a pretty young woman, after all…"

"No… never even once. All the other men, boys really, were just bloody boring or… put off by the colour of my skin or, even worse, excited by it."

Janet clutched her shoulders and, staring into space, pondered the one question that always lurked on the edge of her thoughts. "I've asked myself so many times what Thomas sees in me."

Mairi quickly replied, "Don't sell yourself so short!" Laying a comforting hand on Janet's arm, her mother added, "Perhaps you two were just meant for each other?"

"Maybe…"

Janet leaped to her feet and, buried in thought, began to pace across the tower roof that formed their comfortable sunlit prison.

Eventually she sat again on the low parapet overlooking the gardens below and ran a hand through her still short, cropped black hair. With the fingers of the other, she slowly traced the intricate stonework of the rooftop battlements. The air around her was fragrant with rose and apple from the garden below. But Janet didn't notice. Transfixed by the scene that played out within that garen, she watched The Lady and Her companion walk slowly along the wide pathways. Although Janet was unable to distinguish their conversation, she heard the soft murmur of their voices and the occasional burst of delighted laughter from The Queen. Both filled her with jealousy.

In truth, it was the figure beside The Queen that she watched so diligently. Even though she had not spoken to The Knight of the Rose since they were in the throne room together, Janet knew in her heart that she had forgiven him and longed to tell him so.

When Mairi sat down beside her daughter, they both gazed silently down at the small marble marker, already swathed in rich red roses, which rested in the garden to the side of the path where the two figures walked.

Janet sighed. "I miss Mother Hainter." Her face split into a grin before she added, "Right now we could use her sharp tongue and a cheeky boot in the backside as well."

Mairi stroked her daughter's face. "But at least she's at rest now after all of her years of labour…"

Laying her head on her daughter's shoulders, Mairi asked a question that both women had done their best to ignore. A question that troubled both their hearts. "When do you think we will be able to leave this horrible place?"

Janet scowled, "That's entirely up to that creature down there, and there's nothing we can bloody do to make her decide any faster."

At that moment the two silver foxes chose to leap into their laps, and, as both women begin to stroke the soft, silky fur of the two extraordinary animals, they immediately grew calmer. Janet stared down at the magical creatures before asking, "Yet you two always seem to go where you will. Is there no boundary that stops you?"

"Lady…" said the first fox.

"there are no barriers…" replied the second.

"for such as us." They chorused together.

"We walk…

"within the telling…

"of every story…"

"that has ever been told…

"or…

"will be told.

"New stories…"

"always replenish…"

"the old."

"And the one…"

"we live through…"

"now…

"may finally…

"surprise…

"us all."

Frustrated, Janet sprang to her feet again, barely aware of the fox that slipped gracefully from her lap onto the stone flagging. Pacing back and forth between the low walls of the parapet, Janet finally stopped in front of her mother, "New stories? Are there any brand new stories? How can we fashion a new tale that features us... myself and Thomas and you as well, Mother?"

Looking up at her daughter, Mairi grew serious. "I fear that your knight will never break his oath. To do that would make him a much lesser man than he would ever want to be. Especially in your eyes."

Bitterly Janet spat out a retort. "Then he's just going to quietly follow that bitch's every whim?"

Again, her mother offered advice calmly. "Rash, ugly words will not bring us any nearer to a solution."

"Well fuck this, and fuck your damned solution!"

Clearly shocked by her daughter's choice of words, Mairi asked, "I understand your anger, but must you use such common language?"

"I'm sorry, Mum... but sometimes it makes me feel better."

Just like my anger...

Better, for a moment but that's all!

Janet, though, saw the impact her coarse words had on her mother and resolved to at least try to sweeten her tongue.

Mairi's heart broke, though, when she heard the despair in her daughter's voice as she said, "Thomas swore to me that he had no love left for this Queen, yet he will not break his vow and come with us back to the world where he belongs. I just don't get it!"

Silently, Mairi rose to her feet and kissed Janet tenderly on her tear-stained cheek. But Janet wrenched away, still too angry to be consoled. "That bloody bitch! She promised me She wouldn't harm anyone that I held dear. And She won't, of course! It's that damned Dark Lord who'll grind Thomas under his giant splayed hoof and She will have kept Her fucking word!"

Faced with her daughter's outburst, Mairi sighed. "Our friend, the bottle witch told me more than once to never trust The Queen's word. No matter how carefully chosen an oath may be, it can always be twisted to serve Her purpose."

Despondent, Janet slumped beside Mairi and leaned into the comfort of her mother's arms. She stared down at Thomas who continued to walk dutifully beside his Queen, so far below. "How can I possibly leave Tom here in this wretched place?"

Mairi gathered her daughter into her arms and tried to comfort her in the only manner she knew. "My child, listen to me now, it may help you endure your misery."

At their feet, the two strange fox-women looked up at mother and daughter and smiled their sly smiles. They whispered then, so quietly that none but each other could hear their words.

"Excellent…
"a song."
"But which will she sing?"
"Hush, sister…
"and listen."

As the older woman began to sing, her voice was as soft as a child's lullaby that would calm her daughter's heart. But this was no cradle song.

> "Janet tied her kirtle green
> a bit above her knee,
> And she's gone to Carter Hall
> as fast as go can she."

Instantly recognising the song Janet added her voice to her mother's.

> "She'd not pulled a double rose,
> a rose but only two,
> When up there came young Tam Lin
> saying 'Lady, pull no more.'
>
> 'And why come you to Carter Hall
> without command from me?'
> 'I'll come and go', young Janet said,
> 'and ask no leave of thee.'
>
> He's taken her by the milk-white hand,
> An stroked her silkin' hair,
> And what they did then I cannot tell,
> Amongst those leaves so green.
>
> Janet tied her kirtle green
> a bit above her knee,
> And she's gone to her father's court
> as fast as go can she.'
>
> Well, up then spoke her father dear

and he spoke meek and mild,
'Oh, and alas, Janet,' he said,
'I think you go with child.'

'Well, if that be so,' Janet said,
'myself shall bear the blame,
There's not a knight in all your hall
shall get the baby's name.'

'For my love is an earthly knight
not of the elfin grey,
And I'd not change my own true love
for any knight you have'."

Janet clutched her mother's hands and despite her sadness the girl's eyes brightened as she softly repeated that last verse.

"For my love is an earthly knight
not of the elfin grey,
And I'd not change my own true love
for any knight you have."

Mairi stopped and, looking into her daughter's face, she asked, "Daughter, you say you love your Tom-Lyn?"

"Yes. Yes, I do."

"Then listen to the ballad until its end." Mairi held Janet's face in her two wrinkled hands and began to sing the final verses of the ancient ballad.

"Janet tied her kirtle green
a bit above her knee,
And she's gone again to Carter Hall
as fast as go can she.

'Oh, tell to me, Tam Lin,' she said,
'why came you here to dwell?'
'The Queen of Faeries caught me
when from my horse I fell.

Charles Vess

'And at the end of seven years
she pays a tithe to hell.
I so fair and full of flesh
and feared it be myself.

'But tonight is Hallowe'en
and the faery folk do ride.
Those that would their true love win
at Miles Cross they must bide.

'So first let past the horses black
and then let past the brown,
Quickly run to the white steed
and pull the rider down.

'For I'll ride on the white steed,
the nearest to the town,
For I was an earthly knight,
they give me that renown.

'Oh, they will turn me in your arms
to a newt or a snake,
But hold me tight and fear not,
I am your baby's father.

'And they will turn me in your arms
into a lion bold,
But hold me tight and fear not
and you will love your child.

'And they will turn me in your arms
into a naked knight,
But cloak me in your mantle
and keep me out of sight.'

In the middle of the night
she heard the bridle ring
She heeded what he did say
and young Tam Lin she did win."

THIRTY-SIX

As the words of the song faded, Janet sat silently gazing at the distant figure below in elegant red armour who knelt now in supplication before his Queen. "Thomas, what do I have to do to bring you safely home?" She turned back to her mother. "Good for her but there's more to the song isn't there?"

"Yes. The Queen is left angered and vengeful, cursing the girl and the man she rescued."

Janet couldn't stop her bitter words. "Just like this bloody bitch of a Queen who is set on ruining her Knight's life and his fucking honour."

Mairi considered her long-absent daughter for a moment before almost whispering, "Janet, forgive me, but I don't think such casual doggerel will ever get us the answers we need, or even deserve."

Quietly the older woman continued, "I didn't believe so at first, but don't you think that perhaps even our Queen, unlike the Lady of the ballad, deserves to be left with some small measure of happiness?"

Hands clenched, Janet cried out, "No. I. Don't!"

"Is there no forgiveness in your heart for Her then? For all She has done to my life I do look for it in mine." Janet could hardly believe she was hearing this, given everything her mother had suffered, yet Mairi continued: "After all, there is still some tiny part of The Queen lodged within us both. It always will be."

Mairi's hand rose to gently stroke her daughter's shocked face. "Our friend the bottle witch once explained that there was no reason for either one of us to fear that thought. After all, it gifts us with the sight to see this land and all the beauty that is here."

Janet whispered hollowly, "And all the horrid creatures that live here as well."

Her mother laughed softly, "Yes, that's plain enough. I would be well content to live out all my years without ever seeing that tall horned creature ever again But, daughter, this land, any land really, is a reflection of those that govern it.

"Even in our world…" And here the older woman paused for a moment of reflection before continuing, "If you consider any particular country, you can see the mind of its rulers at work. So, if ugliness, fear, and monsters stalk that land, then that is what I fear you will find within the heart of its Lord or Lady and the advisors who rule with them."

Reluctantly Janet found herself slowly nodding in agreement – she knew what her mum meant – and this seemed to encourage Mairi, "Remember the dead and withered landscape we walked through on our way here?"

Janet's shoulders tensed, "How could I blood… ah, forget?"

"Look around you. From this tower, all we see is a world that is green and growing, lush with life. Breathe the air. Doesn't it set your blood racing? Doesn't that at least speak to there being some element of kindness in its Queen?"

Janet couldn't help replying. "But what about the casual cruelty that we've seen all around us? What about the utter darkness of that Dark Lord's dungeon? Isn't that a part of this world, too?"

Her mother smiled. "Yes, of course, there is some part of that darkness in all of us as well. Yet here, if there were no simmering hatred between this Lord and Lady, then do you think that their two lands would run with so much useless spilled blood? I doubt it."

Janet smiled. "Mother, I've made so many mistakes in my life. If you'd been there to talk me out of some of them I'd be a different person today."

Her mother's hands reached out to hold hers. "Different, yes, but perhaps no better. Your mistakes make you who you are just as your triumphs do. And Janet, you are a fine person. You truly are."

A flash of understanding warmed Janet's heart as she remembered their long journey to The Queen's city and watching as the two older women spent hours and hours with each other, constantly talking and laughing together. "It seems so stupid now, but on our journey here I think I was jealous of all the time you spent with the bottle witch." Wistfully, she continued, "And all I ever did was sulk and feel sorry for myself. I wasn't much fun, was I?"

Janet looked directly into Mairi's eyes. "Forgive me."

"Yes, of course. You're my daughter, and I'll always love you."

At that moment, the foxes roused themselves, to leap playfully from lap to shoulder and back to lap before standing on the stone flooring in front of the Janet and her mother. They stared quietly up at the two mortal women for a moment before looking slyly at each other. Then they began to speak, their voices once more raised in perfect harmony. "This is a sad tale that speaks of a Lord and a Lady who always sit their separate thrones in every story that has ever been told of them.

"Never, never ever, could they remember what they had done to bring them to the same lonely end from one telling of it to the next.

"They both endlessly repeated every mistake they had made, but seldom any small kindness they had rendered each other again and again and again. Most times their story caused great harm to those who pledged themselves to their service and much too seldom good as well.

"But never did this Lord and this Lady ever win to a satisfying resolution.

"So their story begins again and again, always different in its parts but always arriving at the same sad conclusion."

A rush of understanding came over Janet as she considered what the two foxes just said. "Okay. Okay, I get it! Your lady in the story is our Queen and the Queen in that song and the Lord is the devil who's owed his due and that creepy dude with the horns, and maybe if they were happy together then everything here would be better. But what can I... *we* do, to sort out this stupid mess?"

A satisfied smile played across Mairi's face before she replied, "Why, we must change the story that's being told. Especially since this new Queen seems bent on making the same wretched choices as before. Allowing that to happen will only bring us to the same tragic ending."

Janet grinned, "Like the man said, same as it ever was."

The foxes continued to stare up at the girl expectantly, until a look of understanding transformed Janet's features and she continued, "Oh... If the story is changed, then Thomas will be free to do as he wishes and he could be mine again."

Janet slipped her slim arm through her mother's and looked down at the two silver foxes that were curled again in her lap. Then she made a quick decision, "So I... I'm an intruder here. And unlike the Queen or anyone else in this entire cuckoo land, my life in the mortal realms, will be over and finished in a heartbeat. Out, out brief candle and all that bloody crap."

Right Janet... no bloodies, no damns and most certainly no fucks.
You can at least try, can't you?

"So maybe... I don't have the luxury of letting my life tell its story as slowly as if it's on some ancient dial-up connection."

Mairi laughed and shook her head. "Never mind dear, I don't always exactly understand your choice of words, but their meaning is clear enough. Go on."

"Maybe... maybe my 'human' eyes can see what every creature here can't or won't? In a land made from a hundred zillion stories, maybe I can just simply tell a new tale with a better ending and then try to make it true?"

Both foxes sat up straight and began to speak, their words spinning out in their usual sing-song manner.

"Wise Janet...

"must help write...

"a new end...

"to this eternal tale."

The girl laughed, "You mean like 'and they lived happily ever after.' That ending?"

The first fox laughed, "It can be happy...

"or sad." The second continued.

Both foxes intoned together then, "It simply needs a new ending, satisfying to each person who lives it."

THIRTY-SEVEN

When the moon was full once more, riding bright and strong over The Land of Summer's Twilight, Janet and her mother were released without warning or ceremony from their long confinement in the Queen's tower. A formal note delivered to Janet by the two fox-women informed them of their freedom, and, once read, the note simply dissolved into crisp brown leaves that crumbled in her hands.

"You may go now."

Having little to pack, they were quickly ready to leave even though Janet delayed as much as possible, repacking the meagre contents of her traveling satchel over and over again, hoping against hope for a chance to bid Thomas farewell.

I swear I'll take you away from your bloody Queen... somehow.

Just past the arched doorway of their prison, Janet paused, gazing curiously at the elaborately carved leather satchel that her mother had slung over her shoulder. But when she offered to help the older woman carry it, Mairi only smiled secretively and replied, "No, thank you. It's just a gift from our friend the bottle witch that might be useful someday."

"Okay. Let's get out of this bloody... sorry, this place, before that crazy queen changes her mind."

Scampering at their feet but never entangling them, the foxes followed the two mortal women along a broad paved roadway that led them straight and true away from the walls of the great city, until it reached a crossroad where it branched into three equally inviting paths.

Her mother smiled gently, humming a particular ballad to herself. "Perhaps we should just flip a coin?"

Janet laughed, "Do you have a three-sided one, then?"

But the foxes seemed in no doubt; with an assertive toss of their sleek silver heads they kept to the left-hand path. Putting their faith in Aellin and Delian, the two women followed, the foxes' playful barking distracting them from thoughts from an uncertain future.

Throughout the journey that followed, the older woman carried that carefully-wrapped satchel.

Eventually their journey was done, their destination reached.

The two foxes scampered about their feet in the thick heather that pushed up against the foot of one of the seven great stones that marked the boundary between the two worlds. Mairi's voice was full of wonder when she spoke, "Can we really just walk through that stone?"

Janet grinned, "Yes. Anyway, I did it before, so why not again?"

Around them, endless twilight covered the rolling landscape that enveloped the great standing stones. One great enormous slab of granite tilted toward the west, as if it had come to life once and taken a tentative step before becoming immutable stone once more. Its surface, pitted by the wind and rain and patterned with lichen, was a record of its lifetime and its age, old past imagining.

Janet looked up as a brief shower of briskly moving rain momentarily left the surface of the stone glistening in the rays of a sun that never quite touched the true Lands of Faerie. She turned to her mother, "Come on, home is waiting for us."

The older woman's face lit with anticipation. "It will be good to see your father."

Janet crouched down in the heather and smiled at the two foxes. "Thank you so much. We couldn't have done without your help. On the road home and... elsewhere, too."

The soft tongues of the otherworldly creatures licked her hand as Janet continued, "Maybe we'll see you again. Hope so anyway!"

Mairi awkwardly shifted her pack, eagerly reaching for her daughter's hand. "Okay, let's go..."

And then, without so much as a single glance behind them, they stepped toward the great stone and disappeared into its unforgiving surface.

Behind them, the foxes ran in excited circles around the base of the great standing stone and yipped joyfully up at the full moon that hung heavily in the sky over all the land of Summer's Twilight.

THIRTY-EIGHT

On the other side of that long, bewildering step through stone, Janet and Mairi stopped and looked around at the boulder strewn landscape. The rolling hills looked much the same as before, but edging the top of the heather and bracken was a sharp orange light that made the earth here and everything in it seem to glow. Breaking through a tumult of dark blue-grey clouds, the light from a red glowing sun washed over the land.

Seeing that simple beauty, they were relieved to know they were home. As they walked briskly down a lightly gravelled trail, Janet linked her arm through her mother's and smiled warmly at Mairi, trying to mask the worry that continued to tumble through her thoughts.

Okay, we're back, but where the hell are we? Somewhere in the Highlands, by the look of it, but that covered a vast area and the weather could be deadly.

"Mum, can we walk a little faster and maybe find out where we've ended up?"

Over the next rise, Janet was relieved to see the ancient stone bridge that arched over the River Nairn near the road to Aviemore. The familiar landmark lent energy to both their feet. And as they drew closer to the bridge, both mother and daughter saw a figure waiting on its far end, silhouetted against the skyline. Far behind that standing figure, the city of Inverness was vividly lit by the glow of the setting sun.

"Want to guess if the sun is setting or rising?" Janet smiled grimly to herself. "It looks like we'll be able to ask someone pretty soon."

Just don't be that stupid troll creature. I'm too tired to play any guessing games with the likes of it.

Near the ancient bridge they paused, still wondering who the figure might be, when suddenly Janet's mother broke away and ran eagerly across the stone paving. A single word escaped her lips, "John!" before she was enveloped in the arms of the tall, heavyset man who had been waiting on her return for the past eighteen years.

Moments later, Mairi spared an instant to look back and wonder at her daughter's reluctance to join them. Beyond excited, she called through the dimming air, "Janet, it's your father, come to greet us back to our own world." Turning again, Mairi looked up at her husband.

For his part, John Ravenscroft seemed to recognise that her sparkling eyes were clear of the madness that had once possessed her. He embraced his wife again with gentle, bear-like arms.

Janet still hesitated. Genuinely relieved to hear the happiness in her mother's voice, she became increasingly nervous as she wondered just how her father would greet his wayward daughter. Seeing his broad, reassuring smile, though, her pace quickened.

Suddenly, the stone of the ancient bridge shuddered under her feet, and once again, the enormous troll creature stood directly in front of Janet, blocking her path.

Fuck! Has to be sunset then…

This time, more impatient than terrified, Janet raised her voice to the huge beast before it made any demands of its own. "All right, relax, I've got your blessed password."

On the other side of the bridge, John Ravenscroft only saw that his daughter was standing directly under an enormous shadow of some kind. He reacted, as any father would, ready to tear Janet away from whatever it was, at whatever cost. But Mairi put her hand on his arm. "John, wait. I'm sure there's nothing to fear. Our daughter is more capable than you'll ever know. We should just wait."

With an effort, he struggled to trust his wife's judgment. And, with his hands held firmly in hers, John clearly saw the great hulking beast that towered over his daughter. He shuddered. What John Ravenscroft witnessed next made it clear that his daughter was no longer the spoiled, wilful child she had been before she left.

Out on the bridge, Janet looked calmly up at the enormous troll as its deep rumbling breath escapes wetly from the creature's craggy mouth. "My lady, you need no password ever again, your knight has pledged his word and his life for your safe passage on this night or any other." For one brief moment, Janet's heart leaped with hope. "Thomas! Is he here?"

"No, my lady. Upon The Queen's word you will never see the Knight of the Rose again."

"No…!"

"But he has sent you a parting gift and a message as well."

The giant beast fumbled at its belt and from it pulled two enormous leather gloves from the wallet that hung there. Pushing his hands into those gloves, he reached around for the pack hanging across his shoulders. Grunting once, the creature lifted the gift out and casually set it between them both on the bridge, smiling at Janet as he did so. She gasped, then laughed and then wept as she looked at Tom's Vincent Black Lightning, polished and shining as if it were brand new, balanced on its kickstand, resting on the stone flagging in front of her.

Janet swung her legs over the cycle and sat its high seat, lost in memories. When she picked up his leather helmet, the fading fragrance of a dozen sweet herbs, picked in the far distant lands of Summer's Twilight, still clung to it. In despair, Janet looked out into the gathering darkness and whispered, "Thomas! I need you more than this damn bike!" Fresh tears ran down her cheeks as vivid memories of all that they'd done, both the bad and the good, washed over her.

Lost in that swirl of memories, Janet didn't notice at first when the troll gently placed a small sealed scroll in her hands. Her fingers trembled as she unrolled it and began to read,

My Lady Janet,
It is gratifying to know that there can be such great wisdom in one so young as yourself. Never again will I pledge my unconditional oath to anyone, save that person be you.
Thomas

Quietly, she stared at the words scrawled elegantly across the sheet of paper until the sharp scrape of a belt buckle on hard stone broke her concentration. When she looked, up the great beast was clambering over the side of the bridge returning to its station beneath its span. After the deep shadows there swallowed it, she whispered, "Thank you for your kindness."

Softly, hanging in the cool night air, she heard the great beast's reply, "Lady, I am your servant now and always."

Slowly walking the bike across the stone span, she studied her parents at the other end of the bridge, their arms wrapped around each other in a warm embrace. That shared intimacy made her heart break into a thousand pieces as she muttered, "I know our love is stronger than any stupid bloody vow!"

"Somehow... I'll get you away from that damned creature!"

Mairi looked at her daughter and said, "Janet, listen, we must go home now. We need rest. Then we have to tell your father everything… everything that's happened to the both of us." She looked up again at her husband. "From what our daughter has told me, I'm sure there are resources at your disposal that will help us find her Thomas and rescue him from the desperately unpleasant fate that waits for him now.

"Am I right, John?"

Ravenscroft squeezed his wife's hand and then looked down at Janet. Layers of guilt from so many past conflicts simply fell away, leaving behind only deep, unconditional love for his daughter. Janet, remembering those very same fights, bit her tongue, keeping any sarcastic comments to herself. Both women, though, returned his smile when John replied at last, "Yes. Whatever is mine is yours."

Janet gazed steadily at her father before asking, "So, how exactly did you manage to be right here, right now waiting for us?"

"Ah… I remembered your story of the troll and this bridge and thought that it was the best place to wait. As for my excellent timing… Well, I've been here, waiting for you, every evening, for the last six months."

"Oh! Six months, has it been that long?"

"Yes, it has."

His admission more than anything else told Janet that her father had changed from the impatient man she'd lived with for so many years.

Janet's surprise must have been obvious, because he whispered, "Call it penance or guilt or whatever you like, but I want to start over Janet. If that's even possible?"

"I guess… I hope so."

Mairi took her daughter's and her husband's hands with her own and said, "Then, let's go, I want to see my home again."

As they walked toward the small parking lot just beyond the stone bridge where John's car was parked, he glanced at his wife and noticed the burden that she had carried for so long without complaint. "Your pack looks heavy, love. Let me carry it for you."

With a sigh, Mairi shifted the strap from one weary shoulder to the other. "I'm fine."

Then as he opened the car door, he looked back at his daughter as she supported the heavy bike with her body and asked, "It doesn't look like you need a ride?"

Straddling the Vincent, Janet grinned back at her father, "No, da. No, I don't. I'll see you two love birds at home, okay?" And kicking the bike into gear she pulled out of the parking lot and flew up the road toward Inverness.

Her mother looked at John and sighed, "Our daughter has grown into a fine young woman, hasn't she? I only wish I could have been there to see it happen…"

John's words tried to lighten her dark mood, "Quick then, get in. Let's see if we can get home before her!"

Under the stone bridge, curled comfortably in the troll's wide lap, two silver foxes looked at each other and smiled, "Wasn't that nice."

"A family reunion…

"is always…

"so very nice."

"Always."

THIRTY-NINE

Since the night that so many had been slaughtered at his front gates, everyone that had worked for John Ravenscroft had tendered their resignations, leaving him alone to look after the great, empty house. So the lovely singing voice that carried down the hall and into John's office where he sat with his head buried in his folded arms, fast asleep, was the first welcoming sound to counter the stillness that had settled for so long over his estate.

After they had returned the night before, Janet, claiming exhaustion, had immediately retreated to her room. But Mairi had been too excited at being home again to follow her daughter's example, and had walked arm in arm with her husband through the great house. As they did so, she had begun to tell him a little of what had happened in that other land.

For John, there had been six long months alone in a great empty house where he'd spent far too many hours dealing with the aftermath of that single night of mayhem. But it was his intense guilt over the disappearance of his daughter and wife that had given him so many sleepless nights. Determined to devote himself solely to finding his family, Ravenscroft had resigned as CEO of his vast business enterprise and walked away from the myriad boards that had plundered so much of his time.

Later, after Mairi succumbed to exhaustion as well and fell asleep in their bedroom, John had felt awkward joining her after so long a time apart. So he'd gone down the hall to his office and sat at his desk, where he carefully considered everything he'd heard and seen that night.

All that he had learned convinced him that time in the otherworld moved much faster than here. The noticeable change in Janet and her attitude towards him made him certain of it. Still, it cost him great effort to push aside his lingering doubts and simply accept the story his wife had told him as true. What other choice was there? As much as he had tried to convince himself otherwise, he had seen his daughter subsumed by some otherworldly force and the ravening beasts on that night of slaughter. Then just yesterday he had witnessed her interaction with some huge creature – presumable the troll – out on the bridge.

Exhaustion had finally claimed him as well and he'd fallen asleep at his desk with the lights still shining brightly down on him.

Now the rich, fluid notes of what he was certain was his wife's voice woke John Ravenscroft as well as stirring memories buried deep within him for far too many years. Standing, he walked down the hall following the lovely voice, tinged with an intriguing but unfamiliar accent.

>"Moon shine tonight come mek we
>dance and sing.
>Moon shine tonight come mek we
>dance and sing.
>Mi deh rock so
>You deh rock so
>Under banyan tree.
>
>Ladies may curts and gentleman may bow
>Ladies may curts and gentleman may bow
>Mi deh rock so
>You deh rock so
>Under banyan tree
>Mi deh rock so
>You deh rock so
>Under banyan tree"

He found Mairi sitting comfortably in a high-backed chair facing a lace-curtained window looking out over the gardens, the morning light washing across her soft features.

Without speaking, John stood silently, basking in the pleasure of having his wife as a part of his life once more.

>"Come we join hands and mek we
>dance around and sing
>Come we join hands and mek we
>dance around and sing
>Mi deh rock so
>You deh rock so
>Under banyan tree
>Mi deh rock so
>You deh rock so
>Under banyan tree."

Reaching the final verse, Mairi opened her eyes to see her husband looking down at her with tenderness and love. She responded with a warm smile. "There you are, love."

"Mairi, I don't think I remember you singing that song before?"

She laughed. "That's because it's an old Jamaican tune my mother and I used to sing together. The words always bring her and my father back so vividly – which I suppose is why I sang it so seldom in years past… But that will change, soon, I hope."

Her face, momentarily sombre, brightened again.

"But enough of that, let's get started, shall we?"

Soon afterwards they were both seated at the immense oak desk in John's office, waiting for Janet to join them.

Although he knew she was eager to discuss their rescue plan for Thomas, Janet nevertheless entered the room cautiously, perhaps recalling their many confrontations here. Her mother's welcoming smile helped reassure her as she slid into a proffered chair.

From the outset, John tried to dominate the discussion out of long-ingrained habit. But as they carefully walked through their planned abduction of Thomas, he was interrupted again and again by his wife or Janet offering an important piece of information or advice on a subject that he knew nothing about. Finally realising that this was not the boardroom of one of his firms where he would have ordered everyone to do as he wanted, he took a deep breath and simply listened.

After all, their plan boiled down to an all-out assault on what he understood was the High Court of the Faerie, about which he had absolutely no knowledge whatsoever.

Like planning a hostile takeover, but with more at stake. Much more.

At one end of his great oak desk, made conspicuous by no one ever mentioning it, rested his wife's dusty backpack. Occasionally, he noticed when his daughter's eyes lingered on it with a certain amount of curiosity as well. But for the moment, Mairi had chosen not to acknowledge it was there, and he decided to respect her unspoken wish.

When Mairi cleared her throat and spoke, all of his attention focused on what she had to say. "Last night, I tried to explain something of what happened to Janet and I in the last few weeks, but John, I'm at a loss to tell you who Mother Hainter was and how much she meant to us both. We really wouldn't be here now without her help."

Wiping a tear from her eye, Janet finished her mother's thought, "Her death was just so completely unexpected." Then the young woman murmured softly, "She called herself a witch, and she really did have a potion for any ailment you could ever have."

Together they chorused, "And they worked, too!" Both women looked at one another and shared a quick, fragile smile.

John was doing his best to keep an open mind, but couldn't help asking, "A witch? Really?"

"Yes, really."

Concerned that he was missing something vital here, he said, "Well then, can you tell me who or what she was and what part she had to play in all this?

"We'll try..."

Much later, after the two women finished telling him everything that they remembered about their friend Mother Hainter, they looked at John hoping that he understood what she meant to them.

Under their steady inquiring gazes, He shifted uneasily, still finding it difficult to accept a world so radically different from what he had always known to be true. Then, with a shrug of his shoulders, he determined to face this new world with all its dangers.

"Well, I will say that I would like to have met this witch of yours. However, I do still have a lot of questions for you both."

But at that moment, Janet asked a question of her own. "Mum, did she ever tell you where she came from? Or was she just a truly oddball fairy witch?"

Mairi smiled at her daughter, "Well, to start with, dear, Mother Hainter wasn't one of the Fae. She was the last of a race that had lived on both sides of the border for far longer than any of the Fae and most certainly any mortal. I suspect that only her two fox friends are older. Perhaps far, far older?"

John couldn't help himself. "Fox...

Mairi squeezed her husband's hand. "Yes, love, I'm sure you'll meet them soon enough, so I'm not even going to even *try* to explain those two."

Then as John sought to ask more of the questions that troubled him, Mairi brushed his lips with her fingertips. "Hush now, there's much more for us to discuss, so let's get down to it, shall we?

"Because tonight is Halloween. Samhain. All Souls Night as The Queen called it, the night named in the ballad of Tam-Lin, the very night when Thomas will be given to that dark creature's service. The night on which the story we are a part of takes place, a story that we will now try to fundamentally change.

"And only on this very night can we hope to do so."

Many hours later, after a firm plan was agreed between the three conspirators, John leaned toward his daughter and held out his hand. In it was the gun he had taken so long ago from the chief of his security force. "After you were gone, I began to do some research of my own. So, I had the bullets in the clip made with solid lead, because from what I read that will do serious damage to any of the creatures we'll have to deal with tonight."

Janet hesitated, reluctant to accept such a lethal thing when Mairi reached between them. Gently but firmly, the older woman closed her husband's hand around the weapon with her own. "Your daughter won't need that kind of weapon tonight. This, however, will prove most useful."

She pulled a small leather bag from the satchel that she'd brought with her from The Land of Summer's Twilight and placed it in front of Janet. Her daughter fingered the curiously engraved leather for a moment before loosening the drawstrings and pulling out its contents. Suddenly, Janet shuddered, because what she held in her hands was The Huntsman's insidious net.

"Mother! No! I don't want to even touch this..."

"But you must."

"Where... where did you get it?"

Staring enigmatically at her daughter, Mairi sighed. "I may seem old to you, but I still have a few secrets to my name. When she gave me this, our friend Mother Hainter said that it might be useful one day."

Fingering the mesh of the net, Janet guessed why she'd been given this particular gift. "Must I use this horrid thing to hold Thomas?"

Mairi stroked her hand. "The Huntsman's net is gifted with many special properties. One of them is that it will never release what it has caught until the one who cast it gives that command. So, if you want to be certain to bring your Thomas safely home, then the answer is yes.

"Because even though his heart wants to follow you, he will refuse. He is the Knight of the Rose and has sworn to do The Queen's bidding, no matter what it may be. And for him, a man that breaks his word is simply worth nothing."

"Damn! Sorry. Okay, I… I understand that. But he just needs to be bloody careful who he pledges his word to, doesn't he?"

Her mother drew a deep breath before answering, "Yes, of course. We all do." She considered Janet, then her husband for a moment before continuing, "So are we all agreed, then? Since there is nothing we can do to change Thomas' will in this matter, we shall instead change his part in the story. When we do that, then we will change the Queen's too. And just maybe all their stories will end well enough. At least I do hope so!"

All three faced each other around that desk and nodded in agreement. On John Ravenscroft's face, though, there was a shadow of doubt as he tried to accept so much that he had called an outright lie all his life. Mairi saw that doubt, but shrewdly chose not to confront him about it, knowing that what happened this night would put an end to it once and for all. She squeezed his hand briefly before speaking again. "I think now would be the right time to show you both what was put in my keeping by my friend. After all, I brought it with me the whole long journey back to our world so I could show it to you."

She smiled and carefully untied the leather wraps that bound the mysterious object inside her satchel, then slid it across the table. Looking down at the slim folio in front of her, Janet asked in amazement, "Mum, you brought a book all the way from The Queen's tower?"

"Yes. Yes, I did."

Curious, Janet gestured at the book that, to her, and surely her father as well, looked small and insignificant.

"What's in it, a short poem?"

"You could say that. The history of all our worlds does have a certain poetry to it."

"In that? But there can't be more than dozen pages there, if that!"

Mairi's answer was simple. "This book is a record of every story that's ever been told and someday every story that ever will be. No matter how small it may look to us, it still carries a record of every one of those tales in its pages."

Unable to take her eyes off the volume, Janet whispered, "May I?" And after Mairi nodded her assent, the young woman's fingers brushed lightly across the inlaid gold letters of the title: The Book of the Summer Lands.

Opening it, Janet gasped when she saw the story recorded there on the book's first vellum page, yellowed now with age. At once she beckoned her father closer and whispered, "Oh, come see. Come see."

As Mairi watched on, Janet and her father slowly read page after page, each one magnificent enough to be in an elaborate illuminated manuscript. Yet inscribed onto the surface of each vellum sheet was no *Book of Days* or *Biblical Treatise* but the story of a great and devastating tragedy that began when the stars and the moon themselves were newly born. A tragedy that divided the world of mortals from that of The Fae, an utter separation that still blighted both worlds to this day.

Depicted on page upon page, followed by one more page and another and yet others was a world of beauty, shimmering with liquid crystalline colours that glowed from every minute detail of a place and life long forgotten, all rendered with heart-breaking simplicity.

Impossibly long was this tale, yet it was somehow contained within the pages of one slender volume held between the hands of a young woman seated at a desk with her father close by her side.

Looking up, John's hold tightened on Janet's arm as he looked up at his wife and asked, "How is it done? I was inside the story? It was as if I were playing an essential part of it, even as I read the pages where it was written."

Mairi smiled, "Many times I've asked myself the same question, but I was told that it was just another aspect of the book."

Janet's hands began to tremble as they moved lightly across later pages that depicted the inhabitants of each newly created world as they tried again and again to regain that world of heart and mind that some among them still recalled; a sublime world that once was theirs simply for the asking. Yet for all their efforts, those who lived within the borders of those broken lands continued to diminish and weaken.

There were other tales as well. Less important, perhaps, but still told with great beauty and soaring happiness, leavened oftentimes by death and no little darkness. Many were ancient ballads copied out in all their infinite variations. Flipping through those pages, Janet and her father saw that different hands had inscribed different stories. At each story's expected end, there was a single blank page that somehow suggested to both that it waited patiently to be filled someday.

Janet looked up at her mother and asked, "How could anyone possibly know how many pages to bind into this… this *book*?

"I think that Mother Hainter or someone quite like her subjected it to a sort of sympathetic magic, ensuring that there would always be enough pages, no matter the length of any tale inscribed in it."

Finally, minutes or hours later, Janet realised that she was looking at a depiction of the story of The Queen of Summer's Twilight. Spilling across page after page after page was a multitude of tellings, each with minute variations that always ended with terrible tragedy or great loneliness.

Excited, Janet tried to explain to her father, "This is The Queen, the one you'll meet tonight... It's Her story that we have to change."

Janet gasped, though, when she discovered her own life story flowing across the pages and that of Thomas, the Knight of the Rose as well. The tragedy of her mother's madness and her father's retreat into solitude and greed quickly followed. In those stories the writing was fresh and the illuminations hastily executed, as if done by a crude but loving hand.

Mum?

And then she turned to what was, at least for now, the book's final page and saw that it was blank. Looking at that simple sheet of as yet unmarked vellum, it seemed to Janet that it waited, impatiently perhaps, for the outcome of the very story they were a part of this night and then, even, what would follow after in the days and years to come.

John's hoarse voice rumbled in his daughter's ear, "If what's in this book is true, and I'm certain that it is, then I have wasted my life. I've devoted it to only one thing, accumulating more and more wealth. And I've squandered that wealth by controlling other people's lives, bending them to my will so that I could accumulate even more. No matter how substantial that horde of gold and silver, it could never be enough to buy back the beauty of the world that is shown in the pages of this book. No wealth can buy back that happiness, that joy."

John placed his hands gently over his wife's and looked deeply into her eyes before whispering, "I have failed you miserably and... my daughter. And I... I failed myself as well. Can you ever forgive me?"

His wife smiled warmly at him, "Of course... but perhaps, when this night is over, we should all heed the lessons here and live our life together in a different, more gentle manner."

Mairi lifted her hand then to brush away a single tear that fell slowly down her husband's face. "This very book will be our gift to The Queen tonight. Pray that She will accept and read from it or none of us will ever escape the tragedy of the story that She has been a part of for long ages past."

As night fell over the lands of mortals, Janet's family stood once more on the vast moors that swept across the Scottish Highlands. Her mother and father tried to keep their emotions in cheek as they watched their daughter rev the motor of the huge Vincent Black Lightning. But when Janet ran the motorcycle as fast as it would go straight toward the enormous standing stone directly in her path, they turned away, waiting for tragedy. Neither noticed that Janet's eyes were tightly shut, her hands clinched in fear on the handlebars as she hurtled toward that rough slab of granite.

Keep 'em shut! If I don't actually see that damned stone I might actually be able to go through with this... again.

Her father couldn't stop an anguished cry, "No!" Then he was surprised and immensely grateful when Janet abruptly disappeared into the surface of the great stone. He gaped in amazement, though, when immediately behind his daughter two beautiful silver foxes scampered out of the thick heather and launched their graceful bodies through the air directly into the same stone.

I suppose I'll need to grow accustomed to this sort of thing.

FORTY

Bouncing onto the hard ground on the other side of the border between the two lands, Janet gave her brakes a tight squeeze, bringing the Vincent to a stop, scattering a shower of small pebbles and loose bracken. Looking around, Janet realised that this was exactly where she and her mother stepped through the stone.

Was that only yesterday?

Rolling swiftly across the sky above her were ominous blue-black clouds with occasional rumbles from distant thunder. Around her the heather was thick and fragrant. Janet pulled the collar of her leather jacket up and Thomas' helmet down, snug over her head, and hoped that it wouldn't rain until after their task was done.

The borderlands are so freaky.
Rain never happens in Faerie.
A light mist every evening, but never heavy rain.

When the clouds suddenly split apart, illuminating everything around her with the brilliant reds and oranges of the setting sun, she realised that what she was looking at in the distance was her earth and sky.

Right.
The border between them is like a sheet of cling film tonight.

Through another quick break in the clouds, Janet caught a glimpse of the full moon that she guessed was part of the land of The Queen. Despite the daunting task ahead of them, she found herself smiling, eager to get on with it. She revved the engine of the Black Lightning and eased the heavy machine back into gear. As quickly as she could, Janet picked her way through overgrown bracken and high, weathered outcrops of rock.

Okay. Mum said that all I have to do is hide somewhere along the border and The Queen would just come to me.

Later, when the moon had finished playing its game of hide and seek with the billowing clouds and began to softly illuminate the vast landscape around her, Janet heard a sound in the distance. It was a thunder that didn't come from any lightning in the distant sky of her world but the pounding of a thousand of hooves on the ground.

At first sight, the riders looked like a vast moving shadow, hardly substantial enough to be anything real. But as the thundering host drew nearer and every indistinct shadow became a vividly real creature of the Fae, Janet began to shiver. As they pounded past the enormous boulder where she hid, deep in the shadows, some were close enough for her to reach out and touch them.

The Queen sat astride a great, black mare, its streaming mane and ornate, jewelled harness hung with fifty silver bells and nine. Beside Her, mounted on a horse of purest brown, rode The Lord of Darkness and of Death, a smile of great satisfaction twisting his thin lips.

Just behind them both, sitting easily on a milk white, steed was Thomas, the Knight of the Rose, clad in leather armour of deepest red. And following them were a thousand times a thousand lords and ladies of the Fae court, most clutching tall lances bearing great fluttering banners, hued with every colour known to their Earth and some from lands beyond, some woven with intricate designs, displaying the sigil of The Court of the Rose and some few with that of The Court of Shadows.

Tumbling through the air, beside and around and behind each mounted lord and lady was every manner of fairy creature, both large and small, winged and not, horned and goat-footed, web-toed and one-eyed and long of tail, sometimes covered in fur or scales of green, sometimes with skin of palest of purple.

All those there tonight had sworn their allegiance to The Queen and ridden with Her to compass the borders of Her kingdom, ensuring Her continued dominion over it. All save The Lord of Darkness and of Death, and in his heart he wished for more than just a simple allegiance or yet another servant to torment.

With the great host, but not a part of it, unconcerned with hoof or lance or boot or sword, ran two silver foxes barking in utter delight. All, though, were faintly lit by both the fading red glow of a sun that set, not in the Lands of Summer's Twilight but over the trembling, paper thin border beyond in the mortal realms, and their own moon with its attendant stars.

Close behind the great thundering host, her heart pumping, her mouth set with determination, Janet rode the Vincent, forcing her way in amongst the riders. Just ahead of her the two foxes leaped and twisted and snapped joyfully at the pounding legs of the horse drawn Host so close around them. Perhaps they were clearing a path deeper into the midst of that great hosting of the Fae. Help mates or not, Janet smiled giving silent thanks for their presence.

From the riders close around there were looks of dismay and impatience and hatred, too, when they noticed a mortal amongst them. At the first, more than one rider attempted to gain honour unseating the intruder with a casually extended lance or a sharp booted foot, leaving Janet glad for the thick leather jacket she wore. But soon, when the metal of her bike began to leave red smouldering welts on any that accidentally touched it and then swift sickness in its wake, the riders began to draw away from her.

Rider after rider then fell behind the vast host, sickened by that touch, whether accidental or not, and had to struggle to regain their place within it. For if any there sought to give over their place in this Fairy Ride, they would court only anger and crushing punishment from The Queen.

Shifting the bike's engine into higher gear, Janet picked up speed, threading her way past rider after rider. Every horse behind her tried their best to escape the trailing exhaust of her Vincent and those before her pranced nervously away from the unfamiliar mechanical roar and fear of its deadly touch.

Dodging long, sharp lances that were thrust from a safe distance at her shoulder or arm or leg and treacherously placed hooves or the sharp, gnashing teeth of their mounts that nipped at her before and behind, Janet hunched close into the bike, smiling grimly. Certain that every rider on each straining horse wished their mount would trample her under its feet, she cautiously threaded her way into their ranks.

Soon Janet's arms began to shake with fatigue even as her heart leaped when she finally heard the bells of The Queen's bridle over the thunder of the surrounding horses. For it meant that Thomas must be somewhere close in this thickly packed host.

Then, just over a streaming banner in front of her, she saw The Lady. Gritting her teeth, Janet gave the cycle its full throttle. At the same time, she reached into her saddlebag and carefully freed the Huntsman's net. Bringing it up in her hand, she began to swing it through the air above her head.

Suddenly, a heavy booted foot slammed into Janet's thigh, sending her and the Vincent swerving dangerously through the far edge of the Fae host. Janet had one split-second to search for its owner and saw The Lord of Darkness and of Death smile back at her just before she burst from the packed throng.

Desperately trying to recover the cycle's balance, she bounced up a face of uneven rock. Hand on the throttle, Janet sent the bike over the top of the granite boulder and caught her breath when she soared free of the ground. The next moment, the Vincent's wheels hit down hard on an almost level surface studded with sharp rocks. In one smooth movement, Janet powered the bike through a narrow gap between two boulders, jolted down the hillside beyond and was amongst the riders once again.

Directly ahead, she saw Thomas' red boiled leather armour, glowing within the deep, moon-cast shadow from the great stabbing finger of granite they thundered past. Once again, Janet brought the net up, this time casting it through the twilight air.

It'd burn the Huntsman's soul to know what I'm using this for now.
That is, if he bloody had one.

Her throw was near perfect, and the last she saw of Thomas before he was wrapped tightly in its coils was an expression of complete surprise. Firmly entangled in the net, the knight struggled desperately but futilely to get away even as he began to fall from his saddle.

Guiding the Vincent in a gentle, swerving arc with both knees and her other arm, Janet hauled in her catch with her free hand. Forcing Thomas' limp body across her lap, she floored the bike and pulled safely away from the massed riders of the Fairy Host. Before anyone was even aware that she'd kidnapped their Knight of the Rose, Janet and her captive were deep in shadows and bouncing away from them through the treacherous rocky landscape as fast as the bike would travel. Only to at last skid to a stop, in another shower of small pebbles, in a patch of rough heather atop a small hill, brightly lit by the full moon.

She smiled, remembering when her mother had pointed it out on their journey from The Queen's tower. "Remember it well." she had said. "Mother Hainter described this particular hill to me, saying that it would be a useful landmark for our night's work, a hill that was once an ancient fairy mound."

Little witch I miss you… I wish you were here with us tonight.

Janet swung her leg off the bike and, as gently as she was able, lowered Thomas to the rough ground. Through the tight netting she saw his face, distorted with anger. He hissed up at her, "Let me go! Now!"

Ignoring his demand, Janet spared a quick look behind her to see if their escape had been noticed yet. When she was sure that it hadn't, she dropped to her knees and wrapped her arms around his body, whispering, "No matter what you say, I won't let you live in that damned court of darkness. I just won't!"

Thomas' reply was grim and final, "Janet, the words that I pledged to my Queen have not changed. I gave my oath to obey her in all things, even it meant my certain doom."

Desperately, Janet shook her head, trying to explain. "But Thomas, you won't be breaking your promise to The Queen, any more than She broke Her promise to me. You were there. You heard Her give me Her pledge to protect any that I held dear. When She gave you to The Lord of Darkness and of Death, She claimed that it would not be Herself but the Dark Lord that would cause you harm. I'm not letting Her get away with a stupid lie like that.

"All I'm doing is following her lead. It wasn't your choice to come back with me. I dragged you here, and if you weren't in this bloody net you'd be kicking and screaming at me about it. So shut up and get used to it, okay?

Gazing tenderly at Thomas for a moment, she whispered, "I hope you'll forgive me when this is over." Then she turned her attention to the distant sound of thundering hooves that now raced directly towards the hill where she stood waiting.

But it was the striking of sharper and much closer hooves that startled her more. Janet was relieved to see her mother clinging tightly to the mane of a huge, black horse that glistened under the moon climb the hill behind her. Sitting close behind her was her Da, his huge arms wrapped tightly around Mairi's waist.

Reaching the crest of the hill, Mairi dropped to the rough ground and, looking up at the horse and her husband, she smiled, "Pooka, I thank you now for your kind assistance. Mother Hainter told me that you might help, and I'm glad you agreed to carry our burden this night."

The great coal black horse shook its head and mane, "I call Thomas Lynn my friend and pledge the same to any that name him theirs. But in truth, I have never liked this Queen and helping those that would confound Her pleases me more than a little."

Its large black eyes then stared down at Thomas, bound roughly on the ground, "Though I hope you have not treated the knight too unkindly?" Its sensitive ears twitched and lay back against its neck, "But mortal, look to your captive now, for they come!"

"Quickly now!" Janet cried and, at her prompting, John slipped down to join his family.

"Hurry," he urged, "the Host will be here sooner than any of us want! And we've not come this long way to waste our efforts."

He then clasped Maris' hand and the two stood close beside their daughter. Both tried to smile encouragingly at her when the earth began to throb with the pounding of Fae creatures hurtling towards them through the dimness of the twilight lands.

Suddenly, the ground below them was choked with a multitude of riders and their frenzied mounts that circled the small hill, their flowing banners snapping in the air like a multitude of birds in flight. Never slowing their pace, they glowered up at the four companions, their captive, and the Pooka standing above them.

In their midst rode The Lord and Lady, both their faces dark with fury, and close beside them followed a milk white mare, its saddle empty of any rider.

Forty-One

Janet shouted over the pounding of the hooves, "All of you here are on a fool's errand this night."

Only the slight flicker of hands on reins and the turning of Her steed made the mortal girl aware that The Queen had heard her. Then once, twice, three times the mounted Host of Fairy circled moonwise round the hill before coming to an abrupt halt. And there they stood in malevolent silence, rank upon rank, thousands deep, their banners still snapping softly in the breeze.

In the heather at Janet's feet, on either side of her captive, the silver foxes sat and waited and watched with evident curiosity. Then, crouching low, their delicate snouts close to Thomas' ears, they began to whisper such stories to him as eased the anger in his heart.

Above them all, thick, racing clouds broke apart to reveal the full moon and a sky full of tilting stars.

Her eyes locked with Janet's, The Queen stilled the great steed that She sat astride and finally spoke, "Mortal, what are you and these others doing here this night?" Then She turned Her gaze on the huge black mare that waited behind its companions, "And you, Pooka, what business is this of yours? Your antics have ever displeased me and were why I banished you from my court long ago, were they not?"

Without waiting for an answer, The Lady gestured at Thomas and continued, "My Knight is held by stronger ties than any net you may have. His foolhardy vow, given long since, to honour any pledge spoken by Myself makes him very precious tonight indeed."

At her side, The Dark Lord's eyes remained locked on his elusive Queen, as if what took place on the hilltop was of no matter. Seeing that look made Janet even more certain that what she glimpsed in the court of the Queen was true.

He does love her, he just doesn't know how to share that love...

Beside her daughter, Mairi gripped the slim leather-bound book in both wrinkled hands.

Following their hastily conceived plan, Janet bowed awkwardly in a briefly practiced, courtly manner, before pleading, "My Lady, do you not see that what you will to happen here tonight, is wrong. What is more, your desires will only lead you and this land that you once more claim as your own into yet further misery?"

There followed a shocked silence. None in that vast host of Faerie would ever dream of speaking such words to their Queen. The silence was shattered by the Queen's shriek of rage.

Mairi managed to quell the surge of panic that threatened to leave her speechless and instead whispered into the resounding silence that came after, "If all that you want to see here in your land is a reflection of your base desires, then your eyes are as blind as if they were carved from wood, for the story that you call yours is a desolate, barren one. Yet you never tire of telling it again and again and again."

Turning her gaze to The Lord of Darkness and of Death, Mairi continued, "So too does this Dark Lord who rides by your side. You both are so filled with useless pride that I despair of your ever sharing the love you hold for each other."

She began to intone, "Once there was a Lord who understood only his desire to possess a great Lady, and through that selfishness made both their kingdoms a home for only darkness and shadow…"

Janet's mother reached for her daughter's hand, and, grasping it, spoke so that all there heard. "Once there was a woman who loved a man, but she was driven away by madness…"

Her young and very human daughter squeezed her mother's hand and then looked into her father's worn face before adding her story as well, "Once there was a motherless child who thought she hated her father…"

John Ravenscroft looked at his wife and daughter before joining their chorus, "Once there was a father who imprisoned his wife and tried his best to do the same to his only daughter as well…"

With joined hands the family faced The Queen. "Once there was a family that was torn asunder by a wilful Queen and her selfish desires…"

The two foxes leaped gracefully in the air before circling the three figures again and again. Each began reading, one after the other, what was written in the pages of the book they held. And, as if by some magic that the book possessed which was more ancient than the magic of the Fae, The Queen and the Dark Lord and all those gathered there stood silently listening to the words that were spoken on this night of nights.

"Once upon a time…

"there was a Queen…

"who had no true love for the kingdom…

"that She ruled."
"All those that lived there…
"suffered for that lack."
"The land itself…"
"suffered as well."
"For it was left desolate and abandoned.
"Even more…
"this Queen had…
"no love for herself…
"and thus…
"when a proper suitor came to court her…
"She cast him aside.
"And that tragedy too…
"became part of Her story."
"The years grew long…
"and the sadness grew…
"in Her land and his,
"and grew…
"and grew…
"becoming something more…
"a dark madness.
"A madness that swallowed them both…
"and then consumed the land itself.
"Twisting…
"all who lived there.
"We wish for you…
"and your land …
"and your people…
"a new tale."
"And…
"it can be told thus…

The three mortals continued their words, telling that story for longer surely than any there would ever know, their words spinning and falling through terrible deeds and just rewards, through sacrifice and repentance, and so came at last to the end, as every story should, with satisfaction and love.

"And ever after…
"those two sat their high thrones…
"Together."

"Together."

"Together."

Then all on that hill chorused together, "And that has brought us to the ending of this tale but perhaps, the beginning of another."

Frightened of what she might see, Janet scanned the tightly packed host of Fae that circled the hill. On every face there was shared wonder and delight in a story well told. Still, The Queen remained silent. Astride his horse that pranced easily by her side, The Lord of Darkness reached out to tenderly claim The Queen's slender hand, gloved in shimmering samite, and quiet and gentle were his words then.

"There once was a Lord who loved a Lady, although he did not know how to truly tell her so…

Listening intently, Janet let out a small gasp when a firm hand grasped hers. Turning aside, she saw Thomas, somehow loosened from the net, standing close beside her. The two silver foxes crouched by the unravelled ropes below and smiled slyly back at her. The Knight of the Rose then took her face tenderly in his hands, and Thomas' grateful face broke into a smile before he said, "There once was a Knight who loved a Queen, but the years fled by and the land of his birth began to speak to him once more from the lips of a young woman who named it her true home…"

Tears filled Janet's eyes when she heard him speak, his voice soft, his anger gone. "I do love you, and would stay with you always. Always."

She smiled shyly, "Yes… I like that ending… or beginning."

But the Queen continued to stare silently, inwardly, thinking thoughts that none there would ever know. Then, breaking Her silence She asked Janet's mother a question. "This book you hold, are there more tales within it?"

Mairi bowed, "Yes, my Lady, many such tales, but there are also pages left to be written on, more pages than could ever be used, even in your lifetime." Janet, too, bowed low before Her, "Lady, it is our wish that you take the book as our gift." Then she added, "But only if you promise to read all that is in it."

"Oh, that I will, mortal, that I will." And then The Queen of Summer's Twilight smiled, and it was a smile full of new beginnings and new tales that would be long in the telling.

FORTY-TWO

Not long after, all that was left of their company, John and Mairi, Thomas and Janet, moved lightly through the surface of the great standing stone and were back once more in the world of humankind.

Moments earlier, on the other side of the stone, when they had said their goodbye to the Pooka who had become their friend that night, their hearts had been filled with sadness.

From the two silver foxes that sometimes were also women, there was no such final parting at all. The sleek creatures had simply leaped away into the deep heather leaving behind only an echo of their excited barking.

Now Janet looked wistfully out over the vast moor that stretched away from them. It was bathed in rich morning light. Far in the distance, cloud shadows raced across high, rocky crags. She turned and joined the others.

Anyone looking at them from afar would not have seen the heroes that walked there with an amazing tale to tell, but only four small figures moving slowly through an immense landscape toward their home. Looking closer, they might have noticed that one of them was tall and fitted in strange leather armour. He pushed a heavy black motorcycle alongside the others.

John Ravenscroft paused and looked at the man they have gone to such effort to rescue that night and smiled, "Thomas, you shouldn't concern yourself with my wife and I, take my daughter and ride that beast of yours out of here. Mairi and I will be fine." And turning to his wife, he continued, "We have so many things to talk about, don't we?"

The older woman leaned closer into the warmth of her husband's body and returned his broad smile, "Yes, it's true. As true as any story."

Janet laughed and mounted the Vincent behind Thomas. Clasping her arms tightly around him, she cried, "Go! Go!" And the roaring, spitting monster that was his Vincent Black Lightning flew over stone and heather towards Inverness and any new adventure that might come their way.

Far behind them, across a border spun from shadow and dreams that now and perhaps forever would separate the Lands of Faerie from that of humans, The Queen walked too, hand in hand with The Lord of Darkness

Charles Vess

and of Death, returning to a court that they would share now for as long as there was a Land of Summer's Twilight and Faerie.

For every lady must have their lord as every lord his lady. Lady and lord, lord and lady, lady and lady or lord and lord or any combination there of, to see one another safely to the ending of their tale. And so, forever, down through the ages it will go.

> "Oh, I forbid you maidens all,
> That wear gold in your hair,
> To come or go by Carter Hall,
> For young Tam-Lin is there."

EPILOGUE:

"Hey, Jamie, give us a hand."

"Jeez, didna I tell you to quit scarfing down every one of your Gran's oatmeals?"

"Never gonna happen."

"Quick, lift us up then!"

Leaving their bicycles leaning against the other side of the crumbling stonewall, all five boys soon comfortably straddled the cap, their faces breaking into wide smiles.

"I knew it. As soon as I heard that cycle of his, I knew he was back."

"Yeah, that's tha fellow all right."

"Even without those daft clothes I'd know him in a crowd."

Despite the winter chill, Geordie wiped a trickle of sweat away from his forehead and paused to suck in a deep breath through cheeks so bright and red that they seemed to glow, "Hope it's worth the huffin' 'n puffin' to pedal out here."

"Who's the lady, though?"

"Dunno…"

Around them the sun sent bright shafts of light down through tumbling clouds on a brisk, early winter afternoon. The wall they'd just clambered up was ancient and built of moss and lichen-covered stone that had withstood more damage than any set of young boys would ever visit upon it. Enclosing the Lynn Estate, it ran astride a gently rolling landscape far enough away from Inverness for that city to be only a dim memory on the horizon.

Janet stood in the small family graveyard, looking about at the gutted manor house, the overgrown garden, and the tumbled grave markers inscribed with names long since lost to time and weather. Despite the evident neglect of the buildings and the land that they were bound to, the comforting presence of her lover's family sank deep into her bones. She smiled to herself when she realised how pleased they would be to know that she'd brought Thomas home at last.

When Janet noticed the young boys lounging on the wall, she smiled at them, then waved a friendly hello.

Discovered, the boys suddenly grew solemn, expecting instant dismissal. But received instead a welcoming smile from the dark-skinned lady Hesitantly, Geordie waved back.

Careful to not let his voice carry, he whispered to his mates, "Maze me. She's not running us off."

"Not yet anyways."

"Doesn't look like there'll be much fun fer us today, though."

Just in front of Janet, the man who had drawn the boys here was on his knees, bending over a small, freshly dug hole in the earth to the side of one of the ancient graves. Finished, Thomas reached into his front pocket and carefully lifted a small brown object from it. Laying the acorn into the newly exposed dirt, he covered it over. Leaning in close, Tom finished a conversation that he'd begun so long ago, "There, old man of the green, is this far enough away from the city for your children to thrive and to breathe properly at last?"

There was no answer, save the soughing of the breeze through the ancient yew trees that lined the cemetery wall.

Still perched on that same wall, the boys let out a collective sigh of disappointment.

Geordie articulated a feeling shared by them all, "Yep, no laughs for us today. No muddy buddy on his bike slippin' and slidin' inna dirt…"

After a moment, Janet leaned into Thomas and whispered something in his ear. He looked surprised then slowly smiled back at her. Arm in arm, they walked towards the five boys who watched their approach as tentatively as fawns or young rabbits out on the moor.

Stopping just before they reached their dangling feet, Janet cocked her head to one side, looking up at them. "Thomas told me about you and the help you offered him not long ago." Then, with a mischievous grin she continued, "Oh, but we've not yet been properly introduced, have we? This, gentlemen, is Thomas Lyn, the owner of this estate. And I, his lady, Janet."

"For real?"

"You mean you own all that big lump of stones, Mr. Lynn?"

Thomas let out a rueful laugh, "Yes, I do. And one day it will house my court once more. I will rebuild this estate, stone by tumbled stone and rule from here with pride and honour. Would you choose to be my vassals, the first knights of my new realm?"

Confused, the four boys looked quickly at each other, unused to adults playing any sort of game with them. But, shrugging their collective shoulders, first one, then the others in turn grinned and nodded their assent, clearly enjoying this new game.

Thomas said, "With what names then shall I knight my subjects?"

Each boy managed, between giggles, to sputter out his proper name.

"Geordie."

"Jaimie."

"Geoffrey."

"Dougie."

"And I'm Donald."

Nodding toward the distant silhouette of the Vincent, Janet continued, "So, noble knights, my Thomas would never have gotten his gallant steed running without your help that day. For certain, we would not be here now, either of us, without it. Indeed, it saved my life... and his as well. So, we want to thank you. Properly."

Thomas slowly looked them over before rather sternly addressing his assembled champions, "What say you men, to a ride on my stalwart steed?"

For the rest of that short winter's afternoon, Thomas took one boy after another for a long ride on his Black Lightning up and down the lanes and once or twice across a field. By the time each had had his turn, all five were whooping with delight.

As the sky began to grow dark and the wind turned bitter, Thomas and Janet stood once again beside the Vincent, looking down at the grinning newfound knights. "We do want to ask of you a further service." On seeing their wary expressions, Thomas hurried on. "You saw the acorn that I planted here in the graveyard, did you not? I would consider it a great favour if you would make certain that none disturb it as it grows."

Standing straighter, Geordie and the other four each gave their new friend a heart-felt promise to do as he'd asked.

"So be it then, with your word as a covenant between us, I will be content. For I feel that my lady and I have some adventures in us yet before we return here to re-build and begin anew."

Happily, Thomas turned to Janet and lifted her off her feet, swinging the young woman who had rescued him from a life of eternal shadow in a circle, moonwise, about him. Then, placing her on her feet again, he slowly kissed the woman he loved.

Jaimie punched his friend's shoulder, saying, "Okay, mates, let's get out of here."

"Yeah, let's go. That stuff might be catchin'."

Sitting astride the Vincent again, the two lovers casually waved to the boys as they scrambled back over the wall. Janet threaded her arms around the handsome man who sat so comfortably in front of her and began to shift her thoughts toward the future and the time they would have together.

Out of the corner of Janet's eye she could see several small creatures with long curling tails and delicate wings leap and dance among the leaves of the great yew tree that leaned close against the weathered stone wall of the graveyard.

She leaned in close to Thomas' ear and spoke just loud enough to be heard over the roar of the machine's engine, "Those faces will always be out there among the leaves, won't they?"

"Always."

"Good.

"Now let's head downtown to the 320, there's a friend there that I owe some answers to."

Acknowledgments

Over ten years ago I woke up one morning with the remnants of a dream still buzzing in my head. In that dream I was on a high outcropping of rock looking down on a vast yellowed field of dead grass and blackened trees. Riding across that field were two people on a motorcycle that was leaving a burning path of grass behind. Somehow I knew right away that that landscape was the realm of faerie.

As I got up and put my clothes on I started humming the iconic Richard Thompson song "Vincent Black Lightning" under my breath, thus naming the cycle.

Then, driving into my studio that morning, the two people on the bike started talking to each other in my head. I let them.

Over the next six weeks they and other characters kept talking to me and, not being a fool, I wrote it all down. Mornings, before I began work on my art deadlines, became a mad dash to scribble all the words that streamed through my head onto a pad of paper.

When their voices finally grew still I realised that I had a rough story outline with a beginning, middle and an end.

My 'gift', from who knows where, was in fact a novel.

I typed it up and for months, and years to come, I continued to tinker with the story, rearranging scenes and inserting dialogue. In time I began to show my text to writing friends (Stina Liecht, Mette Harrison, Ellen Klages, Delia Sherman, Melissa Marr, Charles de Lint & Liz Phillips, etc.) asking for their advice. They each read my story and made suggestions that sometimes had me rewriting vast chunks of narrative.

In the course of time this manuscript also passed in and out of the hands of two separate agents who both confessed that they didn't know what to do with my story. Mostly they worried about the reception it might receive from today's hyper critical audiences since I was an older, white man writing about a protagonist who is a young woman of colour.

All I can say in my defence is that I wrote the story that I was compelled to write, so please forgive me if indeed I have offended any of my readers.

And now my unexpected gift has had a final polish by my editor at NewCon Press, Ian Whates, which leaves me very happy indeed.

Lastly I want to thank my wife for granting me the time to spend untold hours at my keyboard putting in 'just one more little idea' when I should have been taking care of our home.

– Charles Vess
Abingdon, VA
2022

About the Author

Charles Vess has been drawing ever since he could hold a crayon and crawl to the nearest wall. His long list of accomplishments include cover and interior art for Marvel, DC, Tor and Subterranean Press, as well as many illustrated books and graphic novels for which he has won two Hugo, four World Fantasy, three Chesley, two Locus, a Mythopoeic and two Will Eisner awards.

Charles' art has been featured in many gallery and museum exhibitions across the nation, including "Spectrum: The Best in Contemporary Fantastic Art" at the Museum of American Illustration at the Society of Illustrators and "Enchanted, A History of Fantasy Illustration" at the Norman Rockwell Museum. His work has also been shown in Paris, Spain, Portugal, Italy and the UK.

His four-year collaboration with Ursula Le Guin resulted in a fully illustrated edition of all her Earthsea stories. Published by Saga Press, *The Books of Earthsea* garnered many awards. 2021 saw the release of *Honeycomb* (Saga) written by Joanne M. Harris with many color and black and white illustrations and *The Art of Stardust* (Titan), an informal history written by Vess and with an introduction by Neil Gaiman.

He lives in a house down on the North Fork River in southwestern Virginia where he works diligently from his studio, Green Man Press.

You can find him at www.greenmanpress.com and 'Charles Vess' on Facebook

Also from NewCon Press

Embertide – Liz Williams
Practical Magic meets *The Witches of Eastwick* as four fey sisters, Bee, Stella, Serena, and Luna Fallow, pursue normal lives in contemporary London and rural Somerset. Darker realms impinge on their idyl, however, and they have enemies determined to bring them down.

Rose Knot – Kari Sperring
Kari Sperring, historian and award-winning fantasy author, delivers a gripping tale of love, infidelity, loyalty, misguided intentions and the price of nobility, featuring some lesser known members of King Arthur's court: the sons of Lot, the Orkney royal family.

Queen of Clouds – Neil Williamson
Wooden automata, sentient weather, talking cats, compellant inks and a host of vividly realised characters provide the backdrop to this rich dark fantasy, as stranger in the city Billy Braid becomes embroiled in Machiavellian politics and deadly intrigue.

How Grim Was My Valley – John Llewellyn Probert
After waking up on the Welsh side of the Severn Bridge with no memory of who he is, a man embarks on an odyssey through Wales, bearing witness to the stories both the people and the land itself feel moved to tell him, all the while getting closer to the truth about himself.

The Wild Hunt – Garry Kilworth
When Gods meddle in the affairs of mortals, it never ends well… for the mortals, at any rate. Steeped in ancient law, history and imagination, Garry Kilworth serves up an epic Anglo-Saxon saga featuring warriors, witches, giants, dwarfs, light elves and more.

www.newconpress.co.uk